THE POWER OF HER SMILE

Patti Brady

The Power of Her Smile

A Novel

by

Patti Brady

WWW.GRACENOVELS.COM

Peridot Publishing LLC

Copyright © 2009 by Patti Brady

Peridot Publishing LLC
Woodstock, GA

All rights reserved. No part of this publication may be reproduced, stored in a retrieval system or transmitted, in any form, or by any means, electronic, mechanical, recorded, photocopied, or otherwise, without the prior permission of the copyright owner, except by a reviewer who may quote brief passages in a review.

This book is a work of fiction. The events and dialogue in this novel are imaginary. The characters, except for historical persons mentioned, are fictional as well.

ISBN-13   978-0-9790669-1-7

Printed in the United States of America

DEDICATION

Juanita Hughes—with her writing, her knowledge,
and her own spirited smile,
she inspires Woodstock and certainly me.

Character List

The Power of Her Smile

*denotes a character found in first novel of the Woodstock series

WOODSTOCK

Marissa Manning* – main character, daughter of Christina* and John Manning*

John T. Manning* – father of Marissa, deceased, owner of small manufacturing firm

Nathan Manning – uncle of John Manning

Dave Manning – brother of Marissa, lives in another state

Olivia Manning – wife of Nathan

Allen Manning – son of Nathan & Olivia, died young

Harbin Manning – grandson of Nathan & Olivia through one of their daughters

Hank* & Elizabeth* Averill – main characters from *The Heart of a Child*

Manuel* and baby girl – children of Hank and Elizabeth

Trent Everson* – attorney who represented John Manning in lawsuit

Abby Everson* – wife of Trent, neighbor of Hank, family friend of Marissa

Brian Barton* – local pastor, friend of Hank Averill

Lavon Farrier* – city council member, owner of meter reading business

Uncle Rakey* – aging, special needs dependent of the town

Diana Cannon* – local preservationist, craftswoman, wife of Carl Cannon* construction supervisor

Kristin Arnett* – singer/hairstylist, hair stylist, wife of Phil Arnett* construction superintendent

Max Donovan – teenage stable hand living on Nathan's farm

Vereena Donovan – mother of Max, girlfriend of Dudley

Mr. Langley – owner of Harlequin

Mr. Silverstrike – head of real estate division of a company in Atlanta

ST. SIMONS ISLAND

Daphne Adams – first kitchen helper at *Camellia*
Clemma and Alexa Adams – daughters of Daphne
Shalie – sister of Daphne
Jacquelyn – best friend of Marissa, owner of exercise studio, girlfriend of Russell Lancaster
Zoe – friend of Marissa and Jacquelyn
Isabel – *Camellia* employee
Deke – husband of Isabel
China & Rosalee – servers at *Camellia*
Darrien – pastor of one of the island churches
Irene – mother of Darrien
Byron Hewitt – landscape architect
Harvey Trammel – utility workman and patron of *Camellia*
William Dash – backyard neighbor of *Camellia,* oil rig engineer
Kevin Dash – father of William
Beverly Reginalli – friend of William Dash
Everett Chisholm – restaurant critic
Swamp Sally – animal control person, wife of Armand
Frankie – boater
Whilhelmina – naturalist, nature writer
Mr. and Mrs. Weinstein – first owners of the beach house
Mrs. Kilpatrick – patron of *Camellia*

Chapter One

ONCE in a while there's a certain woman, no matter how visually appealing, who can make a man want to scratch his head with a rake, who can drive him overnight into a bad case of stress-induced shingles, or who can leave him no option but to search for a scorpion-infested bar in Yucca Flats, Arizona, and drown himself there forever. That was Marissa.

Imperceptibly over time, beneath the umbrella of a changing culture, she became unrelenting and hardened. Raised within a loving family, amid the beautiful hills surrounding a north Georgia town, no one could recognize the attractive woman any longer. Unable to find the fulfillment she yearned for, she cut out, to start a new venture on an island, maybe the last good try left inside her. In life, two things she intensely desired always eluded her—business success and a husband. Even so, she owned a smile that could quicken the heart of hopeless old men and could draw children to her. When it happened, her brows relaxed, the precipice of her cheekbones reflected the faintest glimmer of light, and her eyes filled with warmth. For so long, this outward symbol of the womanly part of her was a thing she did not value. Then, she woke from misconception. And she wondered if those abilities she maligned in her early youth and later disregarded had fled her. That was the question haunting her.

One morning on verdant St. Simons Island, Marissa stood at a window and swirled a cloth, making the view to the outdoors keener. Her tearoom, *Camellia Japonica,* languished, vacant of customers on that day in early April. In fact, the place could not boast a single customer for the two weeks since opening. Her arm slowed its striving for perfection, and she spent minutes examining the glass for streaks. She looked past the window for something to give her hope that the inactivity smothering the tearoom would lift. Shifting slightly to the left, she took advantage of the angle cutting from the window, across the alley, and toward the main road lined with souvenir shops, sportswear stores, and an ice cream parlor all designed with more catch-'em than well-made crab traps. Were they the ones stealing her customers? Maybe she was to blame, picking a location down the shady side road. But the old, nondescript building had declared itself a steal. The quirky owner died, leaving the place to his estate. Relatives hankered for a quick sale. On a gamble, Marissa swooped in with her life savings.

Beneath stagnant clouds, vehicles came down the central avenue two blocks away, traveling to the park and pier. Marissa sighed. She was the kind of person who would rather work until fainting than die from boredom. From her vantage point, she could see part of the hardware store. The plain facade with fishing gear and old nets hanging in the window sufficiently engaged a few strollers to enter that place. Next door, a woman on the far side of seventy years came from the village bookstore and caught Marissa's eye. A warm cross-breeze worked through the screens reminding her that *Camellia* would need the air conditioning turned on by noon, but the tightly coiffed woman on that far sidewalk wore a trench coat.

Marissa was about to resume her cleaning task when she thought she saw the woman tap the tip of her nose with her index finger and pull an earlobe several times. Gingerly, the small form stepped from the sidewalk and into the street. Marissa, making a silly grin, shook her head. She pulled back and blinked. She pulled close and squinted, wondering if her eyes fooled her.

After three paces forward, the elderly woman returned to her starting point. On the sidewalk once more, the graying head turned left and right. Her hand rose. Tap, tap, tap. Pull, pull, pull. Marissa dropped her cloth. The woman proceeded, accomplishing more steps this time before she retreated again. A car and a truck slowly passed. She waited. Then, tap, tap, tap, pull, pull, pull and out she moved, making it to the opposite lane before she pivoted, ready to dash back. Done purely for rude effect, tires screeched and a horn blared. The woman flinched so hard she almost withdrew like a land turtle into her too-large coat. She remained frozen, except for twittering fingers. The driver guffawed in tandem with his passenger, and the car moved around the flustered woman, laughter still trailing. Marissa felt like storming over there to pinch the heads off the cruising pair. The gentle woman pulled to her full height again, shoulders relaxing, and she made her way back to the sidewalk for the third time.

Marissa swung her head around, hoping Daphne would come from the kitchen. The kitchen assistant's song rose above the hum of the mixer, and the swinging door remained shut. Marissa turned again to the view, trying to will the frail, tentative woman across what was actually a lazy thoroughfare. The woman, head bent with determination, had already left on her mission once more. With a flurry of steps, she reached the far side of the street where she paused, adjusting her coat and smoothing her hair. She continued, following the sandy road past the antique shop and behind the seafood restaurant. Marissa noted leather handbag, matching pumps, and pearl earrings. She studied the woman's features. The refined lady wasn't one of Marissa's new acquaintances since coming to the island in January. Then Marisa softly gasped. The woman stepped purposely toward the tearoom. Bolting from the window, Marissa rushed around while the fact still registered—finally, after so many days, a customer.

The door to *Camellia* opened. Marissa grabbed a menu and with a warm greeting welcomed the woman inside. Marissa guided her customer to a table near the row of windows that lined either side of the room.

"That's a lovely brooch on your lapel," Marissa said sweetly. The woman dipped her head slightly in response and took the menu.

A minute later, Marissa burst through the kitchen door and glided to Daphne's side. "Our first customer has arrived!" announced Marissa.

"Good," said Daphne. "The pumpkin bread is ready to come from the oven."

"She's an odd one, though," added Marissa. She raced out the door to pour the woman's tea. She returned to the kitchen. Minutes later, with a complimentary slice of pumpkin bread plated gracefully alongside a yellow and purple pansy bloom, Marissa went out the swinging door again. A pleasant, spicy aroma trailed as she went toward the woman bent over her hand that held the china cup brimming with tea. The other hand positioned the final button of a multi-colored row resting on the circle formed by her thumb and forefinger pinching the cup handle. Marissa paused but continued over.

She lowered the plate to the table. The woman remained transfixed with her peculiar task.

"More tea?" Marissa interrupted, unaware her frown peeked out.

The woman covered the ornamented hand with her other and looked up. "I don't believe I shall. Just the bill, please." She swiped the buttons from her hand and slid them into her coat pocket.

Marissa charged into the kitchen. "She wants her bill, already. I don't think she's even going to taste the pumpkin bread!"

Daphne added ingredients to another mixing bowl. "Don't worry. Most things begin with a slow start."

"I hear you. But come take a look. She has a thing for buttons." Marissa turned to exit again, her palm about to push the door.

Daphne's voice grabbed her. "Do you want pecans, walnuts, or macadamias in the banana muffins?"

Marissa stopped. "You decide." Her hand gave the door a shove, and she spoke over her shoulder while moving into the other room. "I guess I haven't told you, Daphne. *I've never met a nut I didn't like.*" Her animated words flooded the eating area. Marissa saw the woman's head jerk at the words. Eyes blinking, head trembling, the woman fumbled with a few things on the table, pushed her seat back, and primly adjusted her coat. In a flash, she found her way out.

The word *wait* tripped over itself in Marissa's throat and failed to make it out. Her extended hand holding the check fell next to her side. She walked to the table by the window where her first and only guest had sat. Marissa found a lone dime. She was about to gather the dishes and stopped, staring at the table. She grabbed the napkin and looked underneath. She scrambled around the floor, hunting the missing item. With a haggard face, like the wind in her lungs was knocked from her, she got up. Then, breath returning, she crumbled into the chair. Daphne pushed through the kitchen door and seated herself on the opposite side.

"That her?" Daphne asked and nodded at the view through the window of a figure scooting away.

Marissa, eyes wide, got to the point. "She stole my grandmother's spoon."

Daphne looked at the table. "Hm. Perhaps she'll return it."

Marissa's face reddened and she let loose. "I thought you said the season had started!" The words came out like barks.

"Has."

"Well what about us? It's not like we're trying to feed them cockroach quiche."

"Takes time."

Marissa responded with an annoyed look at her assistant. "That's just it! I don't have time. Not a minute. My business funds are dwindling, and the years are draining like olive oil through my fingers." She stood and threw up her hands. "Have you any idea what it's like at the age of thirty-seven, trying to make a go of things? One of my oldest friends is already a sitting judge in the Federal Courts. My brother's wife travels to Milan twice a year as a buyer. Myself, I tried the corporate ladder. It wasn't a good fit. However, I *would* be pleased to have a modest little enterprise here. Just a modicum of fulfillment and success is all I ask." Her voice rose in pitch. Her breathing sped up. Her eyes focused on the air as she delivered her diatribe. "And while I'm on the subject of *my rapidly waning life*, I might as well mention that all my former college friends are married and have countless kids. A few women have even moved to their second go-round. *So I have a right to rant about time. Every right.*" Her face had turned into a scowl that could back an ugly flounder deeper in the sand.

Marissa tried to slow her breathing, and she paused to look at her employee. Then Marissa, eyes full of alarm, brought a hand to her open mouth, and she said softly, "Oh, no. . . . Forgive me, Daphne. I'm so sorry. Truly I am."

Daphne rubbed one of her sun-spotted forearms self-consciously. Her gray eyes looked calmly at Marissa. "No matter. I've had a very blessed life."

Around 3:00, as usual, they closed the place, and Marissa went home to the beach house. After bathing, she slipped into a sundress that was so festive she felt ashamed and had the urge to scrub the rough plank floor of the porch with the breezy print. She paced, having an hour to kill before she had to be at her new pastor's home for the Sunset Supper for Singles. As much as she had looked forward to the gathering, she now wished to confine herself at home, flog her tongue, and disallow dinner. Her desolate bed would be her penalty. There she could remind herself of her recurring deficiencies and Daphne's horrible plight. She flopped in a canvas chair by the bedroom window. Her eyes moved around the space looking for something to reverse her mood created by the debacle of the day. The closet door hung open. She went to the black case on the shelf and brought the object down. She opened the latches and lifted the violin. A whiff of the fine wood reached her nose.

She left the house, instrument in hand. The warm sand massaged her bare feet as she walked to the low sea wall that performed no real purpose with high tide never encroaching that far, but it served as a perfect ledge to gaze from. If it was the start of the season, you couldn't tell it. Only two beachcombers wheeled on bikes along the shore. She lifted the bow and laid it on the strings. To punish herself, she picked the saddest melody she knew. Her music rode the air while her thoughts ran in the same vein as the bow and her pressing fingertips requiring little direction because her heart led them. Finally, she laid her violin to the side. In front of her, the wide, endless sea stretched, making her feel worthless and small. *Her life was a wasteland. Thirty-seven years and she had nothing to show for them. Who cared if she lived or died?*

Her mind went to Daphne, a woman who had every reason to complain, regret, resent: a teenage pregnancy, a baby boy put up for adoption, and the child's father who beat and finally left her. When Daphne reached her late thirties, she married a man who loved her well but was taken early on, in a violent car wreck. She raised their two baby girls by her wits and much hard work. Now fifteen years later, her two young daughters would be without their mother after enough months had progressed, according to the doctors' predictions. Marissa pictured Daphne's face—prosaic and unpretentious, stressed by hours working in the sun. With quiet dignity, she had entered Marissa's world. Through February and March, Daphne worked alongside her, getting *Camellia Japònica* ready, always soft-spoken, always singing softly. Marissa had almost resisted hiring her. A hard life had left its marks on a woman who appeared to be more than her fifty-five years. She hadn't looked strong, either, but Marissa was surprised at her endurance and capability. Would those qualities last at least a year? The woman, trim and sinewy, insisted it would. The tiny bungalow in Brunswick was paid for. Employment would allow her to pay her bills and keep putting something in her girls' college fund. Marissa gave in. No one else wanted the job.

From the sea wall Marissa rose. When she reached the house, she brushed off the sand that stuck to her feet and lower legs. She swished the light cotton skirt of her dress and entered the beach house. In the bathroom, she smoothed lotion on the same skin that had been so aware, earlier, of the rough concrete block pushing against her calves. The milky liquid smelled so joyous that she sighed, ashamed of the frivolous hours coming her way. High heeled sandals slipped onto her feet and emphasized legs that could win a trophy. She flipped off the bathroom light. After checking the weather report, hoping for rain, she reluctantly gathered her keys and purse and went out the door. With her present mood, she knew she wouldn't be smiling that night.

Chapter Two

MARISSA opened the car door and swung her feet to the ground where she stood tall and sleek. She took a deep breath, thinking she might as well enjoy herself and salvage the day gone wrong. If she planned her approach, she could evaluate the party guests before they caught sight of her. The rose garden and patio hugged the right side of the house, at a lower grade. As she made her way around the front yard, the high heels of her sandals caught in the thick sod, giving her a jagged rather than graceful walk, but it didn't stop her from checking out the scene below. People crowded the patio. The ratio of women to men was not to her advantage. However, several guys by the barbecue looked promising.

Wanting to present herself in the very best light, she came to the steps that led down to the patio and paused as if standing on a pedestal.

"Hello, Marissa! Come join us," Darrien, her pastor, called from below. Curious faces near him looked at her with interest.

Marissa waved to Darrien and took the first step of her descent. Her eyes widened at the notice of an unanticipated person. Then an ankle buckled, giving her body an awkward jerk and her honey blond hair a toss. Reflexively, her arms flew out to achieve balance making her look like a ridiculous clown she was certain, but at least she saved herself from a tumble. She looked again. The person meandering near the pastor was the trench coat lady, nicely attired for the occasion. Marissa became conscious she was starting to perspire. Reaching the sure footing of the patio floor, she stepped aside, allowing a couple to spring up the brick steps and go gather a cooler from their car. Marissa's sandaled feet tarried over a drainage grate. Ready to move in the direction of her host, again, her right foot lifted to proceed forward. Her left spike heel sank into iron teeth. As her front leg thrust forward, the back heel broke off. Marissa staggered and gasped. Her eyesight strained at the grate. Did one rescue the amputated part or pretend it didn't happen? She left it and hobbled to Darrien, avoiding the eyes of the older woman who had moved close to him.

His face full of concern, Darrien reached out. "Are you okay?"

"Yes, but I've never made a worse entrance."

"That's impossible. I mean, that you could make a bad one, at all."

"Thank you." She shifted her weight to the foot wearing the shorn sandal and was immediately three inches shorter.

Darrien laughed. "We'll have to do something about that. Have you met my mother, Irene?"

"Uh, I believe she was our guest at *Camellia Japonica* this morning." She tried to smile.

The woman didn't return the look. "I really don't recall," she murmured and gave a little sniff.

"Oh. Well, how about loaning Marissa a pair of shoes?"

"Won't work," said Irene. "I wear a five. She requires at least a ten."

Marissa colored. "A nine to be exact. But I'll just dash home and be right back."

"No way," Darrien said. "You can't drive like that."

"Well. . ." Marissa shrugged.

Irene grinned. "I know," she said, speaking to her son. "I do have something. Those slippers Margaret gave me for Christmas are huge."

Marissa checked around, thankful no one else seemed to hear the insults. Darrien concentrated on his mother.

"Thank you, Mom. I'm sure Marissa appreciates your help." Irene eagerly went on her errand. His gaze moved to Marissa.

Marissa's feeble smile came out, and she nodded her thanks. Unfortunately, a church social where the men wore jackets and ties and the women had donned their most stylish dresses wasn't exactly the place to traipse around barefoot. Darrien left to turn the steaks, and Marissa waited by the side door of the house. Irene returned holding blue slippers so wildly furry they resembled a pair of dyed Easter rabbits frightened by a rottweiler.

The woman shoved her offering into Marissa's hands. "Hope you like these gunboats," said Irene, who then turned and walked away.

Marissa schlepped to the different groups, joining in conversation, trying to laugh off her less than fetching look. The main course was almost ready. She helped set the places and toss the salad. Darrien wandered up to her.

"Thanks for helping Zoe get things ready. I hope you're having a good time."

"I don't think your mother likes me," she said.

"Really? You've got to be mistaken."

"Trust me."

"Please, explain."

"Well, she. . ." Marissa looked away. How harsh it would be to give him a clear picture.

Darrien pulled her by the elbow to the side of the gathering. "She's not her best. Thanks for any patience you can spare. The doctor took her off her medication for OCD. Too many side effects. I brought her here from LaGrange, trying to keep her out of assisted living as long as possible. It's not easy for me." He grinned. "She has a strong aversion to my motorcycle."

"I'm sorry," said Marissa. "I know what you're going through. My mother went through a long slide before I lost her two years ago."

"Thank you for understanding. By the way, did I tell you how very adorable you look with exploding pom-poms on your feet?"

"You are the sweetest man! Too bad you're my pastor." She patted his arm and shuffled off to talk to Jacquelyn.

"Did you meet Clifford and Jared?" asked Jacquelyn. "One is an attorney, and the other always cooks for his dates."

"I did, but any confidence I had evaporated within two minutes after arriving. I'm almost ready to call the night over," Marissa muttered and switched the subject to Darrien's mom.

"Amazing. So she was your weird guest today? She hasn't been on the island that long. I hadn't noticed anything unusual about her. Poor Darrien. We ought to pray for the woman."

"You're so right," said Marissa. "And I shouldn't be gossiping about her." Her voice trailed off as she looked past Jacquelyn's head to the corner of the roof edge. Marissa's features drew into a frown.

"What is it?" said Jacquelyn.

"Is that a wind chime attached to the overhang?"

Jacquelyn turned. "How clever. It's made of spoons . . . .Oh!" With a worried look, her attention snapped to Marissa.

Marissa briefly froze then blasted from the slippers and rifled to the object. After mere seconds of scrutiny, she spotted what she hunted. Her hand ripped the spoon from its string, making the wind chime swing like crazy and clang alarm. Darrien's mother let out a long, pitiful wail, pointed one shaking finger at Marissa, and fell to the floor. Almost thirty-six aghast looks aimed at Marissa. With the spoon in her hand and the chime still swinging, she practically ran to the car, and she didn't mind one bit, driving home barefoot.

The next morning Marissa arrived at the tearoom to find Daphne sitting on the front steps, waiting. Two camellias, each taller than a man, in massive ceramic pots defined each side of the entrance. Those deep green, glossy plants and a black and white striped awning were the only ornamentation of the brown, clapboard building.

"Sorry," said Marissa. "I couldn't sleep last night. Here, you'd better take my extra key. With the way things are going, I may start lagging in bed with a case of the blues."

They entered and set about their work, brewing, baking, and stewing, the latter solely in Marissa's case. To her surprise, two workmen entered.

"Don't need a menu," said the man in his forties built like the sparest fence post anywhere. Lean perpendicular folds of skin were bookends for his lopsided grin. "Give me two eggs sunnyside-up, bacon, grits, and toast, young lady."

"We don't serve breakfast. May I recommend the ham and cheese frittata?"

"The whatta?" he chimed. "Don't look so disappointed, Sweetcakes. If it's food, we'll take it. We've been driving all night. Got some emergency work to do at the power station before we can get home to Jesup for some sleep."

Later, cleaning the dessert display, Marissa almost twirled with more lightness than the whipped cream garnish when she saw the men take their last bites, give a good luck rub to their stomachs, and settle back in their chairs to wait for their check.

The thin man playfully lumbered to the cash register to pay.

She laughed.

"I tell you what! That meal was fit for a king, and if it's not real clear, I'm no king. Harvey Trammell's the name. I see you call this a tearoom, but it's still darn comfortable for a man."

"Well, I'm pleased you liked it, Harvey. I'm Marissa Manning. Please tell your friends to drop by."

"Will do. And the music? What kind was that? Not complaining, though."

"Chamber. Friday is chamber music day."

"Real nice. Real nice. You're some clever gal."

The two men drifted out. With the place empty again, the two women sat down with their lunch of tea sandwiches of ham salad and spring baby greens dressed with honey-lime and walnut dressing.

Marissa's fork dabbed at her salad. "At least we're eating well. I exited the supper last night before I got one bite of dinner."

"Oh, how was the party?"

"Awful. By the time I left, I was as appealing as ten-day-old bait in a bucket."

"Goodness gracious, what went wrong?"

Marissa related the events of the evening. It was the first time she witnessed Daphne laugh heartily.

"I'm relieved you got the spoon back, but maybe we shouldn't be using your grandmother's china and silverware."

"If this place is going to draw people, it has to be special."

Daphne leaned forward with an angelic look. "Marissa, they'll come for the food. You'll see."

Weeks went by with a steady increase of customers. People spread the word. The island paper did a write-up, and so, spring continued in that manner. Then summer arrived with vacationers always stumbling on the place, looking for something to eat. Marissa and Daphne arrived by seven in the morning to make enough specialty take-out sandwiches for tourists. Harvey, sure to bring his buddies, popped in occasionally. Every time Marissa looked at her bank account, *Camellia* moved a little closer to getting out of the red and into the black. Daphne's strength held up through the hot months and her doctor felt good about the lab test results. She seemed especially happy. Marissa hired Daphne's young daughters for the summer months—Clemma, brash and playful, and dreamy Alexa with curling cinnamon-brown hair and eyes bluer than the south Georgia sky. Middle-schoolers aren't known for their focus, hampered by social lives imbued with self-significance like over-inflated inner tubes, but Marissa took a chance on them. The girls cleared tables and took food orders well enough, considering the weighty issue of their mother's illness that burdened their hearts. At one o'clock, they walked to the island pool and later, their craft class. They showed at their mother's car by three, and *Camellia Japonica* was shut tight for the night.

One Saturday in late August, at the end of the day, the women set about the weekly clean-up with brillo pads and unforgiving shoulder muscles.

Marissa pushed flopping hair from her eyes while trying to make the mundane, gritty work pass quickly with conversation. "Do the girls like staying with their aunt on Saturdays?"

"Not that much. . . . But it gives them a chance to get used to the situation before I'm gone."

"I see," Marissa responded softly. She turned the radio on, and they listened to a baseball game as they worked.

Minutes passed in which they found some relief from the emotion knocking around in their chests by attacking the bakeware doubly hard. Marissa turned on the sanitizing spray and washed away suds. A billow of steam wafted into her face. She raised her head and stared out the window above the sink. With her hand, she cleared the fogging glass.

"Who's that?" she said, staring at an unfamiliar man across the way.

Chapter Three

SILENTLY evaluating the scene outside, Marissa and Daphne lingered at the kitchen sink. The intense, afternoon heat of August wrapped everything within its sweltering grasp. Sweat glistened on the man's chest as he tossed debris in a construction bin that appeared two days earlier. He picked up the handles of the wheelbarrow, turned it around, and maneuvered through the overgrown lot and past the side of the house until the women lost sight of him.

Marissa leaned her forearms on the sink surround of white tile. Her vision refused to veer, waiting for his return. "So, someone's cleaning up that dilapidated place."

"The For Sale sign is gone," said Daphne. "I noticed a week ago when I cut through, on the way to the library. He was out there yesterday."

"Must be a workman doing renovation."

Daphne chuckled. "Workmen drive pickups not late model sedans."

"I assumed that car belonged to a real estate agent."

Daphne made a sidelong glance at Marissa. "Go say hello."

"You must be kidding. I'll size things up a while." Their attention went to the far corner as he rounded the house again. Marissa leaned closer to the glass. At that moment, the man turned his gaze on the tearoom. The women yanked themselves back. Marissa busied herself wiping the perfectly clean tile.

Daphne tugged at Marissa's apron. "Are you going to be late to your class?"

"Oh my gosh." Marissa ripped off the plain white cloth.

"I'll finish up," offered Daphne.

Marissa lightly squeezed one of Daphne's shoulders. "Thanks. Lock the back door when you leave. See you on Tuesday." Sundays and Mondays *Camellia Japonica* slumbered. "Don't forget I'll have to leave around ten to get to that Business Association thing."

Daphne nodded.

Marissa drove to a commercial area closer to the island interior. Entering the doors of the exercise studio, she heard the familiar music that began the relaxation process of her balance and flexibility class. She changed into active wear and walked into the mirrored room painted a soothing moss green. A placard hung above the far wall. The words *Unknot—Recharge*, in elegant script, set the tone. Jacquelyn's exercise and dance studio was regarded as unique as Jacquelyn's thumbprint. She waited, stationed at the front, skin like polished mahogany, eyes feline and flecked with gold. The music came on and they began their stretching routines. Her voice, mellow as mulled cider, called out encouragement. Every participant followed her lead. Marissa, well attuned to her body, felt her muscles sigh with rejuvenation. Thirty minutes later, Pachelbel's Canon in D lifted them off the floor and into the final phase—turning, bending, and reaching. Afterwards, some of the exercisers deviated to a smaller room and took seats on curving, white leather sofas. Outside the large glass window, a water fountain produced calming sounds. Scented towels waited on a warming tray for anyone who still needed to loosen any stubborn muscles in their neck or shoulders. Jacquelyn poured cranberry ginger spritzers, and the women talked about their week. Soon, most of the women went on their way. Marissa changed clothes, then waited for her friend. They sat in the office.

"So when are you going to try the aerobics class?" said Jacquelyn as she finished paperwork. "It's perfect for you."

"I'll try to make the 4:30 class on Wednesday. Things are smoothing out. Daphne and I have a good routine going. And her daughters were a big help this summer."

Jacquelyn, younger by five years, asked, "Are you handling the pressure better?"

"I'm surprising even myself," said Marissa. "I'll tell you over dinner."

"Where should we go this week?"

"Let's get something from Brogen's and take it to the pier."

They completed some errands and made it to the pier with their boxed food as sunset approached. Ocean winds swirled through the covered portion of the pier. Waves sloshed against the pilings.

"Hey, chil'," a heavy, black woman called. She bent over, placing a crab in a bucket, and raised herself again. Her broad smile was meant for Jacquelyn.

"Mama Townsend!" Jacquelyn embraced the woman. "This is Marissa, my friend. How are you?"

"How am I? Well, don't see how it matters much. You're a successful businesswoman and don't have time to come visit her elders no more."

Marissa grinned at Jacquelyn's embarrassment.

"I do apologize," Jacquelyn proclaimed. "I'll have to make up for it by bringing you one of my sweet potato pies soon."

"All right. That would do it."

Marissa leaned over the bucket. "What have you got in there?"

"Some good eats." She placed her thick hands on her hips and smiled.

"Is that a Dungeness?" asked Marissa looking at the crab. "I've been on a crash course, trying to learn about seafood."

"No. They's on the west coast. This is ol' blue crab. Crafty, but so sweet it's like the meat was dipped in honey." The woman swished her catch with a stick. "How's your mama, Jacquelyn?" The woman didn't wait for an answer and turned to Marissa. "I used to take care of Jacquelyn when she was the size of a pelican chick. Even as a little one, she was always so graceful. In church, we used to say she was as purdy as the resurrection fern that grows on the tree limbs round about. Good chil', too."

Marissa peeked at her friend.

Jacquelyn leaned back with surprise. "Really? You were always threatening to get a switch after me." She chuckled.

"That's why you's so good! Now tell me 'bout your mama."

"She's fine. Still working for the insurance company. Daddy wants her to retire. She comes over on Saturdays to take a class at my place."

"Well, tell her I said hello. I bet that's your dinner in those boxes. Now, don't let me keep you women."

Jacquelyn kissed her cheek. "We'll just take a seat across from you. But better watch us. We might make off with some of your catch."

They posted themselves on the long, continuous bench. Immediately a brown grackle flew to the railing behind them, landing near Marissa's shoulder.

She spoke directly to his dark brown beak. "Skedaddle. You're not getting any part of my hard-earned supper." He turned his umber eye away from her and flew off. She dug her fork into the coleslaw. "Jacquelyn, I had no idea you're from the island. Thought you were raised in Brunswick."

"I'm one of the few young ones who've come back to the island. My parents' first home was in the village section, in an area once owned by descendants of the slaves. Increasing land values and rising taxes drove most people out. Mom and Dad sold and moved to Brunswick when I was in high school. My brothers' jobs took them to Atlanta."

"I know all about the tax issue. I have to speak with my brother and decide what to do with the beach house soon. My grandparents bought the place in the Fifties. No one ever dreamed taxes would reach an astronomical sum for a 1920s bungalow."

"I hope you don't have to sell it. Nothing will ever have as much style and magic."

They concentrated on their food for a while. Their bench station surrounded them with sundry smells associated with ocean life. Half a dozen fishing lines draped down to the water. The sound of the rushing tide underscored the sharp calls of the seagulls. The birds sheared the air with their aerodynamic forms as they hunted for prizes below. Gear and containers of all sorts cluttered the pier. The concrete decking was marked and littered with leftover bait, oily stains, spilled Coca-Cola, a pair of grungy socks, fish scales, and a piece of raw chicken about to outfit a crab trap. An array of people wandered by or posted themselves along the railing. The assortment of women, mostly bingo and lawn chair age, earnest in their fishing efforts, had arms accustomed to work even though the aging skin and muscle hung like swags. The baggy knit pants and mismatched top a white-haired woman wore looked as though it had seen too many seasons. A young black man wore basketball shorts and a team logo shirt. He planted one lanky leg and shoe on the bench to steady his effort of putting a new hook on his line. A vacationing man nearing retirement age, wearing a fine watch and a high-end camera, sauntered by, wearing pale blue shorts and matching socks. The straw hat on his head was circled by a strip of Hawaiian-style fabric. As he passed the women, their interest followed the large marlin portrayed on the back of his poplin shirt. Two overgrown boys, one with braces, the other with a wad of gum in his mouth, challenged each other to a race, and they clomped in their sports shoes thirty yards to pier end.

Marissa and Jacquelyn closed their empty boxes and leaned back. Jacquelyn handed Marissa photos and stretched her arms along the rails.

"Russell?" Marissa asked, placing her blowing hair behind her ears. She studied the pictures of a well-built captain stationed in Afghanistan. "I can see why you miss him so."

"Little did I know at fourteen, with my knobby knees and an overbite, that the guy who shot baskets with my big brothers would someday think I was interesting."

"Oh, even then, he probably could see the rose that would bloom," said Marissa.

The sinking light began to heighten the beauty of the water and all the palmetto palms at the park. The fronds constantly fluttered inland. The women's vision went to the lighthouse farther down the shoreline. People, small to the distant eye, traipsed around the tower catwalk. When Marissa and Jacquelyn looked outward, their sight eventually drifted to the bridge leading to Jekyll. Squint as they might, it was impossible to make out a single detail on that island across the way, other than round tufted forms of dark green vegetation washed with gold by the falling sun.

Jacquelyn turned to Marissa with a confidential tone. "So. You said things are better these days."

"Maybe I'm more comfortable in my skin. I do know things are improving."

"Could be my class!" Jacquelyn chuckled.

"A big help but it's something deeper. . . . On other days, it seems like I have to work at it to stand myself."

"Hey, girl, you're not some obnoxious shrew."

"If you knew me three years ago, you'd think differently."

"What?"

"We probably wouldn't even be friends then."

"Wow. What changed you?"

"A friend in Woodstock, an older woman. She helped me understand myself better . . . and understand men."

"Well, she must have done it with kindness because you seem to value her insight."

"I do. And if Abby disliked me, as a few people were known to do, she worked hard to keep it hidden."

"I'd like to meet her some time."

"The chances aren't favorable. She's very ill. My thoughts should be about her, but I usually get lost in my own concerns. And just when I think I really might own that positive potential she saw in me, I go and show my backside, making it clear her predictions were an error."

"*Marissa*, everyone loves you the way you are. Except this serious side. Let's go bowl our arms off."

They picked up their stuff and said good-bye to Mama Townsend. Marissa handed her two complimentary tea and muffin cards for *Camellia*. As they ambled back down the pier, happily talking away, Marissa stepped on a small fish having flopped from the bucket of a five-year-old fisherman. The boy looked ruefully at his dad as though he ought to do something about the bad woman. The stomped head of the fish made Marissa's insides squirm. She made a wry, see-what-I-mean face at Jacquelyn, and after apologizing to the child, they continued on their way.

Chapter Four

MARISSA worked at her desk in the small office of *Camellia Japonica* the next Tuesday morning, slowest day of the week. They'd be lucky if they saw a dozen customers the entire day. Daphne had come in extra early to do the baking. She would be on her own at lunch hour with Marissa attending her business meeting. Clemma and Alexa had started a new school year.

The blazing part of the day was hours away, yet Marissa ignored the pleasant morning air just outside her office window. As she pored over her accounting, she was also oblivious to the maypop vine that had threaded its way up the window screen to her left. Her spreadsheet blinded her to the passion flower blooming close enough to drip morning dew on the desk. The muted violet petals mirrored the color of her halter dress, and they were smooth as the skin of her revealed shoulders. She studied the figures another hour. Her fingers flashed over the calculator. Her hands came together, and she drew close, checking the numbers one last time. Her face lifted, radiant. She stood and ran to the kitchen.

Daphne added cherry topping to a cheesecake. Marissa whipped the bowl and spatula from her assistant's hands. Then Marissa grabbed those same hands and twirled Daphne about.

"We've made it! We're covering our overhead and squeaking by with a little profit. Whoopee!" she yelled at the top of her lungs.

"Whoopee!" echoed Daphne, who took up the spatula and whirled it like she cheered at a championship game.

They bent over laughing.

"Oh, I hate to have to go to the luncheon today of all days," said Marissa. "I'd like to stay here and kiss each customer who walks through the door."

"Even the trench coat lady?" asked Daphne.

"I told you she's never coming back. Wouldn't dare. Oh no, look at the time. I'd better get going or the boat will leave without me."

Marissa spied a plastic trash bag waiting for disposal. First thing that morning, Daphne had peeled and diced half a bushel of onion, now ready for freezing. The ripening discard permeated the room. With a swoosh, Marissa caught the knot of the bag with her hand and swirled the bag around the kitchen.

"Out with the trash," she proclaimed with a laugh, almost floating with happiness to the door. "Yes! Out with the trash and in with the cash!" Laughing again, she looked back at Daphne while bounding out the door. Then . . . *Bam!* Marissa was instantly, forcefully merged with a man. His hands had flown around to brace her from a fall. The bag had dropped to their feet. She sucked in air.

"Morning, Glory," he said, his arms still holding her snug.

Marissa's eyebrows pulled into a frown. "What?" she blurted.

Letting her go, he grinned and shook his head slightly. "It's an old expression of my mother. But you fit the expression much better than my brother and me."

She jerked the trash bag up and grimly straightened her dress.

He stepped back, looking wary. "Sorry about the collision. You darted out the door pretty fast. I'm from across the way. William Dash is my name."

"Marissa Manning," she said without a drop of warmth. "This is my tearoom. I'm in a hurry. I have a business gathering to attend."

"Uh-huh. Is it me or the onion odor giving you that bulldog look? I simply wanted to say hello."

"You don't have to be rude about it." She moved past, rushed to the wooden steps and down. Her skirt billowed and a gust of wind swirled by, making her skirt fly so high in back, that two lace-covered cheeks felt sunlight. She fought the exposure with her free arm. It looked like he tried to hide his amusement by turning his head, but his shaking shoulders gave him away. Lips pursed, she swung the bag into the trash bin like she wielded an axe.

"Pardon me, I didn't mean to laugh," he pleaded when she reached the top of the stairs again.

His eyes had an unmistakable twinkle.

She shot him an annoyed look and walked past. She slammed the door behind her, in case he didn't get the message.

Daphne stopped the roaring mixer. "What's the matter?"

"I met our new neighbor." She went to the bathroom to put a little cold water on her neck before she left.

Minutes later, Marissa walked in the direction of the pier, mildly energized. In the bathroom, her ire had melted somewhat when she considered the fact that she had precipitated the crash. His smile was magnetic although she resisted. Leaning against him was like pressing into a firm live oak. Making his tan more prominent, his wavy brown hair leaned toward premature silver. Couldn't have been more than forty, she figured. She sighed, removing him from her list of possibilities; he obviously considered her an object of derision. Anyway, she didn't like starting things off unbalanced and without having the upper hand. She learned a long time ago, the right attitude prevented a lot of hurt later.

Marissa stepped from the end of the pier onto the party ship. The captain lightly held her hand and guided her down steps to the main decking. She was glad she wore flats. The ship rocked with the sea rhythm. A sense of excitement always trickled through her when she first found herself in a boat that wasn't so large you lost awareness of nautical motion. The business association leaders greeted Marissa. At the rear of the boat, a man with dark hair stared with interest. She went through the buffet line and took a seat between two members she knew.

The vessel shoved from the pier and moved through the St. Simons basin. The man sat at another table, seeming to enjoy himself with everyone and especially with the two men on either side of him, their laughter and conversation continuous. He wore clothes slightly unconventional, and he wore them with tremendous style. She caught him admiring her again. She wondered when he would approach. Unrevealed to her, he was a man of the game. A foot taller than Marissa, with commanding eyes, he always took his time. So she waited. After the meal, the guest speaker's mouth churned on, an unstoppable outboard motor drowning any interest. Listeners stifled their yawns. Marissa found she could watch a trio of shrimp boats and their active halo of gulls without making known that her focus no longer rested on the speaker but had moved slightly to the right. The dynamic sight of nets and catch being drawn in held her mind. How long she was engaged, she didn't know.

"I see you like the hunt," a male voice said softly near her ear.

Marissa jerked her head to the left. The smiling man leaned back and nodded to the far-off boats. He had usurped the seat of her partner on the left who had gone to the latrine.

She let out a little breath. "It's much more interesting."

"You and I agree." His was an entirely different meaning.

After church the next Sunday, Marissa took Darrien's hand and praised his ability to make her see, to understand, in a way she hadn't before. He thanked her and held her fingers a little longer than usual. She inquired after his mother. Irene was with a sitter and preferred to listen later to a recording of the service. The unfortunate incident six months earlier at the Sunset Supper had been forgotten by everyone as each had gained a clearer understanding of the spoons and their origin. Marissa played the scene over at least once a month, imagining how she could have acted with more grace. Sometimes the rehashing made her miserable. At other times her irritation renewed itself.

Marissa followed Jacquelyn to a plot of fiery-colored croton. After the air conditioned room, the warm sun on their arms and shoulders felt pleasurable. They talked.

"He was . . . quietly fascinating," Marissa said, searching for description, "with his dark curling hair that reached his collar and with the way he wore his clothes. He studied art in Paris and landscape design in England. He also said he spent way too much time in the pubs drinking dark ale and reading poetry."

"The way you describe him, I wonder if he keeps a raven on his shoulder or something equally mysterious. Is his last name Poe?"

"No, Silly. His name is Byron S. Hewitt."

"Him! *He's a pick up artist.*"

"You are totally wrong."

"No, I'm not. He prides himself on how many deals he's closed."

"Stop it! He was a gentleman. You know, Jacquelyn, you don't usually fall victim to envy."

"You think it's a different guy, but did he make sure to mention he's been hired to do work on the grounds of the Sinclair and Bell cottages on Jekyll. Or that he designed the new garden room for the Cloister?"

Marissa's features sank.

Jacquelyn's face took on sympathy. "You're not the first woman on this island he's tried to make a move on. Ask Shanna and Claire about their terrible escapades."

"Well that explains it," said Marissa. "Those two ditsy women go through men like Kleenex. Anyway, Jacquelyn, if it's not something you know firsthand, then you could be way off base."

"I don't think so."

"You should trust *my* opinion," said Marissa. "I've been around much more than you have, and I'm a *great* judge of men." Marissa saw William Dash come from the church with an older man who could have been his father. She grabbed Jackie by the arm. "Let's get out of here."

They put down the roof of Jackie's convertible. They drove to Fort Frederica and walked around until the deer flies and Jackie's arguments against a certain attraction got to Marissa. They marched to the car, not speaking. Once the convertible roared down the road, the wind did a good job yanking their hair.

Chapter Five

MARISSA'S car shot over the causeway bridges and traveled through Brunswick to one of the middle schools. She watched the parade of kids exit the school, kids no one wanted to be, that awkward age when everything in life is determined to shame you in the worst possible way. An understanding smile flitted over her lips, while looking at their ungraceful walks, bad skin trying to hide behind shaggy haircuts or under make-up, and loud talk and laughter meant to give everyone the impression they were knock-the-world-in-the-chin happy. Marissa could well remember it all. She scanned the crowd for Clemma and Alexa.

Her arm shot out the window. "Hey! Over here!"

The girls lollygagged like she had all day, Alexa slightly behind her older sister as usual. Marissa jumped from the car and went to the trunk, waving some more. Clemma's expression turned to one of barely hidden humiliation.

"Hey, girls. Give me your book bags. I'll put them in the trunk." She wasn't certain but it looked as though Clemma rolled her eyes before she ignored the suggestion and slunk into the front passenger seat. Alexa followed her lead and took the rear seat. They both popped earphones in their ears where music played except for the five minutes it took them to run into their small house and pack some clothes. Then the earphones went back in place, for the entire sixteen minute ride to St. Simons and the East Beach area.

At the beach house, Marissa pulled into sandy indentions worn in the Bermuda grass and cut off the engine. She turned in the driver's seat as the girls were about to get out.

"Hold it." Her hand was raised with a flattened palm like a stop sign. She pointed to her ear and mimicked a yank. The girls removed their earpieces. "Listen. I'm sorry this is so sudden and your aunt is out of town." The girls glanced at each other. "Anyway, try to have a nice weekend here, okay? After they observe your mom on the new drug, she'll be back home on Monday."

"They explained everything at school," said Clemma. Alexa said nothing.

They got out of the car. The girls' heads angled up, gawking at the roof deck and the open tower of the weathered house. Rushing wind and the commotion of the sea came from behind the clapboard structure. Marissa led the way through the front door, thinking she had failed to get to know them better over ten weeks of summer, within the hustle and bustle of her restaurant, hadn't had time to, actually, hadn't had the faintest idea of how to talk to two girls so far from her own age.

The girls dawdled just beyond the entryway, slowly examining the bright white interior that made everyone overlook the worn woodwork and rough-plastered walls and discrete plaster ornamentation of another era. Then their study sharpened as Marissa knew it would. She hadn't been immune either, as a very small child, the first time she and her slightly older brother entered the ocean side cottage and noticed the thematic decorations. Alexa spotted one first. She scooted to the entrance light switch where a painted mermaid rested languidly above. A light wash of paint made the water nymph almost fade into the wall as though you stared at her through sea water. Alexa pointed and smiled. Clemma noticed the next one, an octopus scouring the ocean bottom, unmenacing, in the foyer niche. They looked at Marissa.

"They're all over the place," she answered to their unspoken question. The girls dropped their bags to the floor and took off in a search. For an hour they ran around the place searching for the surprise pictorials, finding seagulls in the painted sky above the tub, smiling dolphins on the window sill in a bedroom, sunken ships and treasure chests in the other bedroom, sand dunes and sea oats above the kitchen window, and the most beautiful of all decorating the dining room, a nineteenth-century sailing vessel, sails sending her speedily through the water. They came running to the kitchen, where Marissa prepared dinner, wanting to know about the door in the hall ceiling ornamented with a coral reef scene. She turned off the stove and went to the hall that led to the bedrooms. She brought a stool from the hall closet, reached, and unhooked the latch. The door swung down. She opened its compartment. A rope ladder with wooden rungs fell out. Marissa knew the stairs across the front of the house provided an easier ascent, but she waved the girls up. Forsaking her kitchen duties, she followed. Open on all sides, the tower welcomed every breeze but protected loungers from the burning rays above. They peered at the ocean until Marissa had to return to the kitchen.

Later, they sat down to dinner of a seafood casserole and salad.

"This is the most special house I've ever been to," said Alexa who looked at Clemma for agreement.

Clemma nodded. "Yeah, it is. The way the beds are built like ship . . ."

"Berths," said Marissa.

"Yeah, it's cool. And those round windows are neat."

"Portholes," said Alexa.

Marissa grinned at Alexa. "You got it."

Alexa smiled bashfully. "I read a lot."

"That's for sure!" Clemma blurted. "She's the brain. I'm the jock."

Marissa wriggled her head. "You shouldn't lock yourself in like that. You're much more than one thing, I'm sure."

The girls looked at her as if the idea had never occurred to them, at an age when labels are everything.

Marissa wiped her mouth and sat back. "Anyway, I'm glad you like the beach house. It was a present to Mrs. Weinstein from her husband in 1923. She was an artist."

Clemma eyed Marissa. "I thought you weren't supposed to label people."

Marissa screwed her mouth to the side, then laughed and rolled her napkin in a tight ball. She lobbed it at Clemma's forehead.

Clemma jumped up. "I've got my glove and softball in my bag. Can we go outside and toss for a while?" They cleared the table and went out the back door to the beach. Leaving dishes in the sink was tough for Melissa.

Outside, people wearing pants with rolled-up legs waded through the shallow water. An old couple held hands and pointed out different sights to each other. A young mother squatted alongside her two toddlers digging in the wet muck near the water line for anything catching their interest, especially the tiny holes releasing bubbles when the edge of the incoming tide rolled over the home of whatever lived below.

The game of catch continued for thirty minutes. Alexa had given up in the first five and sat in the soft dry sand near the sea wall, looking out. Marissa could tell from the child's placid expression that her mind was spinning tales. Suddenly, the ball hit Marissa's hands once again, much too hard. She pivoted away and walked to some spreading beach vine where she hunched and admired the plant. Instinctively, she knew exactly how to handle Clemma, no arguing, no begging, calm consequence.

Clemma raced over. "What's wrong? I promise I won't do it again."

"Let's head to the house, now." Marissa didn't frown or try to make her feel bad.

"Okay. . . . Come on, Alexa," said Clemma.

After a long school day, the girls hit sleep quicker than a clam snaps shut. Marissa doused the lights and wondered if it was going to be a discombobulated weekend.

The next morning, they breakfasted on muffins and hot coffee with lots of cream and sugar. Over in the village, *Camellia* wore a sign saying: Closed-Sat. only, due to unexpected circumstances. As it was early September, the sun still burned hot by ten. They scrambled into their bathing suits and played in the sea. Unhappy to part too long with her softball, Clemma ran into the house and came out begging for another session. Once the tossing began, Clemma restrained herself to such a degree that even Alexa stayed in the game. After a long while, Alexa made a poor toss and the ball scooted through some lattice and under the house. Sweating from the exercise, Clemma begged for one more dip before they went on the hunt in the dark environs. All three plunged into the water. Squeals came from the girls. Refreshed, they left the water and headed on their mission.

An elf-size gateway as their entrance, they proceeded under the house positioned on short piers. On hands and knees, they paused letting their eyes adjust to the dimness. No monsters met them, just miniature hills and dales of clean, cool sand. A thick plumbing pipe hung low and required them to tummy crawl to the corner where the ball entered. Marissa thought she encountered a few hard objects but moved forward. She thought she saw a metallic glimmer. Still wet from their swim, skin grabbed sand until they were covered with a thick coat. Alexa fetched the errant softball, and they began to clamber out again.

"What's this?" Clemma grasped a handle and pulled. A large metal spoon perched in her hand. They laughed and sat back on their folded legs. Alexa's hand sifted and came up with a pot. Marissa found a rusted kitchen knife, Alexa, another spoon.

Clemma looked up from her work. "This is fun. Sort of serendipitous."

"Good vocab, Clemma," replied Marissa with a grin.

"On yesterday's Engish test. I studied."

Alexa touched Marissa's forearm. "Why's this stuff here? You didn't have your first restaurant under the house, I hope." The girls laughed.

Marissa leaned to one side, propped by her arm. "No. But my grandmother told me about this stuff. She knew that Mrs. Weinstein buried these things here. If I remember correctly, the Weinsteins, being orthodox Jews, followed certain dietary rules. Cooking utensils were designated for certain foods, and if they forgot and used the implement or pot incorrectly, the item was to be taken from the home and buried in the yard."

Clemma's eyes were big. "Wow. So this is a kitchen graveyard of sorts."

"I guess so," said Marissa.

"Let's take 'em," Clemma said.

"No. We'll leave them here, out of respect," Marissa replied. They returned everything to its hiding place and crawled back to the door. Marissa was the last one out. The girls scrambled away, running full tilt to the water to wash off their sand suits. Their enthusiasm was contagious, and Marissa's long legs went into overdrive so smoothly that her speed was effortless.

The girls already splashed in the water when Marissa's mind made sufficient calculation to let her know that at her current rate she would collide with the two men walking a large black dog along the shore. She slowed and realized at twenty yards that she was acquainted with the younger man who paused. Her only options were to make an abrupt U-turn or face the meeting.

"Hello, Ms. Manning," he said.

"Hello, Mr., um . . ."

"Dash. William Dash."

"Please forgive my memory."

"Well, we didn't have the best of meetings. I figured you were having a really bad day."

"No, just the opposite." She didn't smile. Standing there in her bathing suit, she felt awkward and shy but comforted at the same time by her coating of gray sand. The black lab stayed obediently by the older gentleman's side but seemed entranced by the activity of the bouncing, diving, water slapping girls. Marissa prayed the girls wouldn't bound from the ocean and come prolong things.

"This is my father, Kevin Dash," said William. "He's visiting." The older man held out his hand.

Marissa brushed off her own two with a chuckle and they shook. There was something appealing written on his face. Either kindness or gentleness, she couldn't decide. And she was blown away by the resemblance. "You know you look just like your son." He nodded his head and the two men grinned at each other as though they shared a secret. Marissa tilted her head.

"People tell us that all the time," the older man replied. The girls screamed from the water for Marissa to join them. He continued. "I'd like to stop by your eatery while I'm here. Heard you have caramel cake."

"It's my mother's recipe. I would love for you to visit *Camellia*." With more reserve, she glanced at William. "Both of you, of course." She drifted toward the water.

William nodded.

The men remained for a minute, talking, watching the females bob and swirl their arms. Then the men walked on.

Chapter Six

THAT afternoon on the way to the island stables, Marissa explained that riding was the one thing she did every Saturday afternoon to treat herself. It eased her yearning for Al, Marissa's palomino pastured in her hometown at her Uncle Nathan's north Georgia farm.

Alexa had to be coaxed onto a gentle mare.

"But what if the horse starts bucking and I can't stop it?" she said. "Or what if it wasn't fed this morning and it turns around and bites my leg?"

"Curb that imagination of yours," replied Marissa. "I'm with you and nothing bad will happen if you follow my directions." Finally, Alexa stopped her protests. Marissa turned to selecting a ride for Clemma.

"No, Clemma. That stallion is too powerful. I learned firsthand."

"If I get thrown, it'll be my own fault."

"You won't get thrown, but if you can't manage him, he might take off and you could land on the other side of a fence that became a sudden obstacle."

"Did that happen to you?" Clemma asked.

"*No.*" Marissa wondered how Clemma knew. It wasn't a real lie, Marissa decided, because she had pushed the animal into a gallop and the obstacle had been a hedge.

Clemma's sulky face appeared. "What fun is it going to be if I have to ride something slow as a cow?"

Marissa sensed pressure building beneath her skull. She took a deep breath and spoke calmly. "Would you rather do some cane pole fishing"—Alexa perked up—"or ride Hannah, over there? You choose, Clemma."

Clemma looked at her shoes for a moment. "Okay. Hannah."

Marissa huffed, "You remind me too much of myself when I was a kid."

After a pleasurable and uneventful ride, they bought barbecue sandwiches and drove out to Hampton Point where they sat on the dock and gazed at the river and the wispy cordgrass, which Alexa estimated numbered in the trillions. When they finished their meal, they walked around, exploring the complex of condominiums and the boat storage building. Marissa led them back to the entrance and the broken remnants of tabby foundation walls neither girl had noticed earlier.

"So something was here before all this nice stuff?" asked Clemma.

"Oh, yes. In the 1800s, the whole island was dotted with plantations growing rice and cotton." They read the historical marker.

Alexa looked at the scene with rose-colored glasses. "So this was once a nice little cottage for a family." She brushed her hand across the rough shell exterior. The ruins were situated on emerald green grass that had been carefully fertilized and cropped. The walls were hugged by lush and colorful semi-tropical plants.

"Being in bondage, they probably didn't consider anything in their lives so appealing," said Marissa. "Back then, the yard was probably nothing more than sand and the conditions inside were awful. Two or three families were housed in a structure about the size of your bedroom at home."

Clemma's face went serious. "No way would I take that!"

"Children who survived illness and managed to reach your age worked in the field alongside the adults. And each day, at least at the Butler rice plantation, a child's allotment of food might be a single jar of hominy."

"Hominy?" said Clemma.

"Like big grits," said Marissa.

"That's so cruel," said Clemma. "How do you know all these details?"

"I'm reading a book written by a nineteenth-century actress named Fanny Kemble. She married a wealthy man from Philadelphia. When he brought her down here in 1838 to visit his holdings, she discovered the situation the slaves endured and wrote about it. Her husband wasn't a compassionate man. The more fortunate slaves, if you can call them that, lived on the Cooper plantation."

"Can I borrow the book sometime?" asked Clemma.

"Certainly. See, you're a reader, too. You just want your subject to be real, not fiction."

Clemma smiled and they walked to the car with Alexa jabbering about the latest fantasy she had fallen into.

After dinner, they parked their bodies on a high dune and built a fire. Saturday was coming to a close. Marissa told them to watch for the eerie-white ghost crabs that only emerged at night, scampering sideways along the beach to feed. The girls stuffed on marshmallows until Clemma, regarding Marissa with that now familiar, persistent look, presented an idea. She even put down her stick of perfectly roasted marshmallows, careful to lean the tip against one of the bricks lining the fire so her treat wouldn't be spoiled, and she waited for the answer she wanted to hear.

"I'm telling you, girls," said Marissa, "it's one thing to get a tan in the sling chairs up there. It's another thing altogether to attempt to sleep there."

Clemma stood, continuing to deliver her case with conviction. "Wouldn't it be just like camping out, but up high? Think of the fun of it. I could tell all my friends who always get to go to really neat places. But the tower's no good. We have to be on the roof deck, able to see above us."

Marissa wondered why she just didn't come out and say, *no*. "The roof tiles are still hot in the first of the evening."

"We could take the two small mattresses up." Clemma did all the reasoning. Alexa simply monitored the debate.

Marissa rubbed her knees, looked around. "I give up," she said a little too forcefully. "But we have church first thing in the morning. If you two don't settle into sleep, we're heading indoors."

Clemma yipped and hollered. She plopped down again.

Alexa gave her sister a confrontational stare. "Did you forget, Clemma?" Alexa's tone was hard, and her heart-shaped face looked hurt. Clemma got still.

Marissa stared quizzically, "What is it?"

"It's nothing," Clemma's voice was soft and empty of excitement. "I'll help with the mattresses." She stood.

Marissa turned her face to the fire where a brilliant spark ascended to the sky and flamed out. "Aren't you going to eat your marshmallows?"

"I'm not hungry." Marissa didn't press; she understood why as they all watched another spark float to the heavens.

With Clemma's help, Marissa shoved first one, then the other, twin mattress up the stairs that ran on the diagonal across the front of the house to the roof. Pulling might have been simpler, but she knew her body, and she had decided it was best to test her arms and shoulders rather than her back. They meshed the mattresses together. After a great to-do assembling linens, pillows, and a large blanket, a disagreement broke out between the girls about who should take the middle spot. Marissa volunteered but wondered at the wisdom of her choice the minute she reclined and put her head on her pillow. It was obvious that if a lot of tossing and turning occurred, a gap would open and she would sink.

The night began balmy, but Marissa had insisted they wear sufficient clothing for the breeze that would ratchet itself up as the tide came in around 2:00 a.m. The top sheet and blanket waited down by their feet. Lying on their backs, their faces looked to the milky clouds passing before the moon. For a while no one spoke. The water washed along the shore, without force. The wind swirled gently over them.

"Can you imagine what it would be like if we rode that cloud? The one that looks like a strange seahorse?" said Alexa. "It would be a magic ride over the lighthouse and the pier and the causeway . . . all the way to the hospital. We could look down into the window and see how she was. You know, lonely, or thirsty, or . . . wondering."

Marissa spoke without looking at Alexa. "You wish you could take care of your mother always. Don't you?"

"Yes."

"Most people feel that way at some point in their lives."

"Why's life so mean?" asked Clemma.

"It's not life," said Marissa. "Everything that is life is good. It's the world we're in that's tough."

Clemma's head turned to Marissa. "Could I ask you something?" Clemma said.

Marissa felt a little of her guard come up. Usually when someone started with that question, rudeness, anger, or heartlessness was about to follow.

"I guess so," Marissa replied.

"Well," said Clemma. "I was wondering if we could call you Aunt Marissa. Our real aunt . . . she's kind of a pain."

Alexa giggled.

"I'd like that," Marissa replied. "Now we better try to sleep. Remember, the schedule for tomorrow is church, dinner, read or study, a light supper, and an early goodnight since there's school the next day."

Thoroughly depleted by fun throughout the day, they all slept immovable as a barnacle encrusted boulder on the jetty at the island north end. As the temperature dropped, Marissa remained unaware that an empty space slowly opened beneath her.

A few hours past midnight, Marissa woke when Clemma ejected their covers.

The girl jumped up and stood. A rushing sound from all around filled Marissa's ears. Alexa had snuggled as close as she could to Marissa who felt roof tiles under her spine.

"What are you doing, Clemma?" Marissa grumbled from her narrow ditch and sat up. Clemma beamed a fantastic smile, arms straight up in the air like someone scored a touchdown. The girl's hair streamed like ribbons. Her shirt fluttered wildly.

Clemma looked down at Marissa. "This is the coolest! It's like gale force winds, and the ocean is churning."

"A strong prevailing wind from the northeast and the incoming tide, that's all," Marissa shouted above the crashing water and wind. "Lie back down!"

Clemma obeyed. They all ducked their ears under the covers to subdue the noise. The last thing Marissa heard before she went back to sleep were Clemma's words, "*I love life.*"

Chapter Seven

MARISSA sat on the top step of the deck, watching the landscape crew install the final planting in the back lot of *Camellia Japonica*. In that tranquilizing, dusky section of the village, towering live oaks their high arms adorned with hanging sleeves of Spanish moss provided a canopy of deep shade except in a few random areas and on one quarter of Marissa's lot, the rear portion where the sun shone hot and bright. A raised planting bed, three feet high and placed at the far lot line, held an assortment of immature herbs ready to explode in size. Closer to *Camellia*, a hardscape made of pavers created a twenty by thirty-two foot dining area. The paver design, centrally accented by a leaf and a blossom large as a table, had been artfully executed by a Mexican who at the time kept asking Marissa, "You like? You like?" to which she always replied, "Mucho gusto."

All day across the way, William Dash worked hard without pause, repairing the rotted railing and door jamb of his back stoop. The sounds of his power tools competed with those of the landscape workers.

The finishing touches on Marissa's outdoor dining project came to an end, so Marissa packed the restaurant leftovers of sandwiches and treats to send home with the men. Her soft urgings to take the food danced on the air. The workers' calloused, brown hands received her gifts. The men's demeanor became timid as they looked into her eyes with quick smiles to thank her, and they went away with their bounty that was sure to please a wife or girlfriend. Marissa turned to go back inside the tearoom when she noticed William Dash smile and give a wave. She was about to acknowledge him when a different male voice called hello from the opposite direction.

Byron Hewitt, coming by way of the path alongside *Camellia*, entered the newly created area. He caught her attention like a rare and beautiful beast entering a forest where she stood alone.

"Byron," she said with surprise.

His face unreadable, he approached.

She pulled the kerchief off her hair. "I can't tell you how thrilled I am with the results. But I wasn't expecting you." She straightened her work clothes consisting of jeans and a rose-colored t-shirt displaying her restaurant logo. As he looked around, he didn't seem the least interested in her appearance.

"Didn't I tell you I could create something inspiring while staying within your budget?"

"It's more than you promised. I'll have to avoid glancing out the window because I'll want to be in this garden and nothing would get done."

"Do you like the water feature?" he asked. "And how about that private nook I made for lovers?" He placed his hand at the top of her nape and turned her in the direction of the spot sequestered beneath an arbor of wrought iron and curtained by Carolina jasmine on both sides. Marissa noted the cooling down of the day as his hand on her skin registered warm and pleasant.

"I love every element of the design," she said. "You're amazing, Byron."

"I'm traveling to Charleston in a few weeks if you'd like to come along and see my masterwork that's being done there. Well, that's how some describe it. It's easy in a place with so much historical flair. Can you get away for a weekend?"

"I, uh . . ."

"Hold on. My phone is vibrating." He moved away, flipped the phone open, and began a garrulous conversation. Marissa's sight drifted, and she was surprised to find William watching the scene from his yard. He put down his tools, left the porch, and walked over, entering through the back of the lot by the herb bed. He walked up to her while Byron continued his phone call.

"This is some transformation," William said to her. "Very inviting."

"Thank you," she said and turned briefly to smooth the finely ground bark around a delicate plant with tiny floating blooms in a waist-tall urn. She turned to him again.

William's face questioned as he flicked his thumb toward Byron who carried on with laughter and animated talk.

"My friend, Byron Hewitt," she said. The man she referred to briefly raised his head and gave a nod to William.

Byron rambled on the pavers, tossed his head back, and said. "Miriam, you are a doll. But I've been telling you for six months, there is no use setting me up with more of those beautiful friends of yours. You know how bad my heart was broken by Cecile. So for the final time, I'm laying low until I can give up my passion for landscape design and enter a monastery." He laughed again and ended the conversation. Flipping the phone closed, he began stepping away with a huge smile. "Gotta go, Marissa. People are tugging at me as usual. I'll call you later about our trip." He turned and trotted off. They could hear his sports car out front as it backed over the shell-filled parking lot.

Marissa caught a quick glimpse of him charging down the street.

"I'd be careful of that one," William said.

Her head jerked around. "Don't be unpleasant again."

"Sorry. I just wanted to compliment you on the change here and tell you that I'll be bringing Dad by soon."

"Oh. Thanks for letting me know. I have a yellow cake with pecans that's begging to be dressed in caramel icing."

William left and walked past the herb bed again, wondering how the guy had been able to talk on his cell phone. Service had been down since noon. Wouldn't return until midnight according to his provider's e-mail. Tower repair. He entered his house and re-read the message.

The following day, thirty minutes before closing time, Marissa wrapped food items for storage. Daphne brought cranberry scones from the oven, to be used the next day.

"Daphne, I'm going to hire some help. It's becoming too much to manage, especially now that we have outside dining."

"You know what that will do to your overhead."

"The finances look fine." Marissa came over and squeezed Daphne's hand. "I couldn't have accomplished this without you."

"Working here has really helped take my mind off my illness."

Marissa's tone became reverent. "I pray for you every night." They wrapped their arms around one another. The sound of someone entering the tearoom reached their ears.

"I thought our day was almost over," Daphne said, smiling. "I'll seat them."

"Good. I've got to check the meter outside. I swear they must be inventing numbers. We can't be using that much electricity. Then, if things are slow here, I'll run get the chives we'll need in the morning."

The women took off their aprons and commenced with their plan. Marissa went out the back door and down the deck steps. The meter was on the side of the house, too close to a sharply pointed yucca. She crouched and looked at the turning disk. She brought her hand to her chin and squeezed a little. She stared. How did you read those funny dials? From somewhere in her head, she recalled the crazy method: clockwise, counter-clockwise, clockwise, counter-clockwise, or was she entirely wrong? She heard Daphne exit the back door with guests having male voices. Chairs shuffled against the pavers.

"Hope you men will enjoy our new outdoor dining," Daphne said.

"It's great," said the older voice. "We'll have two coffees and one piece of caramel cake." Marissa's ears perked.

Hidden around the corner, she concentrated on the dials, wanting to take her time before she went to their table with a greeting. She wrote numbers on a piece of paper.

"By the way, where're you from?" the older man asked Daphne. "You look very much like someone I used to know."

"A place you probably never heard of. Inaha. Near Tifton. But I've spent most of my adult life in Brunswick. Daphne Adams is my name."

"Oh well, I'm from South Carolina, but come to think of it, you can't be the girl I knew in grade school. You must be a decade or more younger. But how do you do? I'm Kevin Dash and this is my son, William who lives right over there."

"Nice to meet both of you. I've seen you working on your place, Mr. William."

"Hope the racket didn't give you a headache. It's very nice to meet the woman who makes food with such a fabulous reputation, ma'am."

Marissa's pencil fell out of her hand. Her head raised but she remained crouched. Wasn't she going to get any credit? They were her recipes, her menus.

"I just follow Marissa's directions. She's a whiz at scones, muffins, crepes, and cakes. My talent is pie—peach, cherry, pecan, and apple. Still, you have no idea how lucky I am to have this job."

"Really. How come?" said William.

"Oh, tough times, but I've got the most wonderful boss."

"Yes, she's something," William said pleasantly enough. "Why don't you give me a slice of the apple, and I'll decide whether she took a good risk."

Daphne chuckled. "Okay. I'll be right back with your order."

The kitchen door slapped shut. Marissa got up but stayed invisible.

"So, William," said his father. "You've come to the right place. This Marissa must have a softer heart than you thought."

"You know, Dad, she's like I always imagined. Her height. Her shape. And that face. It's beautiful in its own way."

One of Marissa's eyebrows rose with interest. She turned and leaned against the building. A smug grin came out. She drew closer to the yucca and inclined one ear in the guests' direction.

"Forgive the advice, but be careful, William. You could get hurt. There's no telling what her reaction will be when you speak to her."

Marissa leaned closer and jerked back from the pricking plant.

"Don't worry, Dad. I'm pretty savvy. I'll take it slow. Women are easy."

Marissa bristled and her eyebrows lowered.

"Good. You've worked hard to find her."

The hinges on the back door squeaked. Daphne came outside with the order. Marissa fumed, plastered with irritation against the side of the restaurant. She hardly knew the man who picked her out with cunning and certainty. If he wanted a woman why didn't he just hit her over the head with a club and drag her off by her hair.

"Where's Marissa?" she heard William say. Marissa instantly tried to meld with the wall.

"She must have walked to the market. We need chives."

"Well, if we don't see her, please let her know how much we're enjoying our visit."

"Certainly."

William tapped his plate. "This is the most delicious pie I have ever tasted. The crust melts in your mouth. And the apples have the right amount of sweetness not overcome with tartness. Hope you won't mind if I hang around every day at closing time for the scraps." Marissa heard Daphne chuckle and return to the interior.

It was quiet for some moments.

"Taste the cake, William."

Marissa waited, straining to hear.

"Hm," William finally said. "It's a little dry and way too many nuts."

Marissa's nostrils flared with grievous offense. She exhaled and hustled away to the market. Oh how she was going to enjoy burying that man's heartthrob notions.

The two men finished their refreshments. Daphne came outside with the check.

She handed William the slip and grinned with her hands on her hips. "Well, talking about resemblances, I swanny, you two are spitting images."

"The resemblance is entirely coincidental," replied William.

"How's that, when you're father and son?"

"I'm adopted," William said and extended a very large bill. His father quietly watched the exchange.

"That, so?" She shook her head with amazement and smiled. "I'll be back with your change."

"Keep it. The pie was more than worth it."

Daphne looked at the money. Her hand went to her cheek. "I don't think I can take this."

"You must. In the state we're from, it's against the law not to reward good baking."

"Thank you so much, sir." She went quietly away.

William and his father remained seated for a moment. William looked his dad in the eye. "Man, it's like the stab of a knife, hearing the woman who gave you life call you, *sir*."

Chapter Eight

An exotic orchid, delivered within the hour, sat on Marissa's office desk. It was the third orchid in three weeks. She put the bloom near at hand so she could examine its elaborate form. The novel color of chartreuse captivated her sight. For the first time a card accompanied the bloom, but without a name. She perused the sentiment again.

She is complex, too intriguing to be a common rose.
Time moves quickly.
Mystery must be explored or forever close.

With those words, relief rushed in. Marissa was now certain the orchids were not the offering of her back door neighbor. He could never be that poetic, much too thoughtless to know she had a brain, a soul worth investigating. The only thing that captured him was an unexpected embrace with a stranger and her skirt flying up in back. Those words on the card could have been written by only one man she knew, the one whose call she waited for. She would have to decline the trip to Charleston. Some kind of persuasive tension developed when he was near, yet he seemed the last person to be a threat. Still, she remembered the mistakes she made in her twenties. Mistakes that cost her dearly. She lived wiser now, when she did not overlook the treasure of discernment she owned, ancient words so able to fine-tune her judgment. If only she could believe all of them. . . .

The new girl burst into Marissa's office. "A man out here wants to say hello," said Isabel, her stiff, splayed, black pigtails sticking from the side of her head like cockeyed exclamation marks. "Said to tell you it's Harvey and that you'd know who he was." The girl wearing a short skirt bounced with little surges of energy on her legs covered in magenta tights and on her feet wearing the strangest, black maryjanes Marissa had ever seen. An embroidery patch of Groucho Marx, cigar and all, grinned from each toe.

"Could you lose the gum, Isabel? And the beret is very cute but a bit much."

"Yes, ma'am." She took a tissue from Marissa's desk and tossed the gum.

"Anyway, tell Harvey I'll be there in a minute."

"Okay." Isabel went out the door.

Marissa paid another bill and sat back. She realized William Dash's voice came through the back screen door. Him again, talking to Daphne like a lonely sailor or something. Marissa had avoided the conceited bungler because there was no telling what words she might spew. She exhaled with more force than a baby whale, and she opened the general account in her computer software. Nothing worked so well to clear her mind as studying the numbers.

Isabel stuck her head in the room once more. "He says he's going to start singing along with Josh Groban if you don't come out."

Marissa quickly closed the program and pushed her chair back. Harvey was getting as bad as that self-assured, self-congratulatory William. Her feet wanted to stomp from the room but she restrained herself. She gave the door a shove.

"Sweetcakes!" He jumped from his seat. Several diners and two women enjoying tea looked up. Harvey Trammell was oddly alone.

"Good afternoon, Harvey." She stood at a distance.

"Well, how are you, Kittenface? Have you missed me?"

Marissa bit her lip. "Harvey, could we talk?"

"Sure thing." Next to his empty plate, he dropped too much money and took Marissa by the elbow. "We can take a seat in my truck." As he steered her, his face looked absolutely brilliant. Marissa rushed, glad to get him beyond the hearing of her guests.

He reached for the truck door, but Marissa stopped his hand with hers. "Here is fine." She turned and faced him. The sun seemed to fry her neck, which she knew would actually help her prevail. "Harvey, I really appreciate your patronage but like most women, I'm used to being called by my name rather than ultra-feminine nomenclature."

Harvey looked embarrassed. " Nomen-? *No ma'am.* I wouldn't in any way be vulgar! Especially with you."

"No, Harvey. I'm talking about the overly-sweet references you use about me."

"Oh! Well, I remember you objected, before, to my talk of your 'fetchin'' calf eyes,' but I'll cease my inspired phrasing altogether if that's what you want." He smiled benignly.

"That's exactly what I wish."

He pulled his baseball cap off his head. "Sure thing. But while I have you out here...."

Her eyes went to the steps wishing she could take them by twos.

"Yes, Harvey," she muttered and checked her watch. She remembered that she had to get a call in by three p.m. to her food supplier. She slapped at a fly that tried to drink the sweat forming on the back of her neck.

"Well, I might as well get right to it. My Uncle Tito passed on. Left me his cattle ranch. Two thousand acres of central Florida.... I can't think of anything sweeter than you selling this place and spending your time trying to fatten me up, down at the ranch, just like one of those bulls. I'm talkin' marriage, of course."

Marissa's brow furrowed. "What?"

"Now hold on. You sure do like the way I can chow down on your food. And I think you're the prettiest thing anywhere in Georgia." Marissa fought to engage her tongue. He continued. "But it's like my grandma used to say, 'There's a time when a woman gets a little too long in the tooth, and her thought ought to be to grab the next rooster that happens by.'" He must have read her face. His eyebrows angled with worry. "Besides, Hon, I'll buy you the nicest Cadillac they have at Palmetto Land Motors and you won't have to do another thing the rest of your days . . . except be my loving wife." For the first time ever, she witnessed a serious look on his face.

Her feet twisted in the oyster shells below. "Except for your tremendous way with words, this old girl thanks you for the offer, but *I'm not marrying anyone.*" She jerked around, flew over the oyster shells, and solidly took each step, leaving no doubt in Harvey's mind.

The door slammed behind her. She avoided eye contact with any of her guests; however, the staring serving girl with a retro comic on her shoes caught Marissa's attention. Marissa lowered her head and blasted a fiery look her way. It seemed Isabel's short pigtails trembled.

Marissa was about to enter her office when she heard a man's voice in the kitchen. She froze. William Dash. The conversation still rambled on. He probably waited for her to pop into the kitchen, so he could make an amorous move. His voice sounded muffled. He probably schmoozed Daphne about the excellence of her pies. Marissa would have to be careful to avoid blood spatter on the food when she pulled out his tongue.

Her palm rammed the swinging door open. She encountered his legs spanning part of the floor. He lay on his back inside the cabinet, under the sink. He continued his conversation with Daphne, unaware that anyone had entered the room. Daphne shrugged at Marissa and looked apologetic.

"Just a few more adjustments," said William, "and I'll have this water sprayer behaving again. Next Wednesday would be a good day for me to fix the leaky toilet. Customers like a ship-shape bathroom. Can you hand me the mallet?" Only his arm came out, and without a word, Daphne supplied the tool. "So as I was telling you, I'm retiring a little over a year from now. The company doesn't want me to go. I'm the best troubleshooter they have. Sixty hour weeks for almost twenty years dim the excitement of traveling all over the world. When an oil well goes haywire, an engineer can find himself on a rig off the coast of Morocco one minute and twenty-four hours later, somewhere in the Indian Ocean. Eventually, I'll be doing part-time, inshore consulting, but as I said, life's short and there's only one thing important to me now. Having a normal life and starting a family. Although, I do have to tie up some loose ends first."

Marissa walked over, grabbed his ankles, and yanked with more might than she realized she had.

"Wha-!" His rear slid a foot across the linoleum. He tried to scramble the rest of the way out, hitting his forehead on the inside edge of the cabinet. "Man!"

Daphne put a hand across her mouth and shook her sagging head.

William sat, cradling his forehead. He tilted his head up and looked from the eye on the undamaged side of his face to discover his tormentor.

Daphne ran to him with a wet cloth to halt the blood dripping between his fingers.

Marissa stood over him like a bouncer full of menace.

Daphne's puzzled eyes sought her employer's. "He was only trying to give us a hand, Marissa."

William hoisted himself up and glared at Marissa. "*Lady, just what is your problem?*"

"You're the one with a problem, you cock of the walk!" bellowed Marissa. Daphne's intake of breath could have made the pilot light go out. Marissa propelled William from the kitchen to the deck. The outdoor dining was vacant.

"Okay! What is it?" he demanded.

"Don't come into my kitchen and talk about me being one of your loose ends!"

"Huh?"

"That's right. One of your loose ends that's ready to be tied up, then signed, sealed, and delivered to the altar."

"Altar? You're not making any sense."

"It's all about physical attraction with men like you."

The guy, dumbstruck as a mop handle, didn't move.

"Don't play ignorant. You told your father that I was the end to your search . . . . You know, my beautiful face and so on. Your father tried to warn you that I might not be receptive. But, not to worry, because you're *so-o-o savvy*."

A smile dawned on his face.

Her rage began to boil. At first it appeared he tried to contain his mirth until his lips broke apart with laughter. Marissa took a deep breath. Emotion slung itself inside her head, making her despise him.

He straightened, wiped his eyes, and tried to slow his laughter. Finally, he could speak.

"You must have been eavesdropping," he said. "*I wasn't talking about you.* I was referring to someone else. So put the brakes on your worry." He turned to go down the steps but paused. "By the way, you're the last person on Earth for whom I'd entertain even one mildly romantic thought." He dabbed his forehead, looked at the bloody cloth, and walked home.

Marissa wanted to collapse right there on the hard, dry wood. The splinters would probably feel appropriate; she had made a perfect fool of herself. Men. Sometimes she thoroughly disliked them, but oh how she wanted one of her own.

Daphne had seen and heard it all from the kitchen window. She turned and rested her lower back against the counter. Her arms folded in front of her. Her head hung down. The swirls in the linoleum tile at her feet looked confusing, like threatening wisps of gray smoke that could steal any breath you had left.

Marissa dragged herself through the door and the kitchen. She went to her desk and put her head down. Five minutes later, she lifted her face when she heard a sound at the doorway. Daphne braced herself with one hand, her thumb nervously rubbing the wood of the door surround.

"I'm sorry we upset you, Marissa." Something about Daphne's countenance told Marissa there was more. Her assistant's weary eyes reflected emotions Marissa didn't comprehend. Daphne's hand went to the base of her throat as though she needed support to say the words. "I think he's the son I gave away."

Chapter Nine

A humbled heart wants to hide, shrivel, shrink, but Marissa forced herself from the office and out the back door. She would be the go-between, whatever might begin to right her wrong. She trudged through the patio and past the herb bed, across his neatly cut grass and alongside the semi-tropical plantings to his back door. Her arm lifted, ready to knock on William's back door.

Earlier, Isabel left for the day, and for an hour, Marissa and Daphne talked privately. Daphne presented the major clues to Marissa. William was the name Daphne had given her baby. The man of the same name in the house behind *Camellia* entered Daphne's life thirty-eight years later and was on an important search for someone. The adoptive couple resided in South Carolina. William's wavy hair and blue eyes were just like Alexa's. Interrupting *Camellia's* kitchen routine for an entire week, he visited using different excuses for his presence, asking all about her. Why would he care about a woman who was neither rich nor of any consequence to the world? Daphne made one stipulation to Marissa. Under no circumstances was she to tell him of Daphne's terminal condition. There would be no wavering on the subject. This time with her son should not be shadowed by her illness. Marissa gave her word and headed on her errand.

Her knuckles rapped on the screen door. She thought she sighted a stove. The aroma of lobster bisque met her appreciative nose. The sounds of World Series baseball traveled to her from a television in a room somewhere. The black dog came through the kitchen, its toenails making soft clicks against the floor. It sniffed through the screen. Its pink tongue sprang out and jiggled from an open mouth while the tail hailed a greeting. A figure came around the corner. Her heart beat erratically. Her mouth dried like cardboard.

"So soon to give another thrashing?" he said. "Let me go get my shield." The screen was between them.

"Please . . . I'm so sorry. I can't believe the way I acted."

He opened the door. "You sound like you mean it." He stood in the door frame.

"Could I come in for a minute?"

"Sure." He held the door for her. He gestured at the dog. "Just remember Cammie is trained to attack when necessary. Well, squirrels, maybe. What do you expect from the pound?"

Marissa smiled.

He put one finger up. "Hey. Did I just see a rare phenomenon?"

"I've made a really bad impression, haven't I?"

"Let's call for a new bit. . . . That's oil rig language for starting over."

"Okay." She patted the dog. "I didn't know you had a pet."

"Keeping her for my dad a week or so. Come have a seat in the living room. Watch out for the tools and stuff on the floor. I'm about to take out this wall."

She sidestepped obstacles and followed him to the front room. The screen door on the front of the house allowed air to draft through the back one. For an old house, the interior updates transformed the entire look. The furniture was sleek but simple, the room clean and absent of clutter. He switched off the baseball game. He chose an armchair. He aimed the remote at the baseball game. The screen went blank.

"I hate for you to miss the ninth inning," she said.

"Your trek to my door must be very important, or you wouldn't have come over here."

"My apology was sufficient reason, but there is more."

"What's up?"

She hesitated. "This search of yours, does it have to do with Daphne?"

He didn't answer and looked away. His fingers tapped the arm rest.

She leaned forward. "I'm trying to help, not pry."

He glanced up. "She's the person I'm seeking."

"Daphne thinks you may be the son she had to give up."

"So. . . . She knows."

"Figured it out."

"Is she upset?"

"No. She's afraid you may not understand the decision she made."

"Allowing me to be adopted was a very unselfish act on her part."

"How long have you been on this quest?"

"A little over a year. My mother died. I had a great childhood and a wonderful family, but I needed to know that the woman who made such a sacrifice was okay. I hired a private investigator. He led me here. I bought this house so I could take my time."

"She wants to see you."

"Should I come by in the morning?"

"She's waiting for you now."

He stood. "Thank you."

She smiled and rose. The dog hopped up and followed. In the kitchen, William spoke to the animal and it flopped by the screen door. Marissa and William went out. She looked at *Camellia* from his backyard and realized how perfect the place looked. The cool, pale green of the Japanese maple against *Camellia's* chestnut siding stunned her eyes with color contrast. The gambrel roof needed repair but the attic dormers looked village-quaint. The kitchen window, a bank of panes, required constant cleaning but allowed the interior lights to shine like diamonds at the wane of day. For her, coming from William's yard was a totally new perspective. This reversal of outlook reminded her of times when, as a young girl, she had ridden in the car with her dad, from Woodstock, up old Highway 5 to Canton in the late '70s when little had been built to landmark most of the way. Returning home down the same road, she always enjoyed the false sensation that they traveled a different route. Several houses, country gardens, and woodland hollows had been missed on the earlier ride. A garage arbor covered itself with a climbing rose, a fireworks of red bloom. How could she have overlooked that beautiful feature? They must be traveling a different road, she would say to her father as though she had not made the statement on other trips. Then her dad would glance at her, ruffle her bangs, and smile as they neared home again. She would find herself relaxing against the seat and marveling. Only as she grew did she realize her lesson—humans sometimes required a different way of looking at things to encompass all of reality.

Marissa brought William into the office at *Camellia*, without a word. Daphne sat shyly in a straight-backed chair. Marissa indicated the desk chair for William, and she gathered her things. She told them to stay as long as they liked. They assured her that they would turn off the lights and lock up.

Marissa entered the beach house and dropped her things on the kitchen counter. The refrigerator stood out like a beacon of refreshment. A glass of orange juice relieved her throat. She wandered to the dining room picture window and looked to the sea. She stood there for a moment, thinking. Energy drained from her body. She traipsed to the bedroom and sat on the bed. The clock said six p.m. A quick nap before dinner would be the thing, she consoled herself. She let her head melt into the cool pillow.

She woke with a start. The room was dark. The wind rumbled the tin roof of the shed outside. Her cell phone rang. Byron's mellow voice and moody music in the background greeted her.

He chuckled at her sleepy voice.

"It was *some* day," she explained.

"I was thinking of you," he said.

"Yes?"

"The way you walk like summer. The way you laugh like May."

"How lovely."

"My emotions are in a strange place right now. I'm tired and overworked."

"Is there any way I can cheer you?" she asked.

"Maybe. In some ways, I'm a sad boy who's waiting for the hard school year to be over. And you are standing in the distance, luminous as a pearl, waiting to be my freedom, my best companion teaching me how to play again."

Marissa didn't know what to say.

"Please ignore me," he continued. "This dark frame of mind is causing me to run off at the mouth."

"No. Don't be sorry."

"Let me make it up to you with dinner tomorrow night."

"I'd love that."

They settled on the time. She hung up the phone and lay there. She kept the light off and opened the casement window, letting the ocean breeze pour into her bedroom and over her body. The scent of sea water braced her mind. The deep, trumpet sound of a ship horn bounced across the water. The window screens made that foreign, whistling sound, which undermined the edges of her sense of security. Thoughts rolled in like fog. For three weeks she had waited for his phone call. The suggestion of Charleston had gone up in smoke. Orchids had been the only thing to keep her expectation alive. Orchids which he failed to address. Uncertain, unclear, everything between them remained vague except her growing attraction that she tried to hold down with the whip of her more sensible self.

Chapter Ten

As the next morning sun dappled the trees with clean light, ethereal white egrets swept into the myrtles ornamenting the lake next to the church. Marissa closed her car door as Pastor Darrien pulled into the parking lot. She walked over and gently teased him for arriving as late as she had. He laughed sheepishly; his boyish good looks at thirty-two lightened up the grumpiest early risers attending Bible study class. Zoe waited, watching their approach from the end of the covered walkway. When they reached her, Zoe slipped around to Darrien's other side and they proceeded. Without Darrien seeing, Marissa cast a quick grin to her friend. Zoe, retiring, petite as a dove, smiled back. Once they entered the room and Darrien greeted the group, he went to check on the coffee maker that Zoe already had going.

Marissa pulled Zoe aside. "Well? Have you told him how you feel?" Marissa asked.

"No." Zoe laughed softly and made a cute face. Darrien entered the room again.

Marissa nodded toward the man. "Take action, girl. Like I said the other day, go after what you want."

"For now, being friends is enough. We're taking the youth group sailing today."

"Does a man think like that?"

"Doesn't matter. I'd rather know he feels some attraction, too."

"At this rate you'll never find out. Take charge. You have to admit in this area you're a novice."

Zoe didn't move from her philosophical position.

Marissa smiled and shook her head. "Okay. I see I'm not having any influence. He's about to start class. At least you ought to grab the seat next to him."

Zoe laughed lightly again and gracefully slid into a seat close at hand, on the opposite side of the circle from Darrien.

Marissa sent Zoe a frustrated look and took the place next to her.

After class, Marissa saw Jacquelyn in the main foyer, came over, and entwined one of her friend's arms. They chatted about the recent letter Jacquelyn received from Russell in Afghanistan. Then Marissa was about to tell Jacquelyn the amazing knowledge that had been uncovered about the neighbor behind *Camellia* when their heads swung about.

"Aunt Marissa! Aunt Marissa!" Clemma pranced in their direction. Alexa followed. Farther behind, Daphne walked especially tall, her hand perched on the forearm of William Dash.

Clemma came so fast, so full of news that the girl almost stepped on Marissa's smart shoes. Alexa put one arm about Marissa's waist and hung there, looking up expectantly.

"Have you heard?" Clemma almost shouted, "We have a brother! He brought us to church. Next week, he's coming to ours."

Marissa shook her head. "Yes, I know all about it."

Alexa gestured for Marissa to lean down, so the seventh grader could whisper in her ear. "He's pretty old for a brother but we really like him." Marissa wondered if she had been put in the same aged category.

Daphne came up next and introduced Jacquelyn to William and then Daphne explained the situation.

Jacquelyn was beside herself. "So you're the person living behind *Camellia* . . . and you turn out to be her son!"

"I am," he said.

Jacquelyn turned to Daphne. "You never mentioned the possibility that day you were teaching me how to make a better pie crust."

"Just found out myself. Marissa will tell you all about it later."

Jacquelyn, clearly amazed at the discovery, nodded eagerly. "Yes, we're meeting friends tonight for dinner. I can't wait to hear how everything unfolded."

William grinned. "Actually the day started with a very awkward beginning but she can skip that part." His hand went reflexively to the bandage on his forehead.

Marissa turned abruptly to Jacquelyn. "I can't make it tonight."

Jacquelyn's voice held disappointment. "How come?"

"Something came up."

"Like what?"

Marissa sighed. "A dinner date. At the new house on the marsh."

"With who?"

"Byron."

Jacquelyn shook her head, looked worried. "*Oh*, Mr. Byron S. Hewitt of landscaping fame."

"Does the S stand for shifty?" William sardonically inquired.

The two women stared adamantly at each other, hardly hearing him.

Marissa tried not to show her teeth clamping. "The praise choruses have started. We'd better go in," she said, turning Clemma and Alexa lightly by the shoulders in the direction of the entrance. She led the way into the sanctuary. Sanctuary. She wanted to smirk. She felt bombarded by the silent speculations of her seatmates, making it impossible to listen to a single word of her pastor's message.

After the service, they all said goodbye and broke to go their separate ways. The girls ran ahead. Daphne took a few steps to leave but returned to Marissa. William lagged slightly behind. Daphne hugged her purse to her chest. "I haven't had a chance to tell you how grateful I am for your help yesterday. Thank you so much."

"You know I would do anything for you."

"You must be an angel put into my life," Daphne said and embraced Marissa.

William put his sunglasses on and eased away. Daphne moved off with him as Marissa entered her preoccupations. William tossed a goodbye. She didn't notice.

As her car left the parking lot, she witnessed Clemma and Alexa walk down to the lake while Daphne, William, and Jacquelyn leaned in to one another, engrossed in conversation, which left Marissa wondering what could be so noteworthy.

She crossed over the little land bridge leading to East Beach, and her mind traveled to a certain man, one who seemed admiring of her but clearly unattached. Something about the nature of their developing relationship created a destabilized feeling, although he valued her intelligence, her accomplishments, and above all, her independence. When she got home, she bypassed the kitchen, rested, and tried to read. Then she lit an aromatic candle, put on music, and soaked in the tub before she dressed for her dinner with Byron. Her appetite heightened, she left for her date.

At seven, when she pulled in the drive at the home on the marsh past Cannon's Point, her eyes surveyed the lush grounds of five acres and the sprawling home, casual elegance distinguishing its island style. The evening breezes of that late September evening caressed her skin. The air held smells evocative of vegetation having reached its zenith.

Byron swung open the large front door opening to the veranda and hurried down the steps. He embraced her warmly, something he'd never done before, and drew back with a friendly smile.

"This is some place," she said, her eyebrows raised.

"I told you I have a great deal going on here. I just got a call from the Janzens. They won't be back from Spain until late November."

Marissa laughed. "So you get to enjoy this gorgeous home while you do your work. I'm sure you're going to drag the project until the last minute."

"Hey, now. You don't create a Monet garden overnight."

"No, you don't. How is it progressing?"

He took her hand. They walked up the steps to the home. "Come share dinner with me first. I'll gladly pay for your opinion. That is, of the garden design, not the cooking. I already know I haven't your talent there." They entered the doorway. The smell of pear and patchouli swept over Marissa. She followed him through one large room of high-end décor after another. Finally they reached the kitchen filled with trendy, restaurant-style appliances.

Byron laughed at Marissa's admiration of the room. "I don't know why Carla has all this top-of-the-line equipment. She hates to cook. Hates to eat. Every party is catered."

"And her husband."

"Frederique?" Byron laughed. "He's seldom here." He took a look at Marissa. "Enough of them." He lifted the lid from a pot holding paella. "Senorita, what do you think?"

Marissa put her nose over the rising aroma. The wine sauce, briny clam, and lemon scent caused her stomach to come alive. "Mm. Simply, mm."

After dinner they took their blueberry shortcake outside, to enjoy by the pond. She had to follow him down a narrow path that veered, forked, and made unpredictable changes. Finally the vegetation opened up. He spread a blanket and took the remote control in his hand and turned on the outdoor lighting. Marissa sat down. He joined her on the blanket. They tasted their dessert.

"Monet would be proud," she said. "I feel like I'm in Giverny. The willows dance above the water, and the lilies are like scattered jewels."

"Just a little of my magic. Spring will be the truest picture, when the specially-chilled iris bloom in serene blue. Soon we'll be constructing the bridge." Then his eyes jumped with eagerness. "You haven't seen the best thing yet. Some roosting blue-winged teal. They pass through Georgia in September. Some go as far as Peru." He hopped up and gestured for her to follow. They wended their way along the edge of the pond and threaded into the plantings. He whispered for her not to make a sound. Past stalks of boggy plants, they came to the wispy limbs of featherleaf maple, which sat higher on the bank. The outdoor lighting barely made it through at this point. He put a finger to his lips as a reminder and waved her close. She moved beside him. He pointed down, over a lower limb. On the other side, a group of ducks wearing plumage of steel blue on their heads, tan on their chests, and sides dotted with deep brown slept in the leafy refuge. Marissa turned her face to Byron's, so close she thought he was going to kiss her. He looked thoughtful, but he pulled away. He suddenly withdrew down the path they had come. She tried to keep up.

When they reached the blanket, he sat down. His look was unsettled. She came down to the blanket.

Marissa leaned near. "Is anything wrong?"

He fell back, putting his hands behind his head. He did not look at her. "I'm sorry. I almost kissed you. You've been a great friend. I don't want to spoil things."

Marissa reclined on her side next to him. She placed her hand lightly on his chest. "It won't spoil things," she said.

He kissed her gently at first, but soon, in the semi-darkness that kept them hidden, his warmth increased. Something nagged at her. His hand reached for the remote control to make their privacy complete. The place went black, and the process had knocked their uneaten desserts over. His kisses became more fervent. It registered in her mind that all his hesitancy had snuck away. He knew her much less than she thought. She pushed one of his arms away but he returned. His all-of-a-sudden desire strangely flattered her.

The sound of a car coming down the driveway reached her ears. She gave one strong push against him, and they both sat up, watching through the vegetation as the headlights moved toward the house.

Byron jumped to standing.

Marissa could feel that clumps of her hair had stuck together with the blue goo of their dessert. During the couple's entanglement, blueberry syrup spotted her arms and clothing. She bent over to get up, and a piece of adhered, ropey hair swung and slapped her nose and one cheek with color. Wiping with her hand smeared the stuff more. Each touch or adjustment added new stains. Marissa felt a sting underneath her ear, then another on her arm. She slapped, uncaring if she spread the slime. She stood up and shook herself, trying to be released from prowling ants. Byron seemed indifferent and kept his eyes angled toward what could be seen of the veranda. The loud knocking on the front door carried all the way to their ears. Byron headed for the house. Marissa ran around him and down the path, determined to get to a basin as quickly as possible. A man watched from the porch, the light behind him, his front clothed in shadow. She came closer. He shook with laughter. She raced up the steps and was about to storm inside when she did a double-take.

"What happened to you?" William Dash said.

"Uh. My dessert, that's all." She scratched her neck, mixed-up and enveloped in a weird dream. She simply stood there.

He leaned in, took a sniff. "You smell sweet."

His grin threw her out of her daze. "*What are you doing here?*" she cried.

"Emergency."

"You don't sound alarmed. What is it?" she barked.

Byron walked up. The men did not address one another but took measuring glances.

Hands in his pockets, William casually turned to Marissa. "I was sitting in the back yard, reading, and I thought I smelled something. First, I assumed it was the citronella torch, but then I began to wonder if there might be a propane leak."

She looked at him as though he had lost his mind.

"At *Camellia*," he added with utter calmness.

Chapter Eleven

Her car dashed down the long road while she ranted in her head and used a wetwipe to rub blue smears off the leather seat. She swiped along the sticky steering wheel and crammed the dirty towelette in her purse.

Byron stayed planted at the Janzen home, remembering a few business duties that required his attention. He had put an arm around her and commented on her capability to handle a crisis. William, quietly firm, insisted on accompanying her, which elicited her sigh. Worse than a pestering flea, he was always around, irritating her best moment. One eye on the road, she pulled down the visor and took stock of herself in the small mirror. Her hair not locked up by syrup blew around in disarray. Her splotched face transformed her into a fiend. She knocked the visor in position and gave the car engine a gush of gas.

The two cars reached the village area and turned down the side road. The familiar crunch of the shell parking lot brought mild reassurance as her car pulled in and came to a quick stop. She jumped out and began her run to the back of the restaurant where the propane tank waited behind lattice. William had pulled in also, and as she looked back during her mad pace, her mind caught a snapshot of him ambling casually in the same direction.

All seriousness, she reached the tank and began sniffing with more determination than a bloodhound. She checked the dial. She inspected the connections. Her nose took another survey in the four directions. She moved to the outdoor tables and took another register. Nothing. Up the steps to the back door she stormed. William followed. Her keys flashed in the darkness. They entered.

William's hand covered the light switch. "Don't turn it on. We don't want a spark."

Her head with hanks of glued hair whipped back and forth as she sniffed. She ran to the stove. William came beside her. She eased the door open. They both leaned their noses inside the inky cavern to take a whiff.

They stayed bent. She turned her face to him. "I don't smell a thing."

William shook his head. "I must have been wrong," he said plainly. His face moved in, and he kissed her syrup slathered cheek and then, lightly, her lips. He pulled back and said softly, "I never could resist blueberry."

Marissa jerked up, straighter than a butcher knife. William rose. She took a step back. *"If you ever do that again, I'll chop your head off."*

"Lady, of that I have no doubt." He turned around and exited the back door.

Marissa, still in darkness, went to the sink. Her hands slapped the faucet handles on, and when she felt the water was as hot as she could stand, she put her head and neck under the flow. One hand grabbed for the dishwashing liquid. A hefty dose dribbled onto her hair. She scrubbed every inch of skull and face and neck and arms until she was blueberry and neighbor free. It wasn't until later that she realized just how thorough a job she had done.

When she arrived home, a midnight ebb tide had begun, pulling ocean water, swirling seaweed, skimming fish, and so many beautiful things away from her. She hankered for a long ocean swim, but she was not a fool. She peeled off her stained clothes, took a shower and fell on the bed. Her eyes traveled to her cell phone. She lifted it from the table and flipped it open. Scrolling through her list of numbers, Byron's name came up. She paused, wondering if she should call. She took a breath and selected the listing. After two rings, his voice announcement came on. When the beep sounded, her words stammered. "Byron, uh . . . I, I was hoping to talk. But . . . never mind. I'll catch you later." Her fingers snapped the phone shut, and she lay there studying the ceiling.

Monday morning she bolted into the exercise studio at eight. Jacquelyn kept any questions to herself and seemed to cut her a wide path. Marissa dove in: first stretching, then aerobics, resistance training, step, and a final class of cycling. Over five hours later, coming into the relaxation room from the showers, her rubbery legs wobbled. Wearing a thick terry robe, she collapsed on the lounge.

Jacquelyn walked by, her arms full of clean towels. She dropped them on the table and stood while she folded. "If you wanted to kill yourself, why didn't you have me tie you to the back of my car and make you run to Jacksonville?"

"I'm visiting my old way of handling frustration," mumbled Marissa.

"Men problems, eh?"

Marissa wondered how she knew it was *men* not simply *man*. The room had emptied. People went in search of lunch. Classes paused until three p.m.

"The years must be affecting me," said Marissa. "This old method isn't enough. My thinking isn't any clearer, and I'm plain worn out with exertion."

Jacquelyn put the stack of towels in the cabinet. "I brought a salad loaded with chicken. Want to share it with me?"

Marissa lost her slouch. "Love to."

Jacquelyn went to the refrigerator and brought their meal to the low coffee table. She served and offered dressing. Marissa, ravished with hunger, said a prayer and jabbed her first forkful with a grateful smile. For a time, they remained silent, eating.

Jacquelyn looked up. "How'd it go last night?"

"He's not exactly as I thought."

"Byron or William?"

Marissa looked askance. "What do you mean *or William*?"

"I just meant Byron, of course."

Marissa hesitated. "He surprised me is all I was implying. I thought he considered me more of a friend."

Jacquelyn pushed her face forward. "Amorous or downright froggy?"

Marissa put her fork down and sat straighter. "Jacquelyn, he has respect for me and a great deal of admiration, too." Marissa got up and carried her plate to the tiny kitchen. She could hear Jacquelyn's next words barreling across the other room and into the alcove.

"Yes, he probably told you that he appreciates that you're not one of those weak, needy women he looks down on. Which actually translates into, *"Don't depend on me for anything, certainly not all that sticking by you in sickness and in poverty drivel."*

Marissa dropped her plate into the dishwasher too quickly and it clanked against another plate. She came from the kitchen, her face hardened like the heaviest free weight in the studio.

Jacquelyn met Marissa and blocked her. "I'm sorry, Marissa! I can't mind my own business, but I do care what happens to you."

Marissa's heart softened instantly. "It's okay." She shook her head slowly. "I don't know what I'm doing. . . . I haven't for most of my adult life."

"Cut yourself some slack. You do have a way-too-nosy friend."

October skies turned everything golden in the afternoons as more than two weeks passed. The tourist season ended, and they were back down to a handful of patrons at any hour. *Camellia* welcomed the respite. When Marissa silently watched Daphne move about the restaurant, her hope grew; the woman never seemed stronger. Across the way, William toiled outside, directly behind *Camellia's* herb bed. For days he hauled dirt and plants to the back yard as his strength never seemed to give out. He constructed a planter, equal in length and height to *Camellia's* herb bed and snuggled parallel to it. Interspersed vertical pieces of ornamental wrought iron rose from the new planter. He installed sun loving plants.

Since their last acrimonious words, his foot never stepped once onto Marissa's property. His face never turned in her direction. Marissa, well-practiced at driving men off, chaffed at the all too common situation. Every afternoon, when they closed shop, Daphne treaded her way to her son's place. He drove her to work in the mornings and then home in the afternoon.

"He says it's the best way for us to get to know each other before time is up," Daphne explained.

"You told him?"

"Oh no. Maybe when the situation warrants. I'm enjoying our easy friendship so much. He's leaving soon on assignment."

Marissa put the broom in the closet. "The place is clean. Let's rest for a minute before you walk over." They took cups of tea into the main room.

Settled, Marissa swept back her hair and made a short braid with her fingers. She took a sip of tea. Daphne watched a squirrel playing in the tree outside the window where they sat.

"Well, what restaurant will it be tonight?" said Marissa.

"The old seafood place on Heron Avenue, near the Brunswick docks. I've finally convinced him I'm not one for fancy places. I couldn't talk him into returning those expensive clothes, though. He doesn't know I'll never need them. I don't know why he cares so."

"The girls. Are they fond of him?"

"Oh, my goodness. Every day when we pick them up at school, they insist we give one of their friends a ride home. An excuse to have them meet their handsome brother, they confessed later." Daphne put down her cup. "I asked him if he was one of those swinging bachelors I hear about. Said no. A long-time relationship with a woman in France didn't work out. He wants to find the right woman before he gets too old. I laughed and told him he didn't know nothin' about old."

"So, he's going to be leaving?"

"For a while. I hope not too long. But I know I've got no right to him. The company is sending him back to France and then a rig somewhere off the coast of Argentina. He said he'll return before May when a surprise for you is due to pop up from that beautiful planter back there. Some kind of vine he put in. Can't imagine."

"Well, I hope it's a pleasant surprise," said Marissa, hoping he hadn't started poison ivy, trying to ward her off. Uneasy, she pushed back her chair. "Please tell him I really look forward to seeing those Lady Banks roses bloom in April." Soon they closed and went home.

Sixteen days of self-doubt ended briefly for Marissa on a mid-October evening when she heard Byron's voice on the phone one Saturday evening. As the conversation progressed, however, she realized all intimacy had disappeared. Her self-esteem rose and fell on huge waves that his fluctuating attention created. It was worse than any seasick trip. More pain than pleasure. He talked of his work related problems. The Janzens were due to return in six weeks, and they expected project completion. His conversation changed course, and he gave elaborate description of two parties he attended and the fascinating people there. His mirth had no end, relating his buddies' latest high jinks. Finally, the talk slowed. Marissa waited to hear when he and she would meet again. No hint came. He did not ask about *Camellia* and what if anything she discovered on that night threatening her life's only remaining investment. Someone was at his door he said and ended the call.

After skipping dinner, night came down and Marissa sat alone in her viewing tower, eyes following lights, near the horizon. At least her daylight maritime skills had increased, but at night, she still had difficulty distinguishing between buoys and real vessels. Two forlorn ships traveled across the water. She got up and went to bed.

Chapter Twelve

ANOTHER Monday came, holding no relief from an entire month of disquiet bearing down on her equilibrium like a tropical disturbance. Jumpy, impatient, she set herself into motion without seeking God that morning. As though some sickness forced her, she went outside and got on her bike, a fat-tire beach contraption, and she left her house on East Beach, turned right at the intersection, and pedaled over the land bridge leading to Demere Road. Following that route, her bike moseyed through the old village section of homes until meeting Kings Way. She turned down the heavily shaded road, her legs cranking the wheels along, and after a while, she angled at a corner onto the airport road. Once her bike headed north, up the island, the idea popped in her head. Perfunctorily weighing the pros and cons, she minimized the distance to the Janzen home and she set out. An executive jet coming in for landing seemed to lead her bike as she streamed alongside the airport chain link fencing. She passed The Tabby House Gift Shop and got through the main intersection with the light changing in her favor. As she slipped by the trendy shops of Frederica Station, she saw a frequent patron of *Camellia* and waved. The woman driving a glimmering Lexus looked at her as if riding a bike was beneath Marissa who dodged gray sand encroaching the sidewalk. She pedaled zealously past her observer. Sooner than she imagined the Sea Island Causeway and Sea Palms Resort confronted her. Cyclists coming toward her smiled and made room as they came adjacent to her bike. The air, loaded with the smell of cut grass, inspired her exertion. Although deep into autumn, the warm halcyon day encouraged the island people to dress in shorts and tank tops.

After some time traveling Frederica Road, she reached the fork. She veered right, down the long island road to Hampton Point. The road appeared never ending with ribbons of glassy heat rising and an interminable number of oaks and utility poles marking her progress. Doubts about her impulsive ride filtered into her thinking. She pedaled on. Only the tiny settlement of Germantown and several cruising cars broke the visual rhythm. She looked down at the sheen on her arms, excitement rising in her chest. Her effort reminded her of the cross country races and the swim meets in high school where the waiting prize of victory propelled her like high octane. Except for the hum of her tires on asphalt, few sounds met her ears, except bird calls.

The ever increasing manses on the marsh signaled she had neared her destination. Her calves slowed their spinning, hailed by the long driveway marked by 'Isle of Capri' oleander trees with spectacular yellow flowers and handsome foliage, just like the ones situated in the sunny rear of her outside dining area. The trees had a particular drawback, though. She wondered how something so appealing to the senses could be so decidedly poisonous when ingested. She turned down the Janzen property.

She glided at an easy pace over the serpentine driveway, trying to make her breathing slow. His car parked in the circular drive confirmed her good timing. She stopped and leaned her bike against one of the lampposts. Her intuition sent her to the winding footpath leading to the pavilion. Daylight gave the entire walk a totally different ambience than on the night when she had been under its influence. The sound of a saw screaming its way through wood met her ears. Several male voices communicated in quick phrases. She entered the clearing that held the thicket-wrapped pond where workmen hovered over the massive form meant to put the final touch on his work. There he was, caught up in his labor and creative devotion, white sleeves rolled up, darkest brown hair that shone in the sun. His eyes turned in her direction, altered and slightly hooded by his pulled down brows.

"What are you doing here?"

Marissa's mouth dropped slightly open. "I'm sorry. I didn't realize I would interrupt your work."

"How's that? It's what I do every day of the week," he said. His tensed body lowered a heavy post into the notch of a curved wooden expanse, and he loosened his hold. He straightened. A smile appeared. "Hold on." He turned back to his work and placed a level vertical to the post, took a reading, and laid the level on the ground. A workman secured two thick bolts with a massive tool. Then he came to her. "We're finishing up the railing. Tomorrow the crane is coming to lift it in place. What do you think? After a few coats of paint, will it resemble that famous bridge?"

"It's marvelous. A perfect Monet replica."

"Not the real thing. Still, I have a great deal of pride in it." He unbuttoned his dress shirt and waved the loose halves to trap some cooling air. "When I least expect it, I have to jump in and do the work myself. Wouldn't you know it's close to ninety today."

"I'll let you get back to what you were doing. I was . . . on a bike ride."

"No wonder you're so flushed and sweaty. Considering the distance, I'd have given you credit for more sense."

Marissa looked away. "Exercise does me good."

"Yes. I forgot how rugged you are," he muttered in a disinterested tone and turned to admire his bridge.

Marissa absentmindedly smoothed her hair.

"Look, as long as you're here, stay a while," he said plainly. "Carla keeps two dozen swimsuits in the pool house for her friends who drop by. Go refresh yourself with a swim and then come back here. To the pavilion if you like. As soon as we're done with the railing, I'll send the men home for the day."

Marissa nodded mutely and turned to go back down the path. She realized she had chosen the wrong direction. A ginkgo tree with fan-shaped leaves, their form found in fossils old as time, seemed to block her way and her blind compliance. She turned and took another look at the scene by the pond. He was already absorbed in his work. She skirted the tree and continued.

Inside the pool house, the closet held a variety of two-piece suits. She gave up her search for something modest, being in a hurry for the mind-awakening, heart-soothing water, and she slipped into a bikini. With one leap into the liquid coolness her anxiety lessened and her certainty buoyed. She floated a while. Hunger made itself known. Drifting, she tried to force her mind and senses to go blank. Her eyes opened to the sky above, but the noonday sun made her lids flinch shut. After some minutes, her heart finally slowed, and in the soundlessness of the water, she forgot where she was and she relaxed. . . . Her head jerked up. She sputtered and coughed. Had she fallen asleep? Her arms swirled, bringing her to a standing position.

She put on a cover-up and went around the house and to the pond again. He was laughing with his men when he caught sight of her. He waved. She entered the pavilion made of massive cedar timbers. Each supporting beam, thick around as a pre-cut tree displayed beautiful carvings of winding vine and blossom. Snuggling against several posts and clambering across a portion of the roof, New Dawn roses tried to remind the world of their beauty one last time before a chilling spell in December injured every tender thing. Marissa lowered herself onto a gaily striped chair and watched him.

Most of the workmen began collecting their tools and straggled away. Byron conversed with a man who held a schematic of the design and pointed to the foundation piers. After a time, the man took off, leaving Byron with two jocular helpers remaining. Marissa strained her ears, thinking she mistakenly heard one man ask Byron when he was going to throw another party. Byron threw his head back with a laugh and mumbled something. Soon those workmen also took their leave for the day.

Byron walked over, peeling away his damp dress shirt. "Come on," he smiled and gestured with his head to the path. "I'm sweltering. I need a dunking, myself."

She got up. They started down the fragrant, cypress mulch trail.

"It's great that you came by," he said. "I need your advice on a plan I'm designing for the Williams estate, outdoors connected to the indoors kind of thing."

"Sure."

"I trust your sense of balance, and I've noticed you have a great eye for color. But, when I think about it, you're talented in many ways. *Camellia* says it all."

The path narrowed. He took her hand and then let go.

They reached the front lawn of St. Augustine grass. When they came to the circular drive he said, "I'll go hit the water. Sandwiches are on a platter in the fridge. Would you bring them out? Oh, and make us a pitcher of something cool to drink while you're at it."

She turned to do his bidding. A bounce snuck into her step. Byron continued past the house to the pool area.

Marissa opened the front door to the Janzen home. A rush of cool air washed over her skin. The mirror in the powder room beckoned her. Sun from her bike ride had transfused her cheeks with pink. Her lips presented a happy rose, and her hazel eyes sparkled. Only her hair needed help. She found a comb in the drawer. She swept her hair up on each side and secured the strands high. The back hung loose. She made another appraisal in the mirror and liked what she saw. She stepped from the powder room and crossed the elegant living room. When she entered the casual sitting room off the kitchen, one of the borrowed sandals on her feet snagged on a raucously-colored area rug, throwing her off balance, leaving her bent over the contemporary design. Rising, she became aware of an open laptop situated on a desk in a nook beneath the back staircase. A briefcase sat near by. A landscape plan hung on the wall. The screen glowed in that dim part of the room. Prominent words got her attention. *League of the Lair.*

She puzzled for a few moments. The screen became a fishhook piercing her mid-section, drawing her in with sickening awareness. She sat down and read one area of text after another. The sentences promoted a hedonistic club cloaked as a school for eager but untrained men. The ideals elevated a game and the thrill of the hunt. The site avowed one purpose only. This goal, the text assured, women desired, too, although evolutionarily more hesitant than men. The advice continued. Get your fill. Move on to the next. Seize all gratification before you die.

Marissa fell back in the chair. Her sight returned to the motto—A Male Community for Enjoying Today's World. Marissa, also a product of the current age, had heard the same reasoning almost two decades earlier, thoroughly inculcated by a few of her female professors. Be free like men these proponents declared, convinced unfettered carnality was the source of men's power. Self-deceived by their credo that consequence had died, the cadre of new-thinkers led others, lock step, onto the treacherous cliffs.

One of Marissa's knees jittered up and down. Her breaths pounced on the computer keys fast and shallow. Scrolling down, she read all the techniques that had been used on her. Adopt your own special style. Fake appreciation for lofty, delicate things: babies, animals, the weak and helpless. Praise her. Build her up. But consistently steal her confidence. Claim you're unavailable or unable to respond . . . although, if you were, she'd certainly be the one. Flaunt your talents. Exaggerate your accomplishments. Lie if you have to. Make sure she knows how very much everyone adores you. Keep her in the dark. Mystery, create it or sleep alone.

Chilled by the egocentric principles and the frosty air conditioning, Marissa pulled the cover-up snug and leaned in. The site had an interactive forum. She selected the tab. The rolling conversation shot onto the screen. The most recent post, signed by So Many Passions, iced her more. She read his words: *"It's like a beautiful garden; I would know. You prepare the soil. Then you find a new specimen for your ever-growing collection. You cheat a little, grabbing ideas for success from here and there. The plant does most of the work. And the minor effort you expend is worth it, as you sit back and wait for your reward—a feast for the senses. Anticipation . . .*

it's everything. Right now, I expect her to show up here, one day soon. Walking into my lair. Raging with man-fever. Gladly offering herself to me. . . . I am the master!

She charged from the house still wearing the swimsuit and cover-up. She stepped from Carla's sandals and tore outside to her bike. Her riding clothes stayed in the travel pouch secured to the seat, but she pulled on socks and laced her athletic shoes tight. The journey home was the longest and most uncomfortable ride of her life. As she pedaled in the scorching sun, her skin burned during the long, isolated stretch before she reached Frederica Road. She registered the scent of a dead animal. Up ahead, a turkey vulture the size of a dog plucked at the blood-draining, tangled mush of flesh and organ and watched as she approached. Trying to recall seeing the road kill earlier, she came within twenty yards. The bird squawked and hopped a few feet away to grudgingly yield the entirety of the pavement to her. A few midday hours in the heat boosted the exploding growth of bacteria making the stench trying to wilt her. As she passed, the smell clung to her. Yards later, her lungs gulped air, and she fought to hold back shame induced tears.

The lesson she thought she learned in her twenties had come back like a determined tire scraping her over the Rough Road of Smarts one more time. She couldn't blame anyone but herself. She rose in the seat and pumped the pedals harder.

Chapter Thirteen

THE marathon bike ride home and a shower did nothing but rev her anxiety. Emotion wanted to drown her. Turbulent questioning shattered her nerves.

Marissa phoned Darrien and begged for counsel. He quickly agreed and brought his cousin to sit in the reception area of the church. Linda read a magazine as though the urgent request was normal procedure. In his office, in the gentling hush of evening when the soothing patter of yard sprinklers comes on and yellow light glows from open windows and tired but happy voices emanate from those same homes amid the calming darkness, Marissa told him everything. He listened empathetically as she poured out her pain, her fears, her lack of understanding.

The next morning, sunbeams angled a little too directly into the *Camellia* kitchen when Marissa pushed the swinging door and entered the room. Too little sleep left shadows under her eyes.

Daphne looked up. Her fingers had been deftly crimping a fragile pie crust. "Morning," she said.

"Morning," Marissa muttered while turning on the ceiling fan and opening the back door to allow the screen door to shuttle in some air. "Hope its not going to be another warm day. This is crazy for fall."

"Looks like you had some fun in the sun," said Daphne. "That must hurt a bit, though." She returned to her work.

Marissa ducked into her apron, pulling it downward with a snap but winced as the neck band rasped her inflamed nape. "I'll be okay."

Daphne paused and straightened. Her eyes had the look of someone traveling memory lane. "Reminds me of my first days on the shrimp boat with Ned. We'd only been married six months when we bought that vessel. Pretty soon I was so brown no amount of time could redden me. William's the same way."

"Let's start the custard, okay?" said Marissa. A hint of discomposure flitted across Daphne's face. Nevertheless, Marissa refused to let it bother her and went to the fridge.

"Yes, ma'am," Daphne said.

"Please don't start with that formal attitude." Marissa opened the fridge and peered inside. She turned her surprised smile on Daphne. "You already made the tea sandwiches."

"I came in early. The bridal shower isn't until two, but you know how I get anxious if we're not ready with time to spare."

Marissa shut the refrigerator door. "Your foresight has saved me a dozen times."

The first customers entered the dining room, and Isabel handed them menus. Marissa and Daphne got down to business, not knowing the day would throw them a challenge.

Closer to mid-day, Clemma and Alexa tumbled in the back door, laughing at some private joke.

Daphne transmitted a look of apology to Marissa. "Teacher workday," the girls' mother explained. "Their Aunt Shalie is too busy."

Alexa handed Marissa a gathering of bright pink fringe flower, its tassels dancing. "But please don't put us to work, Aunt Marissa."

"She won't," said Clemma, "once she hears Mom already sentenced us to the library. At least she let us take a walk first."

"Yes, but I didn't think you'd be gone this long," said their mother moving through her tasks.

"We made it all the way to the Coast Guard Station and back. We had fun talking to everybody." Clemma dribbled an imaginary basketball around the work table and laid up the ball in a pretend basket above the back door.

From a corner of the kitchen, Daphne gathered forgotten book bags and dropped one in each girl's hands. "Now, get going. The library opened two and a half hours ago. You can take a break to eat your lunch on the pier. Then get back to those projects. They're due sooner than you realize." Her hands swished in the direction of the door.

"Can we have money for a Mountain Dew?" asked Clemma. The thrust of her outstretched hand overturned a box of corn starch.

"No way." Marissa interrupted. "The combined wallops of caffeine and sugar are the last thing you girls need. Take two bottles of strawberry lemonade from the fridge."

"Thanks, Aunt Marissa."

The girls raced to get their drinks and were about to blast out the door, laughing again, when Isabel rushed into the kitchen.

Her dark eyes were opened wide with worry. "He's here!"

"Who?" her listeners said in unison.

"The British guy. The one from the paper."

"Everett Chisholm?" blurted Marissa.

Isabel nodded.

Daphne turned to Marissa who had frozen like the sherbet bombe in the freezer. "I thought he was supposed to give us a heads up," stated Daphne.

"Wishful thinking on my part," said Marissa.

Alexa let her bookbag crash to the floor. "We'll stay and help, Aunt Marissa. We'll even scrub pots and peel potatoes."

Marissa spied Clemma who looked positively hopeful that she and her sister were about to exchange library dullness for a little drama.

"No," said their mother. "Now out the door." She physically guided them out the back.

Slightly dazed, the three women zipped into a cluster to deliberate. Marissa felt heat flame on her sunburned shoulders, face, and neck. She took a wet towel from the counter to cool her skin.

"We can do this," Marissa said. "Just remember all the positive comments we've gotten. Isabel, act calm and be courteous as always. Daphne and I will be back here ready to dish out whatever he requests."

The visit by the food critic came off without a hitch, it seemed, and the afternoon bridal shower was judged a success. Marissa slumped at her desk, exhausted from the unnerving day coming on the heels of her humiliation at the marsh house. Two fingers wrestled with a paper clip as she recalled *Camellia's* guest, a stumpy, rotund person with a thin mustache riding the wave of his upper lip. A serious man, he had all the power in his tippy tappy fingers, which at that moment, might be spelling out disaster for Marissa on his computer keyboard. His comments while in the restaurant were polite and few, but one statement had left her edgy: "With it being the off-season, I didn't think it necessary to give you a courtesy call first . . . but maybe I was wrong."

Marissa bucked herself up, thinking that the lunch of beef tenderloin on a bed of arugula drizzled with pan sauce, accompanied by a side of delicate scalloped potatoes, and brown sugar pear tartlets served with Earl Grey presented such perfection that the meal would have left an overfed king clamoring for more.

Three-thirty came. Isabel and then Daphne and the girls left for the day. Marissa couldn't make herself rise from her seat. On her arm, she noted a little patch of dry skin announcing the peeling process before the heat of her sunburn had totally died down. She chewed over some bills. The phone rang. She instantly recognized the Spanish-influenced tongue.

"Marissa? This is Elizabeth Averill from Woodstock."

"Elizabeth! I'm so glad you called. I want to let you know I finally braved enough to try your *flan* recipe last week. The customers raved. And Mrs. Bañuelos said the taste and texture were far superior to what she gets at her favorite restaurant in Tampa."

"It pleases me so much to hear it. . . . But I am afraid I have called with bad news."

Later, Marissa phoned Daphne and Isabel to explain the situation. That taken care of, Marissa worked in her office and then in the pantry taking inventory. It would not be good to leave things in anything but perfect order while she was gone for a few days. Around eight, she sipped a cup of tea, standing at the sink and looking out. Her eyes drifted to the other lot. His house was shut tight and dark, just as she knew it would be.

The next morning, after she gassed up her car, Marissa went to the newspaper stand and reached for The Island Gazette. So certain the report would be glowing, she made a vow not to open the food and entertainment section until she reached Macon, two-thirds the way home. Home? She paid the clerk and chuckled. Ten months earlier she left, but still that town had a hold on her. She went to her car and tried to casually toss the paper on the seat beside her. She cranked the engine and pulled away from the pump, thinking, three hours to Macon. She glanced at the paper calling to her from the seat. What was the point of prolonging the suspense, anyway? She swerved the car to a vacant part of the gas station, near the pay phone and the vacuum. Engine idling, her hands flashed through the pages until she found the column.

Camellia Japonica –A Case of Confusion

Dear readers, as is my habit, you are well aware, I took another of my great literary friends, Anthony Trollope, in spirit only of course, along with me ever ready to hear his sage advice somewhere in my head. Yes, I carried my rare copy of <u>Can You Forgive Her?</u> up the steps to our newest server of fine comestibles, to entertain myself as I awaited something special. You know I do not expect the sublime . . . but much more, the divine: simple, fresh food prepared well and an attractive place in which to digest the product. So, what about <u>Camellia Japonica</u>? The owner, Marissa Manning, seems to be off track. The main dish was satisfying. The pear tartlets, rich and rewarding. Service? Efficiently done by a young lady giving too much homage to personal expression. However, for the eatery, I do withhold complete approbation. Here are my complaints. First, the indoor areas, although comfortable and clean, are missing ambience and theme. Colorless and rather dull, in fact. Next, Ms. Manning lists her establishment as a tearoom and sandwich shop. My dear! To identify one's place a tearoom, you must be fully dedicated to that idea. Bagged chips and hotdogs? Please! No standard, boring fare. Finally, how about something from the sea? We are on an island, you know. I would recommend a lobster salad hoagie or a spicy, shrimp-filled roll. Come now. You can do better. <u>Camellia Japonica</u> has the potential to be greater than the confusing way the owner has defined her restaurant.

For once, readers, you find me, your paragon of good eating, straddling the fence. The place requires another visit. Perhaps you should investigate for yourself! I just don't know if Ms. Manning brings anything memorable to our culinary choices, however well she pleases the food wants of the occasional, indiscriminate tourist. The owner's goals are a mystery to me. To be fair, I withhold judgment until another time. Perhaps today's schizophrenic experience has influenced my reading choice for next week: <u>Dr. Jekyll and Mr. Hyde</u>. Until then, Your Trusted Critic – E. Chisholm

Marissa slapped the paper down on the seat. Straddling the fence! Why, he was so overfed he wouldn't last more than five seconds before he fell to either side. She gassed the engine and took off, a rabbit racing for its hole. Her eyes watered. For so long she had needed a good cry about so many things: the sadness of illness, the meanness of a few men, the struggle to accomplish, her clear-cut aloneness, and now Abby. She grabbed tissues from the glove box and let the tears flow, thinking sunglasses are a wonderful thing as she headed north.

Hours later, she left Macon and came up I-75. Marissa turned on music and watched the way the terrain changed, long hill after long hill stretching up the piedmont, ascending to another land. Once near the energy-sparked city of Atlanta, she merged with I-85. The golden dome of the capitol cheered her progress. She came through the Grady Hospital curve, amazed as always at the great conglomeration of commerce. Her car whipped around, following the course snaking its way between and around buildings so never-ending tall, graying out the blue sky, that she pulled off her sunglasses and her dour look fled. She loved this section. It was as though she took a kayak ride skating down rapids through a deep, north Georgia gorge. She came out the other side of a concrete cavern into the open, skimming by the Varsity and Georgia Tech, riding the curves and straights, people moving at the same pace all around her, darting through the Perimeter interchange and the edifices of more corporate giants, and eventually cutting through Marietta. Finally, she veered onto I-575. That's when things softened. Development and industry released its hold on the land. Apartments rose, family subdivisions peeked through the trees that grew in abundance. In no time, she saw the signs telling her welcome to the town of her roots and whispering, *come see how we've changed in the blink of an eye.*

Any inkling of sadness had left when Marissa pulled in the gravel drive. She lowered her window and let cool north Georgia air rush in. Arriving at the house, she glanced at the front porch where fallen leaves had collected. Her daddy's uncle sat in a plain ladder-back chair, coppery hair hardly muted by time, and a face with more lines than the number of bristles in the broom always parked by the door, lines up, lines down, lines crosshatching his light-skinned, freckled countenance. But when he broke into his famous grin, he was beautiful.

She opened her door. "Uncle Nathan! You must have been waiting for me."

"Yes, the sight of you tells me life's still worth livin', even at ninety-three."

She walked over, kissed the top of his head, and hugged him.

Chapter Fourteen

THE year was 2002 on that November day in Woodstock when Marissa lugged her rolling suitcase up the stairs to the second story of the old farmhouse hidden down a hilly drive off Trickum Road. On the hall wallpaper, the repeating, country-style design had dulled with time. The floor creaked. She came to the doorway of the guest room where she paused and let her vision linger over everything.

Aunt Olivia had placed no stops on her decorative urges. Once her daughters had grown and left, it became Olivia's room where she wrote letters to her family, where she did her genealogical research, and where she gazed out the windows to see the fireworks made by the forsythia exploding into curved spires of bold, yellow blooms every February. In the far corner a wicker chaise rested, the perfect although brief escape from all the labor waiting for her. The bedroom, named the green room by the family, owned papered walls displaying a nearly life-size Chinese vision of willows, ornamental maples, flying birds, and coral-pink peonies against a pale green background. It was reputed that Uncle Nathan balked at the extravagance, but Aunt Olivia held her ground. After thirty years, she deserved a special place all her own. He moped for several days until she made a lemon meringue pie. In one small area near the bedroom door, the enchanting garden traveled up the slanted wall where the roof angled deeply into the room forming a cozy alcove for the bed. Short posts carved of maple marked the four corners of the bed having a woven, plaid bedspread in reds and greens and gold. A long bed skirt of forest green cotton sateen billowed with gathered folds. The waist high paneling, door, window frames, surrounds, and baseboards wore soft, spring green paint. The dark floorboards displayed a beautiful hooked rug with a bounty of flowers in a white, oval centerpiece framed by complementary flourishes in red and coral on the black background. On the bedroom walls, lanterns once used by railroad men had been electrified and affixed, illuminating the room. The most intriguing objects in the space were the bureau lamp and a vase holding ostrich plumes. Aunt Olivia had called the opaque glass Jadite, its creamy, pale green hue similar to the woodwork, yet much more vivid. In ultraviolet light, the items glowed. She said uranium produced the color, although without enough radiation to be a hazard.

Marissa rolled her suitcase to the bed and walked to the tall paned windows. She drew the sheers back and gazed at the yard. Uncle Nathan called from the kitchen below.

She took a seat at the 1930s white enamel table while Uncle Nathan filled the kettle with water. Marissa watched his back outfitted in a plaid long sleeve shirt and overalls. His lanky body and long arms hung from the horizontal line made by those capable shoulders, shoulders that had seen more physical work than some twenty-first century men knew was possible.

"Ah-h-h," he said, taking a seat until the water boiled. "Back's been botherin' me." In her direction, he pushed a bowl of apples, gifts from his tree by the well. Marissa selected one of the fruits and lifted a paring knife perched right in the same bowl. She cut a slice and took a bite, looking around the unchanged room.

"Delicious," she said. "Is the well holding out this year?"

"Barely. We're still at low rain level."

"With the recurring dry spells, I used to wonder how everything remained so lush in this county, especially the trees," she said.

"I figure they like extremes," replied Uncle Nathan. "They just grow taller and fuller."

"Everything looked good as I came through town. Spruced up. Some nice shops have opened, too."

"Ugh," moaned Nathan. "Things are happenin' too fast. Kroger and Publix are popping up like chipmunks in a meadow. Wal-mart is still confused. First they show up in our town, back when, and build themselves a store. Yeah, I liked it. Went there all the time. Next, Wal-Mart decides they gotta be bigger. So they tear themselves down along with the beautiful, old Reeves home next door, and they rebuild a bigger store on that same ground. But could they be content? No. They take a fancy to a different spot and move toward my direction."

"But you shop there."

He fidgeted in his seat. "I know." He smiled sheepishly. "They've got anything a person could want."

Marissa rubbed the top of his time-worn hand. "I think renewal and growth can be beneficial so long as we value our past."

He nodded. "Lately, I've been hearing whispers about big doings called Hedgewind or something. I got a peek at the drawings. Really nice. Like nothing this town has ever seen. But it'll be smack in the middle of things." He rubbed the beard stubble on his cheeks. "I don't know. Sometimes we're a town vaguely confounded by all this development. We may get swallowed by progress, and no one will ever know Woodstock existed. Just like the kudzu trying to cover the milking shed."

"Are you still battling that green pest? You don't have milking cows anymore. Why don't you have the area bulldozed and burn the kudzu along with that old shed?"

"And lose my nutritional advantage? That steer of mine is healthy and strong. The best I ever raised."

"You're feeding kudzu to your steer?"

"Sure am. The extension agent said it won't hurt one bit. He calls the vine an untapped . . .uh . . ."

"Resource?"

"Mm hm," he answered with a definitive nod.

"I guess it won't hurt," she said, smiling into his eyes.

He surveyed her face. "You sure look pretty. But when you first drove up, you seemed a wee bit melancholy in the face. I could tell because your . . . um . . ." He got up, pushing the chair back, frustration revealing itself by the way his head dipped. He went to get the kettle. He poured the water and brought the cups over. "because your . . ." He blew air with his lower lip pulled to the side. "Oh, those . . . *things* . . . the fur lines on your face." He eased into his chair.

"My eyebrows?" She held down her laughter.

"Yeah." He gave a shake to his head and looked at her again. "When you're happy, your eyebrows rest softly over your eyes like two sleeping baby squirrels."

She chuckled and leaned back. Her legs extended, and she held her cup close. "Thank you for the unusual compliment, Uncle Nathan. . . . If I looked blue, it's because I'm going to miss Abby."

"You and this entire town." They took sips from their cups.

Marissa put her cup down and crossed her arms. "What time do you want to leave for the service?"

"About ten. I got to gas up the old Chrysler. After the funeral, everyone is invited to Hank and Elizabeth's place to pay our respects to Trent."

"I'll whip up something to take," she said.

His face lit up. "Don't bother. I already have something special."

"All right, Uncle. . . . You look a little tired."

"Don't tell my men friends, but I reserve this part of the day for a lickety-split nap before dinner. Allows me to stay up for the eleven o'clock news."

"You go lie down. You know where I'm off to."

"To see that horse of yours." He took a final sip and he leveraged himself up by leaning on the table. "Got me a new stable hand. Max Donavan. Strong and hard-working."

"You didn't send me word. Did you check him out?"

"For certain. We had a chat."

"Forgive me but you know that horse is like a child of mine."

"I know, girl. Trust me."

They left the kitchen, Marissa trailing Nathan who moved slower than he had earlier. "I'll settle you in," she said. They entered his sleeping chamber, Aunt Olivia's former dining room wallpapered with cabbage roses above the time-darkened wainscoting. He edged to the bed, turned around, and landed his rear quarters on the squeaky springs. Marissa got down and removed his work boots. She lifted his legs to the bed and covered his feet with a quilt. The low hanging Victorian style chandelier bumped her head as she stood and turned to leave. She pulled the pocket door closed. Five years earlier when Nathan's knees had adamantly refused to grind themselves to the second story, a precedent was set that he would follow the rest of his days—he remained on the ground floor. Twice a year, a cleaning woman came to do the heavy-duty housework and to check for spiders and other things that might have taken up residence in the three bedrooms above Nathan's head.

Marissa went out the rear door of the house. The stable sat two hundred yards away, down by the branch that later drained into the creek seeking confluence with Little River. Stable smells of dirt, manure, and hay mingled in the air. Soft whinny sounds came from the stalls. She traipsed around the corner and encountered a boy topped with a shock of white blond hair. He held a pitch fork. He looked surprised.

The same could be said of her. "Oh. Didn't know anybody was riding today," she muttered

"Nobody is."

"Uh . . . hm. I'm looking for Mr. Donavan."

"That's me."

"You? How old are you?"

He pulled his shoulders back, puffed his chest. "Fifteen. I'm just small."

She saw the muscle tone in his arm holding the tool. "Pardon me. I'm Marissa Manning. The palomino is mine." Her head had turned away before her words ended. She scurried through the stable doors. The urge to investigate the state of her animal broke off any more conversation. At her approach, the horse whickered and bobbed its head above the stall door. Marissa poured out her affection in soft words and strokes of the white blaze on the forehead of the animal. She realized that the stable hand, not much taller than one of the stall shovels, had followed and now watched her quietly. Marissa flicked open the latch and entered. The boy leaned the pitch fork against the wall, entered, and continued to shadow her. Marissa scanned the animal. Her hand skimmed the neck and one side. She bent over and crooked a rear leg to examine the hoof. Her head flipped in the direction of the bushy-headed kid who displayed the demeanor of a guard.

"I'll speak with you in a minute," she said nicely. "You can leave."

"Can't, ma'am."

Marissa lowered the horse's leg and she straightened. "What do you mean, you can't."

"Ma'am, I have responsibility for the four horses boarded here. I don't think any of their owners would like the idea of my allowing a person I've never laid eyes on to get near the animals unsupervised, unless I'm certain they are who they say they are."

"But my uncle is taking a nap. Oh. Don't mention I told you that!"

"Follow me." He said and exited the stall.

Marissa exhaled and proceeded behind the sturdy little frame that marched to his contrived office the size of a refrigerator box.

He picked up a clipboard. Focused on the sheet before his eyes, his questions began. "Horse's name?"

"Algorithm. Al for short."

"Birth?"

"February 3rd, 1996."

"Sire?"

"Mansour."

"Dam?"

"Merinique."

"Driver's license." His open palm waited.

"*Driver's license?*"

He nodded.

"This is ridiculous," she spouted, towering over him. "I have to go all the way back to the house. It's in my purse."

Unfazed, he didn't say anything, simply stood there, blank faced, waiting with his clipboard.

She slung herself about and plodded from the barn and back the way she had come. When she entered the house, she checked the bed in the dining room. Nathan's breathing rippled in sleep, resembling one of his equine tenants in their more docile moments. Marissa tiptoed up the stairs. On her way out again, she heard her uncle stirring, but she decided to let him rise at his own pace. The license better be sufficient, she declared to herself, but darn it, the kid was plucky and, she had to admit, he possessed a degree of backbone she admired.

She progressed only ten feet outside the back door before the long shadows and sun-glowing fields melted any remaining irritation. The pastureland of thirty-five acres swam the rolling terrain, allowing the eye-grabbing sunset to etch itself on every viewer's mind. Orange. Violet. Purple. Gold. She folded her arms and breathed in the intriguing smells of autumn. She raised her face to heaven and let the breezes kiss her skin. This town. This place. It filled her senses. It calmed her spirit. It always renewed her hope.

As she lowered her head, her sight was alerted to the boy standing in the stable doorway. The lights were on now, but he stood out as a dark silhouette, one with a ruffled mane. She sped up her walk.

"Sorry. I was distracted for a moment. I know you've got to close things for the night. I won't take Al out this late, but here's my driver's license."

He looked at the item and returned it. "Thank you, ma'am."

"Thank you for taking good care of the animals. Maybe I'll ride tomorrow afternoon. We have a funeral to attend in the morning." She smiled and entered the building. "Let me help you lock up. Your mom is probably holding dinner for you."

"I don't need your help."

With his last word, Marissa noticed a clatter and the distinct smell of something savory. Her sight went to the office. Tomato soup foamed and spewed from under a jumping lid. The kid ran into his tiny headquarters. He jerked the pot off the hot plate that glowed neon red.

Marissa came to the doorway. "See you tomorrow, Max."

He wiped the side of the pot with a rag and kept his eyes from turning her way. "Okay. See you then."

Night had already floated over the farm as she walked up the hill to the house. The kitchen light beamed onto the back stoop. Her uncle could be seen milling about the stove. For him, she had a list of questions already pressing the insides of her head.

Chapter Fifteen

NATHAN ladled onion gravy over Marissa's country fried steak.

Marissa gasped. "This looks wonderful, but you better go easy on my portion in the future."

"Your Aunt Olivia could do justice to a plate like this."

"That's because she worked as hard as you did on this farm."

"Well, child, aren't you running a restaurant?"

"It's hard work, but not the same."

Nathan sat down. They took their first bites.

"Uncle, I met the stable hand."

He looked up. His aged head hung almost the same level as his rolled shoulders, so the food only had a trip of inches to his mouth. "Uh huh?" he said.

Marissa bit her lip and paused. "He's just a kid."

"Works a lot harder than some I've hired in the past. And boy does he know horses."

"Did you know he's cooking his dinner out there?"

The man's eyes returned their focus to his plate. "He won't let me feed him."

"Why isn't he eating at home?"

"This here is his home."

"What?"

"Didn't you see the cot next to the tack room?" Nathan said.

"Where are his parents? Does he go to school? Uncle, you could get in trouble."

"Not unless somebody tells, Marissa." His eyes met hers for a moment.

She continued her appeal. "He is doing a good job, almost too thorough, but there must be a better solution."

Nathan put down his fork down. "His mom don't want him. He got in some trouble with the law. Better for him here. Brooke Waller is supervising his schooling. Some kind of self-teach program. Let me tell you, that boy's brighter than the gleam in an angry bull's eye. Brooke stops by twice a week. Checks his progress. In the spring, he'll have to take a test each year until he graduates."

"He needs to be at the high school."

"Won't go. No use letting him end up on a trash heap somewhere."

They returned to their meal. Neither spoke.

When they finished, Marissa washed the dishes while Nathan watched a new show called American Idol. She found him asleep in the chair. He resisted her attempts to lead him to his bed. She gave up and climbed the stairs.

The atmosphere above the farm swirled pitch-dark while Marissa's sleeping mind fought off her night dreams—dreams of a deceptive, indurate cad. Breaking the spell, the reality of kitchen sounds reached her subconscious. Although weighted by three quilts, her limbs twitched. Coming awake, she chased away the agitation in her arms and legs with stretching, and she fished for her watch on the night stand. She turned on the lamp. Five a.m. Off went the light. After a period of darkness, a hint of gray brought the furniture and walls slowly into delineation. The smell of coffee weaved itself up the stairs and into her room. A half an hour passed in which she tried to shake images of her disturbing dream and the undermining debasement she narrowly escaped. The word *naïve*, echoed in her head. *Naïve*. Even at her age. She yanked herself to a sitting position. The covers fell from her upper body and frigid air surged against her shoulders. She rubbed her face.

A pan dropped below. She shivered. The middle of November was rarely so ahead of itself. The cold snap along with the light had wiggled itself through the windows and past the curtains. She swung her feet to the floor and studied the little fireplace, wishing a fire roared in that gloomy cavity. Her thoughts went to the funeral. To stay warm, she would have to layer clothing and somehow still look appropriate. Then it hit her. A shower in the unheated upstairs would be worse than death. The only solution was to throw on jeans for now and get ready as late as possible. In the past, Woodstock morning sunshine often sent the chill fleeing to some other clime. Her body relaxed. She thanked God she would not be staying in the icebox-like upstairs more than another night.

He was cracking an egg when she entered the toasty room. "Morning!" she called and came by his side at the stove. They laughed when the shell released its contents on the stovetop before reaching the cast iron pan. "Let me take care of this," she said softly. "If I remember, you like yours sunny side up."

"All right. But just leave mine in the pan. I always bathe before breakfast."

"How do you make it up the stairs?"

"I don't. Your aunt's laundry sink is my tub. Folded up, I fit well enough."

"Heaven knows you can't be serious."

"I'd really be stinking if I hadn't been serious about finding a substitute all this time. Luckily, my mother taught me long ago, when you don't have something you need, improvise."

"I never realized. I would have helped you get a bathtub put in. Bet Harbin doesn't know."

"Course not. He's got enough on his shoulders over there in Iraq."

"He's been home for visits."

"I worked things out just fine, missy. And I don't want you worrying him or Louisa about it." He handed her the spatula and went to the laundry room door. "Now keep this door shut or you might get an ugly sight when I get on that step stool and my nekked rear climbs into that basin." He chuckled like a naughty schoolboy and shut the door.

Marissa took her station over the pan, shaking her head and smiling. Gospel music came from a radio in the laundry room. She ate her eggs and cold biscuit. Soon the earnest melodies from another era, old melodies that were rich with simple goodness and the antithesis of trendy, present-day sound, had her moving about the kitchen. She swept. She wiped down the refrigerator inside and out. She made her uncle's bed. The music switched off. He came out wearing the same clothes.

"Now I'm ready for those eggs." He sat down and Marissa poured a cup of coffee. He glanced at her. "Was wondering if you'd give my hair a trim?"

"Be glad to."

He ruffled his red locks. "Don't want to be an embarrassment to Trent and the . . . uh, the . . . hm . . .oh, you know, the boo-hooers."

"Do you mean the mourners?"

"Yep. Didn't mean any disrespect. Words snag me sometimes."

He attacked his breakfast. Marissa washed the dishes.

"Where do you keep your clippers?" she asked.

"In the hall closet."

"Do you mind if I offer breakfast and a haircut to our helper in the stable?"

"You can try. Just pull the rope outside. That's my signal for him to come running."

Marissa cracked two more eggs into the cast iron pan. She added a small slice of country ham she found in the fridge. Uncle Nathan took note but said nothing and watched with a curious air evident in his alert head.

She opened the back door a tiny bit, then wider, finding the chilly air already being mastered by the sun. Her armed reached for the farm bell. She pulled. The call went out.

Moments later he entered and shut the door behind him. He stayed by the door.

"Yes, sir?" the boy said.

"Come sit with us a spell, while I get a hair cut," Nathan said.

"I've got my studies to do."

"Please," interrupted Marissa. "I need to hear how Al's been doing. I want your opinion about that rear hoof. And we have this leftover food." In one second she dished it up and placed it on the table. Her hand waved to the chair. He took a seat.

It looked like the boy's mouth watered. "Thank you," he mumbled. She put a fork in his hand and dropped a napkin in his lap. Before he could change his mind, a glass of orange juice and a cup of hot coffee sat next to his plate. He dug in. Marissa guided Nathan to a stool near the kitchen front window. She fetched the scissors and began beautifying. As she cut, she and Max talked horse talk: hoof problems, gaits, liniments, special feed, and supplements.

"Yes ma'am. I do most of my veterinary research at Woodstock Library. On the computer there. The minute the place opens. There's a nice lady there who gives me the password, so I can get into the research journals. I could read there all day. But Mr. Manning finishes visiting his buddies at Dean's Store in an hour or so."

Nathan looked indignant. "We don't visit. That's what women do. We chew the fat."

"Yes, sir."

Marissa removed the towel from Nathan's shoulders and dusted him off.

He stood. "I'm a new man," he said with emphasis. "Unfortunately, the widurs are gonna start chasing me again. They can't get it through their head that I've loved one woman, and now I plan to remain a . . . whatcha call it?"

"A bachelor," said Marissa.

"Mm-hm. Until the day I leave my Earth-suit behind." He lifted a light jacket from a hook on the wall. "I'm walking to the road to get my paper." He left the room.

Marissa turned to the boy who wiped his mouth. "Max, hop up here. I'll give you a free cut."

He hesitated, put down his napkin.

"Come on," she urged. "Like Uncle Nathan said, you'll feel like you're a new man."

"My hair is coarse, though. Just buzz it."

"Will do." She began her ministrations. The boy sat stiffly.

"Don't worry," she said. "I'm pretty good. I used to cut my daddy's hair when he was alive. He's Uncle Nathan's nephew. I'm Harbin's cousin. His father was Uncle Nathan's son, Allen, who died too soon like my dad . . . Uh. Sorry. You look confused."

"No. It's just that a horse chart containing a five page pedigree is easier to follow."

"Were you born with your love of horses?"

"It's in the genes. My great-grandfather was a jockey."

She held off the clippers. "Oh, really. And how about you?"

"Being on the back of a horse makes me feel like I'm just as tall as anybody, but my dream is veterinary medicine."

"I know your mom loves that." Marissa resumed cutting.

"She doesn't believe in dreams. Except for the kind online gambling can buy you."

"Oh. Well, hold onto your dream. I have a few of my own. Some days I look pretty foolish, but I keep trying anyway."

Marissa was almost through buzzing hair when Uncle Nathan walked in, his sight aimed at the text of his Cherokee Tribune.

"If that don't beat all," Nathan spurted.

"What is it?" she asked.

"The rest of the property near your old place has sold. Gonna put apartments there, starting next month. I hope those Ridgewalk developers know what they're doing. Too bad the seller didn't get a deal like mine." He sat down at the table, back to perusing his paper.

Marissa finished with Max's trim, wiped him down, and got the broom. Palest blond hair formed a miniature mountain on the old linoleum.

Marissa opened the pantry cabinet where her aunt's "take a check mirror" still hung. Max wore a bashful expression. Marissa took him lightly by the shoulders and guided him to the spot. He gazed. He grinned. He thanked her and rushed out the door.

Marissa finished cleaning up by eight-thirty. The thought of the cold bathroom upstairs half appealed to her. She was about to tend to her plan when she paused with a question.

"Uncle Nathan."

"Yep?" He was still bent over the news.

"I was curious. What did you mean by the sellers not getting a deal like yours? I didn't know you were liquidating land somewhere."

"Somewhere? I thought I told you about that real estate fellow, Mr. Silverstrike."

"No."

"I guess I failed to mention he owns the farm now cause it doesn't really change a thing. I do have a nice pot of money in the bank to leave to Harbin when he's home for good, but I'm not going anywhere for a while. Not unless Jesus wants me home. Mr. Silverstrike and I made a deal."

Marissa grabbed the side of the table and swerved her backside into a seat. "Uncle. You didn't sell this place, did you?"

"Didn't I say just that? Now don't get anxious. Max and I get to stay at least three more years. Rent free. Not one blade of grass can be touched. And I'm going to pray my body holds out that long so I can see Max graduate from high school and head to college. . . . Now stop letting those baby squirrels jump all over the place. . . . Oh. I forgot to tell you the most important thing." His tone was all confidence. "We shook. A hearty handshake it was. We're staying. I have Mr. Silverstrike's word on it."

Chapter Sixteen

MARISSA, her face stricken with concern, leaned toward the man and covered his hand with her palm. "Uncle Nathan. Did you have an attorney? Did you get fair market value? Let me see the contract." Marissa's words were yelps to the ear.

"See the contract? What for? I'm happy as a laughing cowboy."

"When did all this happen?"

"Back in January. Right after you took off for fancy island life."

The time stood out on the kitchen clock above Nathan's well-groomed head. "Oh gosh," she blurted. "I have to start getting ready. But Uncle, it would give me great peace of mind to see the papers of sale when we get back. Everything."

"You're thinking tricksters?"

"Sooner or later they cross everyone's path." She rubbed the back of her neck. "I know a thing or two about the subject."

"Sure, honey girl, I'll share the details if it eases your mind. Right now I better begin heating my casserole. I bought one of those carry-things at Wal-mart. It'll keep the dish nice and warm while we're in the service."

She feigned interest, trying to lighten the mood that she had sent to the ceiling. "I saw your creation in the refrigerator. A baked spinach dish?"

"Better than that. It's called King Kudzu Parmesan Pie. I'll need you to transport the thing. I'm feeling a little shaky this morning."

Hankering for a shower, Marissa climbed the stairs. A feeling of dread about the day was well on its way. She took pride in her cooking, and now she would have to present a dish certain to make her the laughingstock of town. In her estimation, only recently had she regained affable footing with so many of the townsfolk she managed to offend and alienate during an entire decade or so in which she mingled with arrogance, resentment, and misguided notions. She let the shower spray pound her skull.

Uncle Nathan backed the '72 Chrysler, the last automobile he once vowed he'd ever need, from the garage. Little had he known how long he would live. Every other body part was winding down, but his eyes stayed sharp enough, and so the license bureau allowed him on the road.

Once outside the tight fitting shed, he stopped and Marissa hopped in the vehicle, holding the casserole. The car surged up the long dirt road, with Marissa begging him not to use a heavy foot. He responded with, "Can't hear ya. Too much ear wax." Marissa faced forward, planted a wan smile, and stoically embraced their uncommon but edible gift of condolence.

Roving from his home place hidden down a dirt lane off Trickum Road was the highlight of Nathan's day during his elder years. When Olivia passed on, he frequented town exponentially to his pain, seeking comfort for his wounded heart. He loved to tour the local roads that had suddenly burgeoned in width, sporting extra lanes to accommodate traffic inflated with newcomers, and he felt urged to explore brand-new thoroughfares being cut through his environment with the audacity of a runaway lawn mower. The metamorphosis of his world was a result of that strange and sometimes overnight metamorphosis called growth. Ambivalence visited his thoughts each day. Hardly a closeted monk, he had seen WWII and a multitude of changes during his span of nearly a century of breathing; however, as he advanced in age, it was his personal world he preferred untouched.

On the other hand, he retained a mental catalogue of all the changes he fondly remembered. He often recounted the paving of Main Street in 1929, and how the kids roller skated down the smooth surface, right past the depot, pretending they were the fastest train on wheels. Highway 92, from Woodstock to Acworth, remained hard packed earth until slathered with asphalt in 1962. Nathan and the other men at Dean's Store sometimes recalled their astonishment when the interstate came through, a bold, expansive slab of cement. Then, in 1984, Towne Lake Parkway was cut, making it quicker to reach Bells Ferry than by way of Highway 92, that is, until the hustle and bustle of the huge subdivisions springing up made the shortcut one irritating crawlway at eight and five. He and the older men, however, most lamented the disappearance of the thousand-acre wood that had welcomed them in their youth with raccoon scouting and rabbit hunts. When the pot of gold, so to speak, was offered Nathan for his land, he came to the conclusion that he would be lacking in sense to refuse such a windfall for his acreage; the land had cost his ancestor a mere pittance compared to its current explosion in value. In fact, he knew his father would be proud. So he bowed to change, feeling a twinge of guilt.

Nathan reached the end of the driveway and wheeled his car onto Trickum Road. In seconds, Marissa and he flew by the stores that were secretly fighting to reproduce like chickweed and inch closer to the farm and boarding stable.

Marissa cracked the window and breathed in cool air as the car rumbled down Highway 92. Thinking of everyone she would see, her fingers fidgeted along the handles of the casserole. Uneasiness had already risen within her. Had they all forgotten the personal changes she made? Did they remember they had forgiven her poorly derived opinions and her self-important attitude? And Trent. Had his estimation of her regressed in ten months absence to the former low state when he must have harbored deep resentment for her coldness and her attribution of failure regarding her father's trial. Did he know she had ceased making Trent, now an old man, the scapegoat for her pain and anger? Perhaps she would never be certain. She took off her seat belt, turned around on her knees, and placed the dish on the back seat.

Uncle Nathan pulled in the Chevron station and insisted on doing the gassing up. He moved with the urgency of a strolling foal. Marissa checked her watch and sighed. Then they were on the road again with her wishing to cross over her uncle, slide him to the passenger side, and take the wheel. But she had been growing in graciousness the past few years, so she kept her urge under control.

They entered the church late and took places in the back of the sanctuary. Few seats remained. Brian Barton stood over the casket, reminding everyone to smile. Yes, she had lost her decade-long battle with breast cancer, he said, but she was perfect now, running through heaven, just as she had run through the Florida tall grass as a girl. Then, knowing how his words would always be lacking in the truest impact, he read the scriptures that lifted their hearts. And they believed. Yet tears flowed. Nathan's handkerchief came from his hip pocket several times. Marissa, more practiced at restraining her tears, felt a burning ache in her throat. The congregation, the town, Abby's family would falter and take a spill on the worst days while bereft of her presence until they remembered her practical ways and how she would likely urge them to get on with things.

Brian closed the service and invited everyone to the graveside ceremony. The music began and Trent rose with his children and their families. Slowly they led the procession. Trent's next door neighbors, the Averills, followed. Little Manuel proudly held his mother Elizabeth's hand. Hank Averill supported his baby daughter in the crook of his arm while he guided Rakey, the town's well-protected charge.

At the back of the room, Marissa wanted to let her line of sight go to her lap; Trent had almost reached her side. At the last instant, she lifted her head. Their eyes met. He stopped. Marissa returned his smile, her eyes watering.

"She knew you would come," he said softly while giving slight nods of his head. He pulled a piece of folded paper from his suit. "She told me to give this to you. Read it when you're alone."

Marissa took the paper. "Thank you."

Everyone moved to Enon Cemetery past the library and across the road from the lively recreation center. With the addition of that relatively recent building, the aspect was no longer quite so forgotten as the old burial spot seemed since 1879 when the church elders chose an in-town location for transplanting their place of worship. At Abby's insistence, Enon was to be the place where her earthly body was laid to rest. After all, she explained to Trent, when that trumpet blast came, calling them to rise, how thrilling it would be to go along with the women who came before her, women dressed in the attire of the 1800s, women who had contributed to the strength of the town when Woodstock was merely a small settlement of people struggling to find a better future.

After the graveside prayer, Marissa and Uncle Nathan left Enon and eventually drove up the hillside path to the lake houses. Marissa glimpsed Abby's cabin standing among the hardwoods shedding their leaves. They traveled one hundred feet more and turned through a pass in the woods until they met the cobblestone drive of Hank and Elizabeth's home. A couple of the men waved Nathan to park in a spot that would make his walk to the cottage easier.

Nathan opened his door and got out. Marissa eyed the casserole in the back seat but said nothing. She eased herself from the car.

"Don't forget our dish, Marissa."

"Yes, sir." *Our* dish? He was already ten steps ahead of her. She wanted to sling the carryall in the woods and jump back into the car.

Friends and family wended their way in front of the cottage toward the walkway that led to the green and the gardens centralizing the compound of buildings which made up Morning Star Health and Recuperation Center.

Everyone entered the spacious assembly building that functioned as a Sunday chapel, dining hall, and winter playroom with a game table and two basketball nets. People visited with each other and extended sympathies to Trent while the women prepared food at a large serving station. Marissa meandered in that direction, hoping to quickly drop off the casserole and then make a beeline for some friendly face on the opposite side of the room.

Lugging the carryall, she heard Nathan's voice call out, drowning the polite talk in the entire room. "Marissa, girl." Those two words hit the back of her head with the sureness of two flying ping-pong balls. Her heart sank. "Don't forget. Leave the warming thing on our kudzu pie until the last minute." She visualized the proud grin he must be wearing. The room remained silent.

"Mm hm," she answered and raced to the table, explaining to the women it was his concoction and that he swore it was safe to eat.

Elizabeth leaned toward Marissa. "I for one will try it," said Elizabeth with her Spanish accent that made anything she spoke ring melodious.

"I'm so embarrassed," said Marissa. "I just couldn't hurt his feelings."

Elizabeth smiled and shook her head. "Ah, yes. We are willing to do anything for the frail ones we love. But I will be most happy to be adventurous. After all, in Mexico, the cuisine in some regions makes great use of the insect world . . . and unapologetically," she said, her brown eyes sparkling. She withdrew, to give her son some direction as he whirled about the room with his friends.

Marissa surveyed the place that swiftly filled with people who knew her on a first name basis. She made the rounds, greeting everyone. Elizabeth's husband, Hank, set up another table and chairs. Kristin Arnett tended the Averill baby while Elizabeth watched over everything else. Trent sat in a wicker chair in the sunlight of a window where his silver-tipped cane shone. More people came by, bent down to hug him or give words of support. Marissa felt discomfort rolling off her back, and she made herself useful opening a stubborn jar of dill pickles and, at the same time, answering the women's questions about her tearoom.

During the occasion, forty tables were seated and fed. Afterward, Kristin pulled out her guitar and sang songs bringing gladness to everyone's heart. When she stopped, the people rose from their seats and began to cover and re-pack the leftover food. Trent's family led him to the log cabin, where they planned to stay a few more days.

Marissa was wiping up a child's spilled plate when she saw a different man walking near, his eyes unfocused. Familiar, brown suede oxfords. Cuffed pants that swam around bony legs. A plaid shirt stained with grape juice sometime within the last hour. She stood, came near, and looked into the aging man's face, a face that only a mother could love.

"Hello, Rakey."

"Hello, Miss Marissa . . . 10 Manning Lane," said the address-obsessed little man.

"No, Rakey. I sold my mama and daddy's place. Remember? For a short while I took an apartment here, but I don't reside in Woodstock anymore. I live on St. Simons now."

"Oh." He tramped straight backwards, pants swishing, arms stiff at his sides.

"Wait. Don't you want to know my new address on St. Simons?"

"No," he called to her as he pivoted and moved off. "I don't know about that planet."

Marissa finished helping with clean-up. For a few minutes, she was shanghaied by Carl Cannon and made to laugh until her side was splitting. Finally, she broke away and found her uncle surrounded by black-haired Manuel and three of the child's friends, two boys and a girl several years younger. Their rapt attention was on every word that proceeded from Nathan's mouth.

"Ninety-three isn't old. Some day soon, I'll be one hundred. That's when all your teeth fall out."

"One hundred!" cried Manuel. "How are you going to chew, Mr. Nathan?"

"I'll carve me some choppers from the hickory tree out my back door. Then I'll go to the hardware store and buy some white paint so they shine."

Manuel, not being taken in at seven years old, eyed his friends and shook his head.

The little girl wedged closer. "I been saving my baby teeth. You can have them if you want." The boys looked at each other and howled.

Manuel burst forth, saying, "Five-year-olds don't know *anything*." He and his friend skipped away. The girl ran after them.

Marissa bent down and lightly pulled her uncle by the arm. "Don't you think we'd better head home?"

"Yes," he warbled, drained from the day. "You'd better drive, though."

"I'd be happy to." She tugged and he came from the chair. They waved goodbye to several folks as they trundled out the door with the surprisingly empty casserole dish. Nathan leaned heavily on his great-niece's arm.

Marissa and Nathan came down the long gravel imbedded road leading to home. Approaching the shed by the white pasture fencing, her attention was caught by a Dodge Ram truck and two men wandering the property.

Chapter Seventeen

STRIDING about the farm as though they belonged there, the men wearing khakis and dress shirts carried clipboards and looked over the land. They didn't bother to notice the arrival of the Chrysler.

"What's this about?" snapped Marissa. Her suspicious query threw Nathan right from his catnap on the front seat. He sat up and squinted through a cold mist hitting the windshield.

"Don't know."

She drove past the Dodge Ram, studying the door graphic, which said Aiken & Aiken, Inc. To her eyes the paint on the truck presented a deceptive snow white. High priced tires had laid down fat tread patterns in a muddy depression on Nathan's dirt drive. The highly reflective hubcaps looked like gigantic jewelry that a gorilla would sport.

She let Uncle Nathan disembark, and she put the car in the shed. Together they trooped toward the men who engaged in conversation on one side of the house. The beefier man of the two pointed to the area where the pond languished just before the rise of a hill. In the cold air, his breath came out like steam from the nostrils of a bison. Well into his fifties, he was padded with extra flesh, and he wore nothing over his long sleeve shirt to ward off the dipping temperature. Marissa advised herself to take a backseat for the moment.

Uncle Nathan walked up grinning, schooled in country ways of hospitable kindness that no longer always gelled with the strangers entering his world. "Howdy? Can I be of help?" He extended a hand.

The man in charge muttered, "Afternoon." He put his strong paw in Nathan's hand and cranked hard. "We'll only be here a few minutes more." Just as quickly, he turned his back and continued his conference with an assistant.

Marissa felt a scowl creeping across her face. The man's back seemed overly muscled, something akin to a full grown bear. She turned and looked at her uncle who took a deep breath and another step forward.

"Excuse me," Nathan said with more force. The contractor's head barely swiveled Nathan's way. "Exactly what are you doing here?"

The man turned fully, showing a bemused smile as though he talked to a child. "Looking at the lay of the land. Pretty spot. It's going to hurt to shave this land, but we're going to try to save the best trees."

Marissa saw Uncle Nathan's face blanch. The contractor chuckled with puzzlement and gave her an appreciative glance. His expansive belly strained to move the shirt from under his belt. She wanted to explode with questions but held her tongue. She knew how her uncle would react if she butted in.

"What the matter?" he addressed Nathan. "Didn't they tell you we'd be out here today?"

"No. They promised they'd leave things alone," whined Nathan.

The contractor developed a worried look. "Well I got my orders. If you've got a problem you'd better take it up with a legal advisor. . . . Oh, my gosh, sir. Please, you better sit down." He helped Marissa lead Nathan to the back stoop. The old man collapsed and put his head in his hands. Brianna, the goat, came to that side of her pen and watched complacently.

Nathan uttered to the ground, "Mr. Silverstrike and I had an arrangement."

Marissa felt her face redden and her heart sprint. She sat down beside Nathan and patted the forearm of his jacket.

The contractor extended his hands in appeal. "Sir, I don't know anything about that." The man deflated and got down on one knee, extending his cell phone. "Sir, do you want to talk to Mr. Silverstrike? I can have him on the line in an instant."

Nathan waved the phone away.

"Uncle," Marissa cooed. "Is the agreement anywhere on paper?"

"No," whispered Nathan, eyes glazed.

Marissa's lips began to quiver. She took a breath and rose from the bench. She blinked, inwardly fighting back the adrenalin that stormed through her bloodstream. Then her lips blew open and she blared, "Why you scheming bunch of wild animals! How could you do this!" The contractor got up slowly, his look unbelieving. Marissa's arms waved in the air. In the background, she could hear Nathan's voice pleading with her but she continued. "People like you should be locked in zoos where you can't hurt anyone! Especially, trusting old men!" The contractor backed up like she came toward him with a cattle prod. She saw Max run from the stable, drawn by her blaring recriminations. "Now get out of here!"

she screamed at the contractor. The man and his assistant hot-footed it to their truck. She ran after them. "You better not step one foot on my uncle's-" She froze as though the truth slapped her down in the mud—her uncle no longer owned even one inch of the land in question. Nathan, Max, the horses, Aunt Olivia's lovely dining chandelier, everything rested on this beautiful piece of earth only at the whim of a man named Silverstrike.

Marissa fixed them a light dinner at five. In thirty minutes, it was almost dark outside because of the time change weeks earlier. Uncle Nathan seemed to be crumbling with fatigue. His sagging eyes would not look at her, and the gloom surrounding them made talk out of the question. His mouth opened only once. "You know, hollering doesn't accomplish a thing." Silent at his reproach, Marissa carried the dishes to the sink. At six, she sat him down in front of his television. If she could keep him up at least until seven, he wouldn't be up before even the rooster announced the first whispers of light.

She put a hassock under his legs. "We'll discuss all of this in the morning."

"Okay. My heart's had too much for one day."

Marissa took a seat on the sofa under the front window. He slouched in his chair directly across from her, angled at the television. Easily, she monitored his state just by a turn of her eyes while her head stayed centered on the sitcom. Without this subterfuge, she would likely be accused of being a babysitter and sent from the room. The times his sleepy head eased forward, she purposely emitted a chuckle, and his head jerked up trying to figure out the joke he missed on the screen.

An hour passed. "You need to rest, now," she said. "Why don't I put the house to bed?"

He didn't quarrel but left the chair and went to his sleeping chamber. The pocket door slid shut. She went about the place, straightening and turning out lights. She went to the kitchen and checked to see that she had shut the oven off, which reminded her of *Camellia*. Her little place on the island had not entered her thoughts in twenty-four hours. She pulled out a kitchen chair and sat. Her eyes wandered. The little curtains with a colorful fruit pattern, needing a wash, hung sadly at the window. She recalled the wide, bright bank of panes at *Camellia* and wanted to be there, looking onto the patio dining area and across the herb bed to the wrought iron ornamented planter. Past that boundary marker, she would see gardenia, climbing allamanda, two large cycads, and elephant ear he had planted in his yard. She pictured him outside, as she often saw him, renovating, shoring up his house, music pouring through the screen door to where he worked.

Marissa fell back in the vinyl chair and felt a dull sadness that the man hated her. She had rewarded his kindness with rudeness and venom. Everywhere she went, she left in failure. Everyone she touched was eventually scalded by her tongue. She belonged on an island, alone, safely put away, a danger to no one, a curse no longer. No wonder she had always been unloved. Who would want their days turned inside out? If she failed Uncle Nathan, she would have to go back to *Camellia* with even less confidence and somehow salvage the damage there. She tipped her chair, holding on to one next to her. Forget the food critic, she told herself. People came to her place, paid good money, and returned. She paused. Her chair slammed down. The dim lighting, the lonely ache, and the failures were too much, and depression pulled her into its deep morass. She stayed at the table doing nothing. Nathan's snores came through the wall. Then she heard the bleating of the forgotten goat. Marissa dragged herself from the chair and put on her uncle's jacket. She turned on the porch light and saw Brianna's face with soft, floppy ears imploring Marissa's help.

Later, Marissa entered the house again, locked up, and hurried upstairs. Shivering, she changed into her sleep clothes, took care of her night routine, and flew under the covers. The room was worse than an ice box. She came out and yanked on socks. She went to the bureau for the flashlight she had seen. She grabbed the thing and her cell phone and tossed the quilts over her body and even her head. She sat up, draped completely, and leaned against the alcove wall. She clicked on the light. Something about the strategy seemed childish, but her sadness was forced to leave. Her body heat warmed her den. She picked up the phone ready to speed dial, wondering if it was right to disturb a woman who must guard every minute of rest. The screen said 8:15 p.m. She made the call.

Daphne picked up. Her hello sounded foggy to Marissa's ear.

"Daphne, it's me, Marissa. I'm so sorry. You were asleep."

"It's okay. . . . I . . . fell asleep when I came home from work. Tired. Not one of my better days."

"Oh, no, Daphne."

"Please don't worry. You know it's up and down for me. I just don't know when the bad days are coming. But I worry about *Camellia*. Marissa, my situation may worsen at any time."

"Daphne. I'm begging you, if you need to end your work at *Camellia* then you're free this instant. It can't be helping things."

"No, not yet. I'll have to face the prospect of a hospital bed soon enough, let me feel alive, creative a little while longer."

"Look, I'll be there Tuesday. If I leave here about four in the morning, I can be there by 9:30. Let Isabel know to have the frittata and scones prepared early, so the three of us can meet before we open. I'm going to hire more help, but my uncle is having a crisis, which is going to keep me here longer. I'll explain later. Tomorrow I'll call and put an ad in the island and Brunswick papers."

"All right. But may I suggest you look for a server? A group of twenty-five got off a tour bus yesterday, and I discovered Isabel is fantastic in the kitchen. She thinks food should be as beautiful as artwork, and you've seen her paintings."

"If you think she'd do well in the kitchen, we'll try it. You know . . . maybe her artwork could lift the place out of dullness."

"We read the article. Mr. Chisholm sure doesn't hold anything back."

"I cried most of the way to Atlanta."

A minute later, the conversation ended. Marissa turned off the flashlight and stuck her head outside the covers as she reclined. Warmed, her toes edged off her socks. The house exulted in silence except for an occasional snap or crack as the components of the home shrunk in the cold night. Her nose recalled the scent of cinnamon rolls she had baked earlier, seeking to get a glimmer of a smile from Uncle Nathan as he drooped before the television. Marissa had bypassed the treat, but she promised herself one in the morning to taunt her boiled egg. She smiled at the prospect. Finally, the thrumming of every nerve in her body since her afternoon blowup subsided. She drifted toward sleep when she heard the sound of Max's radio streaming teen-age music from the stable. Too much din for the horses, she thought. The radio switched off. Good kid. Marissa's face relaxed and she went to sleep.

Chapter Eighteen

WAKING, she wondered how a house could morph overnight into a ringing bell. Marissa threw on her robe and flew down the stairs. The clanging racket refused to cease and led her to the living room. Nathan, fit after a night of deep sleep, raised a titanic wrench designed for a tractor engine and brought the tool down again, flailing the radiator.

She covered her ears and yelled over the clamor. "Uncle! Uncle! What's wrong?"

He pointed with disgust to the radiator. "Useless lump of iron. Needs some jarring. Only the dining room and kitchen are halfway livable once the cold comes."

"Then it's time to update your system," Marissa asserted.

He shot her a scornful look.

"I forgot," she said. "But don't be mad at me. I didn't sell the place."

He let the wrench rest at his side. "Well, you didn't help matters yesterday. A smidgen of diplomacy might shame Mr. Silverstrike into remembering our deal. Now it will be his pleasure to get rid of us." He made an ugly face at her.

Marissa turned away. The wrench clunked onto the floor. She felt Uncle Nathan's hand patting her shoulder.

"Pardon me, girl. We'd better get right to counseling with the Lord before I make things worse," he said.

"Let me get showered and dressed first." She dashed up the stairs and shuddered at the frigid certainty waiting for her.

Max slipped through the kitchen door at the same time Marissa sat down at the table. He wandered to the stove.

"Get ya some grits out of that big pot," said Nathan. "Orange juice is in the fridge."

"Thanks. Can I help myself to coffee?"

"Sure," Nathan said. "You need something blisterin' hot to stay warm in this house. Just look at Marissa hugging her cup. You and the horses have it better in the stable."

Max took a seat and aimed his spoon.

"Angh!" Nathan snapped at him. "Don't dig in until you've agreed with us in prayer." Max froze. "Besides, now you know what might happen around here. If we get the boot, you could end up in some foster home, so you'd better seek some help yourself."

Marissa took a sip of coffee to cover her amusement that Uncle Nathan didn't consider his place a foster home. Wouldn't a horse barn be even lower on the scale of suitable habitation? No telling when the last time was that the kid had a bath, escaped the pungent smells of the stable, or looked out a window and dreamed.

Nathan opened the huge black book. He buried his concentration there. Marissa and Max waited. Nathan carefully turned pages. Max heaved a sigh. Nathan eyed him. The boy apologized.

The second hand of the kitchen clock moved silently as Marissa watched the kitchen tap and calculated. A drop of water fell at twenty second intervals. She caught the boy eyeing the steam rising from his bowl, the aroma thrilling his brain. She mused. He's probably praying his meal won't be cold when the time finally comes to plunge his fork into the creamy white stuff. Seasoned with butter, full of texture and flavor, laced with bits of bacon that would explode on one's tongue with salty, smoky, meat taste, the prospect made anyone's hunger excite. Her sympathy mounted. Max didn't deserve sub-par life or frigid grits. She did. She deserved the congealed, tasteless, molded-to-the-bowl version suitable for cutting with a knife, a perfect substitute for pre-school paste, in snowless winters, a great alternative weapon once mashed into a ball, and a feast only when tossed outside for a hungry-eyed dog wandering by. Marissa's mental drifting ceased. Nathan had shut the book.

Her head jerked up. He pushed the book aside. "Uh-hum," he said. "We can bow our heads now." Marissa watched Max take one last yearning glimpse at his grits before he lowered his eyelids. "Lord," began Nathan, "thank You in a mighty way that You are our provider and a very present help in time of need. We ask that You work Your ways on Mr. Silverstrike. We wish him no ill will, and we forgive him that he has reneged on our deal. However, Lord, You know that man's mind clearly. You can show him how he has been unjust to promise something he never planned to deliver. Lord, this was my home. I was born here in

1909, just as You know, so long ago now; there were only one or two cars in town then. You saw us strive to pull a living from the ground. You gave us the mules that added their power to our plows. I brought my bride here. My newborn son brightened my days and gave me the strength to press on. My two daughters were the glory of my household. When the children left, I still had Olivia and You, Lord. . . . She's with You now and I praise You for that. But I ask one thing. Let me stay here until my last breath. In Your word it says Your favor lasts a lifetime, so I'm not worrying one more minute about the subject. . . . But we want to make some promises, too. Marissa will try to remember that, in Proverbs, You advise her, *Like a gold ring in a pig's snout is a beautiful woman who shows no discretion.* . . . And Max Donavan also promises to remember, *Food gained by fraud tastes sweet to a man, but he ends up with a mouth full of gravel.* (Marissa peeked at the boy who choked a little and dropped his sneaking spoon). . . . And now to me, Your most hard-headed child. Lord . . . I will brand the following words on my brain, *The way of a fool seems right to him, but a wise man listens to advice.* Yes, I confess that I harbored resentment against Trent that day a while back when he volunteered to peruse the offer I received. As You know, I declined his assistance and his lawyering knowledge. I confess my lack of humility and the unforgiveness I still had not done away with. . . . So we offer You our contrite hearts Lord, and we end this prayer knowing, *the battle is the Lord's*. Amen."

Nathan got up, looking totally free of worry. "I'll be about my morning ablutions," he announced. He went to the laundry room, closed the door, and sent his favorite radio station broadcasting throughout the lower floor.

Marissa looked at Max. The boy attempted to swirl his spoon through the grits that already entered the beginning stages of solidity. She grabbed the bowl and went to the counter where she dumped and wrapped the blob in newspaper, aware it was best Uncle Nathan didn't see good food thrown in the trash. Another bowl of hot grits landed in front of Max. She went to the fridge for her boiled egg. A turquoise Fiestaware plate held her cinnamon roll, which she slid next to the boy's coffee cup. She didn't look at him as she sliced her egg and relished her petite meal. He said nothing and roared through his food as he had done the day before.

"I have a lot to think about today," she said. "So first thing, I'll be saddling Al."

He wiped his mouth and placed the napkin by his empty bowl. The wary part of him faded when he sat at the kitchen table. "All right ma'am. I'll go give her a brush. She's already had her oats, and I've mucked the stall."

Mid-morning, Marissa adjusted the cowboy hat her uncle deposited on her head as she tried to leave the house. She sat straight in the saddle and pulled up the collar of the wool fleece he had loaned her. The softness brushed the bottom half of her cheeks. She sniffed the wool and grinned—motor oil, camphor, and cedar from the closet. Her hand discovered something cellophane-wrapped in one of the pockets. Out came one of her uncle's butterscotch candies. The golden wrapper crackled. A touch of scent reached her. She smiled and put his treat back.

She and the horse tarried, positioned on one of the first hills past the stable, the best and most elevated view. From there, everything rolled down the lengthy pasture and to the gate leading to the creek and to the cotton road meadow. Al shimmied and stamped, wanting to stretch his legs into a gallop. "Let me soak it in, Al." She tugged at the reins. The horse snorted and stilled its legs. Her station atop gave her vision the best advantage of a scene that was quite different than her view of sunset two nights before. Now she observed a cloudless sky of blue startlingly rich with vibrancy, the water tower in the distance, marking another high point off Neese Road, and on her far left, the shining symbol atop the monolithic round church that characterized the town's positive vision for the future and that created a landmark by which to label time: B.B.C., before the big church, or A.B.C., after the big church.

The horse shifted restlessly under Marissa, reminding her of its genetic desire to chase the wind. Marissa rose in the stirrups and took a whiff of clean, cold air. She sat again, drinking in the mysterious, crisp, energy of autumn, energy that made her want to stream like a red-tailed hawk over the land. The moment was building, leaping in her blood, tensing her body until her voice commanded at the same moment her feet tapped the animal's side, and they burst down the promontory. Her uncle's cowboy hat zipped off her head and baffled in the wind. Down the sprinters flew and up another rise they charged, ripping the grass with their speed, slicing the air with their excitement. Horse and rider loped down that second hill and dodged a boulder, with Marissa shrieking in triumph at their mutual skill and the electrifying beauty of the morning. Over the third and fourth hill they galloped and then she caught sight of the fencing on the back side of the pasture. Closer and closer they came, and although she wanted to let the horse curl and extend it legs up and over in one last moment of strength and exertion, she reined in her horse and leaned back, bringing Al to a turf-tearing halt. Bending toward the neck of her caramel-hued animal, she patted and rubbed while voicing her admiration. She cantered Al in an imaginary show ring, hoping to bring down the roaring heartbeat of the horse, and then she led the animal into a slow trot toward the fence. She slid off the horse, opened the paddock gate, and led the animal through. After securing the gate, she hopped on the horse again, and they turned left and ambled down the dirt path leading through the woods. The creek had worked its way here, and she dismounted and offered the horse a drink where the water sluiced over the rocks and bounced sparks of light. They meandered thirty minutes before turning back and following the same route past the gate. This section of the dirt road proceeded straight from the gate and headed to the lowlands. Then she walked reins in hand, along the high road, beside the exposed red earth wall on her left, cut from the ridge and flanked on the opposite side by bottom land. On these acres, Uncle Nathan had farmed and his father had nurtured cotton just as his grandfather had also done. Nearby, a short distance down Highway 92, Nathan had attended Little River Academy, the first high school in the county, a clapboard structure long gone, on the methodist church property.

If Marissa continued to follow the dirt road three hundred more yards, the way became overgrown and blocked by a stand of trees, although the half-hidden path eventually reached Neese Road. Instead, she stopped and brought her horse down the road bank and tied the animal to what would, in spring, reveal itself to be a wild plum tree on the border of the planting field. Looking around, she felt certain no eye could witness her, and she reclined on the sloped bank, nestled in the browned grasses. She contemplated the former fields Nathan now allowed to flower in the spring with Shasta daisy, reseeding cosmos, black-eyed Susan, and blue cornflower. Aunt Olivia and her aesthetic sensibility had refused to let the bygone fields remain forever fallow and she had flung seed far and wide one year.

Situated a distance from Trickum Road, traffic sounds did not invade and Marissa listened as though she enjoyed a symphony. Air unusually cold for November added distinctness to every sound, and she identified each instrument: crickets sensing the approach of winter and sawing their final strains, dried leaves rolled by the wind creating periodic rustles, and a crow belching out a call, comical and quick.

Al softly nickered. Marissa snuggled deeper in her grass bed, letting the straw-stems and weedy sprigs muss her hair as the sun thoroughly warmed her as she enjoyed the sky. Her mind traveled to the past, and she remembered the stories she had shelved and permanently cached in her heart.

Uncle Nathan's story, a life-changing day, remained paramount in her collection. The event took place on the red clay road behind her resting head. In 1925, sixteen-year-old Nathan sat beside his father in the wagon that hot September day. They carried a monstrously large load of cotton. For a few more years, people in and around Woodstock would grasp a living from the crop before the bottom of the market fell out. The two Mannings planned to travel to the cotton gin on the south end of town; Marissa knew the spot currently as just south of a new subdivision called Serenade. Nevertheless, Nathan and his father would fail to make it off their own property that day. The elder Manning eased the new team of horses up the bank about fifteen yards from Marissa's position. The team was poorly matched and skittish, but his father favored horses over mules. After a struggle, they made it to the road and set out while sweat painted their scalps and forearms. Father and son shared a joke and laughed, moving along to meet Neese Road. Their leisurely trip had barely begun when rumbling sounds reached them, and they glanced at one another trying to hold down their concern. The horses snorted, stamped, and whinnied. A local man took an uncommon route by traveling the narrow back road. His model T roadster clunked unseen just around the bend. The moment the black machine blustered around the curve, the frightened team detonated with energy, veered off the road as though they transported nothing but air, and bolted back down the bank. Nathan and his father were catapulted ahead of the still-loaded wagon. Nathan turned up lucky, but his father writhed and moaned on the ground, most of one hand sliced away. The only portion remaining connected to what once were the ring finger and pinky, everything now a shredded bloody mass. In that instant of freakish destruction, a grinding wagon wheel had been facilitated in its severing with many pounds of pressure above and a sharp field stone below. The motoring man with a knot on his head wobbled down the embankment as though he had partaken all morning from his infamous bottle of rye. The auto sputtered where it had crashed into the ridge. When the horses and wagon fled across the field and tore through the woods, the lashings broke and most of the cotton cargo spilled. Somewhere, the horses whipped around an out-of-control wagon plowing under half the countryside.

Nathan's father poured blood onto his overalls. The boy thought fast. He wrapped the appendage tight and ran with his limp father on his back, to the nearest neighbor owning a wagon because outside town, automobiles were as scarce as millionaires. Once Nathan placed him in the bed of the conveyance, they ripped to town and found the doctor. Nathan gently carried his father from the wagon to the examination table. The doctor needed only one good look, and he gave his pronouncement. Nathan's father nodded his consent; he must be separated from the useless, dying flesh. The doctor turned clear, direct eyes on Nathan who was needed to assist. And he did, unashamed of his tears. It was the day Nathan stepped from childhood and became a man. It was the day he gave up going out West. It was the day he took over the farm.

Marissa lifted her arms in the air. She wriggled her hands in circles and studied the thin bones and soft flesh. She wondered if any other present day people sensed the ghosts of dramas that had taken place all around them.

A grasshopper jumped across her face, only a blur in her unfocused vision so overshadowed by her thoughts. Her quick mind had grabbed the ill-defined picture, though, and she sat, knowing something with an exoskeleton was trying to claim her. She bent at the waist and shook out her hair, reminding herself to look for the hat on the way back.

Something clicked in her head. She straightened and two fingertips touched her lips with worry. Along with her poor marriage-ability rating and her questionable business acumen, maybe her mind was failing, too. How else could she have forgotten to read Abby's letter? She untied the reins, jumped in the saddle, and took off for the house.

Chapter Nineteen

Algorithm treaded reluctantly toward the barn. Instead of placing him in his stall, Marissa handed her horse to Max, with instructions to tend to the rear hoof and then let the animal graze in the pasture. She entered the kitchen with one aim in mind, but Uncle Nathan stalled her.

"Thank you," she said. "The soup smells great but I'll get some later."

"You're looking for that miniature deck of cards, aren't ya? It's been chiming like crazy since you left on your ride." He indicated her room, by a brief flick of his head toward the ceiling.

"It's called a cell phone," she said.

"Well, you're always grabbing the thing like you wanna see what cards you've been dealt."

She looked at him thoughtfully. "Well, I'd better go see if I have a royal flush or a hand meant for folding." She exited and ran up the stairs. She reached into her purse. The screen shouted: seven missed calls, eight messages, all from Isabel. Marissa skipped reading the messages and dialed.

"Marissa, oh, oh, I'm so glad I reached you. Things aren't good here."

"What is it? Tell me," Marissa demanded.

"Well, first, Daphne. She wasn't doing well last night. She called me very late and said for me to handle things by myself today. That I could do it."

"Uh-huh. Uh-huh. What else."

"Shortly after we talked, her doctor sent an ambulance and put her in the hospital."

"Oh, no," Marissa murmured.

"They're going to try an experimental treatment. She'll be there a while."

"Are the girls with their aunt?"

"Yes."

"Okay. I'd better call the hospital."

"Wait. There's more."

"Yes?"

"The Health Department came by."

"Oh. So no problem there. We always receive a top rating."

"Not this time. . . . Marissa, I was all ready to manage fine until he came by. First thing. Before the restaurant even opened. He's new on the job."

"Mm hm. So what number did he give us?"

"Oh, Marissa, I wish you had been here. The man began by harping on the fact that I considered my beret sufficient hair covering. Well you and Daphne only wear kerchiefs, I told him, and when you're in a rush you forget to wear yours. Then the man tweaks his bow tie and asks why my apron is spotted with something slimy green. I had just come from cleaning the algae out of the fountain. I explained that I was about to wash up and change into a clean apron when he showed up. You should have seen his suspicious look. Well, even I know that our baby turtle out there carries more salmonella than raw chicken sitting on the beach for two days. But did he notice those thick gloves I use? No. They were still out back, sitting next to the goldfish food. Before I can give him all the facts, he's off to the pantry where he utters more questions while he clanks things around in there. Questions like, where's your help? How about the owner? And, Didn't I know that metal canisters were superior to zip lock bags?"

"Isabel, did-"

"Oh! And then he saw the roach motels and he practically screamed! I made it clear that this is an organic, pesticide-free kitchen and that there has never been a bug problem here, but he ignored me and went on to the fridge and checked all the equipment, of which, he could say nothing because everything is kept spotless. But just as I think maybe we'll come out of this okay, he marches up to my face. We were about the same height, looking eyeball to eyeball, and he said, with his finger pointing, 'How long have those *eggs* been out?' My heart sunk, Marissa. I couldn't believe they were still there. Daphne and I had made lemon custard filling for a cake yesterday afternoon. She wasn't feeling her best, so I offered to do the kitchen clean-up while she swept the dining area. Somehow I forgot to return the eggs to the fridge. Marissa, you know the minute I laid eyes on them this morning, they would have hit the trash, but somehow I was blind to them until he pointed them out. . . . Are you there?"

"What's our rating, Isabel?"

"Marissa, you wouldn't believe what happened when I told him that we would never use eggs that had been sitting out twelve hours, but he ignored me and walked away. This smile came over his face like he'd just beaten me in a shuffleboard tournament or something. He starts checking things off on his clipboard. Long sentences dart out of his pen. Now I'm begging him to please give me a break and that I don't want to lose my job when I have a new husband with two jobs and a beach ministry. Not to mention my student loan needs paying, and I hope we can cover new tires for the van before we have a blowout going down the highway."

"Isabel."

"Huh?"

"Our number?"

"Oh, yeah. . . . Are you enjoying yourself up there in north Georgia?"

"Isabel!"

"It's fifty-eight."

"Oh no. Oh my gosh. I'm done for."

"I'm so sorry. So, so, sorry. I hate this. You don't know how I've loved working at *Camellia*. A whole new world of artistic expression has opened for me. I'm remembering how much I liked to bake when I was little. My mom even got me one of those Susan Bakes-A-Lot Ovens for my birthday when I was nine. . . . I should have remembered those eggs, though. . . . Are you there?"

"I'm here. . . . Close the doors. Go home. I'll decide what to do. Lock up and drop the keys with Jacquelyn over at the studio."

"You're really mad at me, aren't you, because most people would be screaming?"

"No, not mad. Mistakes happen. . . . I've got to call the hospital, Isabel."

"Yes, ma'am. Will I hear from you?"

"Don't know. Goodbye, Isabel."

Isabel garbled, "Goodbye," and hung up.

Forgetting all about the letter once again, Marissa flung herself down on the bed and buried her face in the pillow. She spent the rest of the day in the green room, calling Daphne, pleading with the Health Department, thinking things over.

Before dinner, Marissa went to the kitchen for therapy. She asked her uncle what he wished her to fix. He begged for meatloaf. She made her special version that pleased him no end. She went to the stable and passed a plate into Max's hands. Back in the house, she watched Nathan finish. He shunned the dessert and sought the newspaper. After cleaning the kitchen, Marissa ran upstairs, grabbed the penlight off her key ring and pulled Abby's letter from her purse.

"I'll be outside getting some fresh air," she called. She threw on Nathan's jacket and went out the back door. The front of the house boasted a covered porch, but that view held a thick jumble of trees and vegetation forming a visual blockade near the road. Even so, cars passing down Trickum Road never inspired anyone. Most of the family preferred the vista out back. Marissa chose it because, if she mentally blocked two or three things on her right and left periphery, she enjoyed much the same view a person would have enjoyed one hundred years earlier.

She seated herself on the stoop near the goat pen. Brianna, tended to quite nicely that day, came out the small lean-to. She bounded around her fencing.

"No Brianna. It's too late to let you out."

The goat stared at Marissa with one of its placid, round eyes. Marissa inched her rear along the cement, closer to the pen. She stroked the fur of the animal. Then her hand withdrew and reached inside her jean pocket. As she unfolded the paper, she glanced at Brianna's sweet face extended with curiosity above the wire fence. One more unfolding and Marissa would know what Abby's parting words had been. Strangely, a little dash of anxiety flew by. Then the words came before her eyes, unclear in the darkness. She put the paper on the stoop and searched pockets for the penlight. In a flash, Brianna clamped Abby's message in her teeth. Marissa grasped the small snout and with her thumbs pried the jaws apart. The paper, slightly crumpled, was back in her possession. She shined the light on the page.

Dear Marissa,

Lying here these past months, I've had a lot of time to think about Woodstock, about your gentle mother, about your father's trial, and you. I remember the talk we had that chilly, February day over three years ago, and I wish we had become close much sooner. Such an age difference doesn't often allow such a thing, and so I'm glad we disregarded the complications created by the mindsets of youth and old age. That day, I learned some things about myself that had built a wall between us. I realized I had held onto attitudes that needed changing. Also, I believe my words on that occasion weren't rashly spoken but benefited you. It was tough being so frank, and it would've been easier to let you alone, but you displayed such forbearance and surprised me with your willingness to learn.

As I prepare to leave my Trent and this place, it occurred to me that I should also make you aware of a few of those positive traits, so apparent, so appealing, that you possess. These traits will help you advance your goals. Only, let the Holy Spirit guide your use of them.

Primarily, you are blessed with a glorious smile. Seems like a small thing, but in this troubled world, it's not small at all. Also, you are gifted with energy and strength that will bolster you when others are fading. Finally, I know your determination. I understand it. Your perseverance is purposeful, and now it's evident how your resolve is not only directed inward but has turned toward helping others.

When I was a child, a boy who lived nearby, once told me that I probably fought like a girl. How that made me cry! Over time, though, I changed my negative view of his assessment. Marissa, aware of your desires for your future as I am, I tell you, yes, fight for those things close to your heart, but always fight like a girl. As females, we have unique strengths and special gifts. Never forget—although our might is a different sort than given men, in fact, we've been handed amazing power.

Your sister in Christ,
Abby

Marissa laid the paper to the side and switched off the flashlight. She put her head in her hands. Her elbows rested on her knees. Thoughts, emotions streamed through her consciousness. A cold wind blew, but she was unaware. The moon had risen when she eventually lifted her eyes. Leaving her place of solace, she turned and went inside.

Marissa entered the living room. Uncle Nathan woke just as a crime was being solved on television. She took a seat across from him. He blinked and rubbed his eyes while staring at her.

"Why, Marissa, you look fairly wild and full of meaning."

She straightened her windblown hair. "Uncle, we have to go see Trent about this problem with Silverstrike as soon as the proper period of mourning is over."

"Now, that makes me full of astonishment. I heard the Lord say the same thing while I was sleeping."

He got up and switched off the television. Marissa closed up the house for the night. Upstairs, she reached for her phone and dialed Isabel. Later she got under the bed covers. With her, she brought a pen and an old envelope she found in her purse. Lying there, using the illumination of the moon, she wrote at the top of the paper: *Women – Unique Strengths and Special Gifts*. Beneath the heading, she numbered one through ten. She waited. She thought. A cat howled somewhere outside. She shifted. She clicked the pen several times, then brought the clicker end to her mouth. A metal taste registered on her tongue. The arm holding the paper and pen went to the side. She let the items drop to the floor. She turned on her side and clamped her eyes shut.

Chapter Twenty

THE next day, Marissa drove into the downtown area of Woodstock to confer with the owner of everyone's favorite tearoom. The place had barely opened that morning when Marissa handed over the food critic's article and admitted she had not taken her mentor's words to heart.

The conversation from over a year ago came back to gently chastise Marissa, and she cringed remembering each word: "Marissa, it would be best not to define yourself as a tearoom unless that's your primary business. There is a tradition, a certain level of expectation."

That day Marissa jumped in, not the least reticent to argue the point with someone much more experienced. "That's silly," said Marissa. "I can have a tearoom and also cater to the beach-goers."

"That's fine, but why not label yourself a casual eatery with a fine selection of perfectly brewed teas."

During that previous consultation, the words had bounced politely everywhere except along Marissa's ear canals.

On the current morning, Marissa hung on every word her mentor spoke. They enjoyed a cup of roobois and discussed recipes. Later, an assistant from the kitchen sought her veteran leader. The proprietress patted Marissa on the shoulder and wished her good luck.

Marissa's next step had her strolling through Betsy's on Main Street and Christine's Creations for items that would lend personality to the bland interior of her establishment. She piled her finds in the back seat. Next, a visit to the used book store filled her trunk with cartons of hardbacks. *Camellia* would be oh-so-much-more cozy with a reading corner. She remembered seeing a Sixties reupholstered sectional, perfect for lounging with a book, at Island Mews Antiques. Floor lamps and shelves to hold the book collection would complete the distinctive additions to her place.

When she arrived at Uncle Nathan's, she unloaded a frozen turkey and other groceries. The bird barely fit inside the small freezer. With paper and pen, she sat down at the kitchen table.

"Uncle, very early Tuesday, I'm leaving for Brunswick to visit a friend in the hospital. I'm writing a couple of things you'll need to do in preparation for the big meal on Thursday. On my way back home, I'll pick up the fresh produce we'll need. Okay?"

"Sure thing, Hon."

Marissa held the pencil like a baton. "I think we should invite Max's mom."

"Well, yes, but I know she won't come."

"Wouldn't hurt to ask," said Marissa.

"Nope, it wouldn't."

"I'll get back from my trip late Tuesday night, but I plan to work on our feast all day Wednesday."

"Mm, mm, boy, I can't wait!"

"Also, I spoke with Hank Averill," said Marissa. "He checked with Trent and this coming Monday will be fine for our meeting."

"Good. It sits well with me."

One week since arriving in Woodstock, Marissa slipped into her car at four a. m. to return briefly to her island abode. She awoke with what seemed enough vigor to run the entire distance. Brianna came from her shed, blinking her steady eyes at Marissa who spoke a soft goodbye. The car lightly ground the dirt and rocks, backing out. Once the wheels hit Trickum Road, she took off and headed south.

Coming through Jesup, thirty minutes shy of Brunswick and the hospital, she decided to have a breakfast that would fuel the long day ahead of her. She found a Waffle House and pulled in. The thought of blueberry waffles swept her through the door like a gust of wind. She was in a back booth hungrily scanning the laminated menu, when Harvey Trammell walked in . . . that is, Harvey and a woman about forty, with unusually lush hair and a voice holding more come-here-big-boy sound than her bright red fingernail polish signaled. Marissa plucked up the menu to cover her face. She allowed one eye to rise above the edge.

Harvey and his companion took seats on the stools, laughing and chatting, leaning into one another. Harvey, in fancy duds, slung his arm around her waist and whispered in her ear. She jiggled with merriment and murmured something back. Something incredibly bright and shiny flashed on her ring finger. So easily replaced, Marissa raised the menu. Her head fell slightly, and her eyelids dipped with fatigue. To sneak away and avoid an awkward hello, she'd have to glide right past their backs.

The waitress's head popped above Marissa's menu shield.

"Ready to order, ma'am?"

"Just coffee."

She bided her time until Harvey and his new woman dug into breakfast. Marissa rose and went past them, trying to float as soundlessly as a ghost. She pushed the glass door open, not believing her good luck. Her car sat right outside the door. Once inside, encased and protected, she experienced a brief surge of guilt for her unfriendly attitude. She turned the key in the ignition. Harvey burst outside. He grabbed the side mirror as though he was afraid she would drive off. She put on the brake, took the car out of reverse and into park. Her window rolled down.

"How are you, Harvey?"

"Why, fine. Just wondering why you're here. The coincidence and all. You must've heard."

"Heard what?"

"That I'm marrying on turkey day. Now tell the truth; you heard this is where I eat breakfast every morning, huh?" He leaned on the lower window frame.

"Not really, Harvey. I'm just on my way from North Georgia back to the island."

He grinned and infatuation poured from his eyes. "You expect me to believe that?"

"Yes, I do."

"Look, I'm not officially tied in matrimony yet. That's my Corvette parked over there. Did you see that two carat rock inside?" His head nodded toward the Waffle House. He pushed further into her space and gushed, "I'd be willing to put something twice that size on your finger . . . if you just admit what you're up to."

"Harvey, you are terribly mistaken. I-"

Marissa's sight flew to the Waffle House door. The woman with an enhanced package sashayed out, in clothes that left nothing in doubt. From the sidewalk, she stared, and her amazingly plumped lips pouted.

Harvey quickly cranked himself to standing.

Marissa jerked her idling car into reverse and paused, "Harvey. You made the right choice. I'm over my head in debt, my three kids are in juvenile detention, and I just learned the open sores all over my back, well, not only do they give off an odor, they're extremely contagious."

Her car blasted back and then out of the parking lot. As she fled down Highway 341, she thought, there, that ought to do it, once and for all. The shame of it was that one of the statements within her last ditch effort was not a lie. She turned on the radio and let cornpone songs wipe every distressing thought from her head.

Marissa pushed the door to the hospital room open. Daphne calmly rested and Isabel, close to the bed in a chair, spoke in muted tones. Their heads turned in Marissa's direction.

Marissa placed flowers on a counter and rushed over. "Oh, Daphne, I wish I hadn't been out of town when you needed to get to the hospital."

She pressed Marissa's hand. "You have to go about your own life. Thank you for the flowers. I'm doing fine."

Marissa looked at Isabel for confirmation and back at Daphne. "Really?"

"Yes, really." Daphne smiled. "The doctor just came in and said I might be back at work in three weeks if all goes well."

"No, Daphne. That's why I'm here today. We've got to make some changes, for your sake."

A woman with wiry hair and an ivory complexion setting off pink cheeks burst into the room. "Oh. Sorry, Daphne. I didn't know you had company."

"Come in, Shalie. I want you to meet Marissa and Isabel."

"Hello," they both said.

"Nice to meet you. I'm Daphne's sister."

"Yes," said Marissa, "Daphne's told me everything you're doing for the girls."

"That's what sisters are for. . . . I just had a chat with the doctor, Daphne. Sounds like things are looking up."

"Mm hm." Sureness strengthened the sound of her words.

"Well," said Shalie, "I'll go down and freshen myself with a Coke. Will thirty minutes give you women enough time to talk?"

"Certainly," said Marissa. "Daphne was supposed to be getting a break from me, anyway."

"Yes? Well, my visit will be short, too. Tony, Francie, and Gretta are getting hungry by this time. Got to take them by for a shampoo and comb out today. Francie and Gretta want Pink Passion for their nails this time." The woman giggled. "*Girls.*" A hand flitted upward. "Well actually, the photographer is coming by tomorrow." She squeezed in and hugged Daphne. "Be back in a little bit." She turned and walked to the bathroom. "Oh! Wrong way." Flustered she went to the correct door, then came racing back for her purse. She shook her head and made her departure again.

Marissa pulled the extra chair next to the bed. "I didn't know your sister has children. No wonder she's a little hesitant about taking the girls."

Daphne smiled with understanding. "Her son is grown. She was referring to her Pomeranians."

"Oh!" said Marissa.

"Shalie says my girls worry them. But Alexa and Clemma say they stick to the porch swing away from the animals. There's too much yapping if anyone other than Shalie gets near the sofa. Even Clemma is afraid of pint-sized Tony. But my girls are smart, and they'll figure out a way to make friends with them."

Isabel came slightly out of her seat. "The girls told me about those animals, Daphne. You can't make friends with dogs half-mad with territorial impulses and teeth as sharp as needle-loaded badgers." Squashed by Daphne's downward glance, Isabel sank to her chair. "I'm sorry. You're right about the girls. I've watched them. They make inroads with everyone, even the old homeless man, the one who wanders the pier. He drifted behind *Camellia* one Saturday after closing. They brought him sandwiches and asked him about his days in the merchant marine. He stopped his wild muttering, gave them a toothless grin and went on and on, an angel of behavior. . . . Well, his only offense was washing his feet in the fountain."

Daphne smiled. "Well, enough about my worries. Tell us what you're thinking, Marissa."

"Yeah," said Isabel, "you didn't explain anything on the phone."

Marissa took out her yellow writing pad. "I called the Glynn County Health Department and explained the situation. Mr. Burke, he knows our track record. So they're not closing us down. However, I told him we're taking a break until I can get my uncle's affairs settled. As for *Camellia*, you are to say it's undergoing a transformation. Closed for redecorating, so to speak. Until I return." She handed a memo to Daphne and one to Isabel. "Here are the details," she said. "First of all, Daphne, if you wish to return, you will be in supervisory capacity only. Queen of the Kitchen is your title. Your pay will remain the same. Second, you and I are going to train Isabel to assume your responsibilities. Isabel, you will receive a pay raise, of course."

Isabel's pretty black eyes gave a hard blink as she gasped with surprised pleasure.

"Third," continued Marissa, "during this leave of absence and as long as my account holds out, your automatic payroll deposits will continue. . . . Okay, if you two raise your eyebrows any higher, you're going to give yourselves receding hairlines."

They went over more details until the nurses came in. Marissa concluded their talk. Daphne made a request that left Marissa uncomfortable, but she didn't want to argue with an ill woman. Marissa and Isabel gave Daphne some final encouraging words and left.

Chapter Twenty-one

RED brick homes like pretty dollhouses nestled in the shade of an older section of the village area. Isabel led the way up the back walk of one of the dwellings. Marissa, conscious of an errand to come, which had to do with William's place, stepped on one of Isabel's heels.

"Sorry," said Marissa, "I'm tied up by my thoughts." She scanned the back entrance, its decorations of a sailboat ornament on the door and, to the side, a wire topiary covered in variegated ivy. "Cute house, Isabel."

Isabel put the key in the lock. "Thanks, but we rent only this back room. The best room, though, because I can cook our meals."

They entered a sixteen-by-eighteen room, the kitchen. Marissa scanned Isabel's living quarters, making an effort not to show surprise. Every inch of space efficiently performed as storage. Several guitars and two bikes helped cramp the room. In one corner a twin bed sat on a platform an inch above petite Isabel's head. Underneath, a desk and computer squatted in the space.

Marissa found herself staring.

"Deke built it. You like our bed?"

"Well, I was wondering how you both fit in a twin?"

"Actually, it's nice; we've only been married five months and fourteen days. The hard part is below, trying to remember to crouch when you get up from the desk. Deke just laughs when he bumps his noggin."

"Tell him to drop by *Camellia* sometime. I'd like to meet him."

"I will but he hardly has time to turn around. I hope he'll quit his second job now that you've promoted me. I can't wait to tell him."

Marissa turned her attention to the easel next to a window flooding light into the room. "Where are the paintings we talked about?"

"The carport." She took a key from a hook by the door. They traipsed to the back of the lot. "Out here is where I work on my large canvases. Our landlord lets me store them in this unused laundry room." She unlocked the door.

Marissa stuck her head into the dark interior. Mustiness hit her nose, and then she caught the characteristic odor of oil paint and turpentine. Stacked paintings rested along a wall. "You've got quite a few," said Marissa.

"I'll bring them out. The light makes them luminous. Well, I think so."

"Show me anything with a garden or nature theme."

Isabel carried broad canvases out the door, canvases the size of doors, and leaned them against the low brick border at the carport sides. The place turned into a virtual gallery. Marissa found a plastic chair, which she placed in a central spot, and she let the lyrical images speak to her.

"Isabel, these are marvelous. It's going to be hard to make up my mind." She studied the paintings. They discussed them.

"All right." Marissa lightly pulled her chin. "I think I've narrowed it down to six. I'm most partial to the dragon fly, the fern with all the varying shades of green, the pond, the elegant lotus, the ornamental bench with the old man, and the little girl under the sable palm. They'll provide a clear motif for *Camellia*."

"I'm thrilled you like them. I received a very high critique from my professor for the old man on the bench."

Marissa reached into her purse for her wallet. She pulled out a check. "How much do I owe you?"

"Owe me? You can have them. I'm lucky to have a job after what happened."

"No, Isabel. I'm paying. You poured your heart and talent into these. Bring that chair over. I have something else to discuss."

Isabel did as she was told. Marissa handed her a large check.

"Blazing colors!" said Isabel. "Thank you. This means the van is going to have new brakes and a set of new tires. I'll catch up on my student loan. And we can refill our refrigerator and pantry."

"Well, now I have a favor to ask. I need your artistic skills."

"Of course. Anything."

"You said Deke is a whiz on the computer. Could he help you design an ad for the restaurant?"

"Sure!"

Marissa reached inside her purse and pulled out an index card. "This is the text I would like to have in the ad, along with the address and telephone number."

Camellia Japonica

A casual eatery with a fine selection of perfectly brewed teas.
A cool oasis garden.
An escape from the burning sun.
Come.
Let your palate be satisfied
And your spirit be refreshed.

Isabel looked at Marissa. "No problem. We can add graphics to reinforce the garden theme."

"And do you think Deke could help you hang the paintings?"

"I know he would."

"Put three on each long wall above the windows, equally spaced."

"No problem. That big room has the height for it."

"Isabel, I didn't want to go into it in front of Daphne, but in the future, we have to make things easy for her." Isabel shook her head. "I'll be bringing in several servers. I hope the things concerning my uncle are taken care of soon. . . . We'll see. But I have a good feeling about you, Isabel. Are you ready to learn the ropes?"

"I'll do my very best. Thank you for trusting me."

"Start by studying the recipes. You can practice if you like. Just be sure to lock up the restaurant when you leave. Here's your key. And remember, be positive if anyone asks you why we're closed."

"Yes ma'am. To let you know how serious I am, I'm going to dress in a manner that fits my new role."

Mid-afternoon, Marissa sat in one of two beach chairs facing the ocean near the pier. Jacquelyn's car, radio singing, pulled into the parking area. She trotted in Marissa's direction. The sound of children laughing as they scrambled over the playground equipment directly behind the park seating bounced through the air along with the squawks of gulls and the rushing whoosh of seawater pummeling the boulders guarding the shoreline.

"Hi!" Jacquelyn called, coming over. She flopped down. "Tough week, huh?"

Marissa nodded. "I thought I was going to make a quick trip for a funeral, and now I'm yoked to the place a while longer. But I love the old guy." Marissa handed Jacquelyn a gyro and a drink. Bracing themselves against the breezes, they ate commenting on the tolerable weather compared to the cold in the upper part of the state.

When they finished eating, Marissa carried their trash to the receptacle. She returned and stood in front of Jacquelyn's chair. "I know you have to get back to the studio, but can I ask you a question?"

"I'm taking the afternoon off. Mikki's handling things. So ask away."

"If someone told you to fight like a girl, what would you say that means? Figuratively."

"This is about your uncle's situation, isn't it?"

"Yes."

Jacquelyn pondered a few minutes. "Well, for me, fighting like a girl means several things. I'd rely on my God-given female intuition but let His discernment flow through me. I'd also have to avoid the trap of impulsive, reactionary thinking driven by emotion." She paused, looking at the sky, tapping her chin with her index finger. "Then, I would confront gently, humbly despite my confidence that I'm right. And finally, like the story of the woman who sought the judge, I would not give up."

"And this works, every time?" She plopped down again, intrigued.

"I don't know. I should try it more often." Jacquelyn's teeth flashed in the sunlight.

They laughed and recalled all their recent failures.

Marissa settled back and looked at her watch. "I have to get on the road soon, but Daphne's got me on an errand before I go."

"Need me to tag along?"

"If you like."

"Where are we going?"

"William Dash's house."

"I thought you said he was somewhere off South America?"

"Yes, and apparently the world traveler on behalf of oil will visit another continent or two before he returns."

"More assignments?"

"That's what Daphne says. Waylaid by problems, just like me."

"So why are we breaking in?"

"*No.* I have the key. Daphne asked me to bring his mail in from the box and make sure the thermostat is turned to heat. A strange request. Like when was the last time a pipe-busting freeze visited down here? Never?"

"It could happen. I have a photo of the pier covered in snow back in '93." Jacquelyn stood and a grin shot from her face. "This will be fun. Aren't you a little curious?"

"I've been inside, once. Remember?"

"Oh, yeah. *That* day."

Marissa took a half empty pack of crackers from her pocket and crushed them. Hungry seagulls that had been strolling aimlessly in the area like little feathered oafs became of one mind and converged in front of the two women. Marissa tossed the crackers outward and the birds jumped from the ground, catching the pieces midair, like a pack of trained dogs.

Marissa was sidetracked by Jacquelyn's unfocused stare.

"What?" said Marissa.

"Okay. Let's go," said Jacquelyn who started jogging to the parking lot.

Marissa lagged behind and called. "Why the hurry?"

Jacquelyn declared over her shoulder, laughing again. *"He's not home, and you'll be able to peek around."*

Marissa frowned and bent into a run.

Chapter Twenty-two

MARISSA and Jacquelyn walked in the front doors of *Camellia* before going to William's house. The women carried boxes of books and dropped them in one of the front corners of the dining room. Then they went to the kitchen.

Marissa reached for the watering can under the sink. She placed the can in the sink and turned on the flow. Waiting for the tap water to fill the container, her head lifted slowly. She averted her eyes away from the opposite lot. She studied the garden, instead. The trumpet vine covering the old pine on the side of her lot spilled flowers, a cascade of coral. The golden chrysanthemums were at their peak of beauty in the tall urn.

Jacquelyn wandered behind her. "Marissa," her friend blurted, breaking through the haze of a distracted mind. Marissa glanced up. Jacquelyn pointed to a gray cardboard container holding a number of eggs. "They're still here. Isn't this the thing that got you in trouble?"

Marissa calmly turned off the tap.

Jacquelyn murmured, "Is she going to work out?"

"Has to. I'm not worried. She was shaken after that man laid the wood to us."

"But after that, she still forgot to throw them out."

"She's young. She'll catch on." Marissa deposited the eggs in a trash bag and took them outside. She came back in, clutched the watering can, and went on her errand to the potted camellias out front. Returning, she said, "Okay. Things are shipshape here. Ready to go with me across the way?"

Jacquelyn's eyebrows jumped. "Let's go."

Marissa locked up, and they cut through the two yards. Her hand searched her pockets for the key.

Jacquelyn looked around the yard. "That planter, what style. This overgrown lot used to look like nothing. He's pretty handy."

"I guess so. The house sure shows it."

Marissa cracked open the door.

"Why are you hesitating?" said Jacquelyn.

"I don't know."

Marissa first, then Jacquelyn slipped into the subdued kitchen. Marissa kept her head straight, vowing not to look at anything. Then, her eyes went right to his spice rack, wanting to judge the small collection. She felt a hand poke near her right kidney.

"Wouldn't it be funny," whispered Jacquelyn, "if he suddenly came home and found us here?"

"Jacquelyn, you don't have to whisper."

They went down the hall that connected to the living room. It was just as she remembered—casual, comfortable, everything approachable and neat.

"Look at the beautiful lines on that," said Jacquelyn. She pointed to an antique secretary on the far wall. The traditional piece was an elegant contrast to the straightforward, geometric style everywhere else. "I think it's the one they had over at Island Mews Antiques." Jacquelyn walked closer.

Marissa felt pulled by her own inquisitiveness.

Jacquelyn turned to her. "Did I tell you? It has compartments and drawers ornamented by seagoing vessels done in marquetry with ivory accents. Must have cost a fortune."

Marissa's hand shot out. "Jacquelyn! Don't open it!"

"I'm not a snoop. I just want to see if it's the same piece." She lowered the angled writing board, causing a piece of paper to float from one of the faceless compartments and land on the writing surface.

Marissa examined the writing. "Call Beverly," she read out loud.

"Oh, my gosh," said Jacquelyn. "We *are* snooping."

Marissa slammed the thing closed and scooted around Jacquelyn, toward the bedroom hall where she adjusted the thermostat. Jacquelyn mimicked her steps but coasted past her, straight to the main bedroom.

"Where are you going?" said Marissa.

"Oh. Come on. Don't you want to see his bedroom? We won't touch anything."

Marissa didn't protest and joined her friend.

Jacquelyn stood in the doorway, evaluating. "Nice. Quietly masculine. Finally, a pair of shoes out of place. Look. There's a picture on the nightstand."

Marissa walked over. She lifted the frame. In the photo, Daphne, William, and the girls smiled from the sightseeing boat at Jekyll Island.

Jacquelyn moved in and considered the photo. "Nice."

Marissa brought the picture closer and said, "Blue . . . his eyes are the shade of deep sea." She took care to place the frame in the exact spot as before.

In front of *Camellia*, they wished each other well and promised to call over the next few weeks. Jacquelyn got into her car and Marissa did the same. They drove from the village section, and when Marissa's route made her split off, she stuck her hand out the window and waved good-bye to her friend. The end of the day, workmen, maids, and shop clerks rushed off the island with her. As she rolled through Hazlehurst and Dublin, she grew tired of her CDs and turned on the radio hoping to siphon the auditory flavor of the lives of people living in south Georgia. The local news and weather entertained her, but then her ears were smacked by an old tune of Tennessee Ernie Ford, an addictive but defeatist theme that could dampen anyone's spirits: *Sixteen tons, what d'ya get? Another day older and deeper in debt.* Her hands tightened around the steering wheel. Futility wanted to play with her emotions. Her index finger flashed to the off button. Talk about hitting the nail on the head, she thought. It would be a risk to listen to those depressing words. She decided to embrace the safe, predictable idea of Thanksgiving Dinner, going over her choices that would accompany the bird. Everything had to be perfect for Max's mother. By the time Marissa was due to roll into Woodstock, she'd be lucky if a single grocery store remained opened. Her pep fled and her lower back ached. Wednesday would hold at least ten hours spent shopping as well as cooking and cleaning.

Early Thanksgiving day, Marissa slid furniture from the living room to make a place for their banquet. Aunt Olivia's dining set had assumed a quiet life at Samson and Delilah's Antiques ever since Nathan needed a downstairs bedroom. The farmhouse living room would be their dining space. A piece of plywood and two sawhorses substituted as the surface for their feast. Marissa's arms sent Aunt Olivia's nicest lace cloth floating across a table pad. China and pearl-handled silverware took their places. A glass candleholder, the shape of the famous bird, took position at table center. Several times, Max wandered in from the stable, not saying a word, watching the transformation. Marissa thought she detected a slight, periodic limp. At the stove, she made him sample the turkey gravy draping a spoonful of mashed potatoes. His resulting joy sent her, even more, in a flurry to satisfy everyone's expectations. She iced carrot cake while a cherry pie baking in the oven saturated the kitchen with the aroma of comfort, peace, and the sanctity of home.

Noon came and they waited for their guest to arrive. Uncle Nathan, wearing his best wool pants, white long sleeve shirt, and plaid vest, popped a butterscotch into his mouth and trooped back and forth in front of the window, craning his neck to see the advance of his guest. Max sat at the kitchen table, head leaning on his fist, dull-eyed by prolonged hunger. Marissa moved her concentration on a round of the burners and oven, striving to keep the food piping hot. She took a secretive check of Max's expression and, with a hidden sigh, turned back to the stove.

An hour later, her stomach growling, Marissa left her seat on the front porch and went inside the entryway where Uncle Nathan diverted Max with checkers at a small table. For a while, she watched their play. Max made a double jump on the board, took the pieces hostage, and looked at her.

"Max, maybe you should call to see if your Mom changed her mind," she said.

"She's not comin'," he replied

"What makes you say that?"

"She never does what she says she's gonna do."

At that moment, the doorbell rang. Marissa went the few steps to the door and opened. A squat woman stood there with a bland look and a raw, pink nose. "I'm Vereena," she said plainly and pushed inside before Marissa could utter a word. Right behind the woman, a man with traveling eyes and hair cut in an eighties mullet scooted through as well. He pumped their hands, failing to look at his hosts. Eyes roving the furniture, he went straight to the table and claimed his chair like an alert terrier waiting for his meal. The woman moved more leisurely. Marissa offered her name. Neither guest took note.

"The food," said Marissa, "may be a little dried out, but it will be warm."

Max watched his mom as though he waited to see what would happen. She merely turned and took a seat at the table.

Marissa drifted over. "I'll get an extra place setting."

"Oh." said the woman with a flick of her hand toward the man. "My fiancé," was the limit of her introduction. She took out a tissue and blew one long, unpleasant honk.

Marissa peered at the man for help with a name, but he only smiled and let his sight continue its survey. Marissa looked to Max for help. He shrugged his shoulders and closed the gap of his open mouth. By now, Uncle Nathan was unable to hide his perturbation. Marissa was about to right things herself, but Uncle Nathan geared up to take hold of the situation.

The old man strode to the table, drawing little interest from the guests. "Swak!" The guests jumped. Nathan's hand had slapped the wide, upper brace of a dining chair. The guests' faces were riveted on him.

Nathan grinned and jutted his face toward the couple. "Thought I saw a fly. And your name, sir?"

"Huh? Oh yeah. Just call me Dudley."

Uncle Nathan's face poked forward again. "How about Dud?"

The man pulled back slightly, looking apprehensive. "I prefer Dudley," he muttered.

"Fine," said Nathan who introduced himself and Marissa.

Max's mom regained an unfazed appearance. With her knife lifted and her reflection caught in the lustrous blade, she inspected her inflamed nostrils and then the pearl handle.

Marissa jumped in, "Well, so glad you could join us. Max, pull the chair from the hall." He did as he was told. His mother watched.

"Max," said the woman with a snort, "did one of those horses give you a gimp leg?"

"It's nothing," he answered.

"You are too slow to learn," she added and busied herself by lifting the lace cloth and fingering the crochet work like a quality inspector.

Marissa brought dish after dish to the table. Uncle Nathan carved the turkey. The man and woman ate like they bellied up to an all-you-can-eat buffet. Any effort to start conversation with them fell flat. Previously silent, Max vaulted into the awkward scene, talking. His subject centered on the horse that had been giving him trouble, Harlequin, a mighty Arabian sorrel with muscles to match his attitude. Uncle Nathan offered his experienced advice and praised Max for his horse smarts.

Marissa realized the man and woman listened, no longer engrossed by their plates. Marissa tried to hoist a pleasant look onto her features. "So, Vereena, does Max get his love of horses from you?"

"No. I hate the things."

"Really?"

The woman swiped her nose with her hand and took another large mouthful of squash casserole.

The phone in the hall rang. Uncle Nathan, expecting holiday wishes from friends and family, excused himself from the table.

Marissa dabbed her mouth and tried again. "Max does work wonders with the animals. Except that Harlequin, he's a handful for anyone."

The man and woman made a quick glance at each other and stilled their forks.

Dudley cleared his throat and projected a goofy grin. "Yeah. Stable work is tough, tough work. Yes, sir. . . . Matter of fact, Vereena and I've been talking how you and your uncle ought to be sending a little cash our way. The kid's healthy and strong. Doing you a good job, too." With a smirk, he leaned across the table toward Marissa. "Course, some jobs require a real man." His grin grew bigger. His partner watched indifferently.

Marissa clenched her teeth. Her sight flew to the hall, hoping her uncle was ignorant of the crudeness. Max glared at Dudley.

The man mellowed on, his voice silky and warm. "Hey, don't get serious on me. Just joking around. . . . But we wouldn't mind a little hand-out. See, I'm not feeling well enough to work, and Vereena needs corrective surgery."

Marissa hardened her posture. "What kind of surgery?"

He started to speak, but the woman pulled on his arm. He settled back in his chair.

"My eyes need help," said Max's mom. "I must stare at the computer to do my work. Many long hours. Only expensive surgery will save me from going blind."

"Yes, I heard you spend a lot of time at the computer, but I got the impression your hobby dealing with probabilities is the thing taking all your time. But . . . what is the medical name for your condition?"

"Uh–" The woman's expression soured. She blew again, a sound like Jell-O rumbling through a pipe. "You have cats, don't you?" Her voice had suddenly gone hoarse.

Uncle Nathan reentered the room. "No cats. Horses, one steer, and a goat are enough for me."

The woman's palm skimmed the surface of the low book shelf behind her.

She studied her open hand. "Dust mites are making my cold turn to something more severe. I feel strangely weak."

"I vacuumed and dusted really well yesterday," said Marissa. "So you must be mistaken. Let me clear your dishes. As you told me on the phone, you have other plans for the remainder of the day." Marissa was vaguely aware of Max.

The woman held onto her plate and massaged her throat. "Must be the squash casserole," she snipped. "You didn't inform me of the onions." Her sound was accusatory. "I'm allergic. I may have to see a doctor." A warning look rippled over her features.

The man cackled as he rocked back in his chair. "Allergic? I don't think so," he declared, still laughing. "You must've forgotten that mountain of fried onion rings you scarfed down last week?"

The woman's eyes pierced him. He cringed.

The man turned to Marissa and pleaded, "I can tell she's ready to go. Mind if I take one of those turkey legs with me?"

Chapter Twenty-three

MAX dragged himself back and forth carrying dirty dishes from the table to the kitchen while under a bogged down mood. With a more pronounced limp, he disassembled the makeshift table. Marissa scraped the plates and washed them. Max insisted on doing the drying but made it clear he didn't want to talk. Near the end of cleanup, she sent him outside with the trash. He didn't reenter. She leaned around the opening to the living room. Nathan enjoyed entertainment on the tube. She rested against the cool wall and gazed out the window nearby. Leaves on the oak by the garage swirled to the ground. Sadness lingered over the holiday. Her wishes for the occasion were now nothing more than food scraps dumped into the trash.

With several hours of light left and the return of a pleasant temperature, Marissa settled on exercising her horse. She opened the back door. Max sat on the stoop, hunched over his thighs, head resting on his hands. An unfocused stare revealed his absence. Brianna made little bleats, begging for freedom. Marissa opened the pen. The goat kicked her heels and scampered about, making one of the yard hens bolt.

Marissa came around and sat next to the boy. "What's bothering you, Max?"

"My mother."

"Oh."

"My birthday was yesterday. She didn't even remember."

"I'm sorry. . . . So, you're sixteen, right?"

"Yep."

"Hey! Now you can get a license to drive."

"I've never been behind the wheel of a car."

"I'll teach you. A birthday present from me to you. We'll have to find an empty parking lot."

"I could run errands for Mr. Manning."

"More than likely. I don't know how much longer his eyes will hold out." She rubbed the denim covering her knees. "Also, there's something else, Max. . . . If we can get Silverstrike to let my uncle remain in the house, you're going to have to move inside. The middle bedroom has the best view of the stable."

"Why inside? I like living with the horses."

"Cause you're not an animal, that's why . . . and . . . we don't want anyone claiming you're not getting good care. By that, I mean give them a reason to put you somewhere you don't like."

"Home?"

"Well, yeah."

"She says I cost her everything good. Her health, her boyfriends, and too much of her money."

"She may not realize it, but you're the best thing that ever happened to her, Max."

"She laughs at my goals."

"Your mom's been hurt by her bad choices. Honor her, anyway." Marissa turned to look at him. "And I'm going to support your goals. If you study harder than ever before, more than ever before, I'll see that you end up where you want to be."

"You don't know about your uncle's riding lawn mower, do you?"

"What do you mean?"

"I stole it after watching by the thicket near the spring house, waiting for him to leave. I drove it right off the property, back through the woods, and sold it to somebody I know."

"He didn't say a thing about it."

"I was starving, living under a tree, although it was plenty better than with my mom. For the past ten years, there have been five live-in guys that I was supposed to call dad."

"You need a little relief from that painful subject. Let's go look at the cantankerous machine in the stable," she said.

"Wow. I guess you're lookin' for a little more drama today."

"I'll be careful."

They went to the barn, talking about the proclivity of the horse for bone-busting behavior. Never a particularly calm animal, the horse had kicked Max in the thigh the night before, leaving a purple bruise that he swore was the size of an eggplant.

They entered the barn and walked down the aisle toward the stalls. Marissa noted Harlequin right away, his pricked ears and alert head leaning out the opening. Tense neck muscles showed beneath his gleaming coat.

"Okay, Max. He's in a bad mood. Let's just walk by. I don't want to get within nipping range."

"I think he has trust issues. Except for that blast to my thigh yesterday, I was doing okay with him."

"Anything happen to cause his behavior?"

"His owner took him through the paces on Tuesday. When you were gone to St. Simons. Mr. Langley works that horse hard. Then yesterday, I tried to take Harlequin to the paddock for training like Mr. Langley asked me to do. We made it outside okay. But he definitely got squirrelly and then started rearing. Scared me. I got him under control and brought him in. That's when Harlequin thanked me real good. I slapped an ice pack on and kept it there all night."

"How often does the owner come by?"

"Twice a month. Four hours straight. I've been doing most of the exercising. But he responds best to a thirty minute session. When I told Mr. Langley . . . well, he doesn't seem to care all that much."

They walked to Marissa's horse, and she lavished tenderness on Al through her words and touch. Max helped her saddle him. Marissa walked her horse down the aisle, ignoring Harlequin but lingering near, stroking her animal, making Al nicker with contentment.

Outside the barn, Marissa mounted and rode Al toward the hidden trail behind the pond. She chose a lazy pace. Leaves gently rained on their bodies. Up ahead, a wild turkey, blessedly free from anyone's holiday menu, wandered into the path. Marissa chuckled, but immediately thought of her steed and upped her riding concentration. Al never spooked at strange animals, but, once, a plastic bag, upturned over a tall weed, waved as though alive and injected the horse with fear. Caught off guard, Marissa hit the ground hard that day.

They took the south heading trail, past the pond. The water rippled whenever a leaf hit the surface. She let Al take a drink. Moving forward again, he lifted his head, catching the autumn smells. Somewhere, a person raked and burned leaves, and the acrid scent traveled far. The horse lowered his head with a snort and shook his mane. His tail rose and flicked dislike. Marissa turned the horse back and caught sight of the animal in the mirroring water. Everything in his body language communicated pleasure at being a horse, at wandering the land, at convening with nature while all his senses were engaged. She remembered how she always took him for a dip in the pond when summer baked the land until everything on the farm was desperate for refreshing. He had played like some overgrown, happy dog. Marissa's mind brightened with realization. The day slipped swiftly to close. She returned to the pastures and led Al in a finishing gallop over the hills.

The next morning, as soon as everyone breakfasted, she went to the paddock. Max already had Harlequin situated inside the training ring as Marissa had requested the evening before. She wore one of Aunt Olivia's fruit-inspired aprons that matched the faded kitchen curtains. The pockets held the last remnants of apple from Uncle Nathan's tree. Marissa wandered to the fence. She turned to the side, one foot on the lower rail and her right arm on the fence top. Her eyes scanned the horizon of tree tops as though she had no other reason to be there. Harlequin pawed the dirt and watched her. Marissa was careful not to look at him, and she waited, wisely letting her mind journey. She pondered a recipe she saw in a magazine while letting her hand slip into a pocket. Out came a slice, which she bit into and slowly chewed. Apple scent traveled on the air. Harlequin eyed her again and ambled a few feet closer. Marissa switched her position and bit into the apple again, studying the roofline of the house, noting the tilt of the chimney and a squirrel running along a gutter. Without moving her head, she looked askance and saw the horse traipse closer and stop again. Marissa acted as though she had all day to do nothing and that she certainly had no plans, no work required of the animal. A looping, scrambling flock of birds flew overhead to some distant land. Lackadaisically, she turned fully front and leaned into the fence. She let one arm drape over the rails. In her limp hand, apple rested. The animal eyed her, ears pivoting in different directions, searching for information about this different kind of encounter. Marissa kept looking straight ahead at a wispy cedar past the paddock. The horse, off to the left, made a side approach. She watched from the corner of her eye. Soon only ten feet separated them. In her head, she repeated the name of every vegetable she knew, waiting. The animal moved in. Marissa spread her fingers backward, balancing the piece on her palm. Horse whiskers and soft, rubbery mouth wiggled against the skin of her hand as the animal grasped the treat. He then pulled back and munched his gift.

Lazily, her hand went to the pocket again and again, until it was empty.

"No more, Harlequin. Sorry."

Both of her arms now rested along the fence top. The horse studied her, but she didn't try to touch him. He remained planted to the spot. Marissa let her eyes focus on the distance once more. Yet she was aware his head moved in and lowered. An edge of fear swam in her midsection as she felt a puff of warm air through her blouse, right above her navel. The thought of a massive clamp to her abdomen reached her brain, and she stiffened slightly, yet she remained still. The soft nose of the animal nudged her belly, benignly searching, which made Marissa laugh.

"I told you, I'm all out of apples." She stroked Harlequin's nose.

Max wandered up breaking the communion. "Friends, already?"

"You know what? This horse needs to be treated like a living animal, not a machine. It's bored with training. It needs play. Take him for a long, meandering walk near the perimeter of the woods. Let him follow you all the way to the old cotton fields."

Max chewed his lip with hesitancy. "I don't know. . . . I haven't asked Mr. Langley."

"The animal is in our care. So take care of it."

"Okay."

"When you reach the fields, get the horse to lie down on that mound of white sand Uncle Nathan had delivered. Let him wallow and kick up his heels. Then get on him bareback and ride the trails until you're tired. He won't be. Let his mind be stimulated by the odors and the sights and sounds." She handed Max the lead.

"Yes ma'am." He moved along the fence to the gate. Inside the pen, he pulled on the lead. The horse meekly followed. Max paused and turned back in her direction. "Do you still feel like giving me a driving lesson today?"

"Oh. Uh. I . . . I know it sounds like I'm procrastinating, but I've got to get the wash done. How about tomorrow? Is that okay?"

"Yes, ma'am."

Later, as she gathered the wash, the aroma of sweat and horse manure from Max's hamper seemed endowed with the strength to make a person scream for a respirator, but she persevered. Suddenly, the thought of giving a driving lesson wasn't half so bad.

Chapter Twenty-four

A hard cotton boll atop the plant breaks its plain brown casing along the seams and opens to reveal its miraculous inner beauty, that pristine white filament of God's design, softer than a rabbit tail. In the same way, Olde Towne Woodstock slowly opened itself to the day. Entries unlocked. Doors cracked open. Shades rolled up. Marissa walked along the sidewalk that early Saturday morning remembering the way Uncle Nathan explained those plain brown husks. He claimed bolls were made that way so regular folks would remember—something special can come from an unexpected place.

People strolled toward their destinations. Cars moved up and down the street. Diana Cannon stuck her head out the door of Dean's Store and yelled, "I thought that was you, Marissa. Come help us decide something." Her hand gestured, drawing Marissa back the way she had come.

"Hey, Diana," she said, approaching.

Diana swung the door wide and Marissa stepped into the dim, high ceiling room of the 1906 store. Originally a drugstore, the Dean family establishment was forced to change itself only six months after opening. The owner, Dr. William Lemuel Dean, long-suffering with a stomach ulcer, died. His twenty-year-old son, Linton, without certification to dispense drugs or practice medicine but armed with a business degree, adapted; and the store became a purveyor of over-the-counter patent medicines as well as small and big items required for daily life. Some thought the prescient father, W.L., had taken stock of his situation and developed a contingency plan for the family he might leave behind.

Marissa blinked, trying to acquaint her eyes to the dimness of the store that now functioned as the town visitors center welcoming people from far and wide. The familiar smell of peppermint, aged wood, and the barest hint of tobacco reached her. She waved hello to the early-morning gentlemen, mostly retirees and a venerable philosopher or two, rising from their comfortable chairs where they commented on daily happenings of region and nation, or past times like the day Posey Dobbs used his bare hand to hoist a huge, hissing, snapping turtle high for viewing.

Ready to depart, the present-day men donned jackets and allowed surprise to telegraph on their faces.

"How you doing, Miss Marissa?" called one of the oldest gentleman.

"Fine. How about you, Mr. Jenkins?"

"Sweeter than the juice of summer blackberries squished through cheese cloth," he trumpeted. "We haven't seen Nathan this week. Tell him to get himself over here."

"Yes, sir. His lumbago, as he calls it, is bothering him. He'll probably be by next week." Several men nodded toward her deferentially, and the group slipped from the store.

Marissa and Diana walked to the back where a circle of women crowded around a table. Women she had known all her life greeted her.

"What are you all up to?" Marissa asked.

"You know us, always involved in something." said Diana. "But what about you? We thought you headed back after the funeral."

"Change of plans. I'm helping Uncle Nathan with a few problems."

"Oh?"

"So what's happening?" said Marissa, side-stepping giving an answer.

One of the women pointed to the items spread on the table and said, "The library is showcasing town history soon. We're making selections for the display."

"Preserving the past. Wonderful," said Marissa. "You don't know how much I revere the Centennial book."

"Oh, we'll never forget that labor of research," said Diana. "Now help us make up our minds before we break into a cat fight." The women laughed.

"This looks like a great selection," Marissa said. Her eyes perused the items including several patent medicines with labels dulled by time, old-fashioned mourning stationery, and the photograph of the turn-of-the-century soda fountain overseen by the Dean brothers. The younger held a drink concoction absent of ice, common mode of service for the time. The elder brother stared more soberly at the camera, survival of his mother and siblings having fallen on his very young shoulders.

Marissa lifted a glass jug of Coca-Cola syrup sitting on the table in front of her. She examined the dark liquid. The contents appeared unchanged many decades later.

"Want a sip?" joked Diana.

Marissa chuckled and shook her head.

"We're definitely including that jug," said Diana, "but we're limited in the number of items we can bring. Making the final two choices is giving us fits."

Marissa wandered to the wall shelves, drawn by old-timey foot powder, colic preventer, and castor oil. "Well, I know what I'd pick," she chirped over her shoulder.

"What?" cried one of the women. "There are so many things to choose from."

"It's only a suggestion, of course." She turned her head away and pretended to study the items in front of her face. So strong was a growing urge, that she blurted words muffled by a Prince Albert cigar box, "Don't want to be accused of bulldozing my opinions, though." A beam of morning sunshine hitting the shelf showed the lightest puff of dust kicked up by her words vented across the wood. In the past, the charge fairly characterized her attitude on every committee and in every meeting. She had bordered on haughty and much too pushy.

"What's that?" said Diana. "Didn't quite hear you."

Marissa's head swung around. "Oh, nothing. Just mumbling to myself." She walked toward them. "Please, take my recommendation with a grain of salt, but I do have a preference for numbers, so I'd pick-"

"That's right," interrupted another lady. "You used to work in the finance department of Atlanta Accolade."

Marissa blinked. "I wish you hadn't brought that up." The woman grimaced. Marissa laughed. "No, it's okay. It wasn't the right spot for me. Now, what I do uses my other abilities as well. . . . But tell me, where is Dr. Dean's accounting book and the cloth packet?"

The faces of the women jumped with remembrance and delight. Diana walked to the storage cabinet. For a while, all eyes on her, she carefully unloaded the book of ledger lines and the packet constructed from ivory duck cloth. The women parted as she came bearing the prizes to the table, and they all renewed their memory of the items that had piqued everyone's interest at some previous time. Diana gently unfolded the stiff cloth. A dozen pockets, each labeled with letters of the alphabet, lined the interior. Promissory notes filled the insides, revealing that some medical debts were postponed or never fully paid by the turn-of-the-century hardworking folk. In present times, some viewers of the IOUs surmised the kind doctor knew it would be impossible for some but allowed the patients their dignity with a piece of paper announcing their intention to fulfill their obligations. Perhaps, he knew a few slothful or malicious souls never had a mind to pay, but the document kept the doctor in the rights and informed.

Marissa's fingers carefully opened the accounting book. "Ladies, if you recall, this is where Dr. Dean recorded the charges and payments made by each family for medical services." Family names labeled the top of each page. "See, here are the records for Uncle Nathan's father, Wayne, my great-grandfather." Her index finger grazed the numbers written in antiquated style. "Thank goodness, no familial embarrassments here. . . . Although," she flinched and smiled good-naturedly, "once, it looks like three laying hens were remuneration to the doctor when cash was lean."

Diana turned the pages. "So many times the doctor accepted wood or fodder," she added. "I recall gallons of syrup as payment on one occasion. Even a cow once wiped out a debt more costly than the animal."

"Just think," said Marissa. "Dr. Dean didn't have to worry about computer down time or losing data from a power outage."

The women thanked Marissa, and she went on her way to pick up Nathan's prescription at a drugstore suited for current times, down the way. Once she completed the errand, she took a seat on a bench outside the pharmacy and watched her hometown blossom with energy as the morning lengthened.

Then she saw him, a man strong-looking for the back side of middle age, one who walked with his shoulders back and his chin up, a Marine in his youth. He was a man whose teeth she perennially set on edge.

In his meter-business vehicle, he had pulled into one of the spaces in front of the park and then made it to her side of Main Street. Skin buckeye brown, he turned and walked in her direction. She waited. At the funeral, his greeting had been brief and formal. He was about to get a haircut, she figured, but he stopped short of going inside a storefront, realizing who she was, and he continued down the sidewalk.

"Morning, Lavon," she said.

He dipped his head in acknowledgement. "Mind if I take a seat?"

"Please do." She shifted to make room.

He took off his sporty cap and leaning over his thighs, twirled it vertically in his hands. He kept his eyes on the cap. "Glad I saw you. Didn't get to say much the other day."

"You look well, Lavon. Business good?"

"Great. How about you?"

"Well, it's a whole different ball game. You have to own your own business to realize how tough the risks are."

"Yep. It takes guts. But you've got plenty of nerve." He sat up straight. "Sorry, I didn't mean anything ill by that."

"Even if you did, I realize I didn't always behave well. Maybe that's why you're still on the city council, and my district booted me out."

"People say you've changed. Sweet like you were as a little girl."

"Life changes a person."

He looked up, nodded, and smiled. "I found a box this summer. A collection of my grandmother's things. There was a letter from your dad. You probably don't know that when she got sick, he gave her big financial help and swore her to secrecy. I never knew he was the one who paid for her surgery, back when there was no Medicare. He paid for a nurse to help her recuperate, and he had her house outfitted for a wheelchair."

"I wasn't aware of that."

"I respected your father . . . and . . . I'm sorry about acting like the rear end of a donkey sometimes."

She laughed. "Okay, but sometimes I was the one with the brains of a mule."

He grinned and got up from the bench. "You take care, Marissa."

"You too, Lavon. Give my best to Althea and the girls."

Off to get his trim, he strode to his destination and disappeared inside a doorway.

Marissa's ears detected a slow rhythmic movement and the screech of metal. A horn, louder than that of any car, rolled off its long note of warning. She leaned forward and looked to her right. Still unseen, the rumbling train pushed closer, its groaning a controlled thunder when it crawled. Finally, she saw the engine like a noble draft horse powerfully pulling an immense load. Everything else in the town came to a halt, the cars near the crossing, the rest of the traffic motoring through town, people mesmerized as though they had never seen such a sight. Although technology had reached an unimaginable peak, minds easily latched onto the massive machine, amazed by the sheer power and symbolic position of the locomotive in American history. Certainly, thought Marissa, her own town was still enthralled. Just as it should be, she reckoned. The railroad had been its heart and soul, the thing that carved a place for the town in 1879, turning it from a settlement of scattered homesteads after the land lottery in 1838 into a place of permanence and nurturing, a place families could eke out a living and eventually thrive.

The engine was almost even with her when she noticed the conductor, his arm blazed by sunshine and resting on the window. The stalwart train lumbered down the track and the conductor glanced at her. He projected a grin and waved.

Like a schoolgirl, Marissa jumped from her seat and swung her arm in the air. As the train approached the gray boards of the depot, the horn blared once more. For some seconds, the engine moving past the structure wore a beautiful crown—the red tile roof of the depot. Then the procession of train cars roared into the crossing and beyond the park and gazebo.

Marissa's arms hung limply at her side. She took a deep breath and turned in the other direction to find her car. A recollection skipped through her head of a day long ago when she was nine. She and her father sat on a bench like the present one, maybe in the exact, same spot. A different train traveled through that day. L&N, for Louisville and Nashville, emblazoned the cars. She flew from her seat then, too, and flagged the conductor with her hello. Her father, unembarrassed, joined her and yelled, "Ho, there!" And he waved his long arm as though a European prince cruised through in honor of the town, tossing gold coins in exchange for each friendly greeting. A friend of her father's exited a store nearby and took a gander at John Manning.

"It's just the train, John," the man said flatly.

Marissa's beaming father looked at Marissa and said with awe, "I know." Then he took her hand. "Let's go get ice cream." How she loved that man. How she had wished to be his copy in mind and accomplishment.

She got into her car, backed out, and drove home.

Chapter Twenty-five

A gentle argument ensued between Nathan and Marissa. He declared the best way for Max to become a driver was to learn right there on the land. It was the old way, and Harbin could vouch for the wisdom of it and so would Allen if he were still with them. Marissa resisted but, worn down, gave in.

Max put the key in the ignition and turned. The motor in Uncle Nathan's roomy car came to life, effecting a grin from the boy.

Marissa checked her seat belt for the third time. "All right, Max. Push lightly on the accelerator."

They moved, the reddish-brown car trudging like a wide heifer, down the rocky drive toward Trickum Road. At first, the muffler expelled exhaust the way a swollen udder shoots milk.

Max smiled from ear to ear, confidently gripping the wheel. They reached the end point where Marissa guided him in a turnaround, and they came back toward the house, never moving above five miles per hour.

"Okay, Max. Put it in park and let the engine idle." She went over safety rules and made him recall the procedures when preparing to drive a car.

"Check fuel, adjust mirrors, secure seat belt," he said. "This is gonna be simpler than a snoozey trail ride on Dixie."

Her nervous fingers rubbed the arm rest. "Believe me; a car can be more dangerous than a galloping, rebellious horse." She grimaced, cogently aware of the Bennicks' yard, a quarter mile down the road, where a speeding Mustang sailed off the road, careened through a dog house, shocked the poor animal on a tie out, demolished the homeowner's bee colony, and finally wrapped itself, dripping with honey, around a tree. The loopy driver, quite lucky with nothing more than a mild concussion and multiple contusions, wandered mindlessly until the emergency crew gathered him up. But a spot several miles down the way wore a white cross and silk flowers, a constant bulletin of another, more devastating crash. Marissa's hand lightly traced the length of the seat belt crossing her chest.

"Can we take the pasture and the back road now?" he chimed. "Makes me think of Dukes of Hazzard." She scowled. His voice adopted a cool-headed tone. "I'm only kidding."

"Max, we're going to go up and down this road ten more times. You have to get a feel for driving. It's not a teenage lark." He turned the car around and moved forward again. She continued with her warning. "Hope you're cramming the information from that booklet into your head. I'm not about to take you on the real roads until you know everything inside those pages and you pass the written test."

"Yes, ma'am. No problem. Wonder how long before I can get the real thing."

"What thing."

"My solo certification," he said, grinning.

"Max, it doesn't matter. You don't own a car."

"Reality check," he piped.

"But you'll be a big help, chauffeuring Nathan. I just have to convince him. You never know, when you do get your real license, he may let you borrow the car for a date."

"No chance of that. . . . I mean a date."

She was suddenly grateful her better sense had restrained her from telling five-foot Max it would help his driving if he sat on the Atlanta phone book. Instead, he was forced to sit on the edge of the seat to reach the pedals. The seat shifter mechanism had rusted and locked in place, allowing room for Uncle Nathan's long frame. Their talk ceased, and they cruised up and down the long path. She smoothed the cantaloupe-colored cashmere sweater she wore over a white shirt. Tan wool slacks in a herringbone weave completed the favorite outfit. Attractive brown alligator heels graced her feet. Gold earrings gleamed from her ears. An invitation to lunch with the preservation group provided her with the perfect excuse to end the lesson at a reasonable time. Marissa let her mind drift, lulled by the sameness of their ride. Her eyelids dipped like the driveway.

In the woods, something flushed a rabbit. Max stomped the brake so hard Marissa lurched forward.

"Why'd you brake?" she demanded.

"A rabbit. Didn't think you'd want its blood on your conscience or your tires."

"No, but try to give me some warning." She sat back and straightened her tossed hair. Her heart still raced. A headache threatened to come on.

At the end of the tenth trip Max stopped next to the house and put the car in park. He looked at her with expectancy. "That's ten," he said. "You look tired. Do you want to go inside and rest for a minute?"

"I . . . ." She thought how nice it would be to fortify herself with a cup of tea but sensed his yearning, "We might as well go ahead."

"The horses are in their stalls," he said hopefully.

"Okay. We'll try the pasture for a while, then the cotton field road. But be careful there. I don't want to slip off the path and plunge headfirst into the dirt below." Trying not to smudge her make-up, she pressed her eye sockets as her head started to pound.

Max slowly drove away from the house. In the side mirror, Marissa saw a car pull to the spot they left. Uncle Nathan was expecting a friend who needed to borrow tack.

Max eased the car around the wooden garage and by the stable. He reached the gate, got out and swung it wide. Excitement shone all over his face when he climbed back in.

"Be careful, now. Take these hills slow," she said.

He moved into the pasture and approached the high point which led to the lower hills like giant moguls on a ski slope.

Marissa's innate efficiency flagged her. "Wait a minute," she said. "Ted's here to borrow that saddle. Did you remember to leave it out?"

Max slowed the vehicle to a creep and twisted in the seat to look back toward the house. He squinted. "Yeah, I did . . . but that's not Ted. That's . . . my mom!" His foot slipped off the brake and blindly tried to find it again. He hit the gas instead, and they sailed off the hill, landing at the bottom with a hard slam that knocked Max to the floorboard, scrunched within the space. His contorted body with hands and knees flailing tried to right itself and, in the process, flogged brake and gas pedal causing the car to jerk wildly over the next hill. Marissa yanked Max onto the seat and speared the brake with one of her long legs. The car came to a wrenching stop. She threw the engine into park and yanked the key from the ignition. Blood poured from an inch-long cut above one of Max's eyebrows. Marissa rubbed her aching hand that had slammed against the dashboard. The top of her head throbbed after being walloped by the roof during that initial, shocking bounce.

"Max! What in the world!"

"Man, oh man!" He wiped away blood poring into his right eye. "I couldn't find the pedal. My face hit the steering wheel when we landed."

"How'd you end up on the floorboard?"

"I forgot to put on my seat belt after I opened the gate."

"Wow." She threw her head back and sighed. "No wonder parents pay good money to driving schools."

He looked at her with his clear eye and wiped blood on his jeans. "I'm really sorry." Blood dripped all over Nathan's seat. He reluctantly took the sweater she urged on him for a bandage.

Marissa stared at the bridge of his nose slowly ballooning in size. "We've got to get you fixed up. Out. I'll drive back." They emptied the car and switched places. As Marissa got in the driver's side, blood smeared onto her wool slacks. She glanced toward the house, remembering Max's mom.

The woman stood at the crest of the hill near the stable, her hands on her hips.

The car churned its way up the pasture, past a frowning Vereena, and parked in front of the garage. Max and Marissa walked to the horse barn.

Vereena met them. "Maximillian, my child, what happened! You are wounded!"

Marissa kept walking. "The stable has a first aid kit."

Vereena held her face and shook her head. She wrapped her arms about Max and cooed her concern. They followed Marissa who was thinking her chance to continue mending fences with friends over lunch had evaporated.

Inside the stable, Marissa sat Max on a stool and swabbed hydrogen peroxide over the wound. The sweater hung over a railing, so bloody it looked like someone had been killed in it.

Vereena continued with exclamations of worry and dread. "Diseases. No telling what has entered this terrible cut." Max looked perplexed. "He must have a doctor, x-rays. A cat scan may be necessary. Oh my! Who gave my child permission to drive?"

"I did," said Marissa dabbing the wound. "I apologize. I should have checked with you first. He's going to need stitches." She continued with her ministrations.

"This is quite astonishing," said Vereena. "You allowed a minor behind the wheel of a car when he did not have a license. Isn't that against the law?"

Marissa leaned near Max's head and closely examined the cut no longer gushing. "We didn't go on any public roads," was Marissa's retort.

Vereena moved near Marissa. Something about it registered confrontational in Marissa's mind. She straightened and met the woman's angry gaze.

"Ms. Manning, I have had many reservations about Max serving as your family's heyboy. Now I am certain it is time for a change . . . unless you can convince me otherwise." She waited, lips pursed, eyes blinking.

Marissa put down the brown bottle. "May I speak with you in the tack room?"

"If you wish," the woman replied.

"Max, hold this gauze over the wound. We'll be right back."

Marissa and Vereena marched to the room and shut the door.

"Aren't you taking a big risk, Vereena?"

"What do you mean?"

"Well, you're his mother. I can't stop you from taking him. Neither can you force us to become the cash faucet you're seeking. You won't get a dribble. My uncle is old, and I do not possess deep pockets."

"I heard you own a restaurant!"

"My business is mortgaged to the hilt. So you can forget that plan. However, I am head of my father's foundation. We select college scholarship recipients. If Max's test scores are high enough, which I am certain they will be if he isn't further distracted from his studies by your gambling debts, I will personally see to it that his college expenses are paid all the way through college and veterinary school. . . . Now, how will that help you? Think. Once your son finishes his schooling and he is earning a living, he will want to help provide for his mother if she is truly in need."

Vereena, with her arms crossed, turned and wandered the room. She stilled and spoke in a quiet, hard voice. "You are vile but clever."

"I'm sorry you feel that way. Since you remain stumped about your situation, maybe this will help." Marissa slid a very expensive watch off her arm and yanked the gold from her ears, drawing the sacrificial line at her shoes. She placed the items in Vereena's hand. "If you come around again with plans other than to visit Max, he will leave with you. But, keep in mind, any future help that might have come your way through your son will go down the drain."

The woman stashed the watch and earrings deep in her purse and tramped from the room. In the aisle of horse stalls, Marissa watched her step quickly by the boy, without a word.

"Mom, wait. I have to see a doctor!" His words bounced off her back and she was gone.

Marissa walked to him, capturing his hurt expression in her mind forever. "Hop up, Max. . . . I'm taking you."

Chapter Twenty-six

According to the throng of injured and ill at the hospital, it was everyone's worst day. After six long hours in a congested emergency room, Marissa and Max returned to the farmhouse. The kid went to the stable with his fast-food meal, wanting to be alone, and Marissa hauled herself through the back door of the house. Nathan sat at the kitchen table, stomach grumbling loud enough for her ears to hear. He had grown pleasantly accustomed to Marissa handling the evening meal like clockwork. Glasses of water and silverware already sat in position.

She dropped the bag of food on the table. "Your car's pretty much okay. I went by Anthony's. He checked the undercarriage. He's going to do a little work on Tuesday. I'll cover it." She fell into her seat and handed Nathan his fried chicken meal. Then she merely hung over her own dinner.

"My, my, I've never seen you look so positively beat," said Nathan.

She looked up. Her tired eyes wanted to reject the jarring sight of his can't-miss-hair but she retained her focus. "I never knew an emergency room could be so expensive. Cat scan. Stitches. When the bill comes in, I'll have to put the monster charge on my credit card. How do people afford children?"

"Like anything else. If it's important, you find a way."

Her head dropped again. "Since I'm getting poorer by the day, I guess it's a good thing I can't have kids," she mumbled at her mashed potatoes.

"Whu?" he exclaimed.

Her head jerked up.

His eyes were wide open. *"You aren't fertile?"*

"Uncle Nathan! You talk like I'm one of your farm animals. It's not the end of the world, you know." The words had flown from her mouth.

He looked ashamed and spoke softly. "Marissa, I meant no offense. I was simply unaware."

"I know. I know. . . . I'm worn out. I'm going to save this food for tomorrow.

My appetite deserted me the moment I flew over that hill. I better get some rest." She re-bagged the meal and got up.

"I'll keep the television low. You go take care of yourself. The heating man came by while you were gone. Fixed everything. Said it's like Florida up there. . . . Oh, I almost forgot. Fran and Jodie called. They heard you were in town and want you to play in a doubles tournament at Woodmont. Tomorrow afternoon."

She perked up. "Okay. Thanks for the message. I'm going to go shower." She tossed her dinner in the fridge. Trudging up the stairs, the novel warmth of the upper floor drew her to the bathroom, and she flipped on the light. She always bypassed the charming claw-foot tub for the separate shower. Aunt Olivia considered putting in a modern tub years earlier, but her sense of style restrained her. Marissa pulled off her shoes and socks and walked across the scintillating texture of numerous hexagonal tiles the size of nickels. . . . Nickels, even a hundred thousand wouldn't do the trick now that her income had stopped. Expenses mounted with mortgage payments due and with employees still on the payroll. In front of the sink, she stepped on a hooked rug of Queen Anne's lace and purple petunias and opened the wooden medicine cabinet. She reached for the bottle of Bayer. The expiration date was the same year that Aunt Olivia died, five years past. She popped the pills into her mouth, anyway, desperate to be done with the nagging ache. She shut the cabinet and looked in the mirror. The light fixture shone down with harsh reality, and she did not like what she saw. A few, new lines. Frowsy hair that could use a color touch-up. Sudden, faint shadow under her eyes.

She went to the extra-long tub and let the water pour. Steam came up. She wriggled out of her clothes and stepped in the tub. The water filled. She laid her head back. Nubby-brained she languished until remembering her ruined clothes hastily substituted before going to the hospital. Her eyes zeroed on the stained sweater where she had cast it on the floor. How did a person get hours-old dried blood off cashmere? If she had only known the whole driving thing was slated to be a debacle, she would have dressed in old jeans and a sweat shirt. The pricy piece was simply another of her accumulating losses, she told herself while trying to halt the tumultuous thoughts gaining on her. The bubbling, roiling water covered her knees and climbed. Rattled by introspection, she acquiesced and opened the door to the debilitating prompt that the wasted clothing was nothing compared to the horribly distressing void inside her pelvis. Even her uncle had revealed his shock and revulsion. Underneath the water, her hands went to cover her flat stomach. The water line neared the base of her neck.

She shot forward, turned off the spigot, and soaped herself. Lying back again, she feared another raid against her peace. Her sight went over the room. She could hear barely audible snippets of applause and singing from Nathan's television show. The steam had invigorated a dried floral wreath on the wall causing the scent of eucalyptus to gently lift away the tension at her temples. Hopefully, Sunday simply held a predictable day of church and tennis; a rest from her worries would be a blessed event. Rest. Why did that word always ring in her head? Maybe its recurring appeal signified her yearning for respite from perpetual heartache and burden she carried. From the unseen world, calming words drifted down into her spirit.

Washed free of the day, she pulled the plug and reached for her towel.

Aunt Olivia's pink chenille robe lay across the bed. Marissa enfolded herself in the lavender-fragrant garment. Her island robe and nightgown of batiste were insufficiently warming she discovered the first evening of her visit. A search through Aunt Olivia's own bureau yielded the robe. Marissa first checked with Uncle Nathan, wanting to save him unnecessary pain. He insisted the robe was hers to use. That first early morning when she had come down for a cup of hot tea, wearing the wrap, she lost heart when she saw that his pining eyes followed her as though he watched an apparition he once loved now gone to some other dimension. After that, she filled a thermos at night and, in the morning, came down to the kitchen in her regular clothes.

In the green room, Marissa pulled the robe belt snug about her waist. She took a small New Testament from her purse and turned on the floor lamp next to the wicker chaise. Sitting down and bringing her legs up, she caused the wicker to snap and crackle. The exceeding comfort of the cushions eased her mind trying to recapture assurance. That confidence had briefly been hers the night Darrien counseled her in his office. She had spoken to him of a childhood moment filling her with joy as she voluntarily left her seat and went up a church aisle. Humble, trusting, she took hold of her place under the King's strong arm. Her love was tender-hearted in those youthful days but later changed. She shared with Darrien the way in which she drifted from that place of safety and became a young adult flirting with arrogance and feeble worldly wisdom. She took a deep breath and disclosed to him the sad result—a blind decision and the tagging consequences to her being. Darrien listened without condemnation. He reminded her of God's mercy to those who humbly came to Him asking forgiveness. She must renew her mind daily, he said, because the world always fought to crowd in and erode belief.

Within the quiet, altering moments she found in the green room that evening, she turned to the intriguing passage that had recently floored her. *He made Him who knew no sin to be sin on our behalf, so that we might become the righteousness of God in Him.* She considered those words, their meaning so fruitful, and she prayed for her thinking to be transformed.

Later, in the alcove bed, she snuggled under Aunt Olivia's quilts, and the enveloping softness warmed like comforting arms.

Sunday, the farm and stable awoke swathed in serenity and the day followed suit.

In the evening hours, Marissa sat with her uncle and planned their words for the meeting with Trent on the coming morning. She went to bed a little uneasy until she remembered the man's benevolent gaze when he handed her Abby's letter.

The next morning, with Nathan beside her, Marissa drove toward the hidden inlets of Lake Allatoona. On their approach to the house, she was aware again, as she had been the day of the funeral, how different the landscape appeared, stripped of its thick banners of leaves. Above the log cabin, the sky trembled with the beauty of azure while thin stripes of pale gray, the slimmest, uppermost branches of tall sweet gum and the darker twigs of linden pointed and reached for the sky. With almost all that had been green gently released to the ground in November, the cabin assumed its central position as what had really been of importance there amid the spectacular scenery. All else was mere ornamentation for life and the daily tug between happiness and struggle.

They were about to step onto the front porch when Hank Averill exited the house. He held a tray of empty breakfast dishes.

"Hi!" he said. "I saw you getting out of your car. Trent asked me to apologize. The physical therapist arrived first thing. Hope you don't mind waiting. She'll be here about fifteen minutes more."

Nathan shook his head. "Fine, fine." He pointed to a rumpled Cherokee Tribune on the tray. "The Sunday edition?"

Hank nodded.

"Good," said Nathan. "Now I'll have time to read the parts I, uh, uh . . ."

"Skipped?" replied Hank. "Help yourself and have a seat in one of the chairs out here. Marissa, want to come over for a quick visit with Elizabeth?"

"Thank you but it's still so early," she answered. "I'm sure she's busy. Ask her if she would like to take Manuel and the baby to the park in town when we get through here. Someone's hosting a bicycle demonstration and giving away free hotdogs."

"Manuel would love that," said Hank.

"I'll stop by. I would think in about an hour."

"Okay. Goodbye, Nathan. It was good to see you again."

"Same to you, Hank. Bring the kids to see Dixie soon. Without young riders around, she misses stepping down the trails. For you, well, I'd put you on Harlequin. You may be the one person with the strength to match that animal."

Hank smiled. "Will do," he said and drifted away, cutting through to the other yard.

Nathan and Marissa took their seats. Nathan dove into his reading. Marissa looked around the colorless, empty porch. When Abby had been well, a person had to be mindful not to knock over the growing things that filled the porch tables and floor.

"Uncle Nathan," said Marissa, looking at the defrocked woods.

"Huh?" he answered, stuck to his paper.

"What's the other name for the linden tree?"

"Basswood," he muttered without looking up. "A favorite tree for carving. Folks around here used to make all kind of things out of the soft, light wood. Things like food crates, toys, excelsior. But everyone also knew if you wanted good honey, you put your hives near the basswood. Bees love the flowers. Way back when, Indians used the strong inner fibers for rope and mats." He turned to the next page in his news.

"You are a virtual encyclopedia of the old days," she said as she stood. "I'm off for a walk."

"Don't go far. He'll be wantin' to meet with us soon."

"I won't." She chose the wooded side of the house and came around the famous flower bed that delighted guests from inside the dining room. Dried stalks surrounded by lofts of curled, dry leaves gave the only hint that something inspiring owned the spot come spring. She was reminded of the shade garden and went further in the fall woods receiving unrestrained light. The canopy of shade would not restore itself until spring. A path of pavers took her to the illuminated spot, and she seated herself on the curved concrete bench. Fronds of autumn fern tinged gold and brown posed around the small reflecting pool. Leaning over, searching for the goldfish, she spied her reflection. A leaf fell, rippling the water and rocking its predecessors. The water smoothed, and the leaves drifted like miniature boats suited for the woods mice. She grinned at the fancy in her mind and caught her reflection again. She rose and came out of the wood, roving around the back yard. The deciduous weeping cherries had become complex, arching sculptures where wintering birds played. The stretched out lawn had been swept of the seasonal debris by someone, most likely the Everson's kind neighbor, allowing Trent to take cover in his house and grieve. She could plainly see the Averill house; the doublefile viburnum divider had shed its green drapery. Excited voices and the sound of a bouncing basketball traveled from the Morning Star Health Complex. Her vision turned to the lake and Hank's dock. A breeze wafted off the water, lifting her hair. She breathed in clean air traced by autumn scent. She walked to the water edge. Again, she saw her reflection.

"Marissa! Come on up!" With her uncle beside him, Trent called from the cabin deck above.

Strangely absorbed by the man's expression and her failure to measure up to the two stellar men on the deck and so many others she had formerly thought herself superior to, she gave the challenge all she had and raced up the slope.

Chapter Twenty-seven

In the cabin, a fire warmed the great room where they took their seats.

"Thanks for meeting with us, Trent," said Marissa. "We sure regret the timing."

"I know it must be urgent. How can I help?"

"Well, we'd appreciate your advice," replied Marissa. She related their tenuous occupation of the farm. "We've studied the document and there's nothing there."

Nathan shifted in his seat, looking disgusted. "I forgot times have changed when I trusted the fella."

"It's a shame there are always a few untrustworthy folks around," said Trent.

Nathan lifted his shoulders and let them fall with a sigh. The bags under his eyes looked heavy.

"The sale of my old property went very well," said Marissa. "The broker was open and honest." She sat up, offended by her next thought. "But this other guy from some outfit in Atlanta, he had no intention of fulfilling his promise."

"And the problem, Marissa, is that Nathan did get fair market value. Mr. Silverstrike simply did not legitimize your uncle's wish for a contingency. Nathan should have had an attorney look over the contract."

Nathan, red-faced, slapped his knee. "*We know it, Trent.* . . . Oh, heck. I'm sorry. I hate admitting what a fool I was." He scratched an ear. "Is there anything I can do about this fiasco?"

"Were there any witnesses who heard Silverstrike agree to let you remain on the property?"

"Nobody but the little secretary, and she's not gonna go against her boss."

"I suggest taking a different direction," said Trent. "Marissa, I think you could enter that office and be the perfect advocate for your uncle. Silverstrike might be open to reason. All you have to do is show him how his present course would not be in his best interest."

"I'd be willing to try."

"This first step is very important. It shows your uncle's willingness to work things out before resorting to some kind of jurisprudence, which would likely be a civil suit hinging on whether the secretary testifies truthfully."

Nathan lowered his head, saying "And a monetary ruling against the man isn't going to allow me to stay in my house. I guess I'm depending on Marissa to fix this."

"I'm not a miracle worker." She looked to Trent for support.

"No you're not," said Trent. . . . "I do know a fine attorney here in north Georgia who could look into the situation. But legally, it's far from promising."

Nathan mussed his hair. A clump stood out like a patch of ruffled feathers. "We'll have to try to appeal to the guy, like you said. I'm not obligating you, Marissa, but you might make progress. Supposedly, the guy is too busy to even take my calls."

"I'll give it a try," she said without enthusiasm.

They conferred a while longer, then Trent asked Marissa to bring coffee down from the kitchen. "I'd never get a tray down those steps with my poor legs," he stated. She jumped up and headed for the kitchen. "And bring plates. I want to sample this apple-cranberry tart you brought me." With effort, Trent raised himself from the sofa, slowly went to his study and came back. As Marissa reentered the room with a tray, he announced, "I've got something to show you." She served the tart on Abby's majolica dessert plates. Trent went enthusiastic, praising Marissa's baking skills.

When they were settled once more, he spread photos on the low table in front of her. "I've been going through our things. Keepsakes and such. Thought you might like to see these." The film had captured a day when she, a preadolescent, had come over with her parents and brother for Fourth of July. Abby and Trent had moved to town years earlier, but the holiday was always spent at the lake, and everyone was invited. Each year Marissa and her father took their annual swim down the length of the cove and back. He always let her win. They fished afterward, lit sparklers, and sang whatever patriotic melodies came to mind, stumbling over a few lyrics.

Marissa put her cup down, tickled by a picture of her brother doing a cannonball off the dock. Marissa's mother and Abby gracefully watched everything from rattan chairs, wearing seventies clothes and hairdos.

Marissa lifted a different photo, one of her confidently plowing through the water by herself.

"You were a strong swimmer, even at that age," said Trent.

"I used to tell her she shoulda been a boy," declared Nathan.

"I'm just competitive when it comes to sports," she said. Trent and Nathan exchanged wry grins.

"The way you relished the water, you remind me of Abby," said Trent. "She was a champion diver before I came around. . . . Now that I think of it, she was the one who taught you to swim."

Marissa looked surprised. "Really?"

"Oh, she taught a lot of the kids from around Woodstock. Two weeks during the summer, she came all the way out here and did just that. You were a little tyke, though. Maybe only three. And you caught on really fast."

Nathan patted his knees. "Yep, she was a smart one. Spied her saddling the pony when she was little. I wouldn't take Pimpernel from the barn that day, so she decided to rig things herself. To raise the saddle, she used the hay pulley rope and looped it around the pommel and seat in a figure eight. Then, she led Pimpernel smack under the hanging leather above. Right?"

"Right."

"When I walked into the barn, she was already tightening the cinch, and she had pulled a box over, ready to climb onto her pet. We had to keep an eye on that child."

Marissa laughed.

Trent put his empty plate down. "Yeah, I think she can figure a way around Silverstrike. She's got brains." He took a swig of coffee. "By the way, how's the business going, Marissa?"

"Well, despite compliments from you both, it's much more of a struggle than I thought it would be." She took a deep breath, subconsciously hoping the scent of fruit and spices from the remainder of tart would infuse her with forthrightness. "A lot of complication. Some mistakes."

"Part of the process," said Trent. "You know, I always sensed you inherited an entrepreneurial spirit from your dad. He used to say that the real torque in any business was from zero to sixty, those foundational years of the business. After that, it gets a little easier."

"Yep," said Nathan, "you could apply that drag racing analogy to a lot of things in life."

She glanced at her wrist. The white band of skin left by the watch swapped for a boy's future stood out like a pale, sickly tattoo. She returned the tray to the kitchen and refrigerated the tart. Still thinking about their conversation, she lifted her purse, which held numbers posted on her bank statement so worrisome it threatened to dislocate her arm. She and Nathan thanked Trent for his advice and went on their way.

Nathan and Trent chatted on the front porch while Marissa ran next door seeking Elizabeth. Marissa took the path leading to the archway and approached the side entrance. Her hand rose ready to knock but slowly lowered to her side as she watched the beauty inside the cottage. The morning sun streamed through the glass sliding doors onto the domestic scene. She felt awful but could not stop the urge to incorporate the private family moment somewhere in her understanding. Manuel played on a braided rug with a toy truck and action figures. The baby lay on a blanket, stomach side down, back arching, her head lifted and arms and legs raised slightly off the floor, bobbing. Hank and Elizabeth stood at the sliding glass doors. He was behind, his arms wrapped lovingly around his sable-haired wife. The couple talked and looked at the sky. His head tilted down, and he buried his face in the side of her neck. He lifted his face and said something. Elizabeth smiled and pulled him tighter. Then they let go.

Marissa swung her voyeuristic self to the side, so she wouldn't be seen for the pathetic woman she must be. Loneliness flooded her chest. On the back steps sat white chrysanthemums in clay containers. She remembered brushing one of the plants when she first came to the door. A sprinkling of tiny petals knocked loose resembled scattered, snow-white teardrops. A thought worked its way into her mind. The people inside deserved to be lovers, deserved to be parents. Not her. Then the enemy showed up again, telling her the surgery she had five years earlier was punishment for the thing she had done in her youth.

She felt like fleeing. She could shove Nathan into the Chrysler, grab the wheel, and in no time, she could crawl into the bed in the beautiful alcove among the walls portraying a garden.

The side door of the cottage flung open.

"Oh!" said Elizabeth, smiling. "I was about to water the flowers."

"Hi!" said Marissa, hoping she held back a blush, "I was enjoying them. Are you ready to go to the park?"

"Yes. Manuel is very excited. Should we meet you there?"

"Ride with us and I'll bring you home when we're through."

"Thank you. I will get the stroller and our things."

On the entire trip to town, Nathan remained twisted, in order to face Manuel who sat behind Marissa as she drove. Nathan engaged the child's laughter, telling about the time Nathan chased Brianna up the drive and along Trickum Road. "I'm not that fit anymore, so it was tough on me." He handed the boy a butterscotch.

"Yeah," said the boy. "You told me you were older than Mathuza."

"Oh. Right. At the funeral. Methuselah." The boy was momentarily distracted by his tiny sister cooing and gurgling a string of baby nonsense. Nathan looked chagrined and muttered to Marissa. "Quite a memory for a second-grader. Hope he hasn't been repeating the reference." Nathan turned to the rear again. His young audience looked at him with big, dark-lashed eyes, ready to hear more. "Anyway, that naughty goat skipped on her happy legs a quarter mile, then across the road in front of screeching tires, and finally through the parking lot, straight for Publix. I was a wee bit behind, huffing and puffing. Unfortunately, a lady was about to enter the store. The door slid back for her. Well, Brianna thought it was her own personal invite. Did she head for the eggs and milk? The bread aisle? No. I think she could smell all those lettuces and zucchini and carrots. But it was a lucky thing, actually. There she was standing on her hind legs, with front legs in the bin, all spellbound by her banquet. I grabbed her tight."

"Oh, that's good," Manuel chirped. "Were you mad at her?"

"Not yet. Not until she wouldn't budge toward home. I managed to drag her out the door. But my old, bent-over back was hurting. The manager followed me outside. Let me tell you, he looked none too happy. But he broke down and asked if he could lend a hand. I made my request, and thankfully he consented. We lifted Brianna into a shopping cart. Out the parking area and down the road we went. I'm pretty sure I heard a person exclaim, 'Hey, they're selling goats at Publix!'"

Manuel's eyes scrunched with laughter. He wiggled in his seat, overcome with mirth. The baby stared. Elizabeth patted his arm and told him to settle down.

Nathan talked on. "You'll have to meet Brianna some time, Manuel. She's gonna have a kid this winter. That's a baby goat. You can come over for a glass of her milk."

"Euuuuw," Manuel spouted with a contorted face.

"That is impolite," said his mother. "And do you not remember? We sometimes drank goat milk in Mexico."

"We did? But milk is from cows."

As she drove, Marissa snatched glances of Elizabeth's motherly expressions and supervision in the rearview mirror.

At the park, Marissa walked beside Elizabeth pushing the stroller. Workers balanced on ladders, putting up Christmas decorations. Nathan trundled off, bent on finding some old-timers for a chat. Manuel charged playfully in the grassy areas until a group of people left the gazebo, permitting him to take command of the structure. Marissa tried to guess what played in his imagination as he ran around on the platform.

Marissa nodded toward the boy. "Elizabeth. Captain of a vessel or knight in a castle?"

Elizabeth shrugged. "Perhaps I let him read too much."

"Oh, no. An imagination is a wonderful thing."

Manuel stood on the gazebo bench, conducting music. The women clapped. The shopkeepers from the bicycle store on Main Street entered the park, bringing an array of their newest line, obliquely reminding parents of the gift season around the corner. Manuel moved in close, chomping on his free hot dog, watching the proper way to change a bike tire and the procedure for chain lubrication. A young man got on one of the BMX bikes and whirled about doing tricks, wowing the boy.

Marissa and Elizabeth took a seat on a park bench.

Marissa smoothed the silky hair on the baby's scalp. "You have such a beautiful family, Elizabeth."

"Thank you. I am so grateful for my blessings."

"Especially for such a romantic husband, I bet."

Elizabeth looked at her oddly, as though she wondered how Marissa would know such a thing.

Marissa shook her head and stammered. "I, I can just tell."

Elizabeth smiled serenely. "We have been married three years now. I do not expect my husband to treat me like a new bride. But one thing I have found, Marissa. Each day together is sweeter, more precious than the one before."

"Yes, you do have God's blessings, Elizabeth."

"As do you, Marissa."

Marissa sat back, wondering just how much validity existed in Elizabeth's well-meaning words. Some moments, some days, it seemed recklessly optimistic to expect more than forgiveness.

Chapter Twenty-eight

MARISSA stepped outside the glass doors of Woodstock Library. She paused on the concrete and glanced at the novel in her hand. New, highly recommended, the book would see her through the wait to speak with Silverstrike. The guy, impossible to catch in his office, did not return her calls. His plucky receptionist, buried by work, always scrambled to apologize and make excuses for her boss. For Marissa, an entire week and another payroll without the soft pillow of income had slipped by.

Positioned on a rise, she toyed with the book, flapping it lightly against her thigh, and she looked to the road below where familiar, quaint homes with shrub-filled, hide-and-seek-perfect yards lined the other side of the road. The calming view swayed her mood toward nostalgia. Her feet planted shoulder width, her consciousness musing, she suddenly woke and scooted to the side to avoid clogging the entrance for some approaching bibliophiles. Each carried a stack to be returned. Not a bad affection, she thought; with a book you were never alone, and if you left, it always waited patiently for your return.

Earlier, chatting with Mrs. Mellain the library assistant, Marissa was urged to re-visit the Bookworms Club, being that she was in town. Marissa knew she had tried the patience even of those good folk with her ramrod opinions and tendency to hog the book discussion, so she politely declined. While the woman issued Marissa a new card, they remarked on the old library location in the 1908 yellow-brick building located in the center of town. They recalled the long-ago day Marissa escaped her Saturday chores and secluded herself in a corner of the cozy back room where she fell into an entrancing fictional world. From mid-morning until dusk, the town searched for the missing nine-year-old, described by her father as no bigger than a tall cricket. Her parents waxed frantic. So intent on freedom was the girl that even the busy librarians fell short of noticing her as she snuck inside immediately after opening. Marissa found a hidden niche and seated herself to read *The Mixed-up Files of Mrs. Basil E. Frankweiler*. The narrative involved a runaway girl, living inside the Metropolitan Museum of Art in

New York City. As she read about the inscrutable strangeness of the artifact-laden Egyptian room, about the creepy experience of sleeping in a medieval bed where someone reputedly lost their royal head, and about the outlandish necessity of bathing in a coin-filled fountain, the story transfixed her. She simply could not put the book down, and the hours were lost to her.

Later, only slightly older, Marissa learned the earlier location of the library, the corner of Main Street and Towne Lake Parkway, had actually housed the town bank from 1908 until 1970. The librarian gave her a confidential look-see of the vault. Usually mesmerized by all her reading options, the strange portal had previously remained in the background of her notice. On the day she was shown the money room, she considered herself proudly inducted into a special fraternity—Town Guardians of Architectural Secrets.

As people entered and exited the modern, metal-roofed, red-brick library, Marissa felt the strong tug of her past. A slow smile crossed her lips as she made the decision; she had to see the interior again of that creamy-yellow brick building erected at a time when most townsfolk traveled by horse and buggy. She marched to her car and made a quick call telling Nathan her plans. She dumped her purse and the novel under the passenger seat. She donned a navy hooded parka. Off she went through the parking lot and down the sidewalk stretching toward what was the center of Woodstock commerce in the old days. Each building had morphed in its own particular manner over one hundred years, transitioning in various ways: general mercantile, post office, bus depot, casket store, tearoom, grocery, antique store, jail, neon design studio, corn mill, sports collectibles showroom, saw mill, pizza place, barber shop, Indian arts store, blacksmith, bike shop, hair salon, lumber mill, drug store, cotton warehouse, city hall and so on and so on, up and down through time, left and right along several city blocks in front and behind. In fact, the corner building that housed the former library presently functioned as an art gallery lined with Thomas Kincaid paintings, an artist known for his portrayal of light washing across scenes of a bygone era. Marissa's steps quickened. She simply had to know if the rooms of that corner building still contained the ink and paper smell of several thousand dream-filled books.

A gray sky slung itself over town most of the day. Showers came at intervals. December couldn't be denied its rightful place on the calendar, and the cold had no plans to leave until some unexpected day in February when startling sun-basking weather came and went for an afternoon the same way a fleeting mint candy disappears on your tongue. Then the chill fought to stay until pushed off by the surge of spring at the end of March. Feeling a slight exertion, it dawned on her that her decision to walk would be more than a quick jaunt, and winter daylight would be making its dash away soon. Certainly, dinnertime was already ringing in someone's head, but for once, Uncle Nathan and Max could help themselves to the pot of beef vegetable soup she left in the fridge. She was set on enjoying her reverie.

Following the sidewalk up the modest hill that slid around the curve in the road, she pumped her arms harder, keeping her body engine revved and the cold at bay. Down below, car headlights cut through the dampening light, like bright, happy eyes. She came down the slope and crossed Haney Road and the homes fronting Main, where Christmas decorations brightened doors and shone from picture windows. Linton Street was next and she thought about the man for whom that side road was named. Finally Dobbs Road came into view and the elementary school that was dormant, waiting for another turnabout-transformation as the kids and teachers had all moved to modern facilities up Rope Mill Road.

Once she reached the park, she crossed over and soon entered the art gallery. Lush forest green carpet matched the awnings outside. Lilting music played in the background. A clerk greeted her affably and offered coffee. Marissa declined and began to peruse the art—lovely, enchanting, but heaven. Not a real town, not like hers. She had seen the vintage photos of dirt roads, simple dress, work-worn faces, children in bare feet, and women with deeply lined faces whose posture and optimism had been tested by toil, by illness, and by childbearing entrenched with the fact that it would be uncommon for all a mother's offspring to survive infancy and childhood. Those sepia-toned photos touched Marissa infinitely more than the beautiful images on the walls before her. Linked through time by location, she deeply valued her connection to those genuine, salt-of-the-earth people. Her heart's affiliation, bound so tight to the town, would never be broken wherever she chose to live.

She took a deep breath. No book smells. Sandalwood with a touch of spice and vanilla came to her nose. Artsy. Upscale. How time changed things. The clerk discussed a painting with another visitor, allowing Marissa a chance to let her eyes sweep the main room, trying to bring to life the way she had known the space. She stepped down to the smaller back room and took everything in. She thought to herself, she would give her business away if it meant she could visit her childhood for one uninterrupted day of immersion in the innocence of childhood, a nurturing environment, and her parents' unconditional love. Her happy look slipped away. She sighed, let her arms drop to her sides. Heading to the door, she parted with the clerk and left appreciative remarks in her wake.

Outside, darkness had fully arrived. She began her return trip on the west side of Main, and she crossed at the town mural, moving north. She had passed the first storefront when a torrential rain battered her from above, and she darted under the covered entrance of Woodstock Community Church, the former home of First Baptist since 1913, now being housed in the mega-structure shining its light from the eastern reaches of the city limits, close to Uncle Nathan. She moved back within the shelter and sat on the concrete, hoping to outlast the downpour. One of the large double doors became her back rest. She pushed back the hood of her parka. In the high ceiling, a light fixture sent down a tranquil incandescence as she waited for the ruckus to pass. A blustery wind whipped by and, nearby, Annie Hames pulled up in a minivan with her three half-grown sons. They burst from the vehicle, seeking the brick haven. Marissa jumped up. Annie squealed with delight and hugged Marissa's neck, exclaiming her happiness to see a long-lost high school friend. Annie had moved three states away when the boys were small. The women talked, each sharing the events of their lives. Recently, Annie returned to have the support of the town and her family. Her husband had left her. Marissa's sight went automatically to the boys. Streetlights flickered the rainwater overflowing the gutter. The falling streams played on one of the boys' outstretched palms. The other two, older, more somber, stared into the rain. To their mother, Marissa expressed her concern, offered encouragement. She asked Annie to keep in touch as she gathered her sons and went inside. In minutes, other women arrived at the church doorstep, greeting Marissa with such warmth that her heart glowed like the light above. Again, it seemed that everyone had permanently forgotten any strained relationships she created in the town. The start of the prayer meeting, inside, drew Marissa's well-wishers away, and she took a seat once more. It had been a long time since she felt so relieved and confident. Maybe her absence had made people's hearts grow fonder. Maybe, for a long while, she'd been blind to their kindness. The town wasn't perfect. Like every place, it had a few scoundrels and knaves. But one thing she knew—she wanted to be like so many of them: loyal, unpretentious, and merciful.

The rain stopped and, for most of an hour, she remained in her serene hovel watching the parade of life go on before her and the lights come on the decoration draping the ornamental fencing at the park: Peace on Earth spelled with diamond spangled script. She forgot all her problems. In her heart, love welled up, overflowing and bursting forth. For the praying women. For Annie and her children. For every human being.

Her head rose. She sighted a petite figure, a shocking spot of vibrant color, crossing rapidly at the mural. The stylish woman wore a yellow rain coat with a mandarin collar, cinched at her tiny waist. High heels on delicate feet cut freely through the water streaming across the road. Lightest golden curls peeked loosely from under the rim of her umbrella. Shadow hid most of her face. Marissa rose. She had a ways to travel herself. She stretched, rejoicing at the thought of the brisk walk ahead. At the same time, the little woman, on-task as an avenging angel, turned down the path that led to the church, and she seemed to take stock of Marissa. With Marissa's first stride on her journey back to the car, she quipped, "The prayer meeting's right through there. But might be over soon."

The woman stormed up and lowered the umbrella.

Marissa stared. Cognitive dissonance flooded her mind. Confusion tied her tongue as she scanned the woman's face. The pretty green eyes were narrowed by eyebrows squashing them down in anger. The expressive, rosy lips had been tightened with anger. Marissa knew that face; rather, she knew the calm, docile one.

"Zoe!" said Marissa. "What are you doing here?"

"Waiting all day for my conference in Atlanta to end. So I could find you."

"What's the matter? You look like you're ready to punch someone in the nose."

"No, Marissa. That's not my style. But I would like to get something off my chest."

"Are you . . . you can't be upset with me, are you?" gasped Marissa.

"That's putting it mildly." Zoe's cheeks heightened with pink. Marissa's jaw dropped. Zoe continued, "This little side trip to Woodstock is going to have me driving all night to the island, without sleep after a grueling day. *But it's worth it.* The headache I have from trying to get your aged uncle to explain exactly where you were *is also worth it.* . . . Marissa Manning you are *cold-hearted, deceiving, disloyal, and narcissistic. Begrudging, too.* Your behavior is probably stupidly related to my being made president of the Beachcombers Club, when you thought you were a shoo-in. Well I didn't care all that much about being president." She inhaled and spewed a double dose of repudiation: *"But you clearly know how much I care for Darrien . . . you, you man-thief."*

Zoe's heart-ravaged words tore through the damp air at the same time the prayer group exited the church. Annie Hames turned her surprised look on Marissa.

Marissa shook her head, aghast at the tears trailing down Zoe's face. The church women scurried around the conflict. Marissa's point of view switched from woman to woman, frantically trying to read their faces, wondering if disappointment was the thing shrouding their eyes. They moved away. Marissa's last chance to salvage their good opinion was about to evaporate.

Marissa raised her voice in explanation. "No, Zoe. You're wrong. Darrien doesn't care a thing about me. Believe me, no man does." Marissa gulped, unbelieving the humiliating words she blasted about the church front. "Look at you," she continued. "You're twenty-six and as young and pretty as a spring daffodil. I can see forty up ahead and no man who ever knew me well wanted to be permanently tied to me." Heat glowed from her face. "I'm telling you, there's some mistake." Marissa was conscious that the only remaining female spectator entered her car and let the door shut.

"No mistake," contended Zoe. "He's got it bad for you. Told me himself, when I revealed my deep affection for him, *just like you constantly urged me to do*. And you know what he said? First, he looked at me with those warm brown eyes that I've been looking into for almost three dozen dates. 'Zoe,' he said, 'you are so special to me, but I've discovered I have a growing attraction for someone unexpected, someone who hasn't given me even the slightest hope.' 'Oh,' said I, while fighting my pain, and I inquired, 'Does she know how you feel?' He told me that he hadn't been given the opportunity because she was away for awhile. Of course, your name came to my mind. 'Marissa?' I asked. He turned red, stammered. You know he won't lie, so he said nothing. The answer was as plain as . . . as those clothes you're wearing." Zoe broke out with heavy crying. She paused to speak again. "So this is his thanks for the outings and lunches I took his strange mother on. She actually likes me, and she hardly likes anyone. But I'm finished with him. And I'm finished with you!"

"I'm sorry, Zoe. I never should have told you what to do."

"Well great, Marissa. As a future pastor's wife, women will seek your advice. You'd better bone up on guidance principles."

"No, Zoe. I'm telling you, I don't want to marry Darrien."

"I don't believe that. I overlooked the way you were always sidling up to him, wanting to know about this, or help me understand that." Her head tilted forward, and she gave a light shake to her champagne tresses. "You went so far as to pretend you thought of him only as a brother. Amazing technique, Marissa."

"I'm so sorry. I wish you knew the truth."

"Well, please don't worry about me. I've met a new man, one who creates beauty wherever he goes." Zoe sniffed. She looked away as if speaking to herself. "Byron appreciates me, even if Darrien doesn't."

Marissa's eyes flew wide.

Zoe took a deep breath. "Goodbye, Marissa." Zoe pivoted on one of her pointy heels and began her leave-taking. "Oh." She paused and partially faced Marissa. "With time, I will forgive you," said Zoe. Then her index finger speared the air. *"Just don't be handing me any more advice. Ever."* Zoe stormed into the night.

Marissa's shoulders dropped. The town had emptied and gone home to bed. She had difficulty moving for a few moments until someone inside the church doused the light fixture above her head. Everything turned to gloom. Grim faced, she trekked down the half mile of road to the empty parking lot that held her car.

Chapter Twenty-nine

THE sounds of Nathan's bathing in a basin carried to the upper floor. He sang along to songs on the radio. Marissa decided to carry her cup of tea down, to add a touch of honey. She made the dash wearing the chenille robe. Once in the kitchen she spied some food scraps for the goat. Marissa stepped onto the back porch, her interest drawn to the far pasture. Harlequin paced in the training ring as though a distant wolf had caught scent. The horse, eyes open wide, ears back, and head shaking intermittently, revealed its agitation. The early morning air ranged around thirty-eight degrees. Puffs of vapor blew from fierce, black nostrils. Marissa could picture the details of that incongruously beautiful, velvet face as the animal trotted the endless curve leading nowhere. Max was posted at that far fencing, observing the animal. The breakfast Nathan made Max had grown cold on the plate.

Something soft and warm nudged Marissa's slipper-covered toes situated near the side edge of the stoop. Brianna grabbed her feeder's gaze and bleated. Marissa dropped the scraps into the goat pen. A Land Rover pulled by the house and parked at the stable. Marissa scurried inside.

After throwing on work clothes, she trotted outside to the ring.

"Max, what's giving Harlequin the jitters?" she said, walking up.

"I put the training halter on. Mr. Langley called about an early session." Max cast a worried look at her. "He's in the stable, changing from his suit."

Marissa looked puzzled. "Why so early?"

"Just flew in from L.A.," said Max. "He looks tired and grumpy. I can already tell this won't be good." His eyes darted to the horse.

Marissa swerved around, hearing the man's distant approach. When he walked up, she introduced herself and commented on the chilly day while trying to avoid musing over his unblemished clothing more appropriate for a horse show.

He glanced at her briefly, his face drawn into a mask of impatience. "I work best alone. No distractions. So if you don't mind."

The horse paced back and forth, its energy elevating.

Max took off. Marissa stood her ground. She noticed the expensive boots, polished to perfection, unfamiliar with mud. "Pardon me, but may I speak with you a moment." She smiled and casually leaned against the fence.

"I have a conference call soon. On top of a full day. But what is it?"

"With all due respect, you haven't owned a horse before, have you?"

He adopted an amused smirk but didn't answer.

"May I show you something?" She went to the opposite side of the ring fencing. Harlequin stopped his abrupt, disjointed movements and came near. She began her soft communication with the horse. A bag of apple slices came from her jacket. Harlequin steadied and visibly untightened as he focused on Marissa. Soon, the horse placidly followed her back and forth along the far side of the pen, waiting for her command.

Marissa left the animal and returned to Mr. Langley. She spilled everything she knew. He listened, checking his watch on occasion. His blood-shot eyes came to rest on her face and glazed into dullness. She cut off her pitch.

He came to life and chuckled. "You women," he said, rubbing his face. "With you, everything is about developing relationships. Relationships, relationships, relationships." He released a little snort.

Her head tilted downward. She scuffed the dirt with her shoe and grinned. "You have no idea what a compliment that is to me." Her head rose. "Anyway, building bonds, using a little understanding also works with a horse."

"I'll keep that in mind," he muttered and released the latch to enter the pen. Harlequin's glittering eyes pinpointed on him. The man stepped inside and turned to secure the gate. Harlequin charged, snorting and stomping. The cringing man flattened himself against the wood. Harlequin bypassed, wildly whipping about. The man's trembling hands fumbled with the latch. Marissa was already there, pulling him out and securing the gate. Langley bent over his knees, panting. Then both human heads swiveled toward the house. A voice hollered.

Nathan ran and waved both arms above his head, screaming, "Ma-a-a-r-i-i-i-s-s-a!" From her uncle's warbling throat, her name had never sounded so shrill. "Ma-a-a-r-i-i-i-s-s-a!" Teetering, the man's arthritic feet seemed to stab the December-moist earth as he attempted a descent of the first hill.

Alarm slammed about Marissa's chest. Was the kitchen on fire? Had house demolition workers arrived? Her face as well as Mr. Langley's pulled into lines of confusion and questioning. They heard Harlequin walloping the dirt in the pen.

Rear hooves blasted the fence and made the wood rumble and shudder, but they could not take their eyes off frantic Nathan.

Marissa shaded her eyes from the angled morning sun, and she shouted, "What's wrong?"

He was out of breath, and his head fell back slightly as he yelled, "Help me catch her!"

"Who, Uncle?"

He pointed in their proximity. "The . . . the . . . oh! . . . The butting thing."

Marissa and Mr. Langley turned to look. Unnoticed, Brianna had wandered up, gone under the fencing, and stood watching Harlequin flail the air with his body while his mane thrashed like charcoal-colored fingers ripping the air.

"Uh-oh," said Mr. Langley. "This won't be pretty. That Arabian has hooves like scimitars. Your goat will be sliced to ribbons."

"Won't happen," said Marissa with a smile dawning. "Watch."

Langley must have thought she was crazy until Harlequin's frenzied bucking and wheeling quickly slowed and ended. Nathan came running up, undulating like an old camel. Gulping air, he let Marissa brace him and sling one of his arms over her shoulders.

"Brianna will be okay," she assured Nathan as the goat took two small steps forward, then hip-hopped as she was prone to do.

Harlequin gazed at the much smaller goat, seeming to come out of the spell that had driven him to madness, remembering where he was, what he was. He responded like a well-adjusted horse once again, moving toward that harmless member of the animal kingdom, curious to know how the goat felt about the day. The horse, ears at a more relaxed angle, his eyes having lost the circle of white around the dark orbs, let his head bend to meet the soft shoulder of the goat and the horse sniffed. He raised his head and gently shook it as a shudder was seen along his withers, releasing the last of his tension. Harlequin stood placidly as the goat played around the pen.

Marissa reached into her pocket. She bent low and called Brianna. Lured by the apple, the goat came within Marissa's reach. She pulled the animal under the fence and gathered the big lump into her arms and turned to go. "Come on, Uncle," she said to the old man spent and hanging on the fence. Her head nodded in reference to Mr. Langley as she spoke again to her uncle trudging by her side. "You know, if he wants to get himself killed, we can't do the first thing about it." They slowly ascended the hill. Halfway to the house, she looked back. Mr. Langley, retreating to the stable, gave a flimsy wave and a chagrined smile. Before long, he piled into the Land Rover and left.

CHAPTER THIRTY

MARISSA entered the office door of Peach Country Commercial Realty one more time. Two weeks had rolled by, with her negotiating Atlanta traffic, trying to get hold of Abe Silverstrike's ear but being put off with appointment cancellations and rescheduling. She approached the receptionist's desk, praying for success in finally meeting the man who held Nathan and Max's whereabouts in his whimsical hand.

"He'd better be in today. I've just about had it," Marissa said candidly to the receptionist.

The woman bobbed her head. "Your appointment is as good as gold."

"Ahem," said an older man standing in a doorway of the busy lobby. "You must be looking for me." He pointed to his name on the door and grinned in a way that struck Marissa as falsely compliant.

She walked to him and held out her hand. "I'm Marissa Manning."

"Follow me." They went down a hall to a suite of offices and entered his space. He gestured to a chair. She took a seat as the man rummaged in his desk and brought out a miniature television. "You mind? I missed this the first time it aired. I'll put it on mute." He plugged the television into the wall and screwed in the cable wire, not waiting for her answer.

Marissa's brows bounced slightly. "Sure," she replied.

He messed around with some dials. His face lit up, obviously finding the programming he wanted. He sat back in his seat. His vision, disinclined to leave the delight of his eyes, wavered as he tried to post his sight on her. The phone rang. He took the call, asking questions, giving directions to the person on the line while his eyes never left his viewing. Then down the receiver went. It rang again. He punched a button. "Hold my calls, Maybelline, or I'll never get done with this meeting."

Marissa sighed. "Perhaps you mean, never get started."

He looked at her boldly. "Right, right." He absentmindedly reached in his drawer and pulled out a cigar and studied her. He suddenly noticed the tobacco held by his fingers and tossed the cigar into his drawer. "You know, I saw that crinkling of your nose. You remind me of my oldest daughter. Got five daughters keeping me on my toes actually. The elder puts up a fuss if she catches me smoking. Bet you're somebody's health-minder, too."

"He seldom listens, either."

"Right, right. Now what's this about your worries with the contract-" His vision zipped to the screen. "Come on. Sink that putt. All right Phil! Way to go." With one hand, Silverstrike loosened his tie and stayed hunched with concentration at the screen.

"Fears, not worries," Marissa corrected, referring to the contract. He remained distracted. She wanted to scream. But she thought about Uncle Nathan's words, telling her to use reason not confrontation. She leaned in and spoke in a calm tone. "Mr. Silverstrike? Are you listening?"

His head jerked back. "Huh? Oh sorry, sorry. You're looking at a man sorely in need of some diversion. I give too much of my life to this company." He took a deep breath and rested back on his chair. "What can I do for you and your uncle, Miss Manning? Sounds like you have some questions about the contract."

Marissa swallowed and tried to slow her heart. The tension was worse than any budget meeting she had held at Atlanta Accolade. "Mr. Silverstrike . . . my uncle dearly loves his farm."

"O-o-o-o, don't I know that. He took me all over the place and told me every family story he could recall. There must have been a tale for every inch of those acres."

"Mr. Silverstrike . . . that piece of land is the thing that keeps him alive."

"I believe it. That entire area is prettier and filled with more wildlife than a quiet, misty, dawn on the course at Gleneagles in Scotland." He grasped a golf hat from a hook on the filing cabinet behind and pointed to the embroidered name, smiling. "Been there." He gave a dismissive tilt to his head and a regretful line to his lips. "Eight years ago. Last time I saw a vacation."

"That's unfortunate, Mr. Silverstrike. But I'm failing to get to my point. You see, that farm has a lot of value."

"Hold on, now. Hope you're not trying to claim he didn't get a fair price. Because if you are, you can have your lawyer contact my lawyer. Matter of fact, I don't know why you just didn't bring him along today." Dark clouds brewed in the depth of his weary eyes. His shoulders slumped, and he went on a search for his cigar again.

"Mr. Silverstrike, the price was quite fair but-" The receptionist knocked and came through the door.

"The Fed Ex guy wants your signature on the package, Abe."

"Uh!" He threw down the cigar, heaved himself to standing and plodded from the room.

Marissa also got up, trying to release some of the energy building in her chest. Another failure, she could tell. The man wasn't going to budge an inch. She crossed her arms. The barest sound from the television reached her consciousness. Golf talk. She walked around the desk and stared at the screen showing a replay of a tournament earlier in the season. Phil Michelson was making a charge. Marissa's face changed in an instant. She knew that feeling of triumph. Rare but oh so sweet. She sat down. A piece of golfing equipment, a utility club, leaned in one corner of the room, behind the desk. Her hand went to her chin just like her mother was prone to do when she pondered a problem. Marissa reasoned. She hadn't been building bridges with the man. No common ground. No appeal through mutual understanding.

Mr. Silverstrike reentered the room. "Okay. So. Back to our talk. The price. You're bugged about the deal your uncle and I settled on."

"No, sir. . . . I've been trying to tell you-."

"Whoa, miss, if you're claiming our check was no good, that won't fly."

"No, sir. The funds are in his bank account. I came to talk about the agreement. The one you made with him."

"Hold it. Okay, so we're back to the contract. Do you know how many go through this office each month? My memory isn't perfect." He punched the button on his speaker. "Maybelline, bring me the Manning contract. Almost a year ago. From January, I think." He went back to the golf match.

Marissa leaned in his direction and waved her hand. "Mr. Silverstrike, we don't need the contract. What I speak of isn't in there."

The secretary interrupted by entering and placing the folder with a wad of documents before him.

"Are you telling me we left something out?" Silverstrike asked Marissa. The secretary waited, worry plugged into her features. He started slashing through the pages. Marissa started to answer, but he raised a palm, silencing her. He held up two papers for the secretary's eyes. "What's this doing in here, Maybelline?"

"I don't know, sir."

"I'll take care of it. You can go." The secretary walked out. An odd little smile came over his face. "So, Miss Manning. You're concerned about the chat your uncle and I had. About his request to live rent free while the company generously cools its heels before we move into development."

Ire bubbled in Marissa's brain. She fought to calm herself. "Yes, that agreement, but . . . I confess; I'm distracted by that lob wedge you have in the corner. What is that? A sixty degree?"

"Wow. You know your golf. What's your handicap?"

"Mine's a five, but I haven't been playing much," she raced to say. "My business, like yours, keeps me from that pleasure."

"Woo-wee. A five. That's striking. My goal is to break ninety for once in my life. But that dream may be passing at sixty, since I'm not getting any younger."

"I sympathize with you there." Her body gave a little jerk and she smiled. "You know, just the other day in a tennis tournament, I won a round of golf for two at Woodmont. Why don't you meet me tomorrow, and we can discuss my problem and have some fun at the same time?"

"Well . . . ."

She gently cocked her head to the side. "We business people need a little diversion once in a while." She smiled.

"All right. I can't think of anything better." He handed her a card. "Text me the time on my cell. I'll be there. *That's a promise.* Why the surprised look?"

Marissa shook her head. "I don't know." She rose from her chair. "I look forward to tomorrow. I'll enjoy telling you how much my uncle means to me."

"Oh, I already see that."

Marissa departed the office and building. She was about to step into her car when her cell phone rang. She didn't recognize the number. Nevertheless, she plopped down on the driver's seat and pushed the talk button.

William Dash's voice came across the miles, asking if she would breeze on down the following weekend. Clemma and Alexa giggled and talked in the background. He was taking them on a helicopter ride for their Christmas gift. Now it sounded as if the girls were bent on begging as they clamored in the background. Could she join them, William asked? He'd make sure it was worth her while and safe. He would be at the controls.

A wall of reticence came up in her head. Handing over command didn't come easy for her.

Chapter Thirty-one

MARISSA came from her car and noticed a saucer-size, scarlet flower atop a tall stalk in a cachepot that sat on the kitchen stoop. A package lay beside the floral trumpet, safely out of Brianna's range. Marissa ran over. Amaryllis, known for its arresting blooms, transformed the gray, weather-worn steps. An envelope addressed to her rested on a loaf of lemon pound cake. The note was from the prayer women, telling her not to worry, that they knew Marissa well. They felt sure the other woman, the one so distraught on that rainy night at the church, must be terribly wrong. They closed the note telling her that they were praying for both of them anyway, as everyone needed God's help on a daily basis. Marissa gathered the things and stepped buoyantly into the kitchen.

The table was absent of Uncle Nathan, normally waiting expectantly that time of day. Marissa exited the house and checked the front porch, the stable, and the grounds. She reentered the house. He wasn't napping in his improvised bedroom with the cabbage rose walls and the head-knocking chandelier. The house whispered silence, and she hoped to find him near the resting television, asleep where he sat. She moved at the speed of creeping fig vine, down the short hall leading to the living room. Her footfalls barely made a sound. She turned the corner and found him in his big, comfy chair. Seated, the lanky man appeared smaller than normal and slightly out of it. He gazed dully at her across the room, without recognition. Family memorabilia covered his lap, seemingly forgotten.

"Uncle?"

He said nothing, only stared blankly.

Marissa felt a stab to her emotions, and she came closer. "Uncle Nathan?" She stood within touching distance. He slowly angled his head up. "Are you okay?" she asked softly.

"Whu-?" He looked down and seemed to notice the things in his lap. "I. . . I must've been asleep." His large hands fumbled trying to straighten photos, graduation programs, certificates, and newspaper clippings, causing some to fall to the floor.

She knelt down before him. "Are you okay? Are you feeling all right?"

"Yeah. Would you make me a cup of tea?"

"Certainly." She gathered the mementos and went to the kitchen.

She made the tea strong and added lemon and his favorite alfalfa blossom honey. She poured up a cup for herself and took it to the other room.

He reached for his cup. "You were gone a long while today. It didn't work out with Silverstrike, did it?" His tone was solemn. He took a sip of tea as if to prepare himself for her answer.

"We did indeed meet and talk. It's not a lost cause. We're playing golf tomorrow morning. I'll be able to get breakfast for you two before I go."

"What vittles are we having tonight?"

"I'll put a chicken in the oven. . . . Talked to Marie Evans today. About her meal service. When I'm no longer here, it would help to know that you and Max are being fed sufficiently."

"I'll sign us up . . . well, I will *if Max and I don't have to go to the old folks home.*" He snorted and took more tea. "It's for sure they won't let me have goat milk there. And I heard they make you eat tapioca pudding morning, noon, and night. Can't stand the stuff. Course, Max likes anything. But he won't like them widurs pinching his cheeks."

Marissa rose from the sofa, feeling powerless. Condemnation hit her chest like pellets from a rabbit gun.

The next morning, she stood on the steps of Woodmont Golf and Country Club. The day was colder than the polished steel of her putter. Air as dry as stone, the course had somehow avoided a frost delay. Sun rays would change things quickly for the better.

In Marissa's head, an internal debate ensued as to whether it was best to turn her skills down a notch. A win regarding the defective contract needed the bulk of her concentration. She sighted Abe Silverstrike's beaming face across the parking lot. His pace was brisk. Bundled in winter clothing, he resembled a chubby Eskimo so cute you had the urge to hug him. He greeted her with more enthusiasm than a boy skipping school. He threw his bag on the golf cart and jumped in the driver's side.

Her place in the cart stolen, Marissa was brought up mid-stride, her arms frozen in their natural swing.

He gaped at her. "Now you just set yourself at ease. I always squire the ladies around. My wife would be disappointed in me if I didn't serve you as a gentleman should, especially when you've asked me to be your guest." Vapor came from his broad smile.

She got in, trying to forget her driving lesson with Max. She guided Abe Silverstrike around the clubhouse to the practice range where he peeled off a bulky layer. The long expanse of winter rye lazed under the brilliant sunshine and a broad blue sky wisped curling lines of white that signify a chilling stratosphere. They began their earnest hitting. From the side of her eye, she monitored his awkward swings and his deepening frown. She walked near. "Abe, do you know you're twisted?"

"Huh? Can't be."

She laid down a club at the tip of his shoes. The imaginary line shot fifteen degrees to the right of the range pen he aimed for. She corrected his shoulders.

His next swing carried the ball high and dead at the pen. He grinned at her. "By golly, I like that!"

Marissa returned to her own practice, wondering how and when to broach the subject that consumed her. After a while, they began their game. At the first tee, she made an impressive drive. Abe's effort died on the vine. He plopped in the cart appearing a little disappointed and zoomed away, jerking back Marissa's head. She noticed Abe's line of sight switching back and forth as he commanded the cart. It was a stunning day, but his eyes preferred to scan the rough rather than the spectacular beauty of the landscape in its entirety.

They took their next shots. Abe's stroke veered off target, and he went on a search for his ball. Marissa laid up for an easy putt. Par. Irony laughed at her. For once, she wasn't dying to beat the socks off a guy, but losing to her present partner, a crippled dove, wouldn't be easy.

The next hole continued in the same manner, except that Abe's driving became more and more reckless as his emotions became frenetic. Again his eyes scanned the tall growth lining the fairway, not watching where they were going. The cart bottomed out with a bang on a drain but kept going. Marissa's grip tightened on the handhold at the side of the cart roof. Aiming to reach Abe's ball snuggled next to a tree, the cart careened over the next hill. Marissa's rapidly beating heart protested and her unsheathed eyeballs threatened to fall out.

She lightly touched Abe's forearm. "Could you take the hills a little slower, Abe? I don't want to be eating dirt today."

"Oh my gosh, I'm sorry," he said.

"No problem. It's just that I had a close call recently."

Abe's putting fell apart on the green, and he lost eight strokes there. With another rabbit start that threw Marissa's head back again, they dashed to the third tee. While Abe prepared to hit, she wondered what could possibly make the man warm up to her subject. This day, this outing was her last chance. An ache was emerging in the violently flailed vertebrae of her neck. To her side, the wind whipped dead leaves into a crazy dance. She could feel her optimism plummeting. *Whack.* The man hit another slice, straight into the woods. He clearly was not enjoying the day. They zipped to the area, once more causing Marissa's heart to drop in her chest as her driver stormed across the horizontal on a steep hill, leaning her slightly out the side like a floppy golf towel.

Marissa helped him search for his ball among the winter-browned vegetation. He popped up from a mass of winter-desiccated weeds. "It's okay! I found a substitute! A Titleist!" He dropped his find in the fairway and blasted away, landing the ball in a good spot. With another whiplash, the cart plowed on to Marissa's ball. She got out, rubbing her neck, wondering why in the world she thought her idea of building a bond would have the least bit of merit. Utterly imprisoned by his golfing struggle, talking contracts and honor was obviously the last thing on his mind. She should have simply had it out with him in the office and been done with it.

As they traveled to the green, Abe almost veered into a bunker, hindered by his vision scanning the rough like radar.

Marissa worked up a wan smile. "It's a ways ahead, but there's a woodchuck residing in the rocks surrounding the fourteenth green. I take it you're hoping to spy some wildlife."

He shot her an amused look. "Oh. Not primarily. My eyes are always on a hunt to find a few balls to make a dent in the passel I lose on every round. Eases my shame." He chuckled.

"If you don't mind, let me show you another tip for your drive when we get to the next tee."

"You are some nice lady. And what a golfer! You must have had lessons since you were three, like Tiger Woods."

"Actually, you're right. But from my dad. The best coach I ever had."

They putted out and moved to the fourth hole. At the tee box, Marissa made some adjustments in his stance, urged him to come more from the inside. His ball leapt from the club, straight and true. Abe's entire body was animated with happiness; but, mindful, he moved the cart gently down the fairway. She guided him in a layup to the green and made a change to his grip on the putter. She parred the hole and so did Abe. The man tossed his putter above his head and caught it like a baton, singing his college fight song. They were about to leave the green when she noted a foursome that waited to tee off on the fifth hole. Things were backed up a little, and her opportunity had arrived. She would have Abe pause by the water cooler, away from the other golfers. There she could make her case. His grateful golfing heart was now as receptive as every putter's favorite dream: a cup centered and low, within an expansive funnel of velvet smooth grass. A can't miss stroke, a draino, a sure thing, a cinch . . . inescapable victory.

She dropped her putter in the bag and hopped into the cart. They took off smiling. The dry air had begun to chap her lips. Abe whisked the cart off the hill and down the path, speeding along the pond edge. Marissa let go her hold of the cart and leaned far forward to grab the pouch that held her lip gloss. Untethered, blissfully unprepared, Marissa's body was roughly tossed to the right as the vehicle made a sudden sharp turn to the left. She landed on the mud of the pond bank and rolled, ending her descent with a loud splash in the water. Submerged to her waist, she sat like a mystified wader. The foursome ahead, bogged down with ennui as they waited for things to get moving, turned their heads at the commotion. Every man broke into laughter as Marissa rose from her sylvan bath. Their mirth would have been properly dampened and immediately channeled to sympathy if the female victim had been middle-aged, frail, or a child. Unfortunately, Marissa, though dumped, looked incongruously fetching, her hair tossed and free, her cheeks pink with humiliation, her slender form drenched and trembling with cold.

She stormed up the bank. Abe, totally unaware he had ditched his partner, plucked a ball hidden among some rocks until spotted by him moments earlier. He held it in the sunshine, turning it, judging its worth.

The men at the tee box had quieted, aware of Abe's obliviousness until one man shuddered with another convulsion of laughter. That was all it took, and Marissa overloaded.

"Abe! What in the world are you trying to do?" she cried, her fists balled at her side. "You almost killed me!" To drain herself, she stomped her feet and wiggled. A puddle quickly formed.

Abe hunched, frozen with puzzlement. He stared hard at her. He glanced at the cart next to him, as though her twin should somehow be serenely seated there. Shock registered on his face. He pitched the ball into the woods, scooted into the cart, and came to her side. Grave in demeanor, he begged her pardon with exclamations about his gross stupidity.

The ride back to the clubhouse was peppered with Abe's effusive apologies and offers to spring for a different round of golf, on a better day, without his presence. Silent, fuming, she spurned his conciliatory efforts, so fed up with the man and her uncle's situation that it took everything inside her to dam up the tears that waited to break free. Not once had she succeeded in expressing her troubled heart and making an appeal in her uncle's behalf. *Inept. Foolish. Cold and wet.*

Abe rounded the clubhouse and took Marissa to her vehicle. She opened the trunk with her key fob and started to rise from the golf cart. "Marissa," he said, sounding wise and kind like a father. "I meant for this to be a great day for both of us. A little escape for me and something that might please you." He pulled a paper from inside a document folder he had brought along. He put the paper in her hands. "I think you must be looking for this."

While she remained seated in the cart and read, Abe jumped out and placed her golf bag in the trunk of her car. She turned to him. "I don't get it," she said. "Where did this come from?"

"My apologies, again. Nathan's copy was accidentally filed with ours."

"So you *did* sign an agreement allowing him to stay three years."

"Sure did."

"Nathan's memory's not so good."

Abe sat down in the golf cart. "Marissa, I can't coerce a client into having an attorney. And as I suspected, he barely listened at the closing and didn't give more than a quick glance at each paper he signed. I wouldn't take advantage. I've got a reputation to uphold. My business would cave eventually if I didn't. I'm a true capitalist and a true capitalist is in for the long run."

Her eyes watered and she sniffled, flashing him a smile. "Yes you are, and I'm proud to know you." She hugged him. "Don't be surprised if you get a call some day, requesting another golf game."

"I'll be there in a flash, but I'll let *you* drive the cart."

She laughed and stepped out. She gave him a funny look. "What about those people from Aiken and Aiken? They were at the farm a while back, itching to look at the place."

"Oh, the landscape grading company. They accidentally double-billed me on something else. I simply had them make it up by sending them to do their preliminary report in advance."

Marissa tossed her head back with a laugh. "Wow. What a crazy ride this has been." Her expression apologetic, she continued, "Not yours." A grin popped. "Well yes, yours too, but I deplore grudges. Until later, my friend."

"Bye, Marissa."

She thanked him again, and hurried inside her car to crank up the heater. Her sopping clothes almost dried by the time she reached home.

Chapter Thirty-two

ONCE you near St. Simons Island, your nose fills with stimulating scents hinting of the Marshes of Glynn and the Atlantic Ocean ahead. The odiferous air, even in December, suggests sun-heated mud, algae, peat from decomposing cordgrass, seaweed, wet sand infused with incalculable amounts of microscopic things living and dead; and predominately, that magical, transporting odor of saltwater with its specialized combination of minerals. Except for migrating birds, evidence of life appears reduced in winter to the untrained eye, yet the processes of nature are busily cycling onward; and like the beginning elements of a sea change, alterations of the heart slowly roll forward also unseen.

Arriving right on time after the long drive, Marissa entered the island airport office and was directed to the airplane housing area just outside. When she entered, Clemma and Alexa ejected themselves from their seats at a white plastic table and swamped Marissa with their excitement that she would be sharing their adventure.

"He's outside, Aunt Marissa," said Clemma, bouncing on her converse sneakers. "Don't you think this is the neatest Christmas gift in the world? I can't wait to tell my friends. I just hope we don't crash," she added, joking. Her sister, Alexa, suddenly adopted a serious mien.

Marissa's stomach rioted with nervousness. She had forced a plain bagel on herself before she left Woodstock and aimed her car down the length of the state once more. "Clemma, we have nothing to worry about," she lied and took Alexa's clammy hand in hers. They walked to the table. William entered the hangar.

"Hello, Marissa." He approached, brimming with confidence and good humor. Evidence of his extreme annoyance with her seemed to have faded away.

"Hi. Thank you for inviting me."

"I appreciate your being here today. My certification is up to date, but I didn't feel it was right to take the girls up without another adult. As I told you earlier, Daphne can't come."

"I know she'd be here if she could," said Marissa.

"She still has a bad bug she can't shake," he said. "I left her at home with magazines and lunch. Rest and quiet was my prescription."

"I'm planning to visit her when we're through today," said Marissa. "I'll be glad to drive the girls home for you."

"All right. Thanks." He smiled at Clemma and Alexa. "Alexa, you look a little pale. You know you'll be okay, don't you?"

"Yes, William, but could we fly real low . . . kind of skim along the ground?"

"That would be a very dangerous thing for a helicopter pilot to do. Altitude is our friend. More time to correct action. Fewer obstacles." Her expression brightened. "That a girl." He turned to Marissa. "I have to finish the preflight check. Have a seat. I'll be back in a little while." He left the hangar. She could see him as he worked. In the bright sunlight, his tan face exuded health and energy as he performed the inspection.

Alexa slid into the curve of a plastic chair. Clemma merged alongside a young mechanic who left his work table near the wall and headed toward a single engine plane parked inside. She blurted, "Do you think it's safer for a helicopter to be up high or near the ground?" He looked surprised at her lack of timidity as she joined him, uninvited, by the exposed chassis.

"Oh, yeah. High is much safer." He made some adjustments with a wrench. His hand wiggled parts. He peered at the complex innards. "Did you know it's massively harder to fly a helicopter than a plane? Much more risk. . . . The most dangerous time is just before take-off, when the helicopter lifts from the tarmac and hovers three feet above land." He stopped what he was doing and turned his attention from the engine to her.

"How come?" Clemma asked, while Marissa and Alexa tuned in their ears as well.

"That's when all h-. . . well, it's when all kinds of serious trouble can break loose if you're not experienced. A little too much cyclic and the helicopter can tip forward. That's called yaw, and it can cause the rotor blade to jab the ground and crack the machine into a thousand bits. It'd be like one of those brittle cones that hold ice cream being stepped on by your sneaker." Clemma's sight dropped to her foot. "Also, in that same case of hover before take off, if a pilot can't discern the specific vibration that signifies lean, and its not easy because there's always loud racket coming from a copter, well, that means he may bang one of the skids, and just like somebody turned out the lights, its all over. I've seen it on film, one giant explosion of parts the moment the rotor hits hard dirt." He grinned like he enjoyed flicking the teenager's emotions. "Course, it's better than a fall from the sky. But those rollovers have been known to leave a victim or two headless. A loose rotor is a giant knife screaming through the air."

"Yeah?" said Clemma, dumbstruck and moving two inches closer as if he could save her from disaster.

He slammed down the engine cover. "Yeah." He wiped his hands on a mechanic's rag. He flopped it over the fuselage. "But don't worry. William's got more experience piloting than this propeller has slicing the wind." He left the plane and went to another task somewhere outside.

Clemma walked to Marissa. "Did you hear that?" the teenager asked.

"Don't pay any attention. He's just trying to scare us." Marissa said. She took a deep breath, needing something to soothe the gyrations of her stomach. Her hand extended some bills. "Clemma, could you get me a ginger ale from the machine? Get something for you two, also."

"Thanks, Aunt Marissa." Clemma grinned at Alexa who jumped up, ready to accompany her sister who showed amazement that Marissa was actually going to lower her health standards and drink a soda.

Marissa looked outside. He was taking forever. Her emotions had a strange push-pull to them. Her mind tugged to know him better. Her feet shunned the idea of walking to the object that might be the means of her death.

Clemma plopped the ginger ale in front of Marissa who took the can and greedily swigged.

Thirty minutes later, they took their places in the hibernating helicopter. The girls sat in the back, Marissa up front. He began a safety briefing. Marissa's hands already grasped her harness waiting for the start of things. She spied William's questioning glance at her tight hold. She let go.

"So as I was saying, everyone, if you will keep mindful of those instructions, we'll have fun. Also, this helicopter is not mine. Let's keep the machine spotless."

Marissa thought, Oh great. I just hope I don't throw up.

"Where are we going, William?" said Alexa.

"To the ocean. To hunt for dolphins. Then we're making a landing in the middle of the Altamaha River." He paused and looked behind. "Trust me, Alexa." He smiled, reached back, and touched the tip of her nose. "Then I have permission to land at a fish camp farther up the river. We'll take a break and have lunch. After that, it's back the way we came."

Marissa had remained looking forward, her breathing shallow as she waited for him to proceed. Her right hand wound tight around the door handle.

He turned to her. "Any questions?"

She shook her head, afraid any word coming from her mouth would have a slight quiver.

"Oh, one last thing. When I hold up three fingers, I want you to remember the letter W. That will be my signal for Wolf Island. Look down and you'll see an amazing bird refuge. Okay, here we go." He donned his headset and began to work the controls. The machine surged to life. He spoke into the mouthpiece. The raucous engine and the air-beating blasts of the rotors ate up the words before they reached his passengers' ears.

Marissa held her breath until she realized her paralyzed state. Soon the helicopter lifted, and they hovered just as she learned they would. She tried to drive away the mechanic's words from earlier, and she fought not to move in case the slightest shift threw the whirling daggers out of balance. The girls released squeals muffled by their mouth-clenching hands. The machine lifted effortlessly into the sky. Marissa felt like she had unwarily strapped herself to a surreal amusement park ride in a bad dream. The girls, laughing and clapping, looked out and tracked their ascent. Marissa took a deep breath through her mouth and smiled. She looked out the window to the right, trying to withhold a jaw drop at the sight of houses tiny as peanuts and cars moving like rolling pistachios. Her mode of transportation was unlike the large jets she had traveled in and where she sat so insulated. Blithely streaming through the air, the urbane captain on the intercom usually reassured them so well, and the gravity-defying picture out the window became no more shocking than a living room video. But in a helicopter, it was much more real. No denying, she was flying.

William made an adjustment to the stick connected to something the other side of the floorboard. Without warning, they banked sharply to the right and straightened over the island, in the direction of the sea.

Chapter Thirty-three

RESEMBLING sequins lavished across a stunning gown, countless sparks of light reflected the majesty of the sea below them. The helicopter soared toward the horizon and the deep. Despite the spectacular view, a dozen questions flew through Marissa's mind. The only one she had asked on the phone was hardly sufficient, she realized. That day, she had wanted an accounting of his experience. He replied that he had been piloting a long, long time and left it at that. Now she wanted to know: was he instrument rated; had he filed a flight plan; did he remember to fuel up; what should she do if he became unconscious?

The man confidently trailblazing the air sent her a handsome smile. She turned away to look out the side window, deciding she'd rather do a free fall out the door than seem a quaking child. She sat straighter and adopted a placid expression at the air coursing past her view.

Minutes later, above the roar of the motor, William's voice rang out. He directed his passengers to look to the left. Marissa saw nothing. Clemma, behind William, had her face glued to the window. Once the girl sighted whatever it was below, she squealed her elation and pointed to aid her sister. Alexa strained, leaning toward Clemma's window. Exclamations burst from Alexa, but the uproar garbled her words. The enlightened girl jostled her sister like a rag doll. Through the back of the seat, Marissa felt Alexa's kicking feet. Marissa scanned the water, searching. William glanced at her. She responded with a negative shake of her head. He descended and banked into a left turn, causing her to catch sight of a dark moving shape and a smaller one. As they left the turn, he headed north, straight for the animals that slid up and down through the ocean. Marissa readjusted her conclusion from dolphins to a right whale and her calf, a species once near the point of extinction because the animals were easily harvested. Hunters knew right whales preferred the coastline rather than the great deep. A slow swimming speed hindered escape. Once harpooned, a thick layer of blubber made the carcass float. For the small, present-day population, the area off the

Georgia coast was a favorite calving ground. From the helicopter, the viewers enjoyed a once-in-a-lifetime sight.

William talked on his radio again. Marissa tried to decipher his drowned out words. It sounded as though he informed someone of the sighting and the location. Once William reached the spot, he circled, giving everyone time to study the whales and their carefree-rolling, water-spouting travel along the calm, protected coast. The jubilant girls screamed their comments to one another.

William saluted the whales, a farewell gesture as the helicopter route changed. They left the whales behind and headed toward land. As they reached clear sight of terra firma again, Marissa watched miniature waves stroke the vast shoreline. She noted the helicopter aimed for the broad sound marking a river opening, the grand Altamaha, the mighty watershed of Southwest Georgia. From the passengers' elevated vantage point, the river appeared to abruptly stop not so far from the mouth but, in actuality, disappeared into the thick vegetation shrouding the river course. The helicopter lowered in altitude. William's hand came up, making the *w* sign. They skirted estuarine Wolf Island laced with tidal creeks and dotted with white specks, egrets loafing in the limbs of live oak, bayberry, yaupon, and cedar or fluttering their wings in fluid, graceful flight. In the island marsh areas, fresh water mingled with salt as the tidal force waxed and waned. Brackish sloughs, the small ponds formed by seawater filling land depressions at high tide, spangled the afternoon rays. So high above, the observers of the haven missed viewing the teeming life of insects, crustaceans, reptiles, and fish that burgeoned within the life-conducive environment of a nutrient-rich ecosystem. The area appeared totally absent of human habitation or presence of any kind and it was. Wolf Island had been set apart, a sanctuary for migrating birds and a safe rookery for their nests. Upon closer inspection, other winged creatures of varying hues became evident, pelicans, herons, black skimmers, clapper rails, and oystercatchers. A month earlier, the migrating wood storks, plovers, sandpipers, ruddy turnstones, dunlins, and sanderlings had migrated south. "Get closer!" Clemma's begging voice yelled. William dismissed her request. Marissa's heart warmed at his caution. The helicopter moved away.

Their pilot found the wide, dark ribbon of water again, its path straight and sure at this point, a river daily pouring one hundred thousand gallons of sediment-filled fresh water into the ocean. The helicopter moved a short distance up river and began a slow descent toward a putty-colored sandbar squatting in the middle of the river. William eased lower and before touching, stabilized and hovered, one yardstick above the ground. Then he set his passengers down as lightly as a father puts a sleeping baby in its crib. He switched off the engine, and the rotors ebbing energy, finally came to a standstill.

Clemma threw off her harness. She grabbed the seat in front of her and pulled her body forward. "Can we get out, William? Please."

All Right. Let's have a look. They scrambled out. The girls ran around, exploring the tiny island. Marissa took a step out the door and gratefully found the sand to be packed and firm though damp.

William drew near. "Most of this sandbar will be underwater when high tide moves in."

"How did you know this was here?" Marissa asked.

"Dan. The owner of the helicopter. This is one of his favorite places to fish."

In that subtropical region, most of the oaks had kept their leaves, making a canopy along with slash pine, magnolia, and palmetto. The dense understory contained many shrubs and vines. William and Marissa looked upriver, at the broad expanse of water that came their way. The current seemed deceptively placid, except for a few eddies, while disguising a relentless power underneath the surface. Viewing the water from the side made it more clear to the mind that a giant force passed silently by, a massive flow to sea, carrying detritus, tree limbs, and dead animals, perhaps three hundred miles from the spot each item fell in or was snatched and became inextricably joined with the arm-twisting, branch-breaking current. Marissa sensed a lack of strength while standing in the middle of such incredible magnitude of will.

Clemma ran to William. "Can we get in the water? At least to our knees?" She bent down and began rolling up a pant leg.

Marissa's feelings wriggled with objection at the girl's question.

William chuckled. "No way, Clemma. You're skinny enough to get carried off like a sapling. But I have to object for another reason. Bull sharks travel up brackish water looking for rare delicacies."

She laughed and ran back to Alexa who heard and had gingerly moved from the water line.

William spoke wryly to Marissa, "She thinks I'm teasing."

Five more minutes of awed gazing passed. William clapped his hands like he broke a spell. "Okay. Let's load up. Shake your clothes and dust off all sand before entering."

Marissa and the girls did as he said.

The twirling rotors sounded their commanding thunder and the helicopter lifted and continued inland, following the river. They neared the town of Darien. William descended and hovered above a fish camp. A man came from a ramshackle building, waving his arm; the landing zone was clear. A good thing because a heavy duty fish line strung across two trees to air dry clothes, or a meandering truck and oblivious driver, or a running child could create instant disaster. The copter came down safely and everyone disembarked. William spoke with the man then returned to the helicopter to pull lunch from a compartment inside. The group walked a short distance to a picnic table. The girls fussed about the odor coming from a fish cleaning station upwind on the river bank. William ignored the complaining and passed out sub sandwiches he had made and bottles of ice cold water.

"Mm. This is a great sandwich," said Marissa. "Do you like to cook?"

"On oil rigs, with so many hungry men, there are well-trained chefs, but I've done my share of cooking. Nothing fancy. But I do appreciate good food like you serve at *Camellia*."

"Thank you. You'll have to come back. I think you'll like us better." She shied at the innuendo.

He took another bite of his sandwich, wisely deaf to Clemma's and Alexa's quibbling in whiny voices about a few ants traversing the wooden planks of the table. A gust of wind blew his napkin away and he chased it. When he sat again, he glanced at Marissa. "I meant to thank you the other day when I called. For checking on my house."

"No problem," she said.

He looked with directness at her. "I wouldn't have asked Daphne to do it if I'd known she hadn't been up to par for weeks." He murmured, "Kind of concerns me."

His cell phone rang. Marissa swallowed and felt relief the subject was cut short. He flipped the phone open, checking the number.

William got up. "Excuse me. It's important." He walked a short distance. "Beverly! Hello there. . . . You'll never guess where I am. . . . The Altamaha. . . . No kidding. . . . Yes, there's plenty to inspire a photographic artist. . . . Yes, sure I would. Let me check my calendar and I'll give you a call. . . . Okay. Talk to you then." William snapped the phone shut.

Alexa's head pivoted toward him. "Oh, I wanted to say *hi* to Beverly."

"Me, too." said Clemma.

"Sorry. We've got to eat up and hit the air road."

Marissa looked at him. He must have sensed her curiosity.

"A good friend," he said. He sat down and commenced eating. He ate quickly, staring at the river streaming past. The girls talked incessantly about their adventure. William jumped up, threw his trash in the barrel, and trotted to the helicopter. He reached inside and pulled out a camera and added a powerful lens. He moved closer to the bank. "Clemma, Alexa, come here! There's a river otter on the other side." The girls left their seats and raced to the water edge. William snapped photos. Marissa still sat at the table, wondering why he didn't think she would be interested. She rose and joined them. The sleek creature lazed in the sun, then noticing them, dove in the water and tumbled like a hyperactive clown set on making the girls giggle. Done with performing, the otter zipped from river to bank where the animal cleaned and stroked its fur. Someone in the parking lot close by beeped a car horn, and the animal scooted into the water and swam downstream.

Marissa offered to take a photo of William and his sisters. The girls swung their arms about William and he beamed proudly. Then William offered to do the same for Marissa. The girls stood under her arms, chicks beneath her wings, and the image was caught. They headed to the table for a final clean-up when the fish camp manager strode from his office.

"Now that's just *sad* when both parents can't be in the picture at the same time," the manager said, whipping the camera from William's hand. "Line up. I'll get the pic' for ya." The girls laughed. William had an amused look. At that moment, Marissa wouldn't have minded being plucked off the ground and dropped in a far away swamp by the marsh hawk observing all from a tree limb. The manager gestured. "Come on! Come on! Move together. That's right. Good. Now, smile. *Parents, too.*" A photo was snapped, memorializing the day.

They loaded things in the helicopter. William paused before they got in, to explain they would travel a few more miles inland before heading home. He wanted them to see the oxbow lakes, former bends in the river that had become isolated, crescent-shaped ponds and animal habitats once the meandering river had changed its course.

Alexa, crouched and staring at an empty snail shell in the dirt, perked up her head. "What do you mean, William? Why would a river move?"

He leaned down, put his hands on his knees, and looked deeply into her violet-blue eyes. His words came softly. "Sometimes, with the passing of time, a river finds a better path, sort of the way people do."

Marissa got into the helicopter, knowing the worth of those words.

Chapter Thirty-four

THE airport came into sight, and within minutes, the helicopter landed so smoothly that a nearby flight instructor gave a nod of admiration. After the girls unsecured themselves from their seats and bowled William over with affectionate goodbyes where he still sat, they raced to Marissa's car, arguing about who would get the front passenger seat. Marissa lingered by the helicopter. William continued doing the final end-flight steps in preparation for storing the machine.

Marissa had already thanked William, but hesitated shutting the copter door and walking away. Standing in the sunlight, her hand slid across her seat toward him, to regain his attention. He took his gaze off the clipboard.

"I'd like to make amends, again. Seems like I'm having to do that a lot," she said. "Could I make you dinner tomorrow night, since you do appreciate a good meal?"

He took his time with an answer. "Sure. I'd enjoy that."

She handed him a card with her address. "It's not hard to find. A cottage on East Beach. Is seven okay?"

"I'll be there."

"Great." She walked across the tarmac, letting the sunset wash her in gold. Palmetto palms near the hangar ruffled in the wind, and the clump of ornamental grasses waved their funny, tufted heads as she left.

Driving to Brunswick, she worked to think of a way she could get the girls to remove their earphones. Who could blame them, she thought. They probably shielded themselves from the reality ruthlessly approaching and trying to make them cringe in fear. Marissa shuddered at her selfish ulterior motive. Who cared who this Beverly person was? Why should it matter that the girls were acquainted with her? She drove on.

Marissa visited with Daphne and helped the girls relate their amazing outing. Daphne yearned for every detail as she sat on the sofa with her legs covered by a blanket. Later, she sent the girls to the kitchen to heat clam chowder for dinner.

She spoke to Marissa in the softest of tones about the latest medical report. The situation confused the doctors. Lab tests contradicted themselves. On days when the reports looked promising, she felt her worst. Alternatives were running out. The women grew pensive. The happy chatter of the girls sprang from the kitchen. A stirring spoon tapped against a pot.

Daphne fingered the soft tassels of the blanket. She smoothed the wool across her lap. "He's leaving in a day or two. To spend Christmas with his father. I'm glad I've had this time to get to know him. He makes me proud, even though I had nothing to do with who he is today. . . . When I'm gone, he'll understand why I didn't want to spoil my little season of happiness with sorrow."

Marissa glanced through the blinds behind the sofa. In the gray twilight, along the sidewalk, a lonely-looking woman walked her dog. "I think so, too, Daphne. He'll understand."

The girls ran into the room. "It's ready," said Clemma. "Want a bowl, Aunt Marissa?"

"No, thank you. The excitement from our trip is sapping the one ounce of energy I have left, so I'd better scoot home." They parted with affection.

At the beach house the next morning, Marissa scanned the living room, evaluating her dinnertime backdrop. The early hours had dawned overcast and cold, casting plainness and an aloof air about the room. She went behind the house into the utility closet and brought out a load of firewood. Wind whipped her pant legs as she returned. Each piece was positioned carefully between the andirons. Kindling was made ready, but she refrained from lighting the fire. She walked to the dining room, which held a great view of the sea; but for nighttime, a table near the fire would be best, she decided. She turned the round mesh table from the kitchen on its side and brought it through the doorway. Her hands grasped the edge of an aquamarine cloth and floated the linen circle onto the surface. White china took its place, matching the faultless white of the painted brick fireplace facade. The long mantle ledge formed by a line of jutting bricks lacked interest. From the bedroom, she took the tall mirror leaning against one wall, and walked it, by pivoting its corners, to the living room. At the fireplace, she took a deep breath, bent down, grasped the silver-finished frame at the bottom and heaved the mirror to mantle center. Eye-catching, she thought, rubbing her arms. Why hadn't she used her decorating sense on the place before now? She stepped back to study the scene. After a moment, she ran to the kitchen and grabbed a large serrated knife from a drawer. Out the front door of the house she trotted. Her goal was the vacant lot between two houses across the street. She meandered into the overgrown plot and found the perfect saw palmetto. She crouched and began her own sawing until she had two long stemmed, fan-like leaves, the size of giant platters. At the house, she reached for two heavy glass cylinders inside a cabinet. Normally used to house candles on the roof deck, the containers were washed until sparkling and filled with water and a single giant leaf. One on each side of the mirror like statements of importance, their star-like, geometric forms and their rich, deep-green color brought impact to the entire room. Next, she placed polished silverware and goblets beside the plates. Paper napkins, all she had available, would not do. Stumped, she sat down for a moment and then jumped up. She went to the kitchen drawer that held the dish towels. Her hands rummaged through the interior. She came out with a matching pair of towels, plain cotton, not too worn, having a nice white- on-white plaid weave. Her eye caught a spot. She dove under the sink for bleach. Opening the bottle, she said a quick prayer and daubed on the liquid. The stain melted from view. If it were only that easy in real life, she muttered.

Salmon patties filled her stomach at lunch, providing the strength to balance her checkbook. Seated in the dining room, she tapped the keys of her calculator. Minutes later, she came to a conclusion; she wouldn't be serving Chateaubriand. A little kitchen wizardry was required. An inexpensive skirt steak could be turned into fajitas, a manly meal. Anyway, something more formal might scare him off. He certainly had reason to be skittish.

She looked out to sea. Her spirit refused to be dampened by the dun-colored water capped with foam. Desolate gray beach. Gloomy clouds. A gull, like a hungry, lost pet, flew back and forth, head down, searching for something to slide down its gullet. Nothing could tarnish her mood, even the absence of income and a checkbook that held only enough for the meal at hand and nothing more. Tomorrow, she thought, holding herself together. Tomorrow she would form a plan.

She gathered her purse and drove to the store.

That evening, she dressed in navy slacks and white silk blouse. At her throat she placed a necklace with tiny drops of turquoise. Matching stud earrings highlighted the curve of her elegant cheekbones.

Shortly before he was due to arrive, she lit several candles but chose not to create any implications of intimacy by placing one on their table. She hoped that if she did get a good look into his eyes, awkward discomfort would not be muddying their blue hue.

The doorbell rang right on time. She opened the door and welcomed him from the damp chill. He handed her a bottle of wine, which she ran to place in a bucket of ice.

She came back to the room with two plates, each with a single delicate fig wrapped in mascarpone and dressed with almond slices. She offered him a seat by the front window and handed him his appetizer. An almond piece tumbled down her fig. She picked it up and placed it in her mouth. "Mm."

"You must like almonds."

"I adore them. My favorite snack, actually. Do you know the scent of almond can drive away anxiety?"

"Wish I'd known that. Things can get tense on an oil rig, especially when there's indication of an impending blowout. Of course, the guys might consider my snacking under pressure a little dainty."

She laughed. "I love your sweater," she said. "It looks like it came from the brain of Ralph Lauren or Perry Ellis."

"Thanks. I've got several. I used to get them straight from the manufacturer, a plump, widowed lady born to wield knitting needles. She has a tinkling laugh and an eye for design. Her half-hidden shop is on a side street in Lisbon."

"Portugal?"

"Yes. But her wares are more economical than an American designer label." He chuckled. "Crucial, when selling to a boy from Sumter, South Carolina. However, she used to let me sweeten the deal by bringing her a pair of lobsters from the market."

They talked on. She questioned him about his favorite haunts around the world. He seemed relaxed. She brought him into the kitchen. She heated the grill pan and sautéed the onions and peppers, which sent an inviting, hunger-inducing aroma around the room. He looked on, questioning her about the house. She told him the story as she braised the spicy steak strips. He opened the wine and poured glasses. Warm tortilla wraps came from the oven. She pulled a salad from the fridge. They sat down before the fire and ate. They spoke of the island and the magnificent Altamaha. She wanted to know more about his flight training, and she learned he had begun his quest to fly helicopters as an eagle scout at seventeen. He asked about her uncle. She told William of her needless travail on Nathan's behalf. Informed by Daphne about the current problems, he asked about the future of *Camellia*. She avoided worried expression or dire prediction. She tried to be positive. Lightness seeped into their conversation, and soon he was joking about that awful day, telling her the scar on his forehead had only recently faded. Neither broached the subject of the night he had kissed her all coated in blueberry.

Finished with the meal, they rose, and they pulled the table from its position by the fireplace. Marissa angled two slipper chairs in front of the glowing embers. She brought coffee and two slices of snow white coconut cake from the kitchen.

He tasted the dessert. "Wow. You can't find anything this good except in America. My mother once won a blue ribbon at the fair for hers."

"Oh, that's intimidating. I hope mine's up to her standards."

"I can't tell a difference. How'd you know this was a favorite of mine?"

"Pure luck."

They ate and the wind howling outside was unable to disturb their small enclave of warmth and tranquility.

He put his empty plate on a nearby table. His eyes grew serious. "I wanted to speak to you about Daphne. I've been worried. Something doesn't seem right."

"Really?"

"Her coloring has changed over the months. She's thinner. Do you know anything I should be aware of?"

Marissa hopped from her seat and gathered dishes. "Winter," she answered without looking at him. "Every woman loses some of her sparkle without the summer sun. And this flu bug, or whatever she has, will soon pass." She aligned dirty silverware on one of the plates, and she gathered the dishtowels that had served admirably as table napkins.

He rose. "I'd better get going."

She turned and faced him, her mouth parted slightly as she scrambled to think of some way to keep him longer without going so far as to demand he help with the dishes. A dessert plate fell from the stack in her arms, but he saved it.

He took the goblets from her fingers. "Wait a minute. I can't leave you with a messed up kitchen."

A gentle smile spread across her face. "No you can't," she teased.

During their cleanup, they listened to a jazz station on the radio, and they laughed about the bold refrain of an old Dinah Washington song that warned a threatening party, *"My man's an undertaker, and he's got a coffin just your size."*

Another chorus sashayed by. Then the refrain ramped up the strong message again. Marissa washed a dish and mimicked the lyric. Then William acted the part, changing the words slightly: *"That's right. Her man's an undertaker. He's got a coffin just your size."* He whirled the drying rag above his head, then brought it down, snapping it hard in the air like a weapon. They broke into more laughter. They sang louder. The song ended and Marissa and William tried to catch their breath. Then they stood looking at one another for a second but resumed their normal attitude. William looked for something to dry, and Marissa found leftover tortillas to put in the fridge.

The doorbell rang. William glanced at Marissa. "Who in the world could that be?"

"Don't know." She walked to the front door, with William following.

He touched her arm. She paused. "Would you like me to answer it?" he asked.

"Thanks, but no." She pulled the door open, and Jacquelyn spilled inside the house, expelling shrill hellos, her arms thrown wide to hug Marissa. The girls laughed and remained entangled. A man in military uniform waited on the porch. He was brought in apologetically by Jacquelyn who introduced him to Marissa and William.

Marissa expressed her happiness at finally meeting Russell, and she took him further inside the living room where she pulled up two extra seats between the slipper chairs.

"I was beginning to get worried. I've been trying to get you to answer your phone for almost three weeks," exclaimed Marissa to Jacquelyn. "When I called the studio, Mikki would only say you were on a secret vacation. My feelings were starting to get hurt."

"I'm so sorry, Marissa. It was a very sudden departure." She gazed at her man. "I left my phone and laptop behind." Russell helped her out of her jacket. "As a matter of fact, I have something to show you."

Marissa tried to interpret her friend's wide grin. Jacquelyn pulled off one of her gloves. A diamond wedding band flashed its brilliance.

Chapter Thirty-five

THE living room at the beach house was suspended in a vacuum of awkward silence.

Jacquelyn's eyebrows rose questioningly. "Aren't you happy for me?"

Marissa wiped away a few tears. "Of course I am. It's just that my best pal is being taken from me."

Russell chuckled. "I'm willing to share her."

Marissa pushed a smile through, rose from her seat, and hugged the bride and groom.

"Thanks, for understanding," Marissa said to Russell. "Without her, I wouldn't have lasted more than a month on this island."

Russell looked at Jacquelyn and grinned. "I've known Jacquelyn since she was a skinny little girl, and all that time, I've watched her help everyone be something better." He turned to Marissa. "From everything I've heard, you've got the same trait."

"Me? No." Marissa shook her head.

Jacquelyn jumped in. "Yes, you." She turned to the men. "We met at the produce counter in the grocery store. Marissa saw my puzzled expression and explained how to open a pomegranate and the best way to cut a red bell pepper and avoid the seeds. Then I told her about Uncle Fred's diet changes. She made all these wonderful suggestions. We talked like we'd always been friends."

Marissa took over the story. "Actually, we discovered that we're both businesswomen, although Jacquelyn had two years compared to my two weeks. She invited me to her church and gave me a coupon for a free class at her studio. Once I discovered she liked Jane Austen novels and baby back ribs with succotash, she couldn't get rid of me. So for almost a year, we've parked in each other's ear, unable to live without the other."

William joined in, speaking to Russell. "The short time I've known them, they run in and out of each other's lives like basket weaving."

Marissa agreed with William, and she found herself looking at his cable-knit covered arms. She offered coffee and went to the kitchen with Jacquelyn. Once within privacy, the women talked about the things on their hearts. Marissa required a total summation of Russell's proposal. Then Jacquelyn fired her own questions.

"Just a friendly dinner, that's all," Marissa said, explaining William's presence.

Jacquelyn gave her a stare. Marissa refused to elaborate.

Marissa angled her head past the kitchen doorway. The two men had hit it off. They were deep in conversation.

Jacquelyn put her head on her friend's shoulder for a second as they got the coffee tray ready. "I can't begin to tell you how happy I am."

Marissa poured coffee. "And I am so thrilled for you."

"Mama and Daddy are disappointed that I skipped a formal wedding, but I couldn't see any good reason to wait. Time is precious for us."

"Well, Mrs. Lancaster," Marissa said, smiling and picking up the tray, "I am honored to serve you and the captain."

They joined the men.

After Jacquelyn and Russell left, William stood around, quietly watching her carry a few things to the kitchen.

She returned to the room. "Would you like to sit by the fire a while longer?"

"A minute or two." He took a seat in the slipper chair. His glance went from the glowing embers to her on the other chair. "How much longer will you be here?" he asked.

"I have to stop by *Camellia* in the morning. Then I'll be on my way to Woodstock."

"Until?"

"I hope to reopen March 1st. So I'll be back the last week of February. I've got an event to carry off, first."

"What's happening?"

"The foundation my father started has a gala every few years. I plan the entire thing and present the scholarships. The event is held near Atlanta, the second Saturday in February. I was wondering if you would attend? As my escort?"

"I'd be glad to, but this winter, I'll be in and out of the country. More assignments."

"I'll send you an invitation, and you can let me know."

"Is your offer because you heard about the young men of South Carolina? How they're forced at birth to attend cotillion where they're taught not to gag on turtle soup and not to step on their date's gown?"

"Why, yes. Your fine reputation precedes you."

"Thank you. I do apologize, though, for missing the lesson on proper, first introductions with attractive females. On that day of instruction, I was teething, I think. Maybe it was diaper rash that kept me out. Anyway, I sense you've forgiven me for our rough beginning."

"Georgia girls are trained at an early age to be incredibly reconcilable," she said, "although some gentlemen have found them to be, at times, excessively cranky."

He countered with several more jokes. Marissa was sure she had never laughed so much with a man in one evening.

He grinned and stood up. "Thanks for an excellent meal."

They moved to the small foyer. They closed the night with a few last words. He opened the door and a blast of cold dampness blew in. He turned and looked at her before he stepped onto the porch. "Stay warm," he said, and walked away.

Marissa closed the door. She turned and leaned against the wood. The candles still burned. The coals of the fire still gave off heat. The palmetto leaves against the white of the fireplace startled her eyes with their uncommon beauty. Never had she loved the beach house more. How had she ever been so callous as to call it a beach shack? It was a mansion of memories, a cataloguer of life. Her expression lost some of its cheer. Unfortunately, those walls could not tell the future.

She moved about the living room, blowing out the candles, straightening things. She always drenched a remaining fire before going to bed but, that night, she couldn't bring herself to do it. She went to the long settee and pulled off the four seat cushions, lining them up before the fireplace. In the bedroom, a nightgown went over her head. Socks cuddled her feet. With a small radio tucked under her arm, she carried three blankets and several pillows to her sleeping spot and stretched along the length of the cushions. She placed the radio by her head and turned the volume down until very soft. Her eyes watched the glowing embers rise and fall in brilliance. A crackle announced a shooting spark of light that flew in an arc and hit the fire screen where it burned out like a meteorite in the winter sky.

The radio announcer talked of sparkled gumdrops and gingerbread decorated with icing as music from the Nutcracker danced around Marissa's head. The wind rustled outside. Her eyelids slowly dropped. Minutes passed. She found herself in a turn-of-the-century kitchen shelved and stocked with baking items. Her hand reached for an old-fashioned ceramic bowl, yellowware with a line of blue near the rim. She placed the heavy bowl in front of her and allowed her hands to skim the immaculate apron across her stomach. The smell of freshly washed cotton came to her nose. She measured out flour and sifted until it swirled in the air in front of her face. She followed some fantastical recipe that came to mind, a recipe ornamented with an abundance of ingredients, an array too large to be found in any one cake. Two smooth eggs sat on the wooden counter. She cracked them and watched as they rolled like two happy children over a mountain of white softness. The sweetest, freshest, room temperature butter waited in a glass bowl. She continued randomly adding ingredients. Nutmeg caught her eye. She rubbed the hard brown piece across a grater and inhaled the sprite scent. Vanilla from an exotic place came off the shelf and added its golden brown liquid. A touch of honey dripped from a honeycomb. Cinnamon dropped from her measuring spoon. Then she let sugar crystals like glitter spill from a cup. The wooden spoon went into the bowl and she stirred. Around and around the spoon went. More little jars opened and their ingredients went in. Lighter and lighter the batter grew. As she lifted the spoon high, the batter followed, trailing upward, and as the spoon lowered, the batter floated down, circling inside the bowl. She poured her creation into a cake pan and then another. The batter never ended, filling pan after pan. Her laughter provided music for the sun-saturated room. A kitchen hearth, large enough to walk in, accepted her trays of cake pans. Marissa turned around and noticed the back of a little girl seated on a high stool, working at some task, a basket of eggs and a glass pitcher of milk in the background. Her red curls captivated Marissa. The child inched herself around the stool to gaze at Marissa. Loose ringlets spilled on one side of the girl's forehead and by one ear. Her brow was smooth as cream but splotched like her apron with flour. Bright eyes reflected happiness. A diminutive nose, two rows of shining teeth and lips the color of rose-lined peppermint candy led to a pert little chin. In her arms she held an apple pie, the crust flaky and golden. She extended her gift. Marissa found her feet frozen to the floor. As much as she tried, she could not move toward the child. An ache pervaded Marissa's chest. The child turned back to the counter and placed the pie there. She climbed down from her perch and walked to an oval window where she pointed to the view above her head, seeming to know what sight the window held. Then the child skipped from the room, her curls bouncing. For seconds, Marissa remained in her spot, then discovered one of her feet had shifted. She went to the oval window and looked toward a meadow. William worked at a planter, using shears to shape a camellia loaded with blooms. He looked up, saw her, and waited. Her hands donning mitts, she ran to the oven and pulled one of the pans. A pleasing aroma like nothing she had ever known thrilled her nose. She carried the cake to the window. William still waited. The aroma, visible like an iridescent stream, sought him. He closed his eyes and inhaled. The gardening tool dropped from his hand. Marissa fell deeper into sleep.

She woke at six, light softly washing the walls of the beach house. The incoming tide made its rushing, rhythmic sounds outside. She snuggled deeper into the womb of covers protecting her from the chill of morning. Her mind rehearsed the strange dream, and she regretted she had no time to bake. Then realization of everything she needed to accomplish within the hours of that day crashed into her waking, and she jumped from her bed.

She was at *Camellia* an hour later. Inside her office, she sat down at a desk of perfect order, empty of grocery lists, bills, and correspondence. She flipped her laptop open and composed an e-mail to Jacquelyn. Her fingers flew over the keyboard, expressing her concerns regarding Zoe as Byron's latest target. Marissa's anxiety poured forth for several paragraphs. Still flummoxed by the other part of the situation, she held back Zoe's revelation about Darrien's sudden attachment for Marissa. Then she delivered a *caveat*: "Don't respond until you have nothing to do, which considering your present circumstances, might be a long while. I'll figure out a solution somehow." She printed a copy, thinking a reread an hour later would show her whether she adequately conveyed the seriousness of Zoe's switch in affections. She turned off the laptop, pushed it to the edge of her clean desk, and laid the paper on top.

Then she decided her laptop wouldn't do for the next task. Something about pencil and paper made it more deliberate.

She wrote the title: *How to Make the Financial Stretch Until Income Returns in March.*

1. *Contact my brother about an immediate sale of the beach house. (I'd be in the clover if Dave agreed, but the beach house would be out of our lives forever. Consider as a last resort only.)*
2. *Sell Al. (He's boarded for free, taken care of so well, and he hates change. Only a very last resort.)*
3. *Cash in part of your 401K. (Not wise, if you want to eat something other than cat food in your old age.)*
4. *Find a temporary job for January and February. (Hey, dummy, who's going to hire at that slow time of the retail year?)*
5. *Borrow on the title to the car. (Oh, my gosh, you're smarter than that!)*
6. *Rent out the beach house for the winter months. (Hm-m-m . . . would it even be possible?)*

She studied the list, especially the last idea. Her head came up. Someone had entered the front door of *Camellia*. She laid the list down and got up. Her sight went to the e-mail concerning Zoe. She took the e-mail and put it in her drawer. Footfalls came down the hall. She stepped from her office. Byron Hewitt met her there.

Chapter Thirty-six

BYRON'S penetrating eyes were enough to make Marissa do an about-face and go to the kitchen. The hall and office were quarters too tight to deal with an unpredictable south Georgia bobcat.

Byron followed her without a word. Marissa went to the cupboard and pulled a stack of dishes, pretending a rearrangement was crucial.

Byron leaned against a wall. "No smile. When are you going to stop being mad at me?"

"I'm not mad at you. I just wish you would leave."

"See, you are."

She slammed the cabinet doors. "Look, Byron, your and my values are worlds apart."

He stared, not listening. "I've been wondering what happened to you. I don't mean that day you bulleted away without a word on your bike. Incidentally, that was a cute response you added to my blog. Thanks to your comments, I've lost all my fans. But it's all right because I'm reformed now. . . . Anyway, someone clued me in that you were in north Georgia."

"I wish you thought I was still there."

"Saw your car. Only the hundredth time I've driven by this place."

"*So what is it you want?*"

"A chance to be honest. Also, to make you an offer."

"What could you possibly do for me?"

"Well, from a former bad boy making up for obnoxious behavior, how about an interest-free loan? Whatever it takes to tide you over, and I do mean whatever."

She absentmindedly rubbed the edge of the counter and tried to look away. "What makes you think I need help?"

"See, that's what gives you away. If you didn't need a dime, you'd just say so. But you're curious to know how I inferred things are running slim."

"Everyone is not so adept when it comes to subterfuge, Byron."

"No they're not, thank goodness. That's my dominion . . . or was. So, a loan?"

"I'll handle my situation for better or worse."

"Well, you're always welcome if you change your mind."

"Now, kindly leave."

Byron moved closer. "Would you give me a moment to be forthright? I can't guarantee you'll like what you hear, but it will be truthful."

She walked to the sink, hunting for something, anything to wash. The vases under the sink came to mind. "If it will help get you out of here, go ahead." She bent down, opened the cabinet door, and grabbed the vases and a long-handled brush. The sight of plumbing pipes woke up her mind, and she thought of William just across the way, near yet so far. She rose with the items and plunked them down on the counter. She filled a plastic dish tub with hot, sudsy water.

He slid smoothly beside her at the sink and watched her every move. "I'm going to be as candid as it takes. No more games. No more trickery. I'm busted. . . . But what I'm going to say is not a lie." One of his arms went around her in back but loosely. "Like no other woman, you fill me with desire."

Marissa let the brush fall into the sudsy water and she turned to assail him with her words. His index finger touched her lips.

"Listen, for one moment, please," he said. "I'm telling you the unadulterated truth. I admit I treated you wrongly, made you think I was someone I'm not. Nevertheless, Marissa, our union would be worth exploring. You're different. I've lost all interest in other women while I still have hope you'll return to me. Remember I spoke of mysteries to be uncovered and known. I want to know you, completely, in every way our creative minds can conjure." His fingertips lightly stroked her back waistline. "Marissa, let me make you faint with pleasure." He pulled her close. Her hand went into the sink.

"*Get away from me*," she said, breaking from his grasp, holding the dripping bottle brush like a kitchen knife. A space of six feet separated them.

"You don't find me reformed enough, I see."

"No I don't." She tossed the brush into the sink. "Now wipe away your amusement and leave!"

He casually projected a strong look. "You haven't even begun to dissuade me. Come here."

Heart racing, she took a step back and blindly looked out the window. William picked a piece of litter off her dining area pavers and was about to come up the back steps. Her eyes narrowed at Byron. She leaned forward and tried to inject seriousness into the ridiculous words inside her head. "Listen, you'd better get gone. I've already got a man and he's an undertaker! With a coffin just your size!" She raced to the door, opened it, and grabbed William's hand.

Byron's chortling died the moment William was yanked into the kitchen.

William appeared puzzled at their entwined hands more befitting a devoted couple. Then, seeing that particular male before him, his face took on sternness.

Byron stood stiffly. "Okay," he said. "This definitely changes things." He moved toward the hallway. "I'll make my departure. But let me know if you change your mind on either offer." He walked through the hallway and the front room. They heard the entry door open and shut.

"Ugh!" cried Marissa to the ceiling as she dropped William's hand.

"That bad?" he jested. "Sorry. Most males have a reticence for lotion."

A smile almost broke. "Not your hand. It's that man who repulses me. He . . . I dislike him very much."

William's brow furrowed and his shoulders unconsciously pulled back. "Is Hewitt bothering you?"

"No." She put her hand up like a stop sign. "He won't be coming around here again. But now the smarmy guy is about to threaten Zoe's mental health."

"Zoe? I thought she and Darrien were a couple."

"Um, that's over. I can tell she'll be having Byron Hewitt's renewed interest. I spent a while this morning pouring out my worries to Jacquelyn." She flopped into a kitchen chair, exhausted. "Go read the paper on my desk. It explains almost everything."

He went to the office.

A minute went by before Marissa realized what she'd done. She flew from her seat and raced down the hall to her office.

"No. Not that," she said, turning pink. He placed the handwritten page on her desk. She brought the copied e-mail from the drawer.

She sat at her desk. He took the seat across from her and read the e-mail.

After a few minutes, he looked up. "What are you women doing, getting near such a narcissistic guy? Jacquelyn and Daphne already told me about him. They were very worried about you a while back."

"I came to my senses."

"So why did you and Zoe, not to mention a few other women on this island, get fooled by a self-centered worm?"

"Poetry."

"What!"

"I don't know. Call it a romantic air."

"It's all part of his scam. By the way, any man can write a few lovesick phrases."

"But they don't"

"Well, that's why they call us men."

She sat there, voiceless, weary.

"On another subject, forgive me for being a speedy reader. Monetarily, you have a problem, right?"

"Yes."

"But Daphne said you're covering the salaries while the business is closed."

"Only two more months. Their money is safe in my savings account, but that's all the funds I have. *Camellia's* mortgage payment and utility expenses are due again the middle of the month."

"Shouldn't you be looking after yourself and a little less after your employees? You know I'll take care of Daphne."

"Daphne and Isabel are part of me." Fatigue washed over her body, and she put her forehead in her hands. "I can't expect them to suffer a loss of income while I'm away, taking care of family responsibilities. Island activity is really subdued through January and February, which will give me time to have some plumbing work done for my uncle. Then I have the foundation gala to plan." She looked intently at him, hoping to hear assurance that he would try to attend.

"Number six on your list made sense to me."

Marissa tilted her head, confused.

"Six," he said again. "Renting out the beach house."

"Oh." She smiled weakly.

"I've got the perfect solution. My friend, Beverly, is planning to come to the island to do some photo nature studies. I suggested the winter months while it's quiet here." William grabbed one of Marissa's business cards from the desk and wrote down Beverly's name and e-mail address. He handed the card to her. "Won't hurt to try."

She nodded and was about to ask questions regarding William's friend, but he got up quickly.

"You have to journey through most of Georgia today," he said, "so I'd better not keep you. Just came by to drop off some thanks for last night and for checking on my place." He reached into his jacket and pulled out a small, wrapped package.

She tore off the paper. She stared at a beautiful copy of Jane Austen's *Emma*. She breathed in the leather scent. Her fingers skimmed the smooth grain and tooled silver lettering of the petite volume. "Thank you so much. I love this story. It's about a proud young woman who wakes up to her bungling ways." Her smiling had no end.

"That's what the lady in the bookstore said this morning. I thought you might like a really fine copy to leave as an heirloom some day."

Before she knew it, he wished her a blessed Christmas, said goodbye, and left.

Marissa flipped open her laptop and shot an e-mail to the diaphanous, hard to imagine Beverly.

Chapter Thirty-seven

UNCLE Nathan rapped his bony knuckles against the door. "Marissa, are you gonna get up today? We've got lots to do, you know."

Marissa had arrived at the farmhouse near midnight. She answered Nathan, relinquished her bed, and went to the leather case on the small writing table. She pulled the laptop from its pouch and set up. In her e-mail, she found two messages waiting. The first was from Jacquelyn and read:

> *Hi, Marissa. Don't worry about Zoe. Now that you filled me in, I sense the urgency as well. I'm kidnapping her today under the guise that we're going to do some last minute Christmas shopping. On the way home, I'll pull into the Bloody Marsh Monument site on a whim, where I will spell things out to her. Luckily, she is not as hard-headed as you. Sorry, but I will have to give her details of your experience. Should be convincing. It's a shame someone can't speak to Darrien about this. Don't know why things cooled between him and Zoe. Oh well. I'll get back to you later. Almost forgot. Russell says to tell you hello, and that, except for all forms of technological communication, he's backing out of the deal and is not willing to share until he's back on duty. Oh, he makes me feel loved!*

Marissa moved her attention to the next e-mail. She paused at the name, Beverly Reginalli. Marissa's eyes popped at the rapid response, and she opened the message which said:

> *Thank you for your e-mail, Marissa. So glad to learn that your oceanside residence is available. Very few options can be found on short notice. William called an hour ago telling me to check my e-mail. After hearing his description, I feel your home will fit my needs exactly. I like the fact that a former artist owned the place. The interior will have good vibes, allowing me to work much on my photography (gallery showings in April and November!). My internet search led me to nothing so unique and charming as your house sitting on the ledge of the spellbinding Atlantic. I am going to throw in an extra five hundred a month if you will allow me to bring my*

five pets. They are well trained and should not cause any damage. Also, I am an energy hog. I keep the heat up. I never turn a light off when I leave a room. So I will include an extra amount for my extravagant ways. One problem. I must stay through March. My home is being renovated then. If I receive your agreement concerning my plans, I will immediately mail the deposit to the address you provide. Again, thanks so much. I have high hopes of being inspired by nature and capturing the incomparable views in my lens. I will also be entertaining some visitors on and off; and if William is in town, I eagerly look forward to the company of our mutual friend. Beverly Reginalli

Marissa sighed. Through March? *Camellia* was slated to reopen the first day of that same month. Where would she sleep for thirty days or more? Her thoughts traveled to the menagerie. Five. What if they turned out to be Rottweilers attacking and grinding their teeth into the wall motifs? Then again, the pets might be hyper Labs, making clouds of fiberfill while chewing the dolphin-themed French counterpane draped over the sofa. That exquisitely embroidered gift to her mother, found in an elegant linen shop, had set Marissa back quite a few dollars years ago. She shook her head and vowed to shun any more sickening mental images.

Her mind considered Aunt Olivia's beautifully papered green room, so perfectly preserved. Marissa gave a slap to the little table top. She didn't have the luxury of a protective attitude; she was desperate for income. Beverly's short-term lease would hand Marissa the capital needed to cover the first month of operation. Staying out of the red would be Marissa's job. She swallowed, thinking of the personal risk she continued to assume like ultra-painful therapy, necessary but break-into-a-sweat fear inducing. The thought seeped in, to open a line of credit. She knew her father would frown at such an idea. His business stayed financially strong by avoiding heavy debt. By osmosis, her father developed the same fiscally-smart attitude as the town. During the depression, Woodstock Bank remained healthy. Marissa, also, picked up the same sage beliefs somewhere along the way and her goal was to pay off the building housing *Camellia Japonica* in five years.

Marissa replied affirmatively to Beverly's request and turned off her computer. It was odd, feeling so grateful to her unseen lessee, while at the same time experiencing a sneaking, indefinable apprehension. She tossed on her robe and went to the shower.

Christmas preparations at the farmhouse went full tilt. Max helped Marissa revive Aunt Olivia's cherished tradition of garlands strung with popcorn and cranberries. Tarnished but glimmering glass ornaments came from the attic. On the eve, they went to church and afterward, Marissa stayed up late, baking and decorating cookies while the old radio in the laundry room filled the space with a medley of carols. She paused once, imagining the red-headed child laying plates for a meal. Later, Marissa pictured that dream sprite, wearing a forest green velvet dress with a lace collar and short row of pearl buttons, seated at the meal, her hands folded like a miniature church as she intoned a sweet grace.

Marissa plated and wrapped the cookies. She scrubbed the kitchen until the old wood floors smelled like balsam pine, and the white enamel sink shone like a star over a shepherd's field. Then she fell into bed. The following day was full of peace and joy.

Days later, on New Years Eve, Marissa served ham sandwiches and *fixin's* as Nathan liked to call them. Max made everyone put on party hats. Nathan insisted on bringing Brianna inside to celebrate. Max affixed a hat to the goat's head. They clapped as they watched the peach lower from its housing to signify the new year of 2003. Nathan got out his silver revolver and pierced the dark sky twice, once for him, the other for Olivia. As another hour passed, entertainers kept the attention of Marissa and Max, but Nathan dozed in his chair. Brianna slept also, her chin resting on one of his shoes. Finally, Marissa switched off the television.

"Well, Max, tomorrow is the start of a new way of living for you."

"But I like it out there."

"We've been through this before. To keep your human status you need to live like one."

Uncle Nathan suddenly buffeted the walls with a crescendo of snoring. Brianna's head jerked up. Max laughed.

"All right," he said. "I'll move in where everyone is so civilized."

"It must be in the thirties tonight. Put Brianna in Dixie's stall again."

"Yes, ma'am. See ya tomorrow." He got up and whistled to the goat, which popped up and followed compliantly. Marissa led Uncle Nathan to his bed.

The next morning they slept in. First up, Marissa, carrying empty cardboard boxes, walked into the stable before Brianna began butting the stall door and crying for her morning meal.

Despite the little cloud over Max's head, Marissa got him going. His stack of The Hulk comic books was carefully positioned in one of the boxes. She made a mental note for the third time, to take the boy shopping. From doing his wash, she was aware just how worn and limited his clothing was. The day before, a tremendously late but very large payment for her catering of the huge affair of an island company, now defunct, had finally found its way to her. The funds would enable the clothing expenditure and would place a balance in her checkbook once more.

"Leave the hot plate, Max. You can use the kitchen any time you want."

"Oh, yeah."

Marissa lifted a box but returned it to the table. "Wait. I've been meaning to speak to you. Promise that you'll watch over Nathan once I've gone back to the island. He doesn't require much."

"You can count on me."

"I know I can." She picked up the box again. Max took several. She paused in the doorway. "Friday, let's plan to go to Canton for your written test."

"Yes ma'am. I'm ready."

They left for the house. Max stumbled up the staircase, his view obstructed. Once inside the room, he dropped the boxes to the floor, looked around and grinned. Everything about this bedroom revealed that it was a male's sanctum. The utilitarian brown woodwork had lost its sheen. No elaborate wallpaper here, only a discrete stencil design in browns and beiges. Tales of the Hardy Boys, atlases, chronicles of American history, baseball facts, the story of automobile production, woodworking plans, and biographies were a few of the volumes lining the bookshelves on the walls opposite the bed. Framed pen and ink drawings interspersed the walls: the Rope Mill ruins, the elegant 1913 Johnston House, the cotton warehouses, the mule pens, and men laboring over a planing mill, their feet and lower legs buried by sawdust.

"I was worried you wouldn't like it," Marissa said. "Things are old in here. This room belonged to Nathan's son, Allen. Remember, Allen was my father's cousin."

He walked to the far wall. "You're right, this window will make it easy to keep an eye on the stable. . . . And all these books. Cool." He wandered to one of the shelves.

"What was your room at home like?" asked Marissa.

"Never had one. The sofa was my bed. Mom saved on rent that way. We were always moving, zigzagging across Florida. When I was really little and my dad was with us, we lived in southern California."

They went from the room and brought back two more loads. Max helped Marissa pull away a plastic dust cover and make the bed with fresh-smelling sheets.

"Max, you and I have to share the bathroom up here. I'm a cleanliness nut, so keep it that way. *A-a-a-and*, do not get in this bed at night until you've showered. Working with horses is a dirty job. This is a house rule. Got it?" He nodded. They lofted and lowered a coverlet over the sheets.

Marissa opened the top drawer of a rickety bureau with scrolled carvings along the front. A musty smell and then the exhilarating scent of wood reached her nose. She added the things from her arms and gently closed the drawer. She glanced at the nicks and scratches accumulated over time by the mahogany dresser. Max lingered at the bookcases and pulled several volumes, flipping through the pages. "Was your father's cousin a brainiac?" he asked.

Marissa looked up as she gathered more clothes from one of the cardboard boxes. "He was a student of history, if that's what you mean. And he liked to illustrate the past." She gestured toward the pictures on the walls. "He planned to teach one day, but he died young."

"Bet he could tell me a lot about this place."

"I never met him, of course, but I think he would have liked you very much and the way you've been taking care of things around here."

He gave a little rub to his head. "Must be nice to have family and roots. You're lucky."

"Well I lost my parents much too early. But everybody has some bad and good in their lives. . . . Do you know much about your dad?"

"No. He took off when I was three. He's following the horse racing circuit somewhere. He's a trainer. A little too large to be a jockey. That's what my mom says." His face changed. "I got a neat Grandpa in Florida, though."

"Well, for as long as you wish, you're adopted by the Manning family. Which entitles you to a peek into what we call the Legacy Box."

"The what?"

She opened the closet and brought down a wooden chest from the high shelf inside. She carried the chest to the bed and sat down. Max also took a seat on the quilted coverlet.

"This was Allen's prized possession as a kid. Now you become official keeper." She smiled. "We've been hoping someone like you would come along."

She lifted the lid and laid it back on its hinges. Max leaned in to get a look.

A canvas pouch rested on top of yellowed newspaper clippings, old letters with curling script, bent and folded documents. Marissa took Max's hand and cupped his fingers. She unlaced the pouch ties and dropped items into the boy's hand: six bullets, three brass buttons, a cavalry saber plate, and a large gold locket.

"Whoa. What's all this?"

"Civil War artifacts. Do you know about the fighting that came down from Chattanooga, through Resaca, Adairsville, and Kennesaw Mountain before Sherman's men marched into Atlanta? Well, there were skirmishes round about the region, too. In fact, those things in your hand were found here, by Allen."

"You mean here in town?"

"Mm-hm. Woodstock saw fighting just south of the intersection at Hwy 92 and Hwy 5. A Union cavalry division was camped there." She sifted inside the box and pulled out a document. "See, here it says that the fray occurred on June 11, 1864 between Brigadier General K. Garrard's Union division and the Confederate division led by General Joseph Wheeler. The Union cavalry pushed the Confederates south but could not move them past Noonday Creek. Three Confederates and two Union men died in the fight."

Max lifted his gaze to the window where, if he were standing, he would see the stable. "I think about the men in that calamity, but I also imagine those horses. Their wild eyes must have been swiveling in their sockets as they obeyed commands. Gunfire and yelling, smoke and screaming men must have assaulted their extreme senses. Can't you see their hooves trampling the ground with fear as they fought through all that confusion and chaos? . . . Poor, brave horses. They had no way of understanding the fury whirling around 'em." He turned his attention back to the things in his palm, manipulating them, turning them over for examination. "Tell me how Nathan's son found these things."

"Allen learned from one of his teachers about the skirmish. Knowing the Second Union Cavalry Division had been headquartered at the spot for a while, Allen was determined to find some artifacts. He was just a young kid still in grade school when he went searching, probably in the early 1940s. More than seventy years had passed since the conflict. People thought he was nuts, going along with nothing to help him but his eyesight, a pocket knife, and small shovel but he wouldn't give up. Every summer for three years. The locket was his greatest find." Marissa took the large piece from Max's hand and read the worn engraving on the back and front. "To My Beloved Ephraim. Fourth Michigan Cavalry. Your loving wife, Carrie Ann." She carefully opened the locket and showed Max a snippet of light brown hair under glass.

"That's sad," said Max. "The soldier lost the only thing giving him hope."

"Oh, a person needs something better than this to give him hope." She gave a gentle smile. "But maybe Ephraim made it back to his Carrie Ann." Marissa placed the objects back in the pouch and deposited it in the box. "Allen was going to research the family and send the ancestors the locket but he died from sudden illness, about your age." Marissa shuffled the written contents of the box. "These clippings and papers have something to do with town history. As keeper of The Box, you can take a look inside any time."

"This town means a lot to your family, doesn't it?"

"That's true. And like most places, it's full of compelling stories and puzzles if you're willing to investigate."

"I'm curious to know everything." His eyes lifted and followed the shelves around the room. "And the books?"

"For your use and enjoyment."

Marissa's head lifted slightly. She turned an ear to the hall.

"What is it?" said Max.

"Listen." Her eyes had brightened.

Clunking feet and squeaking treads announced a coming visitor on the stairs. Floor planks in the hall clicked, snapped, and emitted several groans as someone walked the hall. Uncle Nathan came around the doorway.

His sight journeyed along each of the four walls. "Been a long time since I've seen this room. It's good to have someone using it again."

"How did you make it up here, Uncle?" Marissa asked.

"I can if I have to, but I don't like to. Makes me sad."

Max got off the bed and stood up straight. "Thanks, Mr. Manning, for letting me stay in this nice room. I feel like I'm part of this town."

Nathan, his mouth pulled tight, nodded his head and rusty-colored locks. "This place will serve you well, son. It will serve you well." The old man turned and went back downstairs.

Chapter Thirty-eight

THREE weeks into January, gray clouds tumbled in the skies like frolicking bears over the rooftops of Woodstock. Snow began to pour, a once-or-twice-a-winter treat, seeming like atmospheric caprice. The townsfolk hunkered in their homes around their fireplaces. Trendy shops closed their doors. The supermarkets struggled under a run on bread and milk. The buses left school early, and children arrived home releasing exultant cries as they cannon-shot themselves from the bus steps into four inches of snow at most. Transplanted northerners snickered, but the natives, friendly-like, paid them no mind. Everything came to a halt, which left Max about to climb the walls with frustration. After passing the written test, his driving lessons with Marissa had gone well. He joked by saying that the little beads of sweat had stopped forming on her brow when he drove her up and down Trickum or up Highway 5 and out the entire length of East Cherokee Road. He had been waiting to take the real test.

Marissa entered the kitchen and noted Max's glum look. Uncle Nathan ignored them both and put sugar in his hot coffee.

"I don't have time to bolster you right now, Max. Who could have predicted snow? I'll be back day after tomorrow. Then we'll go. Just be patient."

"How come *you're* driving?" said Max.

She poured a cup of coffee and bit into a raisin bran muffin, unwilling to justify herself. She knew how to maneuver on icy streets. And the snowstorm had bypassed everything south of Jonesboro. Max was beginning to make her feel like one of those parents hog-tied with consternation and doubt by a cagey teenager wanting his way. Goodness, it was like she was his mom or something.

She realized Nathan stared at her. "You sure look nice, Marissa. Like one of them high fashion ladies. Who are you meeting, all dolled up like that?"

"Dolled up? You're just used to seeing me dressed for housework or riding." She took a final sip of coffee and gave Uncle Nathan last minute instructions.

Once Marissa traveled the interstate, everyone flew down the lanes like things were back to normal, and with the roads scraped of snow so thoroughly, the statement was true for the long band of concrete leading to the coast. Her heavy coat and gloves remained on the passenger seat, unneeded in the well-warmed interior. She recalled Uncle Nathan's compliment. One of her hands came off the steering wheel and smoothed the ivory, knit outfit she wore. Her selection had been made after much wringing of her brain. She liked the way the shawl collar of the cardigan tunic complimented her graceful neck. The matching, loose-fitting slacks spoke of casual confidence. The cream fabric made her hazel eyes greener and her tawny hair more golden.

She reached the island as the afternoon luxuriated. Although the flowers remained dormant, once again the length of the state allowed a different climate in the southernmost region. Sweater weather is what they called it on St. Simons. Usually, just adding a pair of crew socks under long pants and a tee beneath your shirt ensured a perfectly comfortable day in the sun doing whatever struck a person's fancy. The islanders loved the time of year, free of pesky vacationers, sand gnats, and flies. Marissa wanted to be free of something herself—the nagging urge to meet the talented, successful woman living in her beach house. And that entails the frame of mind in which Marissa found herself flying over the causeway that day. She looked at the clock on the console. Her time was just shy of five hours, which meant she had driven much too fast.

Her car had not paused in Brunswick. On the island, her vehicle did not park in front of Isabel's cottage or linger in front of *Camellia* but scooted to East Beach. Marissa parked in front of the beach house and reapplied lip gloss. Her vision roamed the place, making her irritated that she had allowed a stranger to temporarily possess Marissa's own lovely nest. An expensive car rested in the carport. The sun shone so brightly that the mysterious Beverly had cranked all the casement windows open wide. The sheers billowed softly as Marissa left the car and came up the walk. She hoped to get a glimpse of the woman before meeting her. Then a loud, annoying voice near one of the casements, seemed directed straight at Marissa's ears.

"Ooo, she's a stack of dynamite." (Then a wolf whistle.) "Hey, baby."

Marissa froze in her steps. Her brows came down. Just what kind of guests did the woman like to entertain? Marissa took a step backwards.

"Come on, lover. Don't go," called the bold offender.

Marissa was not about to make the acquaintance of the dippy guy inside, even if he turned out to be Beverly's ailing father. She tensed, ready to bolt. Someone came around the back of the house. An older man. Burly. Black hair and a deeply receding hairline. His pants were rolled up just under his knees. Bare feet ploughed over the ground. Strong hands carried a fishing rod and a bucket that sloshed water.

"Hello. Can I help you?" he said in a deep, courteous tone.

Marissa, distracted by the design of his navy blue sweater, lagged with an answer. "Uh . . . no thanks. I was here for . . . ." She flung her hand in the direction of the house, wanting to disassociate herself from the occupants. She turned and continued her way back.

His stocky body remained planted. He stared.

She opened her car door, planning to jet away.

"Hold on. I bet you're looking for me."

"You? No, sir."

Another wolf whistle cut through the air. The man's head jerked around. He pointed to the window. "Please pardon him. I hope he didn't ruffle you. Jimmy's a piece of work."

"Yes. He certainly is." She leaned her body into the car.

"Are you looking for Beverly Reginalli?" he called.

She stopped her retreat and came back out. "Do you know her?"

He gave a hearty laugh. "I'm Beverly. People have been making that mistake all my life." He came closer.

"You? Oh my goodness. Pardon me."

"No problem. My grandfather's name. Mama wanted to carry on her southern side. My father's Italian heritage was a little overpowering. I was the fifth son, so my father figured he owed her something."

She leaned on the open door frame. "Now that I think about it, I once heard of a football player named Vivian, and my uncle used to be friends with a pine logger named Agnes."

He lowered his bucket to the scraggly yard. "My name wouldn't have been a problem in Victorian times when they hearkened to the classics. Now I just get accused of being a gender bender."

"I can see why. You look thoroughly masculine to me."

"Yes, my wife of forty-two years seems to think so. . . . Since you haven't told me your name, I'm going to guess—Marissa Manning."

"How did you know?"

"You look just the way William described you, quite pretty. . . . Please come inside."

Her mouth opened, ready to comply but stopped short. Her sight, in a face that had suddenly lost its receptiveness, flicked to the house and back. "No. You've got company," she said. "I just wanted to see that you're pleased with the house."

"Company? I don't have company. That noisome, bad-talking squirt is my mynah bird, Jimmy. His previous owner taught him some really bad habits."

"Oh." She shut the car door, laughing. "I thought it might be a beer-swigging friend who'd gotten much too bored at the beach."

They laughed and walked together toward the house. Inside, the bird started up again. Beverly mimicked cutting a throat while sending a scowl in the bird's direction. Silence fell in the cage. Marissa absorbed the sight of three other cages. One held a couple of parakeets playing with their toys. In the next, a cockatiel preened while the final cage ensconced a chattering canary.

"So these are the five pets!" said Marissa, at the same time noting a wonderful aroma coming from the kitchen.

He nodded. "Thanks for making the allowance. My wife is on her yearly trip to New York. Business. Dahlia designs jewelry. I promised I would take good care of our babies. The real grandbabies are in Seattle, so this is how we cope. Dahlia's joining me in two weeks."

"That's nice. And is everything comfortable? Is there anything your wife might need?"

"Are you kidding? This place is perfectly outfitted, most importantly the kitchen. In fact, a pan of lasagna is just about to come from the oven. Please join me."

"Well, I . . . ." Feeling like she was intruding, she hesitated to walk into the kitchen of her own home.

"Come on." He waved a hand and led the way. "I want to hear how you and William met." With that statement, she followed right behind.

Chapter Thirty-nine

THE living room birds clicked, clucked, whistled, and chirped to compete with the Italian opera swirling through the beach house. Marissa had taken a seat at the kitchen table. Beverly pulled the pan of lasagna from the oven. He let it rest before cutting, and he busied himself making iced tea and salad.

Marissa asked about his camera and techniques. He presented his long range lens, more costly than his pricey camera, and pretended to drop the delicate optical. Marissa saw he enjoyed her startled look and relieved laughter. He served their meal and paused at times to tell anecdotes about his Old World father and his long-suffering mother who learned to cook Italian dishes under the watchful eye and tart tongue of his grandmother. Beverly said his dis-planted mother never complained about living in Brooklyn because his father was wise enough to bring the entire family, two weeks every summer, to Sumter where the mother's son, Beverly, learned to love fried okra and collard greens.

After the meal, Marissa and Beverly went to the beach. The constant sun had warmed the dry sand like a preheated mattress, and Marissa took a seat just to feel the luxuriant heat permeate her legs. He handed her the camera and asked her to take some shots. She stayed where she was, looking close by. Beach plants hugged the slight rise on which she sat. She turned to the rear and chose the waving shoots of sea oats on the primary dunes. Then she aimed at Muhley grass in a swale farther behind. She faced forward again and focused on the elliptical-leafed succulent sea-purslane, and next, her interest turned to prickly Russian thistle. He questioned why she felt drawn to the subjects she did. "I don't know," she said.

"You have an eye for detail," he said. "And you like the organic." He told her to aim at the interesting orach growing just past her feet. The winter-shriveled sample would normally be overlooked by the beachcomber's eye, yet the struggling plant contained intricacy of design and strange beauty. He gave her tips, guiding her composition, and suggesting angles. He talked of art and expression.

She understood, telling him that baking was similar but applied its influence on the taste buds instead of the eyes.

A young couple walked down the beach, and their Irish setter trifled with the edge of the surf, bounding and charging, scooting away from incoming waves. Beverly stepped from his deck shoes and walked down to the shore, his broad feet leaving a string of imprints in the wet sand. He lifted his camera and snapped every line, form, or color that moved him. The couple smiled for him and moved on. The dog followed. Beverly turned to the sea. A pelican gliding above suddenly streamlined its shape by pulling the wings near its body. The bird speared the water and bobbed to the surface. The camera continually snapped images. Then Marissa could see his short, thick fingers make quick adjustments on the camera. The power lens was taken off and placed in the case hanging from his body. He squatted in the shallow for five minutes capturing the effluence of the tide. He rose and faced the mounds of white sand dotted with sea grasses and the beach house behind. Marissa waved. He lifted his camera and snapped a photo of her. He ran up the sloping ground. Kneeling in the sand twelve feet away, he aimed again while a gust stirred the sand around her for a moment causing her to laugh and cover her eyes. Things settled again.

"Pretend I'm not here," he said. "Relax. Look down the beach. Think of something important to you. Good. Now raise your hand to shield your eyes from the sun. Look far. Think of something you are waiting for. Excellent. . . ." He got up, walked in front of her and then to the side again. "One last pose. Pull your legs in, bent at the knee. Wrap your arms around your legs as if you're hugging them. That's right. Now, take a deep breath and let your head fall back. Shut your eyes, exhale, and smile at the sky. Think of something that makes you deeply happy. Wonderful." He took shots from different angles. "You're a natural."

She grinned, saying, "No. After a delicious meal and a soft perch in the sun, anyone will please a camera."

He packed his camera in the case. "I'll e-mail you the results."

She stood and dusted off her pants. "Thanks, Beverly. And thanks for a very nice afternoon." She pointed vaguely at the sweater he wore. "That cable knit. I've seen it before."

"William gave it to me, years ago. It's a favorite of mine."

"How did you meet William?"

"Ah, I was going to ask you that, but I'll answer first. The oil drilling business. I was stuck on land, though. Not that I minded one bit. Those rigs are fraught with peril. William and I had to communicate a lot when he located the problem. I did the computer analysis in the Jersey division. We finally met when he came into the office one day. He flipped when he discovered this northern-sounding Italian was quite familiar with Sumter. Since then we've kept in contact. He's visited our home in Passaic several times. My youngest son is in college. William's advising him on an engineering project. . . . Your turn."

Marissa sought to dissipate the fluster that must be revealing itself in her features. "Uh, well, he bought the house behind my business."

"Oh. Now I recall. You two actually bumped into each other."

"He told you that?"

"Um . . . in the nicest way. And I have to say, it was a fortunate encounter. You are far superior to that blasé Angelique, who is no angel."

"You have it wrong. You talk as if there's some significance to William's and my friendship."

"Oh pardon me. I made a stupid assumption."

She smiled politely and they walked to the house where she gathered her things, all the while wondering again about another mystery woman, this one for real.

She checked on *Camellia*. A new front room greeted her. The eye-catching paintings were mounted on the wall just as she asked. In a move of independent daring Isabel and Deke had painted the rear wall blue-green, the hue that occurs when copper has aged, forming that patina that compliments the yellow-greens found normally in nature. Marissa found no need to reserve judgment; she experienced an immediate positive reaction to Isabel's gamble. Hints of the same color held a place on the palette comprising a few of the paintings. The pleasing shade softened the dark brown boards covering the other walls. That single splash of coolness on the far wall would draw melting summer visitors deep into her shady haven. In the office, Marissa found the advertisement proof. She called Isabel and praised her for jobs well done.

After puttering around the kitchen a while, she went to the narrow door in the kitchen and opened. The unlit stairway portal led to the attic. Before climbing, she paused, staring at the void above. Her feet took the steps. Her psyche felt squeezed by the narrow passageway. She and Daphne had traveled the stairs several times when first readying the building for business, but she hadn't noticed a stifling reaction back then. They had quickly dumped an old-fashioned sink pump they found out back and a collection of jars from the pantry. When she reached the top of the stairs, her only light came weakly from the kitchen below. Faint, unrecognizable smells met her nose. Stepping lightly around a jumble of things on the floor, she came to the center of the large, blank space. She squinted, trying to quickly force her eyesight to adjust.

On each side of the slanted roofline a dormer window jutted, boarded against some future hurricane while keeping bats and squirrels at bay. She could take down the sheets of plywood and let air and sun and sound circulate. A kerosene lantern would give nighttime light. A blanket would cut any March chill. Making do, is what her mother used to call it.

Marissa left the attic and locked up the place. She drove toward Jacquelyn's studio. Almost there, Marissa was stopped by the main traffic light on the island. She became conscious of a familiar person in the opposite direction—Darrien on his motorcycle also caught by the light. She grabbed her sunglasses and threw them on her face. She pulled the visor down. His legs braced against the ground, he appeared to gaze toward the airport, watching a plane land. The leading green got his attention, and he moved forward, turning through the intersection, right in front of her. He headed out Frederica Road. Marissa felt a wave of relief as he went into the distance.

Marissa entered the studio and went to the main room where light music played. She took a seat with mothers who watched their toddlers as Jacquelyn took them through a play and imagination session designed to deplete their little bodies of energy. Marissa observed the women, their rapt attention on their fleshy-limbed, dimple-cheeked-perfections who giggled and tumbled and hopped.

Soon Jacquelyn ended the session. Mothers wanted to speak with her, know her thoughts, have their questions answered. When finished, Jacquelyn walked to Marissa.

"What a surprise!"

"I'll be gone by morning. I came by to get your recounting."

"Recounting? Oh that," said Jacquelyn.

"But first, tell me. Is this something those mothers couldn't benefit from, by doing themselves?"

"I know. But after seven requests for a class, I gave in. And is it ever fun. Children don't have the self-consciousness that adults do."

"Makes you long for a baby," said Marissa.

"A baby. Hm. Yes, it does. . . . Let's go sit in my office."

They walked into the small room, and Jacquelyn shut the door. They sat down.

"Well, how'd she take it?"

"At first, some brief anger. She doesn't like being relegated to second choice after you, again. Then I gave her the upsetting details. She cried. Disappointment, I guess. . . . What really banishes all reason, she thinks Darrien is in love with you. Can you believe it? You two are like brother and sister."

"Actually, he means a great deal to me."

"What?" Jacquelyn turned off the radio on the shelf behind her. "Did I hear you correctly?"

"It's not what you think. I'm indebted to his kindness. I do love him as a brother and will always love him . . . . I went to him for counseling. He taught me so much about God's grace. It's like a part of me that was dead is coming back to life."

Later that afternoon, Marissa pulled onto Daphne's short driveway. The girls dragged her inside, fighting for her attention.

Clemma pulled on her hand again. "You'll sleep in my bed. Alexa and I are gonna unfold the sofa sleeper. Mom rented us a movie. You can watch, too."

"Thanks but some other time. Where's your mom?"

"In her room," replied Alexa with a worried look. She went in the other direction down the hall, curling her fingers with a "follow me" gesture. Clemma didn't follow. Marissa paused in the doorway. Daphne, dressed in slacks and a long sleeve sweatshirt, slept. Marissa started to back out when she heard Daphne call softly.

"Marissa, you're here." She took the clock into her hand. "My goodness. I lay down for fifteen minutes and now the afternoon is over."

"It's all right Daphne. You need your rest."

"This latest trial medicine makes me tired. I'm so sorry. This is no way to greet a guest." She sat up.

"Please, I should apologize for asking to stay."

"No, no. Of course not."

"I didn't want to interrupt Jacquelyn and Russell. He leaves soon."

"You were thinking wisely." She straightened her clothes, smoothed her hair, and stood up. "I've got chili in the crockpot. Let's go dish it up."

At dinner, Marissa heard about the girls' school days and Isabel's visits to soak up Daphne's kitchen expertise. Clemma and Alexa went into groanings about their Aunt Shalie's newest acquisition, a companion for the other dogs, a fierce, protective Chihuahua. Marissa glanced at Daphne who held her head as though it was too heavy for her spine.

Clemma's bellyaching continued. "You should see her, Aunt Marissa. She lets that bug-eyed dog sit on her lap like he's a prince and she's the guarded kingdom. If you get near her, the dog goes wild, snapping. Got me right on the elbow. Boy did that hurt. She's always sorry, but says there's nothing she can do because the dog is so small and delicate."

Marissa chuckled. "I don't think a sharp *no* will break one of its bones."

Alexa looked at her mom and said dryly, "*No* is not in Aunt Shalie's dog vocabulary."

Daphne started gathering the used bowls. "Girls, I would appreciate it if you would not speak disrespectfully of your aunt. I'll talk to her about the Chihuahua."

Clemma sat up, her face scarlet. "You don't see how she treats us, Mom. She tells us we're wasteful and spoiled. She sets a timer and turns off the water at the intake if we stay in the shower longer than five minutes. The light has to go off at eight-thirty whether I'm done with my homework or not. She gets madder than a hatter if we interrupt her hour-long chats on the phone. Even if I'm dripping blood. Her apology and a milkshake later don't matter to me." She fell back, slumping in her chair, her arms crossed.

Marissa broke the uncomfortable silence by insisting on giving Clemma and Alexa a break from doing the dishes. The girls left the kitchen to put on their movie.

The women remained at the table. They talked and prayed.

Afterward, Marissa looked directly at her friend. "Daphne, I don't think your sister really wants the girls."

Wringing her hands, Daphne murmured, "I have no choice."

Marissa took a deep breath. "Maybe I should take them."

Chapter Forty

THE snow around the farmhouse melted, dripping from the icicle-festooned gutters, creating slurry in potholes in the drive, forming rivulets of cold water along the front sidewalk. Clumps of snow remained beneath shady overhangs and in protected corners, on the north aspect of buildings, bushes, and trees.

Marissa drove up and soon felt like she had entered some out-of-kilter world. Her first strange sight out the windshield was Brianna yoked to an elfin wagon painted neon orange, prancing playfully, laden down with garden tools. On the back of the goat an ostrich feather attached to the leather rigging stuck straight up. Then an unhappy prospect jolted Marissa. The Chrysler parked in the rickety garage displayed a left side smashed like a discarded piece of crumpled foil. Her anger flared. Her eyes searched for Max. He flew around the perimeter of the main pasture on Harlequin with hooves hurling dirt clods like they were about to win the Kentucky Derby.

Marissa slammed the car door shut. She raced, legs kicking high in back, to tell Max to cool it. She came around the springhouse when, from the side, her sight was grabbed by Nathan on the top step of an eight-foot ladder with absolutely nothing to brace him, pruning the tops off the hemlocks. Her route immediately changed. She swallowed her voice, not wanting to startle him while he hummed a tune. She approached softly from the rear.

"Uncle," she almost whispered.

He stopped his vocals. He resumed cutting with the lopper.

Marissa came further around and repeated her call.

He stopped and looked down. "Hello there! What do you think?" He stood straighter. "If I hold the loppers like a torch, do I resemble the Statue of uh, uh, whatcha-call-it?"

"Liberty! Please get down!"

He climbed down, looking sober. "I didn't mean to worry you. I had a hundred soft branches to grab if I fell."

She moaned while tramping in a circle.

He added, "Snipping helps them grow fuller."

She leaned over, hands resting on her thighs, trying to catch her breath. "*What's going on?* Max is out there setting records, the break-your-neck kind. Brianna looks like she's joined the circus, and you're ten feet in the air, testing God."

"Oh. No. I don't want to do that. He's let me live so long. I apologize to Him and to you."

She stomped off and yelled over her shoulder. "I've got to go stop Max."

As she came across the yard, Max and the horse had disappeared. She marched to the stable. She found him in Harlequin's stall, brushing down the stallion. She stood there for a second. He kept brushing, not willing to face her, it seemed.

"Max!"

He turned, appearing scared.

She felt surprised, uncomfortable, but she steeled herself. "Come into the house. I need to speak with you."

They sat at the kitchen table eating canned vegetable soup and Marissa's slapped-together egg salad sandwiches. No one said a word. Marissa stared in the air above their heads, grim-faced, chewing. The recent word *liberty* jumped to her mind, and she thought how much she would relish some herself. The two males finished eating but stayed put until she removed the dishes and sat back down.

"Listen," she said. "I am tired of worrying about you two. I put my whole life on hold, risked financial ruin, and probably made a few more enemies just so I could help with your situations. I come home and find you acting like children. Uncle Nathan, what would Aunt Olivia say if she were here?"

"Well . . . she always had a conniption fit if I got on a ladder. And she would be plenty mad that I took one of her ostrich feathers to decorate the goat. . . . It did help me find Brianna, though, when I needed another of my tools." He projected a sheepish look. "But I'm going to manage myself more wisely in the future."

"I hope so, for the sake of all the needless trouble I went through to settle the issue that you have a secure spot here on the farm for a few more years. You could have landed yourself in a nursing home today, flat on your back for the rest of your time."

His eyelids drooped sorrowfully. "You're right," he muttered.

She turned her fiery eyes on Max. "And you! Riding a twenty-thousand-dollar horse like you own him and couldn't care less if he snapped a leg."

"I'll never do it again. Never."

He looked so distraught that Marissa again wanted to soften, but she maintained her demeanor. "Max, if you get hurt, the county will yank you out of here so fast that bristly blonde cap of yours will be blown off like it's a cheap toupee."

He jerked back, ran a hand through his hair.

Her eyes aimed at Nathan. "Guardianship is a big responsibility, Uncle. You've made a promise to watch over this boy. You'd better step up to it."

Nathan gave an earnest nod.

"All right," Marissa said, folding her arms and falling against the chair back. "Exactly what happened to the car?"

Nathan and Max glanced at one another and dove into a shared explanation that began with Nathan needing to run to the hardware for spray paint to finish the wagon. Marissa had just left on her trip. Although freezing, the sun had come out, and they heard the ice plows moving down Trickum Road. Nathan was certain Max could manage the drive. "Besides, I like being chauffeured. I get to see more of the changes around town." He patted his chest and grinned. "You know, in town there's a nice coffee shop with a weird name, something like Calm Bean or Restful Nut. We'll have to try it." Marissa put a hand up and shoved the story back on track. Max took over the tale, making the point that he only got behind the wheel at Nathan's insistent urging. The problem developed after they made it to Morgan's Hardware. Max fidgeted and then spilled the beans. "Uncle Nathan's words were something like . . . he wanted to see how the neighborhoods had been prettified by the snow," stated Max, avoiding Nathan's eyes. Marissa shot the man a scornful look. Everyone around Woodstock knew that it didn't matter if the main roads had been cleared. Refreezing at night turned melting snow into hard pack and slabs of ice, and the most treacherous roads lurked inside the subdivisions for days. Marissa gestured for Max to continue. He said they rode through Nowlin Hall Subdivision, carefully negotiating their way, and came down Washington Avenue toward the intersection with Neese Road. Max braked too hard for the stop sign waiting at the bottom of that slight hill. Momentum and the icy road caused the car to fishtail. He lost control. Agonizingly slow, the car slid down the road sideways and careened into an unsuspecting truck in the intersection.

For a minute or two she did not move, too stupefied. "Guys," said Marissa, making her chair squeal as she slid it back, "I'm really tired after that long drive, but I'm going to change my clothes and go outside to finish topping those hemlocks." She rose from her chair. "I'd better do something before I start tossing Aunt Olivia's beautiful cranberry goblets at the wall. You two can do the dishes."

Outside, she struggled with the ladder, wondering how Uncle Nathan dragged the thing to the hemlocks. Then she remembered seeing him toting it once before, his arm slung through the third opening and his shoulder functioning as a platform, as though he carried an air-filled inner tube. The ladder opened with a squeak sounding like the cautionary advice of a field mouse watching from somewhere near. She nestled the ladder deep into the branches of the tree. She climbed, armed with the lopper. Two more steps would take her to the top platform, the place where Uncle Nathan had played like a statue. A warning label stared her in the face. She kept going, knowing that three trees had been chopped and two remained to be brought in line. She made the ascent to the top step where she quivered until she demanded that her body stop. Now she was convinced angels braced the vulnerable circumstances of old men. She made quick cuts and came down. Satisfaction welled in her chest. The ladder scraped two grooves into the wet earth as she lugged it to the next tree. Determined to make record time and lessen the risk of her perilous climb, she rushed. The ladder wobbled. She froze and lowered her forehead against a ladder rung, her fingers squeezing the sides. Why was she doing this? Why must she take on everyone's problems? She took a breath and lifted her head. She climbed slowly, rose to standing, and snapped the loppers, sending the feathery stems falling.

Her rear sank carefully until she seated herself where her feet had been. Fear drained away. Her eyes enjoyed the vista. Bright sun made the needles in the pines by the pasture fencing glisten. The nandina near the old well laughed at the winter weather with clusters of bright red berries. The train was coming through town. She could hear the horn blow and the low roar as it moved over metal. Her hand went out and stroked the short-leafed conifer caressing her from the side. Nothing softer, she said to herself.

She remembered the time she and her brother had built a lean-to at the old house, the house now gone near Ridgewalk. The tree-trimmer had been by. Marissa and her brother snatched every severed hemlock branch and built a fragrant hangout. They badgered their parents until they agreed to have a game night inside the outdoor room. Her dad brought a camp lantern, all the light they needed. Her mother carried a pitcher of fruit punch. With seats of softest green needles, walls, and a roof of the same, the family played Scrabble and Uno for hours. Marissa's pout failed to convince them to sleep in the bower, and her dad let her ride piggyback to the house, trying to console her.

The cell phone in the pocket of her quilted vest woke her from reminiscing. She remained where she was and answered. William said hello from company headquarters in New Jersey. The day before, he went through his forwarded snail mail and found the invitation. He joked that no man in his right mind would miss an event that was black tie, and quickly apologized, saying he hoped she didn't take it the wrong way. In fact, he looked forward to the gala. He was up past midnight tying a perfect bow tie while blindfolded, and he even spent a horrible two hours in training, chug-a-lugging turtle soup while maintaining his composure. Then the humor went out of his voice. Unfortunately, he might be a little late, he said, and would she mind him meeting her there? Marissa assured him that it was okay. Then William asked what she was doing. He said he thought he heard bird calls and a horse neighing.

"I am situated at the very top of a ladder among the limbs of my uncle's hemlocks, my favorite tree in the entire world."

She sensed his smile through the phone when he asked for a detailing of its virtues. She began. He listened, did not rush her. She told him of the bower of her childhood where she missed out sleeping on a bed so amazing that even a wakeful princess would forget about two dozen peas. He laughed with her, wanting to know exactly what her threshold for peas might be.

Their easy conversation continued until he was needed by a coworker to look at some analysis. He reminded her that he was leaving for another oil rig in the morning and would be out of touch again, until the gala. They ended the call, leaving Marissa wanting to tumble happily into the branches waiting to catch her.

Her memory canvassed the past year. After a long dry spell, three men who she did not want, exhibited unexpected attraction. Yet, the lionhearted man filling her with a new kind of yearning had been whipsawed into nothing but pitying tolerance. Marissa's failure forced her to forfeit a lofty mood, and she came down from her high spot on the ladder.

Chapter Forty-One

ON the second Saturday of February, Marissa stepped inside the ballroom of an event facility, an august mansion in the old district of Marietta near the square. Her eyes reflected the gleam of the winter wonderland inside. White glitter played over branches and twigs, across white backdrops, on a birdbath and wrought iron garden gate. Scores of paperwhites bloomed in crystal vases atop each velvet tablecloth the color of an arctic hare and trimmed with a wide, lustrous border of ivory-colored embroidered satin. The frosty hues made a perfect foil for the deep brown paneling of the mansion constructed in 1890.

Outside, the climate leaned toward spring, and all about north Georgia, daffodils, crocus, and hyacinth were poking their colorful heads from the ground. But inside, a dreamy farewell to winter had been created, and guests arrived at the gala for the John T. Manning Foundation. Marissa and several other members of the board greeted them. Max, wearing a tuxedo, advised guests where to leave their coats. When the rush of arrivals slowed, Marissa moved near Max's side giving him encouragement and telling him how sharp he looked. He complained of the tux and stuck two fingers inside the collar of his starched shirt and pulled against the constraining band. She reminded him to do his job well; when the time came for his consideration in two years, the board would be well acquainted with him. From appearing totally out of his element, he immediately transformed himself into a pleasant young man, and he bolted to the entry and Mrs. Cherbourg, releasing the elderly woman from her heavy coat. Max's expression told Marissa he had been warmly thanked. She watched him advance to the band area and assist the musicians preparing for a night of playing. People found their place cards and took their seats at one of twenty-five round tables. The musicians had solved the microphone problem, and the stringed instruments began warming their bows. People wandered from table to table, greeting one another. The foundation board moved to take their seats at the long table up front.

Marissa went to the foyer. Peering out the front window, she could see the parking area had assumed orderly stillness again. Not a single soul could be found running in late. She glanced back through the hall toward the ballroom. Conversations carried on as people waited. One of the kitchen help with a question strode to Marissa. She gave direction and took one last look out the window. Nothing. She returned to the ballroom.

At the dais, Marissa welcomed the guests. "My father was indebted to the place that imbued him and several generations of Mannings with a love for this country. Their hometown instilled them with an admiration for hard work and honesty, and gave them a respect for God. My father knew the importance of education and wanted to do his part to make it available to those with a dream. I feel certain the recipients on this list will honor the good will behind these gifts." She read the students names, having them stand. Amid applause and congratulations, they came forward to receive their award and tell something of themselves.

The small orchestra played softly as dinner was announced. A server walked up holding two plates of food. Marissa placed her hand over the empty place next to hers, shaking her head. The server moved on. Marissa went to the dais again and asked Mr. Townsend, a board member, to say a prayer for the assembly.

Several bites into her meal, Marissa smiled at Mr. Townsend seated to her left, and she sat back in her chair. His bushy gray eyebrows danced as he spoke about an antique Ford he was restoring. Marissa nodded and laughed at his charming witticisms. He was distracted by the board member on his other side, and Marissa gazed at the people. Max sat next to Catherine, one of the recipients. A tall, husky girl, she had taken an interest in Max. He spotted Marissa's smile. He wiped the mildly harassed look from his face and turned an attentive ear to the girl who showered him with talk about her likes and dislikes.

Marissa neglected her dinner but let the raspberry sorbet sweeten her mouth and her mood. She looked down at the shimmering gold of her gown and wondered if she would experience the skirt swirling to music as she had planned. Her hand briefly touched the bodice that emphasized the beauty of her female form. Finally, she realized she could sit still no longer. Remembering it was time to announce the singer and musicians, she gratefully rose from her chair. She spoke to the guests telling them to enjoy the rest of the evening with dancing. Near the musicians, a young man walked to the microphone as preordained. Marissa introduced him and he began a lovely song sad with regret and weighted with yearning. Marissa departed quickly, went into the kitchen to praise the kitchen staff, and came out again drawn by the poignant lyrics of *"I'm Coming Home."* The young man crooned the words well. Marissa looked into the audience. Every woman in the place seemed spellbound, recalling a certain time in her life . . . waiting for her man to come home.

Marissa felt her stomach draw in with her breath. A funny ache haunted her. She escaped to the rectangular room off the ballroom, a secluded anteroom that held a staircase breaking left and right at the landing, leading to the second story and the restrooms. She took a seat on the staircase in a space that invited melancholy with more darkly paneled walls and low lighting. Pots of dieffenbachia made a weak push through the grimness, but the quiet and isolation helped ease her disappointment. The music beyond the swinging doors still reached her. She leaned against the banister, letting her head fall to the side, listening. Suddenly, the doors opened and he stood there.

"You look like a burst of sunshine in this room," William said. He extended a hand. "Come have a dance with me. You don't know how I love that song."

She got up without a word and taking his hand started to move with him toward the doors to the ballroom.

He lightly pressed her fingers. "No. . . . Here."

One of her hands went up to his left shoulder. She laid the other in his palm and he led her lightly, sweetly. For minutes they danced around the room they had all to themselves, and she hoped the music would never end. And with that thought, the melody stopped. They stood to one side, near the paneled wall.

He faced her and kept her hand. "The sconce above your head is making you gleam," he said. "I'm going to take this image and that song back with me. . . . I have to go."

"You can't stay?"

"I have to get back to the airport. I arrived just a while ago from the South China Sea. I showered and changed at the home of some good friends in Atlanta, and I have to be back for a meeting on the other side of the world in the time it takes to fly there and no longer."

"Are you kidding me?"

"No."

"You came all this way, just so you could be here, even though you have to leave again?"

"That's right. And I didn't step on your gown, did I?"

She smiled radiantly. "No, you didn't."

"Oh. And I brought you something." His hand reached into the pocket of his tux, but everything changed as he was slammed by the swinging door propelled wide by someone's arm. Catherine and two other girls barreled through the doorway and raced up the staircase on the way to the restroom, chattering like maracas, oblivious to the fact they had knocked William into Marissa.

He stayed there looking into her eyes. The girls were gone and the room was quiet again, except for a new song. He bent his head and softly kissed her.

She smiled.

He kissed her again.

Her fingertips brushed his jaw line. "If that's what you brought me, please come see me whenever you can," she uttered softly.

He smiled. "I really did bring you something." He went into his pocket again. He drew out a folded, white paper. He handed it to her. "I've got to go. A taxi is waiting outside."

She glanced at the paper. "What is it?" she asked.

"A poem," he said, grinning.

She gasped. He went out the doors. She stood there, amazed at what had taken place. Her attention went back to the item in her hand. Her fingers started to unfold the paper, but Catherine and the girls came stomping down the stairs. His words would go into her evening bag, she decided, until she could read them alone and hear his voice coming through each syllable.

It was midnight by the time Marissa and Max started the drive home. The streets were nearly empty. Max held a container of leftovers and used a toothpick to stab boneless buffalo wings. She urged him to be careful and asked how he was still hungry.

"Hey, I disassembled the platform. Then I stacked chairs and tables for an hour." He munched happily. She drove, quiet and thoughtful.

He resealed the container and wiped his mouth. "I did good tonight, didn't I?"

"*Well,* you mean. Yes, you did well. You were the most dapper young man around."

"Dapper? That sounds like I'm some old-fashioned dude."

"Nothing so horrible. . . . Tonight you were stalwart, handsome, and gallant."

"*Gallant?*"

"Oh boy. You'd better start working on your vocabulary, Max. You won't fly through the SAT just because you are a whiz at biology and horse behavior."

"Catherine's gonna help me with British lit next year."

"How's that? You don't see her."

"I've been thinking I'd like to go back to the high school." She weaved, letting her eyes off the road a second. "*Careful,*" he said. "You know, you could let me drive."

"You really think you'd like to return?"

"Yeah. Next year. Catherine said I might be able to get early dismissal for the afternoons. I'd still be able to take care of the horses and run Uncle Nathan around."

"Sounds good," she said.

They rode quietly again.

"Catherine's nice. You like her?" Marissa asked.

"Never hurts to have a friend. And I don't have the first one."

"Yeah," she said. "The world's a hard place without them. You're making me proud, Max."

Later, she and Max trudged up the stairs. He grumbled about exhaustion as he entered his room. Marissa knew she would have a hard time falling asleep. In the soothing green bedroom, she slipped out of her gown and got ready for bed. She hopped on top of the covers, leaving on the train lamp above her head. She waited. The paper nestled in her lap. The faint smell of his cologne floated up. Her fingers trembled. She unfolded her little missive and read.

For the Love of Marissa

I will make her a bed of the soft hemlocks she knows,
I will delight her eyes with yellow Lady Banks rose,
With warm hands and sweet almond oil,
I will stroke her feet.
My caresses will comfort her with more solace than healing teas.
Her staunch heart, it draws me softly, earnestly, from across the wild seas.
I will.

Marissa paused, dwelling on his words that sounded like a wedding vow. She studied his penmanship, which was masculine, direct, clear. She left the bed and went to the writing desk where she opened the narrow drawer. She selected one of Olivia's fine pens and tested it to see that the ink still flowed. When she was assured, she took the paper and using her best handwriting she wrote the date and penned these words: *Given to me by William Dash on a very special evening. Marissa Leah Manning.*

She folded the paper and placed it inside the pages of her Bible as though the paper contained a prayer. Under the covers, she closed her eyes and said goodbye to the cold winter wanting to permanently claim her life.

Chapter Forty-two

A lavender dawn heralds the nearness of spring, a season infused with newness, a time of starting over. Above the town, that pale water-color curtain, sheer like the finest organdy, fluttered and subtly changed with Earth's turning. The sky projected promise as though it held startling words on a beautiful banner proclaiming—an unexplainable, unmerited, incomprehensible change toward something incomparably better.

A week had passed since the gala. On a Monday, in the pitch black of very early morning, Marissa sprang from sleep and dressed while the farm rooster remained too somnambulant to rouse himself. She went downstairs to the kitchen and made a cup of tea. Her packed bags waited at the kitchen door, placed there the night before. She detoured with her cup to the living room, wanting to see the approach of the morning. Transfixed by the sky show outside, she lingered, thinking, until her ears perked. Uncle Nathan's snorts coming through the cracked door of his bedroom preceded his usual period of twitchy wakefulness, and she scurried upstairs, wanting some alone time before she said goodbye.

She stripped the bed of its linens, gathered her towel and wash cloth from the bathroom. At the writing desk, she jotted down reminders for Nathan and Max. The pen fell to the desk. She let her eyes roam the space. In a few years, the room would no longer exist except in her memory. The Chinese garden walls, the charming bed, and the unique accessories would never be treasured by anyone again. Marissa longed for Aunt Olivia, for the loving hands that had created the sheltering abode. She longed for her mother, her father. She longed for the good things of her past.

Like a soft white feather falling into her hand, her spirit was reminded that a day of reuniting waited for her. Comforted, she got up, pulled back the drape, and drank in the view of the farm and stables, the mixture of trees waiting to be outfitted by a new season. Her focus went to the horizon and to the mist now disappearing above the town as clusters of life and commerce making up the environs shook themselves awake. She smiled, telling herself that as long as she lived, she would still find herself traveling roads that led back to the town.

The sound of Max's footfalls marked the hall and the stairs. Through the window, she saw him go to the stable to check on the horses. One arm encircled the bundle of linens while the other grabbed her purse, and she went down to the kitchen where she drank a cup of coffee.

Uncle Nathan, puffy-eyed and hair mussed, walked into the laundry room as she loaded the washing machine. An aura of sadness had followed him.

"Come here, Marissa," he said, his arms open wide. "I'm gonna miss you something fierce."

She joined him in a bear hug, next to the new shower stall. "Come on. I know you're worn out from my nagging," she said.

"Not so, child. Not so."

Max, limbs still half-awake, stumbled in the back door. She handed him his list of reminders. She urged him to work hard on his studies. He loaded her suitcases in the trunk of the car. After a few more minutes, she was out the door and on her way to the island.

When she drove up to *Camellia*, she arrived with a prioritized mind. After taking her luggage into the front dining room, she went back to the car and the open trunk. Her fingers unscrewed the bolt holding the cover to the spare tire compartment, and there it was, a crowbar. She took the metal rod and closed the trunk lid. She marched up the stairs to the attic and slowed once she entered the inky black space. Moving toward the closest dormer outlined by thin slices of light, she almost tripped over an unseen object. She inched her way, stubbing her toes on only heaven knew what. She reached the dormer. Afternoon light snuck in at several places around the plywood storm cover, enabling her to see where to wedge the crowbar. She pushed and shoved until the tool lodged. Then she grasped the other end of the crowbar and slowly wiggled, leveraging the sheet of wood, millimeter by millimeter. Her heart pumped. The plywood pulled away from the window, about a finger width. She moved higher on the window and repeated the process. She stopped for a breather and discovered she was perspiring. Several more times her arm rocked the crowbar, and she was able to pry the board back a foot on one side. She continued the process around the perimeter. The board released. She fell backward with the three-by-four piece in her hands as an explosion of brightness flooded the man-made cavern.

She glanced around the dismal, dust-laden room. She recognized the pump and the boxes of jars they had dumped a year ago. Trash and piles of other things along with old wooden boxes littered the room. She moved to the window opposite the one she had just freed. Again, after much labor, the plywood pulled away, and immediately a rejuvenating cross breeze strolled through panes absent of glass. She applied her efforts to the final window, and she twirled around the expanse when she was done. Light illuminated the tall space above her head, all the way to the rafters. Her counting began. Forty-three missing or broken panes would require her attention. The floor, covered in grime and what seemed the dust of ages, had been made of some wide planking, maybe the famous live oak of the island. She roamed the history files in her head, remembering that in the early1800s, warships cut through the water on trusty frames built of the massive tree sections. A spiraling wood grain lent enormous strength to the timber known to resist rotting and weathering. Nothing could be hewn and carved so expectantly into reliable ship bow stems, ribs, and keels, than those broad trunks and curving limbs. At one time, the island was almost denuded of every live oak tree.

Marissa felt a strong pull to investigate the jumble of novelties lying about the big room, but a bed came next on her list of priorities, since of sleeping arrangements she had none. She ran down to the kitchen and looked at the clock clearly announcing the work day almost over. She flashed through the phone book and called the rental store. They agreed to send a foldaway within the hour.

Her shoulders settled with relief, and she moved to the kitchen sink to gaze out the window at William's house suspended in time until he returned. She went to her office and busied herself until the bed arrived. Two men carried it up the narrow passageway. She asked them to plant it smack in the middle of the space, away from all the rubbish lying about the perimeter of the room. After they left, she went to the pantry and grabbed cans of white beans and chicken stock. Celery and onion sautéed in a pan. The freezer, low of items, hid some leftover chicken in foil. Sausage was nowhere to be found, so she fried up bacon Isabel had left in the fridge during one of her practice sessions. Everything was combined and herbs added. Opening a bottle of white wine to layer in more flavor was an indulgence she prohibited herself. A poor woman's version of cassoulet simmered in a dutch oven. The quantity was enough to last her for days, seeing how she had so much to do. Only seven days remained until *Camellia* would swing her doors wide again.

Leisurely seated at the kitchen worktable, she ate her meal. As it had many times before, her thoughts went back to finding solutions to the reviewer's negative comments. She had succeeded in dressing the interior of *Camellia* with more ambience and theme. Now the time had come to create a signature dish, a pretty dish—a clever dessert. Somehow her creation must have a seaside theme. She ransacked all her recipe books, unsatisfied. She considered a molded chocolate boat filled with dollops of ice cream and crowned with a sail made of fondant but scratched the idea. A mass of dark chocolate was too intense for diners beaten by the hot sun, and ice cream was all too common on the island. Cake might be the answer but how would she make it beachy, other than cutesy sunbathers lying next to a sea of blue icing? She could imagine the smirk on the food critic's face. Her body fell into a slump. She rumpled her face with thinking. Finally, she gave up and carried her plate to the sink.

Rinsing the dish, she looked up and caught sight of the dimming light. The clock on the wall snickered at her fear. She slapped the spigot off, barely dried her hands, and grabbed her purse. Out the back door she raced. She cut behind a duplex, a business, and a clothing store until she came to the main shopping avenue. She spied the hardware store with its swags of shrimp netting, its window display of fishing rods, boogie boards and floats. She crossed at the same spot a little lady with compulsive desires had gone back and forth on a day when newly opened *Camellia* waited for its first customer. Closer to her goal, Marissa's mood deflated at the sight of darkness inside the hardware. Illogically, she pulled again on the door handle resisting her. She knocked. No one came from the back to sell her a kerosene lantern. In her opinion, no charge would be too steep for a candle, if she could just get inside to buy one. She turned around to face a street with vehicles straggling their way toward home. Even the pier was deserted, typical on a pre-season Monday night. Her gaze went to the water turned dull by the twilight. Tall lamps in the parking section came on.

On the return walk to *Camellia*, she considered the option of sleeping atop the kitchen work table. She thought about the morning light and the bank of windows and delivery men showing up bright and early, so that alternative was flipped from her head like a scorched pancake from a griddle. Once inside her place, she searched the kitchen drawers for a flashlight but came up empty-handed. Dusk faded fast to deep darkness. Her body dragged. She went to the linen closet and gathered four banquet-size table cloths to serve as bed linens. Then she drove her weary legs up the stairs to the attic. At the top, carefully making her way, she vaguely discerned the outline of things in the room. She made the bed by feeling her way along the task. She reclined in her day clothes and realized the only solution for a pillow was her purse. Lying on her back, her sight grew accustomed to the dark and traveled the long, high ridge made by the roof rafters. She wondered if anything lived in that shadowy realm. After a few uncomfortable minutes, the lumpy handbag was yanked from beneath her head. Outside, a streetlamp sent a soft, restful glow throughout the room. Her body and mind mellowed into sleep.

Hours later, the night grew cooler. Drafts traveled about the room. Marissa woke and raised herself to straighten the twisted coverings. She was about to fall back when, from the side of her eye, she spied the slightest glimmer that told her something slithered along the baseboard. Her brain trembled with the word *snake*. She scrambled onto her knees and glued her sight to the baseboard that was intermittently blocked from view with objects and boxes. Every story she had ever heard about bold reptiles came to mind. And where there was one snake, there were always more. She shook her covers, felt each lump. Her head jerked around, straining to detect any masters of stealth coming from behind. A rustling sound emitted from one corner. The sliding form emerged beneath a piece of newspaper among the piles of junk and came into enough light to enable Marissa to see the snake clearly. It paused. Then the serpent writhed toward the center of the room. Marissa evacuated her bed and stampeded down the stairs. She slammed the attic door tight.

She threw on the kitchen light and paced. After a quarter hour, she stopped in her tracks and sighed. From the linen closet, three more tablecloths were yanked from their spot. She folded one into a pillow. She enveloped herself in the other two, dashed out the light, and climbed onto the worktable. Her head turned to the side to check the bottom of the attic door, searching for evidence of space thicker than a sheet of paper. "Hurrah for old-time construction," she said out loud. Lying there, out of answers, she tossed her cares on God's wide shoulders and then was able to sleep.

"Marissa, Marissa, wake up."

Her eyes blew open. Isabel, for once, stood above her.

Marissa swung into an upright position, still wrapped like a swaddled babe. One of her hands wiggled up and rubbed her face. "Hey," she mumbled at Isabel.

"I let myself in. Look's like you didn't have a good rest. How can you manage like this for a month?"

"Somehow." She blinked eyes slightly swollen and slid off the table to standing. "Help me out of this thing." She moaned. "I hurt all over." She shook off her discomfort like a troublesome coat.

"How can you grin after a night on a hard plank of wood?" Isabel asked as she unwound.

"Don't know. This morning everything seems possible even though a snake was after me last night in the attic. My real bed's up there." Marissa let the tablecloths fall to her feet. She straightened her rumpled clothing.

"What?" said Isabel who walked to the attic door and reached for the handle.

"No, don't!"

Isabel's hand jerked back.

"Would you make some coffee? I'm going to call one of those critter killers."

"They don't kill them."

"Believe me, this one needs killing."

She went to the drawer that held the phone book. Isabel started a pot of coffee.

Chapter Forty-three

EVERY circumstance always looks better, less daunting first thing in the morning. The aroma of coffee filled the kitchen of *Camellia*. Isabel came from outside where she fed the goldfish. She carefully washed her hands at the sink. Marissa finished her phone call to Island Critter Control. Isabel sat down with two steaming mugs of brew.

"He's not coming?" said Isabel.

"Can't. Booked for the day. He's sending a woman who lives outside Folkston."

"Uh, that sounds like alligator-infested no man's land. Hope she makes it out. Don't you want to wait a day or two for Island Critter to do the job?"

"Not if she's willing to get here today."

The women sipped their coffee. Marissa got up and opened a few windows. Sounds of life in the village area drifted into the room making them take heed. They talked of their plans and how much there was yet to do. Conversation drifted to Daphne. Marissa confessed her desire to raise the girls but omitted her trepidation. Isabel exclaimed her support and promised to keep it a secret until Daphne fully considered the idea.

Marissa lowered her cup. "Oh no. I've got to get myself cleaned up before the animal control woman arrives."

Isabel looked stumped. "Yeah. So?"

"I don't have a tub or shower here. What was I thinking when I came up with the half-baked idea of living here?"

"Could you make do, somehow?"

"Now you sound like my mother. I don't plan to hop in that big sink even though it would suit my uncle's bathing requirements just fine."

"I'd offer you our tub, but it's communal between us and the other two renters inside the house."

Marissa snatched her purse and went to the door. "I'm going to Jacquelyn's studio. Be back as soon as I'm freshened for the arrival of our intrepid serpent extractor." A confident lift to her shoulders, she waltzed out the door into the sunshine.

Marissa chatted with Jacquelyn, showered up, and beat it back to *Camellia* within an hour. Her purse held an extra key to the studio, thrust upon Marissa by her friend who insisted the locker room was Marissa's to use at any time.

Isabel and Marissa stood in the dining room discussing the table arrangements when they heard rapping at the front doors. Marissa shot Isabel a relieved grin and trotted to the door. Greeting them, an impish woman unlike anyone they had ever seen, introduced herself, speaking a strange patois.

"Swamp Sally, here. I'm straight from the Okefenokee and gonna get you varmint-free."

The words rolled over Marissa at the same time a strong odor, similar to sweaty socks and wet dog, mixed with strange herbal notes, socked Marissa's nose with directness.

"Oh . . . .hello," Marissa croaked, waving forward the woman with skin pale as forest moonlight. Marissa tried to take small breaths until her nose could get accustomed. She glanced in Isabel's direction to see if the scent had traveled that far. Isabel's squirming features affirmed the suspicion.

Swamp Sally, the height of a fourth grader, tiny boned and lighter than marsh gas, looked about the restaurant. A long piece of Spanish moss hung from one of the pockets of her grimy linen jacket having so many wrinkles a person might assume the beige covering had been wadded nightly into a tight ball. Sally lowered a cage to the floor. Her other hand held a pole. "So. You got yourself a little snakey wanting to live har. Them's an easy job. Not like wrestling a bar. Brown. I don't do grizzly." The middle-aged woman shook her petite skull to confirm her statement. Her three dozen braids, gunmetal gray in color, had come to life, although weighted with scalp oil, a few leaves, and bits of unidentifiable debris. "I'll stop my joshin'," she said plainly. Her small hand extended a yellow paper that listed her prices toward Marissa. "I think you'll find my charges far."

Marissa's mind was on delay, overloaded with impressions. "Huh? Uh. . . . Yes. This is quite fair."

"Whar's the animal?" The woman's small mouth grinned; her little teeth with gaps between each one caused her to resemble an oddly endearing, woodland creature.

Mesmerized, Marissa jammed her hand toward the ceiling. "Up thar. Uh, I mean up there." She turned away for a moment, chagrinned by her rude gaffe.

"Let me show you the way," she enunciated carefully. "We're so grateful you can help us."

Marissa led the woman whose tall rubber boots slapped along the wooden floorboards. Isabel, her hand covering her nose, lagged a score of paces behind. Marissa opened the door to the attic and pointed the way.

Sally took off her jacket and folded it with affection. "Okay. Be back in a minute or two." Her snagging pole clamped in her armpit, she reached for the heavy-duty gloves tucked in the loose waistband of her size two Carhartt pants, and she catapulted up the stairs. "Shut the door," she called down. "No need to give the varmint a way of escape."

For fifteen minutes, Marissa and Isabel heard their deliverer rumbling around upstairs. They sat at the work table, listening for every sound. Finally the woman tromped down the stairs.

The door flung open. The familiar gagging smell wafted into the room. "Got it!" Sally belted. She held the caged animal high. Isabel walked over and took a look. Marissa rose from her seat but hung back. Sally continued, "What ya got har is six feet of thin white rings around glossy black. Known by common folk as the cow sucker, horse racer, or oakleaf rattler. Harmless fellow. You'd probably call him the Eastern kingsnake."

Marissa came over. "I've seen one or two. But he sure looked menacing in the dark."

"You whar smart not taking a chance," said Sally in a serious tone, her round black eyes shining with understanding, her cute little nose twitching with empathy.

"I opened the windows yesterday," said Marissa. "He must have fallen from a tree and landed inside."

"No. I can tell he's been living up thar a while." Her nimble fingers vigorously scratched her skull like she fought a flea.

"How do you know?"

"You got mice."

"I do not!"

"You got a whole village of 'em."

Marissa blanched.

Isabel edged into the conversation, carefully. "Remember . . . the one that stray cat caught out back."

"That mouse is the *only one* I have seen this entire year."

Sally put the cage on the floor and took off her gloves. "That's cuz they don't need to come down har."

"Why's that?"

"Come on. I'll show you."

Marissa and Isabel followed Sally to the attic.

They walked to the far corner. Sally's boot pushed aside some old coffee tins and tipped open a paper bag lying almost on its side. "Dog food," she declared.

"Dog food?" said Marissa

"Yep."

"*Oh no*. The previous owner left it here. I haven't had a chance to clean out all this mess."

"Well the snake's been har a long time, too."

"You don't mean it. I never laid eyes on a snake in all this time."

"Like the mice, he stayed put too. A good thing. Kept the population down. Otherwise, you'da been run from this place."

"You're right," quipped Marissa. "I guess he liked all the easy lunches."

"Mr. Ernie," said Isabel. "The snake must have been his pet."

Marissa turned to Sally. "Slightly eccentric. The man died. I bought this place from his estate."

The three women went back downstairs.

"Well," said Sally, "I'll head to my truck with this snake. You do want me to get rid of the mice, don't ya?" Marissa nodded hard. Sally shook her head with regret. "I'll have to use killin' traps, the only way." With starch in her posture, she hiked resolutely through the place and to her vehicle.

Isabel and Marissa looked up with guilty faces when Sally reentered with her laundry basket full of dulled guillotines. Marissa followed her to the attic despite another reacquaintance with the heave-inducing odor. As Sally worked, Marissa took the time to discover, in the light of day, what else was housed in the giant space. She rummaged through the junk until she felt she would need another bath. She came to a decision; a trash hauler was required. The attic collection consisted mostly of rubbish. She did find two things that interested her, and she brought them to the kitchen to show Isabel. The first box contained a vast assortment of beach pails, a few with flecked paint. Made of tin, some were plain but most pails sported children playing near the sea and others portrayed nautical themes, all in bright, happy colors. Isabel forgot about the grocery list she worked on and thrilled at the retro designs on each bucket. Marissa sifted the contents of the other box, examining the shells it contained.

Sally sauntered downstairs. "Well, that should do it. I'll be back in a week to pick up the dead. You wouldn't want anything fouling this place."

Marissa battled a smile. "No. No, I sure wouldn't." She started to hand over a check.

Sally waved it away. "I'll get that when I come back. Don't want you worrying that I'll leave a bunch of stiff, little carcasses up thar."

"Can I ask you a question?"

"Sure," said Sally.

"Working with food as I do, I'm puzzled. What's the reason for the items in your top pocket? Mint, basil, thyme and rosemary."

"Them's my good luck charm. Armand, my love, he gives 'em to me. He's a cook, too. Out thar on the edge of the Okefenokee, we got plenty of free eats. Anyway, he says, if I carry this charm, it's a way a lettin' them slippery varmints I'm trying to catch know thar gonna end up in our pot instead of go free in that swamp if they don't cooperate. Makes 'em snag-easy every time." She grinned showing her little animal teeth again. Hands on hips, she glanced around the kitchen. "I'll have to bring Armand sometime, to sample your table. So long," she called, departing the kitchen and clomping through the dining room on her way out. Her multitudinous, gray braids swayed goodbye.

Marissa lowered herself to a chair, already pooped from the stressful morning. After a brief discussion about the odd visit, Isabel returned her attention to the grocery list. Marissa's hand went inside the box of shells, some much too exotic for the beaches of North America. One more common shell fit nicely in her palm. Bleached beautifully white, the scallop shell striped with flattened ridges, fanned out four inches in width. A sculptural gift of the sea. Simple. Exemplary in design. Marissa realized she had seen similar shells in her cooking catalogues. The text had suggested the shells as servers of scampi or crab imperial. She turned the shell over, rubbing the surface with her fingers. For a time, she sat there hardly moving as she studied the shell. The room basked in quiet.

Her head bobbed up. She put the shell down. "Isabel! I have our signature creation."

Chapter Forty-four

A signature dessert. How hard could it be?

Innovate, produce, fashion, fabricate, design, contrive, correct, devise, construct, build, erect, shape, compose, perform, mold, forge, imagine, conceive—these are words that quicken the heartbeat of man. Gentle deposits drift down from the Master Creator, inspiration which quietly waits to be invited. Having a father's heart, He is achingly aware of our world that holds us captive—its slough of boredom and despair, its prison of hard toil and physical pain. Create? He's speaking to everyone all the time. Marissa was learning to listen.

Isabel looked from her grocery list to Marissa. The assistant stuck the pencil through the base of one of her pigtails. "Really? A special dessert? What's your idea?"

"If you recall, the reviewer nicked us for a lack of ocean influence regarding our food. Then I found this box this morning." She reached inside and handed the scallop shell to Isabel.

"A bite into that would be awfully unpleasant," said Isabel.

"Not if it's made of lightly sweetened shortbread," Marissa replied. Isabel screwed up her features, looking doubtful. "I can do it," said Marissa. "I'll use the shell as a baking mold." She went to the pantry and pulled down the items she needed. "My signature dish will be made of two shells, seated as though they've opened to reveal a treasure. The bottom shell will hold a dollop of whipped cream cuddling strawberries painted with sweet glaze. But the tongue's surprise will be the shell lining underneath the whipped cream: a thin coat of white chocolate flavored with mint . . . pure unexpected pleasure."

"O-o-oh," said Isabel. "Refreshing, scrumptious, *and* beautiful to the eye."

Marissa turned on the radio. Ingredients went flying, and she hummed along with the music. Isabel washed the bowls and implements as Marissa finished with each. The oven came to life. The shell, covered with a thin layer of dough, went gently inside the appliance. Isabel raced to the grocery. Their grand experiment emerged from baking. After cooling, the shortbread cookie released from the shell. The women prepared several glazes on the stovetop. They did taste tests and comparison. Recipe proportions changed. Another attempt was made. Satisfaction finally arrived. Marissa scribbled notes on paper. Using her expertise, melted white chocolate releasing a mint aroma rolled across the inside of the shell-shaped cookie and, next, hardened in the fridge. Marissa brought the mixer close, telling Isabel her secret for superior whipped cream—a metal bowl chilled in the freezer. The mixer whirred. Luscious white peaks lofted until the women deemed them perfection.

They assembled their creation. They took a step back, gazing. Both slipped a fork into the whipped cream, broke into the bottom shell, and scooped those two elements along with a piece of gleaming ruby-red strawberry into their mouths. The women's eyes went wide open and sparkled. Their feet danced in celebration.

That evening, Marissa ate more of her cassoulet. She searched online for scallop shells and ordered four dozen. She walked outside in the twilight and sat in the garden area. Right in front of her, squirrels scampered, unafraid. Marissa knew the snake was gone, but for some reason the prospect of another night in the attic was more than unwelcome. One of her feet gave a slight stamp to the ground. The day had blown by and she found herself facing another night without a lantern or flashlight. She reasoned. She cajoled. Finally, she got firm with herself. Still, her feet lollygagged across the entire length of the patio dining area. Every azalea needed examining. The leggy, over-wintered begonias needed pinching. It took a mosquito hovering at her elbow to send her inside voicing threats to call the sprayers a month early.

In the dark space, she crawled reluctantly into bed, and once again, the island atmosphere eased her into rest. Quiet, peaceful hours went by until . . . . Crack! Her eyelids flew open. A queasy feeling washed over her. She had forgotten about the traps scattered among the trash heaps, traps ready to snap the necks of hungry little travelers, but her other option, the unyielding kitchen table, seemed as horrible as her present bed. She grabbed her purse nearby. Her hand ransacked inside. She rolled tissue into balls and stuffed them inside her ears. But paper wads perform poorly as barriers against the din of sharp, slamming death, so her sleep was jagged and her dreams unsettling. By the time morning came, thirty-two tiny mice with little rodent teeth and gunmetal-gray fur threatened *Camellia* no longer.

The trash haulers arrived at eight a.m. She moved with the speed of a sleepwalker but managed to produce breakfast burritos, coffee, and mouthwatering cinnamon rolls. The trash men succumbed to her bribery and agreed to empty the traps and discard the wretchedly cute remains. A week spent waiting for Sally's return was too long to share a room with dead mice.

After the trash men left, she couldn't get to the studio locker room fast enough. Several women stared at her disheveled state as she came through the doors. Marissa pretended she wore blinders. She found blissful peace in the shower as the warm spray soothed her. Afterwards, she slipped into fresh clothes. When she dried her hair at the mirror, Jacquelyn came in offering for Marissa to bunk at Jacquelyn's house, especially with Russell deployed again. Marissa declined, saying she had made her bed, and she was just going to have to lie in it.

Coming back, Marissa went past *Camellia* and on to the library to put up a flyer announcing the reopening of the restaurant. She pushed the library door and entered. Immediately, three library workers swamped her, exclaiming their happiness that their favorite eatery was almost back in business. Where else could they get their tarragon chicken salad sandwiches on croissants so light and buttery the bread nearly floated to the ceiling? They continued with more rhetorical questions designed to compliment her until she chuckled at their flattery. A frequent guest of *Camellia*, Mrs. Kilpatrick heard the discussion and came from the children's book section, pushing her stroller with the newest babe. Three rowdy kids followed close behind. Mrs. Kilpatrick chatted with Marissa and insisted on scheduling a large birthday tea for her mother that moment. Marissa whipped out her purse calendar and penciled in the date. They discussed possible menus until two of the children wiggled a little dance, begging for a restroom visit.

Marissa continued her round of the village area, stopping at the announcement board in the pier-side park and leaving flyers with a dozen retail owners on the shopping strip. Her last stop was the hardware. They let her put a flyer in the window. She purchased a lantern that could brighten the worst dungeon. Soon she walked down the sandy lane, behind a row of parked cars. A tired ache built in strength, right behind her eyeballs. She craved a nap. The roar of a motorcycle garnered attention. The rumble came closer and her enthusiasm drained more.

He pulled beside her. She stopped and turned. Darrien flashed that boyish grin everyone loved.

"Hey," was all she could muster, knowing that disappointment in love hurt worse than a wipe-out going sixty across skin-shredding, hot asphalt. She still wore a few scars herself.

"It's really you," Darrien said. "I thought you were never going to get back to the island. Would you like to go for a ride?"

"I'll have to drop these things at *Camellia*, first." She nodded at her dirty clothes, the flyers, and the lantern.

"Hop on. I'll run you by. Then we'll head over to Epworth. I want to show you that section of marsh this time of day."

Inside *Camellia*, she spoke with Isabel for a few moments. Darrien waited in the parking lot. She went to her office where paperwork drew her. A list of invoices and her adding machine even suggested she take a seat. The phone rang. Her hand reached but stopped. She let the answering machine receive the message and she left the building.

They zoomed down the road, the roar and the breeze a part of them. As they swung through the long curve where the needle rush on either side of the road repeated endlessly, she was forced to hold onto him. He tossed back a smile. Finally, they pulled into Epworth-by-the-Sea, a retreat center snuggled under live oaks streaming with moss. They got off the bike, and he directed her to a concrete table nestled close to the marsh. He waited until she chose her place and then took the spot directly opposite.

"This is great," he said. "You. Me. Plenty of time to talk."

"Yes," she said, looking out. The causeway and intercoastal waterway filled the panorama.

"Is something wrong?" he asked. "You look almost as pensive as that evening in my office."

She turned to him and smiled. "Oh no. I'm fine. . . . You know, you turned things around for me that night. Your words were full of significance for my life. Each morning when I wake, I remind myself, I am washed whiter than snow. And I renew my mind with those words that tell me why that is."

"That meeting was important for me too, Marissa . . . which is why I asked you to come out here."

She took a breath, tried to steady her gaze.

He started to reach for her hand but withdrew. "I need to be candid with you," he said. "Lately, the idea of finding a wife comes to me."

"That's nice, Darrien."

"After we talked that day in my office, I realized I had missed something all these months. Marissa . . . I have deep feelings for you."

"Those feelings aren't well thought out. You're full of compassion, Darrien, and you know my deepest regrets. Don't misinterpret those feelings."

He looked down at her hands. "I knew you'd state things exactly as you perceive them. . . . But what about your heart? Does it beat for me in the smallest degree?"

"I admire you in every way. And some woman is going to be very lucky to have you, but I'm not the best choice for you. Not by a long shot."

He got up, stared at the marsh, came back. "Why wouldn't you be perfect for me . . . in case you allowed me a chance to romance you?"

"Well, first, if I were right for you, you would have sensed some attraction long before now. Second, I'm five years older than you. Third . . . well, your mother drives me nuts, and I'm not gifted with patience."

"I wish you had known her when she was well. You would have liked her, Marissa. She had me when she was forty-six. My dad was fifty-eight. After all those childless years, they were shocked but happy. She quit her job as a court stenographer to take care of me. Now, her doctor says she's showing signs of dementia. He's suspected it for over a year. Twice, she left the house at night and wandered. I wasn't even aware until I got a call from the sheriff's office in the early morning hours. The doctor advised that I put her on a waiting list for assisted living. . . ."

"I'm so sorry. I know that particular pain. It has a frightening element as you watch them become someone you've never known."

"Your mother?"

"She had Alzheimer's."

"We have a lot in common. I'd like to spend time with you. I believe it could develop into something more."

Marissa sighed and watched the wind shiver the grasses. "Darrien, I don't have what it takes to be a pastor's wife." She watched him, knowing she said the thing that trumped all things. He loved his calling and performed it well.

He turned his body to the side, obviously weighing her words. "So what necessary trait do you seem to think you're lacking?"

"An important one. Sainthood. You know there are always a few people who go through the motions but understand nothing about salvation. Still deceived, they use hard criteria: perfect house, perfect children, perfect past. It takes only one or two people like that. I would rebel loudly under the scrutiny. . . . I would be no help to you, Darrien. I might even be a hindrance. It requires a gentle, tolerant soul to be a pastor's wife."

"Wow. You've got me depressed."

"Temporary. You'll see the sense of my words soon."

"At least walk with me a while."

She agreed. They traipsed the grounds. A group of ladies carrying their lunches came from one of the buildings. Marissa and Darrien moved towards the marsh and surprised an egret feeding in the tidal creek. On graceful white wings, the bird launched into the briny wind. A yacht with three fishermen passed beneath the causeway bridge. Marissa pointed down the contour of the upland to a place at the edge of the marsh where a platform sat on a pole. An osprey perched regally in a nest of tangled twigs. Marissa and Darrien talked about the inspiring scenery around them. They examined the oyster beds attached to the creek bank. Their hands chased the fiddler crabs. Soon they joked and laughed like dear friends again.

The picture of a feminine face and lightest blonde hair jumped into Marissa's head. She got creative and cagily noted the beauty of a yellow bunting singing in a myrtle, then the joyful pot of golden tulips in a window, and finally the warmth of that citron diamond shining overhead. "Funny," she said offhandedly. "All those things remind me of Zoe."

Chapter Forty-five

ISABEL stopped spooning batter into baking tins when Marissa entered by the deck door, back from her trip to Epworth. Isabel wiped her hands on a towel and walked to the laptop resting on the work table. Situated on the same table, thirty beach pails had been clustered in groups. "Marissa, you have got to see the prices of these pails on the internet. Amazing, is all I've got to say."

Marissa poured herself a glass of lemonade and drank it to the bottom of the glass. "They're vintage. I know."

"No. You don't know all of it. Look"

Marissa came over. She lifted one of the Fifties pails. The sharp smell of sheet metal tickled her nose. Isabel tapped the computer mouse. Pictures of online pails, similar to the ones owned by Marissa, filled the screen. Having small original prices, they were listed decades later on the internet, for around a hundred dollars. Marissa pulled up a stool and read more. "That's nice," she said shortly and got up.

Isabel blocked her from moving. "Well guess what? I couldn't find this bunch online, so I called Barbara at Island Mews. She came over and really studied them. Then she pored over the books she brought. She wanted to wait til you returned, but she had to get back to the store. She showed me the pictures and dates. Says you need to get her estimates verified by a toy expert. These four might be worth two hundred dollars each. And these twelve pails . . . yeah, the plainer ones, she believes they're 1880 or '90. Because they're very rare and in mint condition, they could bring . . . well, look at what she wrote down." Isabel handed her a slip of paper.

Marissa laughed. "I don't believe it! Well, actually I do." Her fingers tapped the work table. "Hey. Wouldn't the pails look cute on a shelf along the back hall leading to the bathrooms?" They ran to the corridor and measured the wall length.

One of Isabel's eyebrows rose. "They'd really brighten this dingy hall. But you'd better nail 'em down."

"*Camellia* caters to people above stealing."

Isabel shrugged and recommended Deke's construction services. Marissa liked the idea. Isabel rushed to call him. He normally used his day off from his main job at the Home Depot in Brunswick for his studies, but he sprinted to the restaurant.

Marissa welcomed him inside. She explained the shelving she needed. He thanked her, telling her he always looked for ways to bring a few extra dollars home. Marissa suggested the job of repairing the missing panes. The three of them climbed the stairs.

"Wow," he said, admiring the huge open space. Afternoon sun streamed in, highlighting specks of dust floating in the air.

"Unfortunately, this attic room has its negatives, mainly no wiring, no toilet and no shower," Marissa said.

Deke folded his arms and looked around. "A bathroom could be easily added. You'd simply need to have the pipes brought up from that corner."

"Well, I don't plan to live up here for long."

"I can easily take care of those windows," he said.

"You're hired."

Deke and Isabel had helped Marissa lug buckets of water up the stairs. A vacuum and mop stood ready to remove all grime and vestiges of creeping, crawling things. Deke prepared to leave, promising to get to work whenever a smidgen of time fell into his lap. For the moment, he had to finish a project for his marketing class and then get ready for his moonlighting gig. He clarified by saying Wednesday evenings he entertained on guitar at the knitting center in Brunswick, a big improvement over providing background music on Tuesdays for Pitcher o' Beer Night at Gordo's where few listened and things were known to get rough. He claimed his guitar was good defense if needed.

"Thursday nights, we lead worship singing on the beach," he said. "Sort of a ministry of ours for the high schoolers. Feel free to join us sometime." Marissa nodded. Next, he turned to Isabel who received a peck on the lips. His wife's sight followed him lovingly as he trotted down the stairs.

The women went to work cleaning the floor and destroying cobwebs. After an hour of elbow grease, Marissa leaned the mop against the wall and surveyed the improvement. Together they lifted the sash and dumped the dirty water out the window next to the side yard. Back in the kitchen, Marissa threw her unusual bed linens into the washing machine. Isabel pulled sea oats from a bag and put them in tall urns. Fortunately, decorator sources for silk plants provided relatively good replicas. Leaving the real ones on the beach was essential. Both women knew that specialized plant protected the dunes, which in turn, anchored the shore line and kept erosion from stealing more of the beach. For decades, St. Simons had battled the scouring effect of the Brunswick River and hurricane-fueled, seawater encroachment. Marissa directed Isabel to put one of the urns in each bathroom. Then the women sat down and planned the next day. Their Thursday agenda mapped out, Marissa urged Isabel to head home.

Around six that evening, the atmosphere hunkering over the sea changed. Marissa took one look at the remaining cassoulet and swung the refrigerator door shut. She stepped outside and meandered on the deck off the kitchen. The wind blew stronger than usual but the sky directly above shone clear. She went back inside, grabbed a sweater, and locked the place. She went through the patio dining area and paused at the planter William had erected in early autumn. The surprise he had promised had not shown itself, but the buds of the Lady Banks roses quivered in a little draft of air swirling by, waiting to break into bloom. She cut through his side yard and ambled down the street to the main road leading to the pier. Her vision was fixed far out, to the sky, a flat-looking wall of troubling dark gray and an even darker squall line blasting down on the white caps. A few gulls, closer in, their whiteness contrasting brilliantly with their somber backdrop, tossed wildly in the gales. When she turned inland to check the opposite vista, she was surprised by a serene sky toward Brunswick. When she turned back again, the distant storm pounded the northeast portion of Jekyll Island. She descended the pier access to the beach. Her shoes came off, and her toes dug into the wet sand. She surveyed the shoreline. Breakfront boulders jutted their sharp angles into the air. Energizing breath filled her lungs. Seaweed and marsh wrack made jagged lines where high tide had deposited the items and left. The damp wind swatted her face with her hair. She passed the lighthouse and hiked up the beach, always monitoring the storm to her right. She sighted a faraway, blazing sword of light as it shot downward. A squat boulder made a seat to watch the squall rage and slowly dwindle. Daylight faded. She realized a chill had crept up her back. She slipped her shoes on and moved to hard sand. Although tired, she trotted the entire distance to *Camellia*. Every beach lover and every villager had scattered to avoid the rain escorting the coming night. Breathing hard, she barreled into the kitchen, finally revived enough for food. As her hand reached for the refrigerator handle, the phone rang.

Daphne's sister, Shalie, stammered and cried. That afternoon, an ambulance had rushed Daphne to the hospital again, her situation critical. Her blood work, her vital signs had fallen. Shalie begged Marissa to come as soon as possible. Marissa apologized for her frozen voice. Whenever she arrived, it would not be sooner than she already wished. Marissa phoned Isabel with the news and hurried to the hospital.

Around two in the morning, a nurse commented that an unstoppable heartbeat was the only thing that tethered Daphne to this world. Everything else was failing. She had refused life support or any kind of heroic measures. Shalie took the girls home to get some sleep. Marissa stayed to keep vigil. All sense of fatigue had fled Marissa's body. She prayed. Daphne, although unconscious, never looked more beautiful, more faith-filled to Marissa's eyes. She spoke with the night nurses and asked to assist in any way they needed her. She wished aloud there was some way she could take upon herself the physical discomfort her friend might be suffering. One nurse explained, as deaths go, hers would be a soft landing.

Marissa fell into a chair, letting her mind drift to the girls' future. Shalie had dissuaded Daphne, saying kin should remain with kin. Marissa held no resentment, aware her complete lack of parenting experience, her financial situation, the nonexistence of a husband, and only a year of acquaintance probably became part of Shalie's reasoning. Maybe Shalie was right. She closed her eyes and turned to the side with her legs pulled into the chair. She thought about Daphne's days on the shrimp boat with Ned in the early days of their marriage. After his death, Daphne sold the boat and opened a lunch stand on the docks where she sold sandwiches and her famous pies to the seamen back from a hard day on the water. Her face always braving the wind, she kept her dignity, lived with integrity, and supported her baby girls. The words, *unstoppable heartbeat* again came to Marissa's mind.

The next afternoon about the time the shrimp trawlers, their work done, pilot back into Brunswick port with their sea catch, Daphne left this world and headed home. And the girls cried.

When it came time for them to leave, Alexa, her curls capped with a halo of mussed hairs like netting above the rest, still heaved with an occasional shudder of whimpering. She moved slowly to Marissa's side and stayed there. Clemma, her eyes so inflamed her vision probably blurred, stared at her sister. Shalie gave another blow into a tissue and told the girls, everything would be okay. Once home, they'd snuggle in with the dogs and eat waffles with maple syrup.

Then Clemma tossed an accusatory look at Marissa but spoke to her sister. "Don't hang onto her Alexa. She's got her restaurant to tend to. She'd rather spend her energy fighting for that."

Alexa stayed where she was and pretended not to hear.

Shalie stuffed her tissues into her purse, saying, "Now, now, that's all settled. Things will be just fine." She walked over and took Alexa firmly by the hand. The girl's head turned, and she took one last look at her mother's lifeless form. Clemma did not look back and followed, tight-lipped and stony-eyed. Marissa stood in the doorway watching. The girls, somewhat dazed by the event of their lives, wandered down the hall with their aunt. Marissa went back to Daphne's side and whispered a farewell to her friend.

Marissa slept deeply through the night in her cleaned-out room. When she woke Friday morning, she remembered nothing of those hours. It seemed she had laid her head down moments earlier. Two cups of hot tea leaching the calming properties of naturally occurring theanine steadied her. She e-mailed William, asking him to call her if possible. The idea of putting the awful news in an electronic message seemed repulsive. When she did hear from him, how would she say those unexpected words into a phone? He would be totally unprepared to hear them, retained by a cold, barren, metal structure on the other side of the world. Wondering exactly how she should proceed, she climbed back into bed, watched the sky out the window for an hour, and dozed again. Lunchtime had come and gone when she woke. A minimum of food had reached her stomach in twenty-four hours. Jacquelyn came over with fruit salad. She made Marissa grab a change of clothes and forced her from *Camellia* and into the studio for a shower. After the stretching class, Jacquelyn put her assistant in charge and took Marissa to Mullet Bay for all the seafood they could eat. At Jacquelyn's house, they watched a comedy and played cards until Marissa went home.

On Saturday, back at *Camellia*, Isabel came over, her hair several shades away from coal black and closer to her true honey brown.

Sad-faced, she said, "It's not going to be the same without her, but I'll do my best."

"Your pigtails are gone. Your hair looks nice," said Marissa.

"I promised I'd try to look more professional. I bought tan slacks and white, long sleeve blouses for work. Three sets. Deke and I found them slashed half price. Just please allow me the shoes, which no one will notice anyway because I'll be here in the kitchen." Her black maryjanes wore birthday cakes that day.

Marissa smiled. "You wouldn't be you without them." She handed Isabel a card containing a gift certificate for the artists supply store, since oils per ounce were more expensive than food, and Isabel's painterly visions required big canvasses.

They talked more about Daphne's passing. They discussed the days ahead. The restaurant was due to open Tuesday, the same day as the memorial service. The opening was postponed a day. All the pre-planning and preparation for their guests was now compacted into one day since Thursday and Friday had been lost.

The women turned on the radio to scatter any painful thoughts. They put their heads down and their hands to work turning out four dozen dessert shells to be stashed in the freezer. Windows were washed and floors scrubbed. The refrigerator and stove sparkled inside and out. The new servers came for training, China, a young girl of nineteen, and Rosalee, a mother of four wanting to fill her time during school hours. Deke mounted the shelf to the corridor. The dining patio received a good sweeping. Colorful annuals were added to the planting beds on that first day of March, much too early for planting in Woodstock where her mother had always cautioned, nothing tender in the ground until tax day had passed. Only southernmost Georgia allowed an early gardener's celebration.

Sunday morning, Marissa skipped the study class, but arrived for worship service twenty minutes early. With a preoccupied mind, she strolled in the meditation garden near the orange, pink, and yellow snapdragons gleefully making their stance among azaleas getting ready to pop in two weeks with their own rich color. Marissa bent down to pluck some dead leaves crowding one of the plants when she spotted someone nearby.

Chapter Forty-six

DELICATE shoes and the lightest floral scent confirmed Marissa's worst fear as she remained crouched down. Was she going to have to endure another blasting, even on a beautiful Sunday morning when her heart still mourned? She rose to standing and looked into Zoe's face.

Zoe threw her arms around Marissa. "I'm so sorry for the way I acted. Can you ever forgive me?"

"There's nothing to forgive."

"Oh, yes there is. I feel so ashamed. I acted like an out-of-control harpy."

"You're taking this to mythological proportions."

"Sit and talk with me a moment."

They moved to a bench and sat down. They crossed their womanly legs, shifted, and angled themselves toward one another.

Isabel wiggled self-consciously in her seat. "I feel so awful. Thanks for having Jacquelyn speak to me about him."

"I would have told you myself, but you weren't believing anything I said that night."

"I know. I was half-crazed with hurt."

"Zoe, even if no one else in the world could have understood your pain, I certainly did."

"Marissa, you don't have to exaggerate like you did that night. Men adore you."

"Thanks, but I still find myself alone . . . however, I'm holding onto hope. A certain guy keeps giving me moments in which time stands still."

"William Dash."

"How did you know?"

"You must be blind. An eligible bachelor comes to the island, and all eyes can see that his eyes are following you."

She chuckled. "Most of the time, his watching was fueled by irritation."

Praise music billowed from the church. The women's heads turned in that direction. Inside, hands clapped in rhythm to the lively melody.

Isabel stood up. "Ready to go inside?"

"I think I'm going to enjoy church outside, today. The windows are open, so I can hear everything. By the way, you look beautiful. Pause just a second in the doorway before you enter the room. He's bound to notice. Don't be surprised if he wants to spend the afternoon at your side."

Zoe, with her open-hearted face, chuckled, gave Marissa a knowing, lenient smile and left the garden.

Monday came through Marissa's life like a consoling kitten, warm, purring, reclining in her lap. Most of the day, she did nothing but ramble through *Camellia*, sunbathe in a chair in the garden, and listen to a symphony on the radio. Things were going fine until about four in the afternoon when she decided to read the saved Sunday paper. Her new ad looked appealing. Maybe it would re-spark interest. Then she stumbled on the food critic's column. He had jammed the article with more pithy, tongue-in-cheek comments about some poor man trying to make a go of things with a BBQ place that served iced tea in mason jars. A cute idea, not stupid, she thought. Didn't the harsh Everett Chisholm comprehend that she and all the other restaurateurs were simply trying to make a living, trying to survive? As long as their food didn't explode from either end of their customers' bodies, couldn't he cut them some slack? She crumpled the section of newspaper and threw it into the trash.

The front doors of *Camellia* wore a sign on Tuesday that read: *Closed. Attending a memorial service. Opening Wednesday.* Some grumpy person, probably dealing with low blood sugar, had scrawled in bold marker, **"Why don't you quit messin' with our heads? Are you open or aren't you?"** Marissa walked up. Tired from the service and disappointed by the clammed-up attitude of Clemma and Alexa, she jerked the thing down. At the same time, a couple with their four children appeared. Marissa explained the situation. They drifted away, the hungry children whining and the mother's annoyed voice reaching Marissa's ears, "I thought somebody recommended this place." The more reasonable father responded, "How were they supposed to know it was closed?"

Once inside her office, she dropped her things on the desk and stared out the window at the family moving off toward the main drag, their heads turning this way and that in a search for food. She plopped into her chair, and she spoke to the window screen where the passion vine crawled again, "Not even open and I've already exasperated half a dozen customers, not including the ones I'm not aware of." She reached for her cell phone that had been turned off during the service and found a message from William. She played it, enjoying the sound of his voice that also generated some nervousness in her. He still knew nothing of Daphne's death. He chatted briefly about the rough weather on the Texas offshore rig and a billiard tournament going on. Any minute, he was headed for a job off Nigeria and would be out of touch, again. He asked that she keep a certain Saturday evening open. He would fly in the night before and would need to sleep through his jet-lag during the day. He said he missed her and couldn't wait until they could spend some real time together. He hadn't been able to reach Daphne either, but asked Marissa to relay his love. He said good-bye.

Marissa eased her phone down on the desk, wondering how eagerness and dread could possibly dwell together in her head for a little over a week until he returned. She went upstairs and changed into comfortable clothes. A run would do her good.

The next morning, she was up at five, chiding herself for the self-centeredness of wishing she had Daphne, her good luck charm, to help her open the eatery doors. She was back from her studio shower by six, making the soup of the day, and grating potatoes for a satisfying frittata intensified with green onion and Gruyere. Isabel arrived at six-thirty, looking every bit the role of sous chef. She commenced with the bread making, tossed salad and made three different vinaigrettes. At nine-thirty, Rosalee and China arrived and donned aprons. By ten o'clock the first guests, a book club of six, wandered in, and the place sang with activity.

The day went more smoothly than Marissa could have hoped. People left *Camellia* raving about the changes. She looked forward to every day that was to follow.

Deke stopped by one afternoon to work on the panes. Marissa first made him sit and eat leftovers from the day. After he had been laboring above for a while, he came downstairs looking like he had experienced a eureka moment.

"Marissa, Isabel tells me you have to travel to the other side of town just for a shower. I was thinking. I can put you a tub up there, real cheap. It'll increase the value of this place."

"You must not know how tight my budget is."

Isabel interrupted. "If there is anybody who can figure out how to save a dime better than we can, they'd be hard to find."

"My dad's an electrician," added Deke, "and he's offered to do the wiring. He knows how you've helped Isabel and me. I have this plumber friend that owes me a favor. We can put bathroom fixtures up there for next to nothing. No walls of course, but that can wait. My store gives their employees first chance at the returns and scratch and dent. A lady just sent back a tub and toilet after she decided the blue wouldn't be as complimentary to her décor as she thought. She doesn't mind the huge loss she's taking, but now my employer has to get rid of something pretty specific. They usually sell misfits for a song, to building supply liquidators. I'm employee of the month, which means I have a fifty percent discount on their low price until April. So I can get them for you at the price of a new dress and a pair of shoes."

Marissa sprang at the offer. Deke made a few phone calls. They moved ahead with the plan.

Thursday evening, Marissa had just gotten into bed when her phone rang. Shalie's voice sounded shaky. Her nerves had been on edge since the service. One of the dogs had developed a cough, and her patience had worn thin with the girls. Marissa agreed to have Clemma and Alexa visit on Saturday. Marissa got it through the woman's head that there was no place for the girls to sleep over. Shalie countered by suggesting they pile into Marissa's bed, until Marissa clarified that her bed was only three inches wider than a cot. Shalie offered a final thought. Then Marissa was forced to reply that sleeping bags in a dull, lifeless attic were unsuitable for girls whose mother had been gone only one week.

Saturday, Clemma and Alexa landed on her doorstep by seven-thirty. Marissa gave the girls warm scones and tea with lemon and honey. She sat down, across the kitchen work table from them, reminding that it was a work day for *Camellia*. Isabel, at the stove, nodded her head in agreement. Marissa told the girls if they needed to get outside, they must stay together, just as their mother had always insisted. The girls vaguely listened, lost in some other world. Clemma's face had new breakouts. Alexa chewed the skin near her thumbnail. Still groggy despite the tea, they sat for a while as Marissa and Isabel rushed about. Rosalee and China came in, aware of the girls' situation. The women spoke gently to them but failed to pull the girls from their shells.

Uninspired to expend any energy, Clemma and Alexa pulled their bookbags onto the table and slowly dragged their books from inside. Soon Alexa was making headway in American literature, but Clemma remained in a stupor with her book flopped open, failing to turn one page of biology text. Marissa walked by and noticed Clemma's mouth hung open a little and dark circles marked the white skin underneath her eyes.

"Yuk," said Marissa looking at the splayed and pinned-back dissection of a frog. "I hope at least they spared you the real thing. Myself, I cried and lost my lunch all over the floor the day I was directed to cut through a stinky squid just so I would discover they have a beak like a bird. Must be the reason I was demoted from captain of the soccer team." She chuckled and watched for even a glimmer of mirth around the girl's eyes, but Marissa wasn't rewarded.

Clemma slammed the book shut, making Marissa start. "Come on Alexa," said Clemma. "Let's get out of here for a while."

Alexa's eyes lifted. She pried herself reluctantly from her book, probably noting the storminess of Clemma's look.

"Okay, girls, be back around twelve for some lunch," said Marissa, scrambling to hand a tray of plated quiche to Rosalee.

An hour past noon, Marissa wondered where the girls were. Alexa trailed in the door and returned to her book. Marissa put down the girl's lunch and asked about Clemma.

"She'll be here in a minute."

Thirty minutes later, Marissa had finished seating the party of twelve, Mrs. Kilpatrick's birthday lunch for her mother. Rosalee brought in their orders and prepared the teapots. Isabel scrambled, assembling the dishes. They all had requested Strawberries on a Shell for dessert. Marissa applied herself to making the whipped cream. The glazed strawberries waited in the fridge. She paused and put her attention on Alexa.

"So exactly where is Clemma?"

Alexa had just taken a huge bite of her sandwich. She produced garbled sounds, giving an answer that emerged unintelligible.

"What? It sounded like you said, *guy*. Chew that and swallow."

Alexa chomped and finally gulped down her mouthful. "She's sitting under the pier, talking to this guy we know."

"She's what?"

"We've seen him before. He's always real nice to Clemma."

Marissa let go of the mixer and rushed closer to Alexa. Simultaneously, Rosalee, China, and Isabel let everything grind to a halt so they could listen. Marissa bent low and put her hand on Alexa's forearm. "Who, Alexa? What's his name?"

"Frankie. He's in the Coast Guard. He's gonna take us for a boat ride sometime."

Marissa jerked up. "Okay. I have to leave." A worried look planted itself on Isabel's face. "Rosalee, you work at the whipped cream. China, after you serve lunch, plate the shells, white-chocolate-coated-ones on the bottom, plain to the side, ready to be propped against the whipped cream. If I'm not back, assemble and serve."

"But . . . ." Isabel's voice died. Marissa had grabbed her phone and was out the door. Isabel let her extended hand drop. She turned her concentration to the stove.

Marissa found them sitting on a boulder in relative privacy, underneath the shade of the pier. Their faces melded sloppily at the lips, arms clasped around each other. "Hello," Marissa said calmly. Their eyes jumped open. Marissa realized the young man was at least twenty-one. A pack of cigarettes and a tall beer sat to his side.

"Aunt Marissa," said a stunned Clemma.

The young man stood up as though he wore dress uniform instead of the ratty t-shirt and jeans.

"You didn't come in for lunch, Clemma."

"How do you do ma'am?" he butted in.

She grinned, pulled her cell phone from her pocket and snapped his photo from several angles. "Very good. That takes care of it. A rash of photos with several," she lied, "of you smooching an under-age female." His mouth gaped. She took a handful of Clemma's shirt and dragged her away from the spot.

"I'm not a child. I'll be fifteen in October," Clemma yelled while being coerced up the steps to street level.

"No, you're *not* a child," barked Marissa in response. "Any child knows better than to make friends with a stranger."

They plodded in silence the rest of the way to *Camellia*. Later they had a long talk.

Chapter Forty-seven

YEARS earlier, a very young Marissa on the cusp of womanhood believed that two wildly beating hearts were all that commitment required. Older, wiser, she knew shared values are the truest bonds tying a couple together for a lifetime.

By the next Saturday, the end of one week, Marissa immersed herself in her brand new delphinium-blue tub as soon as *Camellia's* last satiated diner bounded out the door and kitchen cleanup was finished. The dim attic corner, suddenly jeweled with vibrant-colored porcelain, had inspired her the day before to shop. She found a small table and a reupholstered chair at one of the flea markets across the waterway. She purchased a floor lamp from a discount retailer.

Presently soaking in her tub, she glanced around the airy expanse of her room and realized she had grown accustomed to the space. Curtains on rods simulated bathroom walls, but she had pushed them back to have the view while she soaked. One story above most of the businesses and buildings nearby, she was hidden from eyes and could enjoy the light flooding in from east, north, and west. She mentally prepared herself for her date with William, not having a clue when he would come by or how to dress. The approaching moment when they would be together again was complicated with the heavy news she would have to deliver. She forced herself to contemplate the lobed leaves of a red mulberry tree that met one window view. Her body relaxed.

By the time she let the soapy water slide down the drain, light streamed predominantly from the westward window. The cool, refreshing scent of her bath salts remained in the air, a pleasant change from the timber smell of the room. She stepped out and dried off. Her ears captured the sound of her cell phone ringing in the kitchen. Wrapped in a towel, she tore down the stairs and grabbed the phone. The caller was gone, but a message from William popped up. *"I'll pick you up around seven. Dress casual. Let's go for a drive and then have dinner somewhere. I've had ten hours sleep. Now I'm headed for a steamy, head-fog-busting shower. See you soon."* Her head lifted. She adjusted the terry cloth. Her sight traveled through the garden, past the planter, to the rear windows at William's house. His car was on the side. The blinds were open. He really had come home.

She messed around the kitchen for a few minutes, taking care of a few things she wanted ready for the evening. Someone gave a quick rap to the back door. Mrs. Kilpatrick stepped right in, holding the chocolate curl shaver Marissa had loaned her. "Oh pardon, me!"

Marissa blushed. "It's okay. I, uh, have a tub," she stammered.

"I should hope so. The heat's coming soon," Mrs. Kilpatrick said with a chuckle. She looked Marissa up and down. "You know, it's fortunate you're not married. With that nice shape, it's for sure you'd have a dozen kids by now." The women laughed. "Anyway," Mrs. Kilpatrick continued, "my husband loved the Black Forest Cake. Your recipe was easy to follow. Thanks for your help. Everyone is so glad you're back in business." She put the kitchen tool on the counter and hurried out the door.

Marissa ran up the stairs to the attic and yanked the little calendar from her purse. She counted the days until she'd be back in the beach house, while knowing all the complications of her life were worth her present situation. As she dressed, she thought about the thick agenda notebook and the heavy briefcase that used to stay glued to her side just a few years earlier when corporate duties had run her life. She had worked longer and harder than anyone. Since then, she had changed in so many ways. Miraculously, without always having to try so hard, life was going her way.

At the appointed time, William stood at the back door. She opened. A little stilted, they looked at one another. She slipped her arms around his shoulders and pressed the side of her face to his, chasing away the awkwardness of separation, and she brought him inside. She poured cool refreshment and handed him a glass.

He drank and put down his glass, looking at her intently. "It's so good to be home. In all my years of travel, America has never looked so lovely."

She kissed him on the cheek.

He ambled into the dining room to see the changes.

"Wow, Marissa. A reading corner with lamps for cozy lighting. Beautiful paintings. This room is so welcoming that people must want to stay awhile."

"Thank you."

They walked back to the kitchen.

"Daphne's phone must be on the blink. Tomorrow, let's show up and take the girls and her for breakfast."

"William. Please sit down. I have some serious news."

His face changed. "Have you re-thought things?"

"No. It's not about us."

"What, then?" He remained standing.

"While you were away, Daphne had another bad spell."

"I knew it. A cell phone doesn't help you thousands of miles at sea. I was moved from oil rig to oil rig this time like I was a chess piece." He let his glass clunk on the table. "I am so glad this job is really ending in the fall. . . . Is she better?"

Marissa, with a painful expression, shook her head.

"Oh no. What hospital is she in?"

"She died, William, about two weeks ago."

Frowning, he pulled out a chair and sat down.

Marissa took a seat. "She was very sick for a long time. She wouldn't let me tell you. I promised her, William. Although I knew it was coming, the suddenness of her death caught me totally off guard." Marissa related the day she met Daphne and the courage Daphne displayed as her health deteriorated.

He looked out the window as twilight came on. "You don't seem sad," he said.

"I am. It's only that I've had an entire year to get used to the idea. Almost from the moment I met Daphne, I had known she was terminally ill."

"She told my father and me that she was so lucky to have her job. Now I understand. She liked to say that you were the kindest person in the world and that you made her life so much easier. She was actually talking about her dying. . . . Where are the girls?"

"Shalie has them."

He exhaled and rubbed his face. "This great night has turned into a horrible nightmare."

"I know. Let's take a walk on the beach. When we come back, I'll light the candles outside, and we can have a warm bowl of chowder in the garden."

He nodded and they left. On the beach, he took her hand as they strolled without a word. A tearing breeze usually roared itself across the beach about then, but the night was especially calm. After a while, he turned to her. "Please," he said, "don't ever keep anything from me again."

The next morning William embraced the girls and spoke loving words, hoping to close their deep wound. He and Marissa brought them to church on the island. The singing had begun when Clemma refused to sit next to Marissa and made a commotion switching seats with Alexa.

Outside, after the service, the girls recognized a high school friend, and they walked over. Marissa watched as Clemma and Alexa stood lackadaisically and responded to their friend's queries with grim responses.

William turned to Marissa. "What's wrong with Clemma? Why'd she treat you like that earlier?"

"She's mad at me."

"Why?"

"She's grieving."

They spotted Zoe and Darrien, holding hands, headed in their direction. Walking up, Darrien expressed his sympathy for their loss. Zoe politely reinforced his words. William invited them to join the group for lunch. They could use some help dispelling the sadness, William said. He gave a troubled nod toward the girls still occupied with their friend. Darrien suggested a new place off I-95, run by a former alligator farm owner from Florida who now grilled the best steaks around. Darrien thought the stuffed reptiles on display might prove a brief diversion for the girls.

The two cars traveled down the highway. Marissa tried to find some music their passengers liked. Clemma asked for quiet. In the restaurant, despite the staring reptiles, the girls remained sullen. The knife and fork by Clemma's plate never moved. Her expensive steak was packaged for the ride home. "The dogs will get it," she mumbled and wandered to the window ready to be gone from the place. Darrien glanced at William who shrugged. Darrien silently mouthed the word *sorry*.

On the way to Aunt Shalie's, Clemma and Alexa brightened unexpectedly. Then Clemma came right out with the question, asking William if she and her sister could live with him. He was caught by surprise.

"I'll always be your brother. Nothing will ever change that. And I'll be butting in your lives like a pest whenever I can. But they'd never let me raise you girls."

"Who's they?" demanded Clemma.

"Judges and such. The people who allow such things."

Clemma didn't speak another word the entire ride home.

Monday, *Camellia* rested as usual. Early in the morning Marissa and William took sea kayaks out. They drifted slowly through the tidal creeks, spotting turtles, watching the occasional fish flip itself into the air. The soothing pace and silence helped them gain equilibrium in their shaken hearts. They found some open upland and pulled the kayaks onto the bank. They ate pita sandwiches Marissa had prepared. The isolation allowed them the perfect setting for intimate talk. She told him how much she cherished her poem. He revealed how often he studied the picture of her at the fish camp, with her arms around the girls. And lately, he enjoyed the memory of her looking like a golden princess lighting up a dark hall. Best of all, he liked to recall how, that same evening, she returned his kiss so convincingly. They lay back on a piece of canvas and watched successive banks of clouds move north up the coast. Their hands united and Marissa felt she could die from the sweetness of lying beside him.

They didn't speak for a while. Birds fluttered by. The sun warmed them. Then William returned to the subject that disturbed him, the situation facing Clemma and Alexa. Marissa shared the story of finding Clemma at the pier, snared like a prized redfish by some wily dude.

William became agitated and sat up. "If I catch that guy coming around her again, the police will be at his door if I don't take care of him first. I hate the way the world pulls you this way and that. With all the bad that goes on, sometimes you feel you're in a war."

Still reclined, she tugged gently on his sleeve. "Hey, remember me?"

He turned his head to look at her. The worry in his features disappeared. She felt captivated by his handsome smile. He drifted down. "Yes, ma'am. With you, every problem disappears." He wrapped her up and kissed her.

Soon they shook themselves from their tender embrace. They packed the kayaks and headed back. The tide was changing. If they hurried, they still had time to play a game of tennis before they cleaned up and went to the beach house. Beverly and his wife had invited them to dinner.

By evening, Marissa showed peachy-skinned evidence of their day in the sun. William's perpetual tan was dialed up a notch. Beverly dragged them inside with garrulous greetings. Cloths covered the bird cages. Dahlia gave William a hug like a mother's. Plump and effervescent, she introduced herself to Marissa, going on about the loveliness of the house. Dahlia paused her compliments, having to check something on the stove. Marissa followed, asking about her jewelry designs. The women became entrenched in conversation. When they came back to the living room, the men talked of the oil business and how much Beverly enjoyed his retirement. Marissa wandered over to a large photo of the couple's grown children, some with families of their own. It was clear to Marissa that William didn't take his eyes off her even as he listened with one ear while Dahlia fell into joyous descriptions of her children's lives.

Over dinner, Marissa described her confusing, initial encounter with Beverly that thoroughly ended her misconception about his name. Howling laughter came from the group hearing about her indignation while crossing paths with Jimmy, the mynah bird.

"At first, I couldn't make sense of how a nice man like Beverly would have guests so rude."

Beverly put his fork down and leaned in her direction. "You must have also wondered about William owning such a bad bunch of friends."

William broke in. "Wow, Beverly, you almost messed things up for me. I've had hard enough time convincing this lady I don't drag my knuckles along the ground."

Beverly's thick eyebrows showed puzzlement. "Really? When did you stop?"

"Cut it out," William spouted through a grin.

On the way home in the car, William pulled into the public parking near Goulds Inlet at the upper end of East Beach. They watched a gibbous moon animate the water. He kissed her passionately. They spoke of their innermost thoughts. They discovered more of their likeness of mind.

William looked deeply into her eyes. "Marissa, it's not too late for us. I want a lifetime with you."

Chapter Forty-eight

In April, Marissa moved into her beach house again. Beverly and Dahlia had returned to New Jersey, missing the most resplendent month. The island vibrated with flowering things. Hedge banks of brilliant red, fuchsia, pink, lavender, and coral azaleas were capable of making pacemakers skip a beat. The time-worn trees had fully leafed out with wispy, fluttering green hair above trunks resembling craggy-faced wood nymphs. Shrimp boats churned across a pleasant sea to bring in their catch. Children scrambled over the playground at the beach park, laughing and calling out each other's names. The putt-putt golf place did heavy business. People balanced cones holding three tiers of different colored sherbet and strolled along the pier.

During the previous weeks, Marissa and William spent time together whenever she was free of the restaurant. They danced at night or went to concerts. They played on Sunday afternoons. Several times they took day-long bike rides on Jekyll. They explored the millionaire cottages. They brought Clemma and Alexa, one moonlight evening, to witness the sea turtle hatchlings make their daring scramble to the sea, and for a few, brief hours, Marissa and William saw the hardness encasing the girls' hearts crumble.

One day, William and Marissa sat alone in Jekyll Island's famous Tiffany stained glass chapel. Over the weeks, the couple talked of marriage as they did that day. One of his arms draped around her shoulder. She eased her words out, softly. "Some things in my past . . . well, I'm not proud of them," she said. "I was young. The world's influence was heavy on me."

He looked at her with understanding. "We're not kids, Marissa. We have a past. Any mistakes we made are going to stay there. I'm in love with the Marissa that sits beside me today."

May came, bringing the awareness that William would have to leave again for a final long stint of problem solving on the oil rigs. One morning, he burst in the back door of *Camellia*, during the first rush of morning customers. He took her by the hand and pulled her along, telling Isabel to take over the restaurant while he absconded with her boss. He assured Marissa they'd not be gone longer than ten minutes. They went outside and he paused on the decking.

"Notice anything new?" he said.

She looked down into the dining area, about to say, no, when the brilliant sunlight at the back of the lot drew her vision. White, lavender, blue and rose blossoms decorated the lengths of ornamental wrought iron rising from the planter. Her head tilted back with breezy laughter. "Morning glories!" she said, and ran down the steps to the back of the lot. He met her at the planter where she gazed at the blooming pops of color.

She turned to him with a smile. "Promise me something."

"Anything you ask."

"When we're married, for the rest of my life, wake me up with those words."

"Morning, Glory?"

"Yes. I don't ever want to forget the day you walked into my life."

"Collided is more correct. You know, that day I received quite a scathing look in return for the greeting, so I might be a little timorous the first morning." They fell into laughter. "Now I'd like to ask something of *you*," he said. "Be my guest for a dinner cruise tonight." His thumb wiped off a smudge of flour on her cheek. "And if you look any more feminine and beautiful than you do right now, I may sail away with you forever."

"Me, feminine? Now that's funny. Most of my life, I wanted to disassociate myself from that word."

"Just when did femininity become a dirty word?"

She shrugged. "Years ago, I took the words of two feminist professors a little too seriously. They linked femaleness with three things: weakness, vulnerability, and stupidity."

"What weird logic. Don't they know how powerful women are? And why are they always thinking men have it so good? They must not be aware how much of our blood poured onto the ground in defense of the land women freely walk on. Think of the men who died falling off a bridge construction or who were asphyxiated while trapped in a mine simply in the effort to put bread on a woman's table. How about the men who took a bullet in their chest or got smeared across the front of a Mac truck trying to protect a woman from menace? I could go on and on." He plucked a blossom from the vine and tucked it peeking from the point of her v-necked shirt. "Yes, at times women have suffered terribly, but the world bears down on both sexes."

That evening they boarded the small ship, and Marissa soon asked about the other passengers. He replied that there wouldn't be any. He had rented the entire boat. Her heart did begin to beat wildly. With dessert, he handed her the box with a ring. He made a formal proposal. She cried with happiness and accepted. He took her onto his lap and said. "If your Uncle Nathan refuses to give me your hand, I'm sunk, but it's time I see this place that always works itself into our conversation." They made plans to go the following weekend. William went up front to the ship's housing and came back, a photographer trailing. He introduced Marissa and said to the man. "Aren't I the luckiest man alive? Now take lots of photos. We're going to need them for our children and grandchildren."

A week later, they left for north Georgia before the paper boys had slapped the front lawns with the island news showing Marissa's engagement notice. They pulled next to the farmhouse and found Uncle Nathan washing his steer like one washes a car.

"Sorry," Nathan said, "didn't know you'd get here this soon." He used his overalls as a drying cloth. He and William shook hands.

William looked quizzically at Nathan. "I thought the animals were walked through a dip station or received drops of a heavy-duty chemical on their back."

"Oh this is more fun, especially in nice weather. Bart doesn't mind. He likes it. Don't think I'll be able to send him to slaughter next spring and he knows it."

Marissa looked lovingly on the two men. She kept her ring hidden from view.

They walked from the pen to the house. Uncle Nathan peered closely at William as though he checked for the right answer. "So how do you like our town?"

"Nice. I'm looking forward to seeing more of it. I've discovered Marissa has a lot of memories tied up here."

"We're glad to have you enjoy it a few days. Now let's step inside and have a glass of goat milk. Nothing like it for the digestion."

Marissa looked aghast at the veiled test. William gave her a reassuring nod.

They sat at the kitchen table. William braved a drink. He asked Marissa to show her uncle the ring. Nathan's eyes almost popped from his head. William asserted that he must have Uncle Nathan's blessing first. Nathan claimed he was about to go apoplectic, but he certainly agreed with the marriage. He knew William must be the right one, since Marissa had been telling him on the phone about a special man in her life.

In the other room, someone raced down the stairs. Max walked through the doorway. He grinned sheepishly at the sight of Marissa. She introduced him to William, showed her ring. Max peered at the man, like he was going to need to get used to the idea.

"What are you up to?" Marissa asked. The boy had slipped back into high school sooner than she thought.

"Got a big paper due on Monday. The Carolingian Kings of France. Not my thing. Would you look it over?"

"Sure. But how'd you get such a topic?"

"Couldn't think of anything, so my teacher got impatient and picked for me. Now I just gotta deal with it." He sat down. Nathan poured him a glass of goat milk. Max didn't pass on it like Marissa had. Quick with easy male talk, William got Max to open up. Max promised to give him a tour of the stables. Slowly he revealed the story of how he ended up at Uncle Nathan's, how Marissa influenced him, and how she was enabling him to reach his goals. William listened, never distracted by Brianna making a fuss outside the door. He asked questions that further brought out the depth of the narrative. He promised to take him to meet a friend of William's from childhood, a man who now taught in vet school at the University of South Carolina. Max thanked him and got up from his chair like he had been re-energized for the drudgery upstairs. He offered to saddle the horses for Marissa and William. Marissa told him they had other plans for the day. He left the room expressing his gladness that an extra male would be around sometimes because Marissa easily overwhelmed two. She frowned. Max left the room chuckling.

Marissa looked at her uncle. "I'd be happy to whip up some dinner tonight, if I just had a simple cup of tea right now."

Nathan nodded and got up. "The meal service brings nice food but not like yours."

Marissa exclaimed she had accidentally left her phone in the car. She went out.

Nathan paused with the kettle, eyed William, and leaned in. "So, you like kids?"

"Love 'em. Want a few, myself."

Nathan winced.

"Are you okay?"

"Uh huh. I was just thinking what a good thing adoption is."

"Oh yeah. I was adopted myself. But I have this funny need to start a blood line. Don't get me wrong, I love my parents deeply, but there's always been this tiny thread of disconnectedness that makes you still yearn for your own flesh and blood. . . . It's an odd thing. I'm not even sure it's right." He shook his head with mild self-disgust. "Wow. Can't believe I told you all that."

Marissa walked in from outside. Nathan got busy boiling the water. Marissa sat down and quickly put in a call to Isabel. All was well at *Camellia*. For weeks, business was so brisk Marissa had brought in another kitchen helper for Saturdays. She sipped her tea. William brought their bags from the car. Nathan went outside to finish washing his steer.

Marissa showed William about the house, explaining every nook and cranny. He admired the green room. They stuck their heads in Max's quarters and gave him, bent over a pile of books, the thumbs up for his effort. Then, Marissa took William to the far end of the hall, to what had once been Nathan and Olivia's bedroom. She apologized for the modest simplicity. He said he was humbled to sleep there. She told him that Nathan and his sisters had been born in the room while she politely omitted the fact that several people, as in every old home, had died there. She went to freshen up. They made plans to meet downstairs in ten minutes. Marissa was taking him to town.

They stopped in Tea Leaves and Thyme, back then the gray rough-block building that was formerly the old post office. The couple had a wonderful lunch, except that the head of every woman there swiveled like a weathervane as they tried to sneak a look at the new man in town. A few ladies stopped by the table to say hello and share a childhood story about Marissa. William was gracious and thoroughly entertained. Next, they visited Dean's Store, where she introduced William around. The hostess filled his head with all the aspects of interest. He studied the items in the cases and on the shelves. Then they went on a walking tour where William read aloud the historical plaques attached to the storefronts. She showed him the old homes, homes exhibiting charm and character. Several now housed businesses, their revenue holding at bay further aging, or even worse, obliteration. Marissa related the stories of the families that had lived in each turn-of-the-century home.

"And how about yours? The one with the sleeping porch and huge magnolias?"

"Gone. We lived farther up the road. I'll show you. Near Enon Cemetery. A new road and new development wiped it away."

"That must be sad for you."

She nodded. "I didn't always fully appreciate this place. Now I wish I could lock it all inside a time capsule."

"Is there a preservation effort going on?"

"We celebrated our centennial in 1997. Folks did interviews with the old ones; they documented things, hunted for photographs. A book of town history was released. I wish I had gotten involved."

"It's never too late."

"What are you saying?"

"These are the things we need to discuss over the next few months. Once my job ends, I can do my consulting from anywhere. If you closed *Camellia* for the winter months, we could come here each year."

She squeezed his hand, touched that her interests were also his.

They went to the park and sat in the sun. The mellow temperature and the roses blooming their heads off practically slew the couple with contentment. People walked about setting up booths for the artists fair. Marissa looked up and saw Trent entering the park with Hank and Elizabeth and the children. Marissa threw up a hand and waved. They changed their route and came their way. Manuel broke off and headed for the gazebo. Marissa told William that someone who had been a part of her life came their way.

Marissa jumped up and hugged Trent. William introduced himself around. Marissa asked Trent to please take their seat. He gratefully complied, exclaiming how happy he was to hear about the impending marriage, explaining that he accepted only good news from the grapevine. Marissa expressed astonishment. It turned out Nathan had already been on the phone, calling everyone. Hank and Elizabeth laughed and feigned disappointment that they had not been part of the press release network.

Trent gave a spirited shake to his cane. "So glad this girl of ours has been talked into marriage," he said to William. "Her father and I were good friends. I've known her since the day she was placed in a hospital nursery." He began to tell

William of her past. First, he spoke of the day she swam, only elementary school age, from the cove and into the middle of the deep lake to save a lone duckling chirping the alarm for its lost mother. "She carefully placed it in a plastic bin like it was Moses in a boat of rushes. Then she floated the baby animal back and raised it at home in a wading pool." He went on, creating self-consciousness in Marissa. He related the time when a teenager, she started a summer reading club to tutor local children who struggled. Manuel came over distracting everyone. Marissa was careful not to reveal her relief Trent didn't travel further up the age scale. There wasn't much positive to find once she entered college, unless you counted the frivolous, like the number of sorority socials she planned and the ease with which she found the best price on kegs of beer.

Sunday after church, the couple took Nathan and Max with them to visit Rope Mill Park along the Little River a tributary leading to Lake Allatoona. The group stared at remnants of stone foundations, all that remained of the old site where many pounds of rope were produced in the cotton mill each day until 1949. Nathan talked of the little industrial settlement that had drawn his ancestor looking for work in the grist mill there in the late 1870s. Early on, there had also been a saw mill and a woolen mill. Nathan shared the childhood tales he had heard, tales never truly documented of two men in the late 1800s, who died in separate accidents. A man with the goal of closing the water channel walked along the narrow stone wall of the cotton mill raceway. After reaching the wheel attached to a shaft that would lower the gate, he fell, unseen, hit his head on the wall, and drowned. The other accident victim was robbed of breath one desperately hot afternoon, under a broken loft and toppled bales of cotton. Before the Child Labor Act of 1916, it wasn't unheard of for a little one to be working in the rope mill, Nathan said. He reminded his listeners that times were tough then. Money could pay for medicine, a halter for the mule, or a little extra food on the table. The labor of Nathan's ancestor purchased the initial acres that were cleared and farmed during succeeding generations. Nathan recalled how he and his friends, when boys, waded knee-high in the river section past the rock dam during the worst days of summer. On the river bank they liked to watch the water channel through the raceway and the sluices toward the mill. Nathan said the boys' greatest wish was to be allowed a look inside the turbine housing.

"Now I see how deep the Manning connection runs in this area," said William.

"Mm-hm," said Nathan, "we're woven into this place like the trees that have stitched themselves to Earth, roots lacing up and down through the soil. Irrepressible, we are." He grinned big and proud. They took another glance at the site and returned to the car.

That evening, Nathan cornered Marissa in the kitchen while Max and William talked outside. "You'd better lay it out, Marissa. He has a right to know."
"I will, Uncle, just not now."
"It's a mistake to put it off."
Marissa returned to what she was doing at the stove.

Chapter Forty-nine

EACH evening, it was difficult knowing William slept just down the hall. Marissa was thankful Max's room jutted in their minds like an invisible barrier. William had accommodated Marissa's wishes throughout the weeks. He told her it was a good thing he was going away soon. Otherwise, he would immediately drag her to the first minister he could find. She reminded him not to confirm his Neanderthal ways.

Monday morning they took the horses out and traveled every pasture, every hill, the pond, up the front yard to Trickum and back. She led him to the old cotton fields. They slid off their horses. Marissa watched as William went to the same spot she liked, as though he knew the gentle slope of grass. He sat down. Trouble seemed to brew in his demeanor. She came down. She questioned him. He explained he did not want to leave her. A few times, he thought his life might end on those rigs, and there was something indefinably threatening about a final stretch of time on the sea. He told her about the terrible accidents and explosions that had happened since the time someone considered it plausible to situate men atop a potential conflagration, in the middle of nowhere on the cold sea.

"Five years earlier, a good friend of mine was burned from head to toe and blown from a rig. The fall itself should have killed him. A rescue team fished him from the water. He probably wished he had drowned. Blind, totally disfigured, he managed to kill himself in the hospital."

"I had no idea it was so dangerous," she said softly.

"The chance of something happening is very rare but always in the back of your mind. When Larry died, I wondered, what if that had been me? I had no wife to mourn me, and I'd leave no legacy of love behind. In the end, what did my life matter?"

"But now you matter to me."

"Yes. And that fact gives me courage to go out there one more time."

"You've never told me much about your work. Give me a picture. From the beginning."

"When I was deciding on a career, what I envisioned left out bits of hard reality. I got my chemical engineering degree, and I studied petroleum engineering, thinking of the exciting life ahead that would be filled with world travel and high pay. You could say the glamour of it all drew me. I never counted the cost."

"What cost?"

"For me, it was the worst possible situation. At first, I thrived on the high-powered nature of my situation and the uniqueness. A lot of prestige for a small town boy who had just turned twenty-four. . . . But I wasn't prepared for the isolation. I felt cut off from all I had known, cut off from my family. Letters came, showering me with admiration, but I couldn't tell them about my loneliness. They were so proud of me. So I poured myself into my work. When my twelve hour shift was over, I stayed at the computers and dials and lab for another two. I was good at what I did. Very good. A mud engineer must be exceptionally accurate and intuitive, or the drilling comes to a halt."

"Exactly what does a mud engineer do?"

"On an offshore rig, certain fluids are added to keep the drill cool. At first, water. Then, the deeper you go the hotter the situation gets. A mud consisting of oil, water, chemicals and barite is combined at specific calculations made by the engineer. It's basically a coolant, crucial for good operations.

"Over time, the company promoted me and sent me from place to place to assist when another mud engineer came to an impasse. My savings accounts and investments soared. Eventually, I got used to the separation from my family. I met women. I explored foreign cities. I delved into their cultures. Finally, I fell in love with a woman from Paris. Angelique."

Marissa considered William's expression, then spoke. "Beverly mentioned her. Sounded like she wasn't exactly good for you."

"It took a while for that to sink in. She wasn't a beautiful woman but stylish and extremely attractive. She understood men completely. And she loved them indiscriminately, I later found out. Our shifting, unstable relationship lasted twelve years. Marriage was passé, she said. And I discovered truth had little meaning to her."

Marissa swept the ground with a spray of pine needles at the end of a fallen twig. "When did you decide you were ready to retire?"

"Not long after my mother died. I had been thinking a lot about her. She was a good, loving mother, but she was plagued by fears. She would not let my father tell me I was adopted. He finally put his foot down. I was twelve. At the time, no one knew that the announcement sent me into an emotional spiral. I kept my confusion and shock well hidden. Two years ago, after my mother's funeral, I was on an oil rig thinking about my past and staring at the sea on an overcast day. Land is nowhere in sight. If your vision's unimpeded, you can turn three hundred and sixty degrees, following that thin horizon line. It's an odd sensation. Your mind tricks you, telling you nothing else exists. I went down to my cell that's usually sized to package sardines. Beige metal walls, a narrow bunk, a blaring little TV. I turned it off and chucked the remote in the trash. I switched off the light. . . . The sounds on an offshore rig are eerie. You can hear the metal stanchions groaning under the sea. For a time in the dark, I imagined the rig centered on a flat earth covered by a circular sea. I was there, far out, on the edge of that ocean disk, feet skittering on top of solid water, the plane tilting, me crouching to retain balance and leaning away from the void. Then one foot slipped into black nothingness, and I fought to grab anything as the slant grew steeper. In that sickening moment of awareness, I decided I was done. Done with Angelique. Done with isolation and impermanence. Done with the unconventional, free-wheeling life. . . . Now, the land is what I seek. And all the good tradition, all the tried and true. I've returned to the beliefs I held when I was young. They're more real to me than ever before. I decided to take early retirement, although they offered me a spot in the southeastern headquarters. I went home to South Carolina and spent lots of time with my dad. We fished. I helped him rebuild the back deck. We talked for hours. He encouraged me to search for Daphne. When I found her, I got an additional surprise. This intriguing, honey-blonde woman kept entering the scene. Sometimes, I think it was no accident I was there." He grinned. "Now, our children will be my reward for recognizing you, my unexpected blessing."

Immediately after they left Woodstock and returned to the island, William went on a quick trip to Sumter. One late afternoon, Marissa closed *Camellia* and called Jacquelyn, begging her friend to come sit with her on the beach. Marissa needed her advice.

Jacquelyn was soon planted in the sand next to her. Their low beach chairs enabled them to stretch out their legs. Marissa explained her problem. Jacquelyn flopped back, flabbergasted. She warned Marissa that she already knew what to do, and she had better do it soon since William was leaving on assignment in a week. "Have some faith in him, Marissa." Jacquelyn communicated that she deemed the subject closed by jumping up to wander the beach. Marissa stayed, all energy drained by her mental battle.

She watched as a sandpiper flitted along the water edge, looking for polychaete worms. Under the rays of the sun, Jacquelyn's brown skin glowed like bronze as she struck up conversation with an older woman who was portly and handsome. Her expertly cropped gray hair curved obediently around her skull. She stood with erect posture, and appeared comfortable in her one-piece bathing suit and gauzy cover-up. Her hand held a wide-brimmed straw hat. She smiled at Jacquelyn and talked deliberately as though she dispensed information, but Marissa could not hear her words above the wind and waves. The woman pointed to things at different points on the beach. Then she walked a few feet farther drawing Jacquelyn with her. They bent down. The woman again pointed like she described something. A surprised smile beamed on Jacquelyn's face. The woman scooped something from the sand. Marissa leaned forward trying to see what it was, but her sight was blocked by the angle of her view.

Marissa pushed herself from the chair and walked over. Her shadow announced her presence. Jacquelyn's head turned up. She rose when she saw who it was.

"Marissa! This is Wilhelmina. I've just learned some fascinating things about the ocean front that I've never known in all the time I've lived here."

The woman graciously shared her knowledge about the best way to discover where sand dollars were hidden, saying to look for a slight depression in the sand, a subtle ring with five evenly spaced indentions. The shell would be found underneath. The group of three shifted about and came up with two more. The woman advised them how to clean sand dollars until they gleamed white. She began telling them about the beautiful shells she'd found on the beaches of Thailand, Tahiti, and Hawaii. Jacquelyn asked why there were so few on St. Simons. The woman explained that the wide continental shelf of Georgia created gentle waves without the power to bring shells into shore. Marissa asked what she did for a living.

"I'm a naturalist. I do beach surveys. Illustrations. My data is used by scientists. . . . My husband deals with food."

"Really," said Marissa. "So do I. Please come visit my place sometime. *Camellia* is a casual eatery with a fine collection of teas."

"Oh, yes, I've heard of it. I will have to visit."

"Actually, I'm anxious about a visitor of another sort these days."

"Yes? Who are you expecting?" Despite the woman's reserved, refined appearance, her eyes invited confession.

"A man who gives me hives. He critiques the restaurants around here. You may have seen his column."

"You sound worried."

"That I am. He doesn't seem to understand he has the power to make or break a place. How can he destroy someone's dream like that? I'll admit ol' Everett is quite the authority. He's traveled the world, studying the gastronomic creations of the greatest chefs. Two of his books are in the library, here, if you ever want some cooking inspiration. Why he decided to retire on this little dot of land, I don't know, but frankly, I wish he was sequestered in a house all the way on the west coast, with a bad case of agoraphobia. It wouldn't bother me if he lost all sense of taste and had a stomach so touchy it could only tolerate custard. . . . Pardon me. I didn't intend to sound so mean."

"Gee," said Jacquelyn, "you can really go on about the subject."

Marissa laughed. "It's not like you have to worry about gym critics snooping around your business claiming you refold the used towels and put them back on the shelf for the customers. Or what if some guy wrote you up in the paper and said the exercise teachers were twenty pounds overweight and showing too much cellulite."

"I'd kill him."

"See. You don't go on. You just get heated." The two friends laughed. Wilhelmina only smiled.

"Well," said Wilhelmina, "you two will be just fine. I can tell. So I'll be on my way."

"I'd love to have you come talk to our women's club, Wilhelmina," said Marissa.

"I would be glad to. Just phone. I'm in the book." She started her departure and gave a wave. "The name is Mrs. Everett Chisholm."

Marissa's eyebrows flew up. She sucked in her lips.

Wilhelmina had already reached the wet sand where the sea foam surged against her fancy flip flops. She paused and turned back again. "Oh, by the way, if my mind serves me correctly, his schedule says he will be calling on *Camellia Japonica* tomorrow." She donned her hat, gave a little wink, and walked away.

Chapter Fifty

EVERY woman knows that a refrigerator never goes on the blink at a convenient time. At eight o'clock that morning, the repairman did some adjusting, replaced a broken part, told Marissa the old appliance she got for a deal would last a few weeks at most.

Two hours later, Marissa rushed around the kitchen. Isabel hovered over her tasks with a worried look. Marissa could already feel the tension building, and they still had twenty minutes before Marissa went to the entrance and placed the chalk board announcing the special for the day: creamy crab soup and pot roast in a wine reduction sauce. Up since four a.m., Marissa was aware of a little ache at the back of her neck, the one that cropped up when she felt overly stressed. She got on the phone and called her supplier who had yet to deliver that day. No one answered. She went back to the stove, lifted lids, tasted everything. Out front, she straightened tables and checked the flowers. A panicky feeling wallowed in her stomach. She went inside her office and shut the door, trying to get hold of her emotions. *What ifs?* dragged her deeper. She put her forehead in her hands trying to remember what it was that her mother always said at such a time. Marissa pictured her mother's face. The smooth forehead, the hazel eyes, the gentle mouth came to her mind and Marissa remembered. Whenever she had been hampered by fear, her mother always said, "If you want something distressing to die, you have to stop feeding it." That was Marissa's cue to think about other things. So she sat there in her office, letting her mind travel to the day she hid high in the limbs of one of the magnolia trees during hide and seek with her brother and two male cousins. They searched everywhere, begging her to come out. They offered bribes of bubble gum and a slingshot. They gave up and went inside to dinner. The boys were eating dessert when she blithely walked in, telling them everything they had said, including a few things she didn't like. For that, she would never reveal her hiding spot, at least not until her brother promised to take her to hunt for crayfish.

A chuckle came up. Marissa entered the present again, hearing China and

Rosalee put out the silverware. Her heartbeat had stopped racing. The pain was gone. She looked at the clock and got up, ready to put the sign at its station. The unwieldy easel and chalkboard rocked in her arms as she opened *Camellia's* front door. Outside, she positioned the easel on the top step but noticed one of the rubber tips from the tripod legs had fallen somewhere. A search inside yielded nothing. Outside, one touch and the easel wobbled. Very sloppy, she judged the presentation. She got down on her knees, thinking the best solution would be to remove the tip from the back leg and move it to the front. The easel would lean a little to the rear, but it would not appear out of kilter with the message going slightly down hill. She unscrewed the back tip when, head bent, she heard a vehicle pull in sounding like a truck with a hemi engine. She smiled to herself. Even rugged men enjoyed the place because her food was good tasting and soul satisfying. Vehicle doors slammed. She began the process of securing the tip onto the front leg when a sinus shriveling odor wafted her way. She remembered the garbage cans across the way. The traveling lids refused to stay on. Things were getting bad. She'd just have to say something to her neighbors, if she could ever catch them at home. The smell became more intense, overwhelming in fact.

"Hello thar! Brought my Armand for a taste of your cooking pot delights."

Marissa released her bent over back to oven door straight and up. Still on her knees, she hoped she wouldn't stagger as she made it to standing while clean oxygen was in short supply. "Oh! So glad you could come." Her mind raced. She looked over Armand, who towered over Sally, a man nearing sixty who wore camouflage pants that could hold a dozen Sallys.

"How do you do, ma'am," he said kindly, a sound so mellow and richly masculine that Marissa could not reconcile the voice with the unshaven, dirty t-shirt wearing, balding, salt-and-pepper-strands-in-a-pony-tail package.

Marissa returned his greeting and brought them inside. She noted the absurdity that he carried a copy of the New York Times. Her blood pressure surged at the heightening complications of her situation.

"Can we sit ourselves right down anywhar?" asked Sally.

"Yes. Help yourselves to any table."

Rosalie, at the back of the room, behind the dessert counter, must have already sensed the foul odor. Normally swift to bring a menu to a customer, she walked like her feet were formed of lead. China came out with a key lime pie to place in the case but froze in her tracks until Marissa spoke.

"Today the birds are singing loud enough to wake the ghost crabs." That was the pre-arranged signal for all hands into the kitchen for conference time.

Rosalee took the drink orders and zipped through the kitchen doors right behind Marissa and China.

Marissa grew afraid she was going to break down in tears. She threw her hands up and carried on an incomprehensible conversation with herself as she paced the floor. Rosalee and China filled in the information gap for Isabel.

"I don't know who they are," replied Rosalee to Isabel's question. "All I know is they are carrying more stink than the rear of a septic tank truck."

"O-o-o-o-o," said Isabel suddenly full of awareness. "This is not good."

Marissa looked out back, once again wishing William was available to consult. Then an idea came to her. The bountiful flowers spilling over the planter and the vines climbing the wrought iron suggested a solution. Marissa announced confidently, "I'm going to seat them outside. Tell everyone else garden dining is closed today. As soon as I've got them out back, throw open all the doors to air out the place."

Marissa returned to the main room, thankful there were no new guests. She walked to Sally's table.

"Sally, it is so nice that you've come all this way that I would like to give you the most beautiful seat in the garden."

"Aw heck. Don't trouble yourself."

With a pen, not pencil, Armand raced through the N.Y. Times crossword puzzle as though he were Grand Champion of the lexicographical sport, but he paused to look up and nod in agreement.

"Please," said Marissa. "Do it for me."

"Well sure, if it makes your heart glad," said Sally.

"Oh thank you," wheezed Marissa. "The flowers are going crazy, trying to outdo each other. You're going to like it. As a matter of fact, the meal is on me."

"Hey now," said Sally. "You paid *me* for my varmint catchin'. And ever since, we've been stuffed with cash. So I'd be offended if you didn't want at least a Jackson and a Lincoln or two." Armand slapped his finished crossword puzzle down on the table. He nodded again.

Marissa led them out the front doors and down the side path to the back garden. Once they were seated, she strung a ribbon out front, at the start of the path. Cars had pulled up. Three groups, a total of ten guests, were about to go inside. She praised God for the breeze that had kicked up and the fact that Everett Chisholm was nowhere in sight.

The island approached noon hour. Out back, her garden guests had finished their meal but lingered. According to Rosalee, Sally had two squirrels eating crumbs directly from her hand. Armand was entrenched in the business section, the stock exchange page to be exact.

And then it happened. Wearing an impeccably tailored, wheat-colored suit with a pink shirt and striking rose-colored tie, Everett Chisholm entered the front door with more aplomb than Chief Justice of the Supreme Court. China seated him. Marissa glanced up as she cashed out a customer. A young girl wandered in, right after Mr. Chisholm. She wore shorts. Her bare feet and legs were covered with beach sand. She walked to the counter and made her request.

Marissa let her answer carry across the room. "No, I'm sorry, sweetie. We don't sell hotdogs and chips any more. You'll have to go over to the Sandcastle for that." Marissa bent down low and whispered. "Their dogs are *the best*. I go there myself sometimes." The child thanked her and wandered out.

Marissa took a deep breath and went to Mr. Chisholm who had flipped open his small leather notebook and began taking notes. She stood there not knowing whether to interrupt him. He stopped and glanced up.

"Hello, Mr. Chisholm, I'm so glad you decided to give us another try. I hope you will see that I took your advice to heart." He gave a polite nod. Marissa swallowed and continued. "May I recommend the day's special."

"I never order the day's special. It's already simmering in a pot back there. I'm more interested in what you can do on the spur of the moment. How well you can dance on your feet, so to speak. I think I'd like the lamb in plum sauce."

Marissa broke in. "I'm sorry, my supplier failed to deliver the lamb."

"Then why is it on the menu?"

"Well, I . . . I'd have to . . . . Are you suggesting I mark on the menu with black marker or have back up menus ready for any possibility that could occur?" She forced a smile.

"Of course not, Ms. Manning. However, your hostess did not inform me, which should be done as soon as a guest is seated and studying the menu."

Marissa felt blood rising in her face. "You're quite right. May I suggest today's fish, filet of red snapper?"

He wrinkled his nose. "From frozen, right?"

"Definitely not. China, your server, makes an early morning stop at the docks at the Brunswick fish market, before she comes here. She selects exactly what I need for the day. And I require the freshest."

"All right. But if you want to try and dazzle me, prepare a perfect béchamel sauce to accompany the fish."

"Good, sir."

"And I'll have the sugar snap peas and the rice pilaf."

"Good, sir. I hope you enjoy your dining experience." She backed away and headed to the kitchen.

"Oh, Ms. Manning," he called.

She stopped and turned with her most pleasant expression.

He gestured to the surroundings. "I can see you've upped your game. I'll expect excellence."

Marissa nodded and left the room. She dashed to her computer and brought up several recipes for béchamel sauce. She called Isabel over with the news of Chisholm's arrival. They conferred and selected a recipe from the *You're a Gourmet* site. They prepared the fish for the oven. Marissa gathered the ingredients for the sauce. She began preparation. Meantime, they juggled the other orders coming in at a time of day when almost every seat was taken. They flitted around the food stations like busy wrens. More careful than performing brain surgery, Marissa prepared the sauce. Finally, the timer chimed. Marissa pulled the snapper from the oven and plated it artfully alongside the side dishes. The sauce was poured over the midsection of the filet. Isabel made an artistic suggestion to dress the sauce with long slivers of red bell pepper to bring out the beautiful seafood color. Marissa wiped the edges of the plate. The two women grinned at each other.

Marissa walked into the dining room, holding a warm plate of irreproachability. Her confidence died the moment she noticed Irene, Darrien's mother, coming in the door alone. Marissa looked away, hoping the confused woman would not recall *Camellia* as the place owned by the wind-chime-destroyer. Irene's shrill cries would break the drinking glass in every guest's hand.

Marissa placed the meal in front of Chisholm.

He breathed in the vapors of the creamy sauce and salty fish. "Hm. Not bad. We'll see."

Marissa forced herself to walk away. She heard Rosalee talking softly to Irene who ordered a cup of Christmas tea although spring would soon dip into summer. Nothing odd about that, Marissa comforted herself; she often did the same.

Darrien's mother might be doing better. Several times she had been in church, snuggled next to Zoe like a trusting child. Today the trench coat was gone. Her nice appearance and the fact that Darrien had let her ramble the village area must be a good sign. Marissa said hello to several guests and entered the kitchen.

"He liked the presentation," said Marissa to Isabel. "We'll have to wait and see if we made the grade."

"Just think," said Isabel, "after today, we'll never have another day as hard as this one."

"Yes, but we still have to make it through this one."

Rosalee and China came in with dirty dishes.

"He doesn't look unhappy," was China's report. "I refilled his water. He asked about the paintings."

"Really?" said Isabel with a flip around of her head. She turned back to what she was doing at the stove.

"Asked about the old man reading. If it's for sale."

"No, it's not," said Marissa, "but she will be happy to paint something on commission."

"Would I ever," said Isabel.

Marissa turned to Rosalee. "The older woman you waited on, the one in the blue dress. Keep an eye on her."

"You don't mean the sweet little lady who ordered Christmas tea, do you?" said Rosalee.

"She can surprise you," replied Marissa.

"How about the couple outside?" asked Rosalee. "They paid an hour ago. Still sitting there."

"*Oh no.* I forgot all about them." Marissa ran to the back door and looked out.

Sally and Armand had left their chairs and approached the kitchen.

Marissa loped out the door, her breathing quickened. "I've been so busy I haven't had a chance to get out here. Let me walk you around the building to your truck."

"Thanks," said Sally, "but Armand wants to see your cooking stove."

"Oh, I can't do it. Strict regulations. The health department."

Sally looked a little peeved.

"We understand," said Armand, warmly. "Please excuse my excessive interest, but the great medley of tastes making up our meals thrilled me with their piquant flavors and masterful preparation. The last time we dined out was nine years ago. But now I have a new standard to work toward, although my readily available ingredients are quite different." He chuckled and his belly shook, making him seemingly aware of the strangeness of his circumstances.

Marissa's hand had settled lightly on her chest. "Oh, thank you!" she said, more puzzled than ever by the man.

"No need to walk us," he said, turning to the pathway, smiling affectionately at Sally.

"Right," said Sally, barely coming up to his elbow, two of her fingers latched on a side belt loop as though she was his adored pet.

Marissa couldn't believe the next words that came out of her own mouth. "Please come back sometime," she called to the couple who departed and trailed a double dose of reeking miasma.

Marissa ran back inside the kitchen. Isabel took glazed strawberries from the fridge.

"That is exactly why my mother worried every time I went camping," said Marissa. "Something happens out there. One day you're civilized. The next, you're one with the woods."

"More truth there than you realize," said Rosalee. "He told me he escaped the draft in '70 by turning his back on his brand new business degree and hiding in the Okefenokee. Now, he's quite comfortable there. . . . Oh. I'd better mention I'm a little worried about the lady in the blue dress. She's still in the bathroom."

Marissa went to check on the situation. She had to go out, anyway, to see if Mr. Chisholm was ready for dessert. At the bathroom door, a wavering voice replied, "Occupied," to Marissa's knock. Not dead, thank goodness. She drifted away and went to Mr. Chisholm's table. His hand scribbled furiously inside the leather notebook.

She told him about her signature dessert.

"Signature?" he said with a slight warning tone. "Then you realize it *must* be very special. But, I'm not indulging in dessert these days."

Marissa wanted to beg but knew that would squelch a positive report for sure. She tried a different angle. "Oh, I'm surprised. You're looking trimmer in that handsome suit."

"Well." His head angled up. He looked at her from behind his half glasses and shut the notebook. "I guess I'll try it. Too many years have passed since a lovely young woman used the word trim or handsome within a sentence addressing me." Marissa smiled sweetly and went to prepare his dining finale.

Later, as she served the dessert, she thought to check on Irene again. She didn't have to. Rosalee stood at the back of the dining room, her mouth open, her hand waving. Irene had come from the bathroom and walked down the hall. A large portion of the valuable antique pails looped each arm like elegant handbags to accessorize her blue dress stuffed with sea oats. Marissa halted Rosalee with a shake of her head. A meltdown from Irene would throw the entire room into disarray. A few ladies neglected their food and looked up. In the reading corner, three gossiping teenagers nibbling tea biscuits with lemon curd let their mouths hang open. Marissa's eyes flew to Chisholm. His head tilted down. His eyes had plugged themselves into Marissa's creation. He seemed lost in every bite.

Marissa watched as Irene primly departed *Camellia,* carrying collectibles worth the cost of a commercial grade fridge.

Chapter Fifty-one

WILLIAM returned from his trip to Sumter. Before *Camellia* opened, before the dawn fully burgeoned, Marissa and William had breakfast out, and she told him about her day of trials. He said she deserved a medal for resourcefulness and quick thinking. She voiced the opinion that any medals should go to her loyal staff who ran out and cordoned off Irene. Any celebrating would be premature, she said, until the restaurant review hit the paper and she got a look. Again, Chisholm had left her place with words that were polite but noncommittal.

They ate their eggs and bacon and made plans for that night. He insisted on doing the cooking. He got on his cell phone and asked Darrien to bring Zoe and join them for dinner. Jacquelyn was out of town, so it would be only the two couples having a quiet meal in William's backyard. He had planned a special weekend. It had to be. Three days separated them from seven months of being apart. He was leaving Tuesday morning for his last assignment. Marissa's task was to prepare for their wedding to take place when he returned to the States in November.

That evening the landscape lighting, soft music, and soothing temperature put everyone in a jovial mood. Darrien seemed lovestruck by the young woman he had almost lost, the woman so perfect for him. Marissa made much ado about the blazing yellow diamond on Zoe's ring finger and about the wedding that would take place in July. William jokingly asked the couple to wait until he returned. Darrien replied that he was not about to take a chance and let Zoe sneak away. He thanked Marissa again for the call alerting him that his mother had been seen wandering the village and that Isabel and China had confined her to a bench by the beachwear shop. Like dear granddaughters, they got her talking about her days as bridge champion of the island until he arrived to take her home. Marissa left him blissfully unaware that Rosalee had calmly confronted Irene outside *Camellia* and transfer of the stolen pails proceeded with amazing smoothness.

William and Darrien monitored ribs on the grill. In the kitchen, Zoe and Marissa talked and shared their happiness. They laughed about the drizzly, December night encounter in Woodstock when Marissa was feeling blind love for everyone and Zoe felt like destroying the world. Their laughter fluttered through the window and made the men look up and wonder. Marissa poured the champagne Darrien had provided, and the women carried glasses out to the men. The ribs landed on a platter. Zoe uncovered side dishes she had made. William and Darrien promised to do clean-up. Everyone meant to give Marissa some rest. But things don't always go as planned, just as in summer in the salt marshes when on some unexpected day the oppressive heat along with the great quantity of detritus suspended in the water drastically reduces the amount of dissolved oxygen, resulting in a fish kill. Soon even the tortured blue crabs emerge from the water and climb onto the mud banks to breathe.

They sat around the table enjoying the food and the affable gathering. All serious subjects were banned. Marissa spoke of Jacquelyn and the wonderful Russell Lancaster whom they all had briefly met and were anxious to know more fully when he returned in July. Everything looked auspicious for many good times in the years ahead.

William began to speak of north Georgia and the town so close to Marissa's heart. He proudly shared the story of a boy named Max and the aid and encouragement she was giving to his future. William asked Marissa to describe to their friends the land and the farmhouse, her family and the townsfolk. Through her eloquent words, everyone sensed her attachment.

Marissa's eyes sparkled. Joy rumbled around in her chest at the cozy friendship and the safety found in a convening of hearts with like minds and good will toward each other.

"Darrien," said William, "I wish you could meet Uncle Nathan. He's something out of the ordinary. At ninety-three, he's still strong. He leads his steer around as easily as a person leads a dog. And he still enjoys sitting in a saddle, at least when Marissa isn't around worrying. His appearance is remarkable, too. Tall and slim. And in case you are in doubt of his presence, he owns a head of the reddest hair." He chuckled. "Wouldn't it be great if his genes get passed down and Marissa and I have a child with hair that striking? We'd never have to worry about losing our kid. A child like that stands out in any crowd. . . . What?" He stared at Darrien.

When Darrien spoke, puzzlement riddled the sound of his words. "What do you mean, William? You know Marissa can't have a child."

William's face lost its buoyant look. Shock registered on Darrien's face. William looked at Marissa whose head hung down. Her fingers pinched the bridge of her nose as if she were in pain.

"Marissa," said William. "Does he know something I don't?"

"I was going to tell you." Her tears began to flow. She turned to Darrien. "Why don't you spill everything? You're my pastor. You know it all. Tell him about the hysterectomy that left me devastated at thirty-two. Tell him about the supposedly liberated years I spent right out of college and the pregnancy I terminated at twenty-four like any smart, modern girl would do." Her face turned to William although her words were still directed at Darrien. "Unfortunately, they don't inform you about what it does to you, the creeping corrosion that eats day by day at your heart. Tell him about the years I mistakenly thought God was punishing me with emptiness in my life. Tell him about the self-loathing. Tell him how warped and angry I became. Tell him." She buried her face in her hands. Zoe lightly held Marissa's shoulders. "I was going to tell you, William."

William got up slowly. "Exactly when?"

She did not answer.

He cleared his voice. "I thought you knew I already had all the deception I could ever take. I need honesty. That's what I longed for. . . . You're no better than she was." He left the table and went into the house.

Minutes passed with Zoe holding Marissa. Darrien went inside. A heated exchange tumbled from somewhere inside and to the yard. Things quieted. Marissa sat up, wiping her eyes. Fear rose in her heart, and that fear was confirmed when Darrien returned, alone. He told her that he and Zoe would take her home. They left the table as it was and went to the car out front. The drive to East Beach did nothing but humiliate her. At the beach house, Darrien coaxed her to hold off her runaway thoughts; morning would soften William's heart. Zoe begged to stay with her, but Marissa pushed her offer away. Her friends left, promising to check on Marissa the next day.

The morning dawned brilliantly. Like a mean joke played on her by the weather, the beauty out her window seemed surreal to her swollen eyes. She stayed in bed. She answered Zoe's phone call with brevity. Jacquelyn phoned next, ready to leave her sick aunt's home. Marissa flared and unintended words came out. Jacquelyn ended the call. Marissa turned into her pillow and cried. For hours she listened to the sea as the tide came in and the tide went out. Finally, she couldn't take it any longer, and she showered and dressed. She drove to his house and went to the door. He didn't answer the bell. She went around the house to the back where he usually left only the screen door in place in order to catch the breezes. Today the wooden door blocked entrance. The blinds refused the view. The grill had vacated its spot. The table, the white linens had disappeared. The yard had been swept of everything not tied down. Her stomach clenched with apprehension and heartache. She returned to the front, realizing his car was gone. He had abandoned her for the sea. She got in her own car and drove away. She never noticed the small envelope lodged in the wrought iron amid the morning glories, on the *Camellia* side of the planter. A curious crow, head angling, hopping along the branch of a tall pine came down, plucked it out, and carried it off.

At the beach house, she dragged the beautiful French counterpane up the stairs across the front of the house to the tower. She sat down and pulled an elastic band from her pocket to gather her hair and restrain the strands batting her eyes in the wind. The other chair became the support for her legs. Settled in, she watched the sea, thinking. As night fell, the first frontal assaults began. Doubt infested her mind. Her skin tightened in reaction to the cooling temperature. She wrapped herself in the counterpane. And then accusation stormed in, followed by up-ending prediction. She was cut loose and adrift, his love for her an absolute error.

For a while she sank under the crushing weight of those censuring thoughts. Wind whipped through the tower and buffeted her covering. The roaring sea mimicked the chaos in her mind. She opposed the onslaught of condemnation by wielding eternal words like a sword. The night seemed to hold off the dawn, as though it wanted to slow Earth to a confused, self-destructive crawl. With prevailing belief worn like armor, she persisted, strong and steadfast, and slowly but surely, she pushed back the ponderous force threatening her.

When she could finally see the shrimp boats dotting the horizon, down she came from the tower, shaky-legged, her body figuratively bruised. She fell into bed and slept until afternoon.

Chapter Fifty-two

THAT afternoon when she woke, hunger finally registering, she feasted on plain chicken broth. She longed to be outside and decided to take a walk. First, she checked her phone, which showed no messages. She left the house.

The high winds of the beach would be too much for her she knew, so she traipsed down the beach lanes full of vacation homes and eventually reached the half-mile strip of high land that connected East Beach and Demere Road. At the small bridge crossing Postell Creek, she paused and leaned over to observe a mysterious, reclusive clapper rail. Her emotions numb, she watched dully as the funny bird with a gait like a chicken cruised awkwardly along the bank, searching in the mud for aquatic animals to fill its stomach. Its head came up. The sleek bird suddenly made itself conspicuous with calls reminiscent of laughter. Head bent again, the marsh hen continued its search. So often Marissa had heard of this favorite island bird, and today she was rewarded with the rare sight of one. Something inside her emotions shifted.

She came down into the marsh, unconcerned about the dark mud attaching to her sport shoes. Instantly, fiddler crabs guarding their burrows under the bridge took cover in their homes. She made herself into a frozen statue, waiting for them to emerge again. She closed her eyes and listened to the restful silence of the marsh. An occasional car passing was the only thing to disturb her peace. Voices met her ears and her eyes opened. Two cyclists turned down the road cutting through the marsh and were soon gone. She turned only her eyes and glanced at the burrows. Several crabs lingered in their doorways, sizing up the situation. One crab came out and waved its large claw in defense. I know how you feel, she thought, and continued across the soggy marsh exposed at low tide. The countless shafts of cordgrass swept softly against her legs as she made her way exposed in the sunlight, although shadows of wax myrtle and several cedars at the marsh border stretched far and painted gray streaks across a salt pan. She reached a small patch of upland like a tiny island and found a place to sit. Her eyes drew in the view. The rustling bushes and bird calls sent her body into relaxation.

"You like nature?" a gentle voice questioned.

"Oh! Yes, ma'am."

Around the corner, ten yards down, a very old woman with white hair cut in a short pageboy plunked her fishing hook into the tidal creek that meandered close to where she stood.

"Didn't mean to startle you," the wizened lady said. "It's not often someone else discovers this choice little bump of land. It lends itself really well to catching a mullet or two. Course you have to be out of here before the tide comes in or your shoes get ruined."

"I'm not here for the fish. I'm hoping the scenery will refresh me. Things haven't gone well of late."

"Nature is the perfect setting to wash away your worries. I like what Michelangelo said, 'Gazing on beautiful things acts on my soul, which thirsts for heavenly light.'"

"Yes, the creation stirs me, too," said Marissa.

"Good thing He understood we would need to gaze on hope when it seemed there wasn't any."

A frantic, repeating call, "will-will-willet," broke their conversation. A bird with flapping black and white striped wings hovered in the air.

"Look at that willet making a display," said the old woman who raised a wrinkled hand and pointed. "He's trying to impress a female somewhere on the ground. It's their time of year." She baited her hook once more and lightly cast her fishing line. "Well, I'll lend you back to your solitude again. Much good thinking can be done here." She smiled.

Marissa returned with her own smile. The first in twenty-four hours. She resumed her observations of the specialized environment. In the marsh below her perch, periwinkle snails moved along the lengths of grass stalks, eating algae that had been left behind when the tide retreated. Darker snails traveled the surface of the mud. A tiny worm crawled from its hole. She watched the water drift by in the creek. She shut her eyes again and listened to the sounds trying to identify each one. A plane hummed high in the sky. The willet made his call again. A mockingbird fluted a song. Children's laughter skipped across the road and down, into the marsh, which made her recall the times, as a very young woman, she brashly remarked that the thought of raising children made the hair on her neck rise. After her surgery, the painful irony of those words often occurred to her.

Despite her regrets, poor decisions, and unfortunate circumstances, she was too full of life to let go of whatever God had planned for her. Five years earlier, at the point when she lost the very seat of her femaleness and could not get back what she had not esteemed, she slowly began to change and be changed. Desperate, she had returned to the One who brought her peace and cherished her soul. Her soul. Created for its own uniqueness. Admitting her crippled state and willing to be helped, she was guided, shaped, and refined. Now, life multiplied in her all the time. So fertile, she went about her days, dropping fruit in people's lives without her even realizing it.

The tide had begun its return. She knew because the increased sounds at the shore traveled the short distance inland with a consistent *sh-sh-sh-sh* of growing wave action. The level of the creek had risen slightly. The hole from which the worm had come now closed, a millimeter of water shrouding the opening. She ignored the idea of departing her resting place. The depression hounding her had fled.

She crossed her arms on her knees and rested her forehead there. Before long, she imagined a dive into an ocean lagoon of crystal clear water. In her daydream, she pulled her body down to sparkling sands below the surface. Filled with unlimited breath in that aqueous world, her hands shimmied into the sand, parting the grains on either side of a mound. Her fingertips touched the handles of a chest she could not lift. She grasped and held on but did not pull. She would not let go of her treasure. She would wait, aware of the unmerited favor that sustained her. If weeks passed, that was fine. If years, so be it. If eons passed, life was worth it. She was in a position of total trust. Her dependence was outside herself. And then one day, slowly the treasure chest would tremble and rise. Streaming sand would fall away. Effortlessly for her, the treasure would come, and she would float with it upward. Breaking the surface of the water, her next breaths would be unstrained as though she had lived on something else while waiting.

On the small hammock, Marissa lifted her head. She brushed her shorts and rose. She turned to say goodbye to the woman who was no longer there but had somehow left without a sound.

Chapter Fifty-three

MARISSA entered the beach house at dusk. She called Jacquelyn and apologized. They talked about the situation, and Jacquelyn empathized as only a woman could. Their chagrined laughter came out judging the visit by the food critic ridiculously unimportant in comparison to the present problem. Nothing was left to be said. They were about to hang up when Marissa ended the call with heart-heavy words. "Jacquelyn, thanks for not saying, 'I told you so.'"

Minutes later, she got a call from Aunt Shalie who thanked Marissa for offering to take care of the girls the next day. Since Alexa was fighting a cold, Shalie decided to let both of them miss a day of school. "It's like those two are glued together. I try and I try. I even bought them a cell phone to share. You'd think that would break the ice. I wish they knew how much I'm hurtin' about their mama. So I'm awfully glad for a break. I'm driving to Savannah for the day. A big dog apparel and accessories show." She giggled. "My babies are going with me." Marissa struggled to remember exactly when she had agreed to the girls' visit. Shalie chirped on as Marissa politely listened. Shalie finally wound things up. "I'll have them there at seven, just like you asked. Take care."

In the morning, Marissa forced herself from bed. She got ready for work and arrived by six. She sat Isabel down and briefly explained that William had left for his final assignment on a really bad note. "I might be a little spacey," said Marissa. "If I seem out of it, push me back on track." At seven, the girls did not come in *Camellia's* front door. By eight, Marissa wondered if Alexa's cold had worsened and required bed rest. Around nine, she finished drizzling a lime glaze over a poppy seed cake, and she called Shalie who replied that she dropped the girls off at the pier just like Marissa asked. A long pause ensued. Marissa instantly surmised duplicity. Her ire began to climb. Shalie chattered about the convention hall and the beautiful city. Marissa interrupted and said there had been a miscommunication, but she didn't clarify that the girls had lied. Infusing calmness into the situation, Marissa predicted she would locate the girls soon. In closing, Shalie informed Marissa that Alexa might need a visit to the doctor. Her fever had worsened. *Fever?* thought Marissa. Then, spotting old friends, Shalie had to go. The problem had dropped squarely in Marissa's lap.

Marissa conferred with Isabel and sprinted out the back door. The village area and the pier gave no evidence of Clemma and Alexa. At the library, with the aid of the helpful library workers, a search was made up and down the stacks. She left and questioned the man at the putt-putt golf, one of the girls' favorite stops. He had not seen them, but it stood to reason; only five minutes earlier he was having his tires rotated.

Arms swinging, legs pumping through the sand, she began her march up the beach. She questioned strolling people and children playing in the surf. Her progress amounted to the pool area when a voice rang out calling her name. Isabel ran down the beach, still wearing her apron. Her waving hand held Marissa's cell phone.

Isabel reached Marissa and spurted, "It's Clemma. She won't tell me anything." Marissa took the phone. "I've got to race back," said Isabel. "It's five until ten. People are collecting outside." She turned and jetted in the opposite direction.

"I'll return as soon as I can," clamored Marissa.

Isabel yelled back, "I can handle *Camellia*. Do what you need to do."

Marissa put the cell phone to her ear. "Clemma? Where are you?"

"Aunt Marissa," she whimpered. The next words zoomed into Marissa's ear. "You're going to be really mad at me, but we're stranded in the marsh. At first we were walking in shin deep water. I kept thinking I saw gator eyes poking up. My phone is dying and I'm scared." She finally stopped and took a breath.

"Where are you, Clemma?"

"I don't know. He put us out of the boat cause I didn't want any beer."

"Who put you out?"

"Freddie."

"Him! Where can I find this guy?"

"He hangs out on the beach, right past the Coast Guard station."

Marissa rammed her legs forward in the sand. "All right. I'm going to go nab him. Don't waste any more battery. I'll call you soon."

"Aunt Marissa, Alexa isn't doing well. Her cold's a lot worse. She wants me to find her someplace to rest. What should I-" The phone went dead.

"Clemma? Can you hear me?" Marissa stashed her phone in her pants pocket and changed gears to a jog. The lighthouse and the King and Prince Hotel marked her way. She jetted past all the strolling beachcombers and sunbathers. The Coast Guard station eventually came into view. Within minutes, she spotted the guy lolling across a small sailboat as though getting a tan outweighed everything in the world.

She stood over him. He must have felt the chill. He put a hand up to shade his eyes. He squinted and it looked as if he tried to recognize the face projecting a fierce expression.

She bent low. "Where are Clemma and Alexa? If you don't tell me, I'll have your commanding officer here in a second."

"Give me a break, lady. We went for a boat ride. I got annoyed and left them near the Frederica River. They've probably made it home by now. So stop fretting about your cubs."

"Get up," she said firmly.

He didn't speak but sat up.

"Why are you always out of uniform?"

"I don't own one. Never have."

"You lied to Clemma."

"What's wrong with a little imagination?"

"Look, do you know where they send guys like you? Not far down the road. It's called the State Penitentiary, a hop, skip, and a jump from here in Reidsville. Now, you take me to where Clemma and Alexa are, or I'll spend my last drop of sweat and blood, making sure the police lock you up there."

"All right. All right."

Marissa glanced around the collection of boats and a rental sign with prices. He pulled an inflatable raft toward the water.

"Well, come on," he said gruffly.

They heaved the boat through the sand and things became easier once they hit the water. They moved to a depth of two feet. A little dinghy, tied to the rear, followed. Marissa got into the boat with sopping pant legs and shoes. He lowered the outboard motor and got it going. With her in front, they moved up the coast and reached the Hampton River sound where he piloted the boat into the waterway. Marissa fought to keep a mental picture of the geography. Little St. Simons snuggled the right side of the river for eight long miles, she calculated. She knew the river from the 1838 descriptions by Fanny Kemble. Her reading mind had devoured everything about the island. After a while, they went around the bend near an oppressive place called Five Pound where recalcitrant slaves had been punished with isolation. The boat navigated the dark waters.

She turned to him at the rear of the boat and yelled above the motor rumble, "Are they near the Frederica Monument?"

"Don't know where they've wandered. We'll have to find them."

Marissa wished she could blaze holes in his skull with her angry eyes. She turned forward and scanned the landscape, looking for one sun-blond head and the curly brown tresses of the other. The river twisted and turned. Soon they entered the Mackay River and, a mile and a half later, took the left fork and traveled the turbid, brackish Frederica River. Marissa intensified her efforts.

A long series of hacking coughs rang out. Within minutes, they spotted the girls standing among the tall cordgrass lining the low levee formed by the sediment-delivering river when it overflowed its banks. The boat reached the spot. Glassy-eyed Alexa inclined limply against her sister. She scratched her neck and gave a muddled look at her rescuers' arrival. Clemma glanced sternly at the boat captain. Marissa sprang from the boat. Her footing unsure on the slimy bank, she fell back into the river. Wet to the waist, she clambered onto the marsh that slowly drained with the ebbing tide. The moment she took hold of Alexa, Marissa's heart leapt with fear. The girl burned with fever. Wheezing breaths emitted from her throat. Clemma cried. The sound of the motor starting up hit their ears. Freddie, their coast guard imposter took off, leaving them with only the dinghy. Marissa ran back down the bank. The small vessel already held a pool of water. A test of its seaworthiness required her to step in the rotting boat. Immediately, water gushed through a hole that had been above waterline. She stepped out and climbed the bank where they watched the craft drifting slowly beneath the surface. Marissa reached in her pocket for her phone. The moment her fingers touched the device, her awareness lit up; a dunking certified the death of any electronic device. Their circumstances loaded with obstacle, dilemma, and threat, Marissa couldn't help but note the name of the place. If her memory was correct, they stood in the vicinity of the Hazzard brothers' plantation melted long ago into the earth.

Getting Alexa free of the stressful conditions took preeminence in her mind. They walked to a small patch of upland holding a magnificent red cedar. To the west, Brunswick sat in the distance, but they would have to walk a long way through marsh and swim the wide intercoastal waterway. She sized up the cedar and its abundance of strong branches. She climbed, hoping to receive a